selected
Leo Tolstoy

maple press

Published by

MAPLE PRESS PRIVATE LIMITED
office: A-63, Sector 58, Noida 201301, U.P., India
phone: +91 120 455 3581, 455 3583
email: info@maplepress.co.in
website: www.maplepress.co.in

Reprint 2022 in India

ISBN: 978-93-50334-29-4

CONTENTS

CONTENTS

A PRISONER IN THE CAUCASUS

---⚬⚬⚬---

I

An officer named Zhílin was serving in the army in the Caucasus.

One day he received a letter from home. It was from his mother, who wrote: 'I am getting old, and should like to see my dear son once more before I die. Come and say good-bye to me and bury me, and then, if God pleases, return to service again with my blessing. But I have found a girl for you, who is sensible and good and has some property. If you can love her, you might marry her and remain at home.'

Zhílin thought it over. It was quite true, the old lady was failing fast and he might not have another chance to see her alive. He had better go, and, if the girl was nice, why not marry her?

So he went to his Colonel, obtained leave of absence, said good-bye to his comrades, stood the soldiers four pailfuls of vódka as a farewell treat, and got ready to go.

It was a time of war in the Caucasus. The roads were not safe by night or day. If ever a Russian ventured to ride or walk any distance away from his fort, the Tartars killed him or carried him off to the hills. So it had been arranged that twice every week a body of soldiers should march from one fortress to the next to convoy travellers from point to point.

It was summer. At daybreak the baggage-train got ready under shelter of the fortress; the soldiers marched out; and all started along the road. Zhílin was on horseback, and a cart with his things went with the baggage-train. They had sixteen miles to go. The baggage-train moved slowly; sometimes the soldiers stopped, or perhaps a wheel would come off one of the carts, or a horse refuse to go on, and then everybody had to wait.

When by the sun it was already past noon, they had not gone half the way. It was dusty and hot, the sun was scorching and there was no shelter anywhere: a bare plain all round - not a tree, not a bush, by the road.

Zhílin rode on in front, and stopped, waiting for the baggage to overtake him. Then he heard the signal-horn sounded behind him: the company had again stopped. So he began to think: 'Hadn't I better ride on by myself? My horse is a good one: if the Tartars do attack me, I can gallop away. Perhaps, however, it would be wiser to wait.'

As he sat considering, Kostílin, an officer carrying a gun, rode up to him and said:

'Come along, Zhílin, let's go on by ourselves. It's dreadful; I am famished, and the heat is terrible. My shirt is wringing wet.'

Kostílin was a stout, heavy man, and the perspiration was running down his red face. Zhílin thought awhile, and then asked: 'Is your gun loaded?'

'Yes it is.'

'Well, then, let's go, but on condition that we keep together.'

So they rode forward along the road across the plain, talking, but keeping a look-out on both sides. They could see afar all round. But after crossing the plain the road ran through a valley between two hills, and Zhílin said: 'We had better climb that hill and have a look round, or the Tartars may be on us before we know it.'

But Kostílin answered: 'What's the use? Let us go on.'

Zhílin, however, would not agree.

'No,' he said; 'you can wait here if you like, but I'll go and look round.' And he turned his horse to the left, up the hill. Zhílin's horse was a hunter, and carried him up the hillside as if it had wings. (He had bought it for a hundred roubles as a colt out of a herd, and had broken it in himself.) Hardly had he reached the top of the hill, when he saw some thirty Tartars not much more than a hundred yards ahead of him. As soon as he caught sight of them he turned round but the Tartars had also seen him, and rushed after him at full gallop, getting their guns out as they went. Down galloped Zhílin as fast as the horse's legs could go, shouting to Kostílin: 'Get your gun ready!'

And, in thought, he said to his horse: 'Get me well out of this, my pet; don't stumble, for if you do it's all up. Once I reach the gun, they shan't take me prisoner.'

But, instead of waiting, Kostílin, as soon as he caught sight of the Tartars, turned back towards the fortress at full speed, whipping his horse now on one side now on the other, and its switching tail was all that could be seen of him in the dust.

Zhílin saw it was a bad look-out; the gun was gone, and what could he do with nothing but his sword? He turned his horse towards the escort, thinking to escape, but there were six Tartars rushing to cut him off. His horse was a good one, but theirs were still better; and besides, they were across his path. He tried to rein in his horse and to turn another way, but it was going so fast it could not stop, and dashed on straight towards the Tartars. He saw a red-bearded Tartar on a grey horse, with his gun raised, come at him, yelling and showing his teeth.

'Ah,' thought Zhílin, 'I know you, devils that you are. If you take me alive, you'll put me in a pit and flog me. I will not be taken alive!'

Zhílin, though not a big fellow, was brave. He drew his sword and dashed at the red-bearded Tartar thinking: 'Either I'll ride him down, or disable him with my sword.'

He was still a horse's length away from him, when he was fired at from behind, and his horse was hit. It fell to the ground with all its weight, pinning Zhílin to the earth.

He tried to rise, but two ill-savoured Tartars were already sitting on him and binding his hands behind his back. He made an effort and flung them off, but three others jumped from their horses and began beating his head with the butts of their guns. His eyes grew dim, and he fell back. The Tartars seized him, and, taking spare girths from their saddles, twisted his hands behind him and tied them with a Tartar knot. They knocked his cap off, pulled off his boots, searched him all over, tore his clothes, and took his money and his watch.

Zhílin looked round at his horse. There it lay on its side, poor thing, just as it had fallen; struggling, its legs in the air, unable to touch the ground. There was a hole in its head, and black blood was pouring out, turning the dust to mud for a couple of feet around.

One of the Tartars went up to the horse and began taking the saddle off, it still kicked, so he drew a dagger and cut its windpipe. A whistling sound came from its throat, the horse gave one plunge, and all was over.

The Tartars took the saddle and trappings. The red-bearded Tartar mounted his horse, and the others lifted Zhílin into the saddle behind him. To prevent his falling off, they strapped him to the Tartar's girdle; and then they all rode away to the hills.

So there sat Zhílin, swaying from side to side, his head striking against the Tartar's stinking back. He could see nothing but that muscular back and sinewy neck, with its closely shaven, bluish nape. Zhílin's head was wounded: the blood had dried over his eyes, and he could neither shift his position on the saddle nor wipe the blood off. His arms were bound so tightly that his collar-bones ached.

They rode up and down hills for a long way. Then they reached a river which they forded, and came to a hard road leading across a valley.

Zhílin tried to see where they were going, but his eyelids were stuck together with blood, and he could not turn.

Twilight began to fall; they crossed another river and rode up a stony hillside. There was a smell of smoke here, and dogs were barking. They had reached an Aoul (a Tartar village). The Tartars got off their horses; Tartar children came and stood round Zhílin, shrieking with pleasure and throwing stones at him.

The Tartar drove the children away, took Zhílin off the horse, and called his man. A Nogáy with high cheek-bones, and nothing on but a shirt (and that so torn that his breast was all bare), answered the call. The Tartar gave him an order. He went and fetched shackles: two blocks of oak with iron rings attached, and a clasp and lock fixed to one of the rings.

They untied Zhílin's arms, fastened the shackles on his leg, and dragged him to a barn, where they pushed him in and locked the door.

Zhílin fell on a heap of manure. He lay still awhile then groped about to find a soft place, and settled down.

II

That night Zhílin hardly slept at all. It was the time of year when the nights are short, and daylight soon showed itself through a chink in the wall. He rose, scratched to make the chink bigger, and peeped out.

Through the hole he saw a road leading down-hill; to the right was a Tartar hut with two trees near it, a black dog lay on the threshold, and a goat and kids were moving about wagging their tails. Then he saw a young Tartar woman in a long, loose, bright-coloured gown, with trousers and high boots showing from under it. She had a coat thrown over her head, on which she carried a large metal jug filled with water. She was leading by the hand a small, closely-shaven Tartar boy, who wore nothing but a shirt; and as she went along balancing herself, the muscles of her back quivered. This woman carried the water into the hut, and, soon after, the red-bearded Tartar of yesterday came out dressed in a silk tunic, with a silver-hilted dagger hanging by his side, shoes on his bare feet, and a tall black sheepskin cap set far back on his head. He came out, stretched himself, and stroked his red beard. He stood awhile, gave an order to his servant, and went away.

Then two lads rode past from watering their horses. The horses' noses were wet. Some other closely-shaven boys ran out, without any trousers, and wearing nothing but their shirts. They crowded together, came to the barn, picked up a twig, and began pushing it in at the chink. Zhílin gave a shout, and the boys shrieked and scampered off, their little bare knees gleaming as they ran.

Zhílin was very thirsty: his throat was parched, and he thought: 'If only they would come and so much as look at me!'

Then he heard someone unlocking the barn. The red-bearded Tartar entered, and with him was another, a smaller man, dark, with bright black eyes, red cheeks and a short beard. He had a merry face, and was always laughing. This man was even more richly dressed than the other. He wore a blue silk tunic trimmed with gold, a large silver dagger in his belt, red morocco slippers worked with silver, and over these a pair of thick shoes, and he had a white sheepskin cap on his head.

The red-bearded Tartar entered, muttered something as if he were annoyed, and stood leaning against the doorpost, playing with his dagger, and glaring askance at Zhílin, like a wolf. The dark one, quick and lively and moving as if on springs, came straight up to Zhílin, squatted down in front of him, slapped him on the shoulder, and began to talk very fast in his own language. His teeth showed, and he kept winking, clicking his tongue, and repeating, 'Good Russ, good Russ.'

Zhílin could not understand a word, but said, 'Drink! give me water to drink!'

The dark man only laughed. 'Good Russ,' he said, and went on talking in his own tongue.

Zhílin made signs with lips and hands that he wanted something to drink.

The dark man understood, and laughed. Then he looked out of the door, and called to some one: 'Dina!'

A little girl came running in: she was about thirteen, slight, thin, and like the dark Tartar in face. Evidently she was his daughter. She, too, had clear black eyes, and her face was good-looking. She had on a long blue gown with wide sleeves, and no girdle. The hem of her gown, the front, and the sleeves, were trimmed with red. She wore trousers and slippers, and over the slippers stouter shoes with high heels. Round her neck she had a necklace made of Russian silver coins. She was bareheaded, and her black hair was plaited with a ribbon and ornamented with gilt braid and silver coins.

Her father gave an order, and she ran away and returned with a metal jug. She handed the water to Zhílin and sat down, crouching so that her knees were as high as her head, and there she sat with wide open eyes watching Zhílin drink, as though he were a wild animal.

When Zhílin handed the empty jug back to her, she gave such a sudden jump back, like a wild goat, that it made her father laugh. He sent her away for something else. She took the jug, ran out, and brought back some unleavened bread on a round board, and once more sat down, crouching, and looking on with staring eyes.

Then the Tartars went away and again locked the door.

After a while the Nogáy came and said: 'Ayda, the master, Ayda!'

He, too, knew no Russian. All Zhílin could make out was that he was told to go somewhere.

Zhílin followed the Nógay, but limped, for the shackles dragged his feet so that he could hardly step at all. On getting out of the barn he saw a Tartar village of about ten houses, and a Tartar church with a small tower. Three horses stood saddled before one of the houses; little boys were holding them by the reins. The dark Tartar came out of this house, beckoning with his hand for Zhílin to follow him. Then he laughed, said something in his own language, and returned into the house.

Zhílin entered. The room was a good one: the walls smoothly plastered with clay. Near the front wall lay a pile of bright-coloured feather beds; the side walls were covered with rich carpets used as hangings, and on these were fastened guns, pistols and swords, all inlaid with silver. Close to one of the walls was a small stove on a level with the earthen floor. The floor itself was as clean as a thrashing-ground. A large space in one corner was spread over with felt, on which were rugs, and on these rugs were cushions stuffed with down. And on these cushions sat five Tartars, the dark one, the red-haired one, and three guests. They were wearing their indoor slippers, and each had a cushion behind his back. Before them were standing millet cakes on a round board, melted butter in a bowl and a jug of buza, or Tartar beer. They ate both cakes and butter with their hands.

The dark man jumped up and ordered Zhílin to be placed on one side, not on the carpet but on the bare ground, then he sat down on the carpet again, and offered millet cakes and buza to his guests. The servant made Zhílin sit down, after which he took off his own overshoes, put them by the door where the other shoes were standing, and sat down nearer to his masters on the felt, watching them as they ate, and licking his lips.

The Tartars ate as much as they wanted, and a woman dressed in the same way as the girl - in a long gown and trousers, with a kerchief on her head - came and took away what was left, and brought a handsome basin, and an ewer with a narrow spout. The Tartars washed their hands, folded them, went down on their knees, blew to the four quarters, and said their prayers. After they had talked for a while, one of the guests turned to Zhílin and began to speak in Russian.

'You were captured by Kazi-Mohammed,' he said, and pointed at the red-bearded Tartar. 'And Kazi-Mohammed has given you to Abdul Murat,' pointing at the dark one. 'Abdul Murat is now your master.'

Zhílin was silent. Then Abdul Murat began to talk, laughing, pointing to Zhílin, and repeating, 'Soldier Russ, good Russ.'

The interpreter said, 'He orders you to write home and tell them to send a ransom, and as soon as the money comes he will set you free.'

Zhílin thought for a moment, and said, 'How much ransom does he want?'

The Tartars talked awhile, and then the interpreter said, 'Three thousand roubles.'

'No,' said Zhílin, 'I can't pay so much.'

Abdul jumped up and, waving his arms, talked to Zhílin' thinking, as before, that he would understand. The interpreter translated: 'How much will you give?'

Zhílin considered, and said, 'Five hundred roubles.' At this the Tartars began speaking very quickly, all together. Abdul began to shout at the red-bearded one, and jabbered so fast that the spittle spurted out of his mouth. The red-bearded one only screwed up his eyes and clicked his tongue.

They quietened down after a while, and the interpreter said, 'Five hundred roubles is not enough for the master. He paid two hundred for you himself. Kazi-Mohammed was in debt to him, and he took you in payment. Three thousand roubles! Less than that won't do. If you refuse to write, you will be put into a pit and flogged with a whip!'

'Eh!' thought Zhílin, 'the more one fears them the worse it will be.'

So he sprang to his feet, and said, 'You tell that dog that if he tries to frighten me I will not write at all, and he will get nothing. I never was afraid of you dogs, and never will be!'

The interpreter translated, and again they all began to talk at once.

They jabbered for a long time, and then the dark man jumped up, came to Zhílin, and said: 'Dzhigit Russ, dzhigit Russ!' (Dzhigit in their language means 'brave.') And he laughed, and said something to the interpreter, who translated: 'One thousand roubles will satisfy him.'

Zhílin stuck to it: 'I will not give more than five hundred. And if you kill me you'll get nothing at all.'

The Tartars talked awhile, then sent the servant out to fetch something, and kept looking, now at Zhílin, now at the door. The servant returned, followed by a stout, bare-footed, tattered man, who also had his leg shackled.

Zhílin gasped with surprise: it was Kostílin. He, too, had been taken. They were put side by side, and began to tell each other what had occurred. While they talked, the Tartars looked on in silence. Zhílin related what had happened to him; and Kostílin told how his horse had stopped, his gun missed fire, and this same Abdul had overtaken and captured him.

Abdul jumped up, pointed to Kostílin, and said something. The interpreter translated that they both now belonged to one master, and the one who first paid the ransom would be set free first.

'There now,' he said to Zhílin, 'you get angry, but your comrade here is gentle; he has written home, and they will send five thousand roubles. So he will be well fed and well treated.'

Zhílin replied: 'My comrade can do as he likes; maybe he is rich, I am not. It must be as I said. Kill me, if you like - you will gain nothing by it; but I will not write for more than five hundred roubles.'

They were silent. Suddenly up sprang Abdul, brought a little box, took out a pen, ink, and a bit of paper, gave them to Zhílin, slapped him on the shoulder, and made a sign that he should write. He had agreed to take five hundred roubles.

'Wait a bit!' said Zhílin to the interpreter; 'tell him that he must feed us properly, give us proper clothes and boots, and let us be together. It will be more cheerful for us. And he must have these shackles taken off our feet,' and Zhílin looked at his master and laughed.

The master also laughed, heard the interpreter, and said: 'I will give them the best of clothes: a cloak and boots fit to be married in. I will feed them like princes; and if they like they can live together in the barn. But I can't take off the shackles, or they will run away. They shall be taken off, however, at night.' And he jumped up and slapped Zhílin on the shoulder, exclaiming: 'You good, I good!'

Zhílin wrote the letter, but addressed it wrongly, so that it should not reach its destination, thinking to himself: 'I'll run away!'

Zhílin and Kostílin were taken back to the barn and given some maize straw, a jug of water, some bread, two old cloaks, and some worn-out military boots - evidently taken from the corpses of Russian soldiers, At night their shackles were taken off their feet, and they were locked up in the barn.

III

Zhílin and his friend lived in this way for a whole month. The master always laughed and said: 'You, Iván, good! I, Abdul, good!' But he fed them badly giving them nothing but unleavened bread of millet-flour baked into flat cakes, or sometimes only unbaked dough.

Kostílin wrote home a second time, and did nothing but mope and wait for the money to arrive. He would sit for days together in the barn sleeping, or counting the days till a letter could come.

Zhílin knew his letter would reach no one, and he did not write another. He thought: 'Where could my mother get enough money to ransom me? As it is she lived chiefly on what I sent her. If she had to raise five hundred roubles, she would be quite ruined. With God's help I'll manage to escape!'

So he kept on the look-out, planning how to run away.

He would walk about the Aoul whistling; or would sit working, modelling dolls of clay, or weaving baskets out of twigs: for Zhílin was clever with his hands.

Once he modelled a doll with a nose and hands and feet and with a Tartar gown on, and put it up on the roof. When the Tartar women came out to fetch water, the master's daughter, Dina, saw the doll and called the women, who put down their jugs and stood looking and laughing. Zhílin took down the doll and held it out to them. They laughed, but dared not take it. He put down the doll and went into the barn, waiting to see what would happen.

Dina ran up to the doll, looked round, seized it, and ran away.

In the morning, at daybreak, he looked out. Dina came out of the house and sat down on the threshold with the doll, which she had dressed up in bits of red stuff, and she rocked it like a baby, singing a Tartar lullaby. An old woman came out and scolded her, and snatching the doll away she broke it to bits, and sent Dina about her business.

But Zhílin made another doll, better than the first, and gave it to Dina. Once Dina brought a little jug, put it on the ground, sat down gazing at him, and laughed, pointing to the jug.

'What pleases her so?' wondered Zhílin. He took the jug thinking it was water, but it turned out to be milk. He drank the milk and said: 'That's good!'

How pleased Dina was! 'Good, Iván, good!' said she, and she jumped up and clapped her hands. Then, seizing the jug, she ran away. After that, she stealthily brought him some milk every day.

The Tartars make a kind of cheese out of goat's milk, which they dry on the roofs of their houses; and sometimes, on the sly, she brought him some of this cheese. And once, when Abdul had killed a sheep she brought Zhílin a bit of mutton in her sleeve. She would just throw the things down and run away.

One day there was a heavy storm, and the rain fell in torrents for a whole hour. All the streams became turbid. At the ford, the water rose till it was seven feet high, and the current was so strong that it rolled the stones about. Rivulets flowed everywhere, and the rumbling in the hills never ceased. When the storm was over, the water ran in streams down the village street. Zhílin got his master to lend him a knife, and with it he shaped a small cylinder, and cutting some little boards, he made a wheel to which he fixed two dolls, one on each side. The little girls brought him some bits of stuff, and he dressed the dolls, one as a peasant, the other as a peasant woman. Then he fastened them in their places, and set the wheel so that the stream should work it. The wheel began to turn and the dolls danced.

The whole village collected round. Little boys and girls, Tartar men and women, all came and clicked their tongues.

'Ah, Russ! Ah, Iván!'

Abdul had a Russian clock, which was broken. He called Zhílin and showed it to him, clicking his tongue.

'Give it me, I'll mend it for you,' said Zhílin.

He took it to pieces with the knife, sorted the pieces, and put them together again, so that the clock went all right.

The master was delighted, and made him a present of one of his old tunics which was all in holes. Zhílin had to accept it. He could, at any rate, use it as a coverlet at night.

After that Zhílin's fame spread; and Tartars came from distant villages, bringing him now the lock of a gun or of a pistol, now a watch, to mend. His master gave him some tools - pincers, gimlets, and a file.

One day a Tartar fell ill, and they came to Zhílin saying, 'Come and heal him!' Zhílin knew nothing about doctoring, but he went to look, and thought to himself, 'Perhaps he will get well anyway.'

He returned to the barn, mixed some water with sand, and then in the presence of the Tartars whispered some words over it and gave it to the sick man to drink. Luckily for him, the Tartar recovered.

Zhílin began to pick up their language a little, and some of the Tartars grew familiar with him. When they wanted him, they would call: 'Iván! Iván!' Others, however, still looked at him askance, as at a wild beast.

The red-bearded Tartar disliked Zhílin. Whenever he saw him he frowned and turned away, or swore at him. There was also an old man there who did not live in the Aoul, but used to come up from the foot of the hill. Zhílin only saw him when he passed on his way to the Mosque. He was short, and had a white cloth wound round his hat. His beard and moustaches were clipped, and white as snow; and his face was wrinkled and brick-red. His nose was hooked like a hawk's, his grey eyes looked cruel, and he had no teeth except two tusks. He would pass, with his turban on his head, leaning on his staff, and glaring round him like a wolf. If he saw Zhílin he would snort with anger and turn away.

Once Zhílin descended the hill to see where the old man lived. He went down along the pathway and came to a little garden surrounded by a stone wall; and behind the wall he saw cherry and apricot trees, and a hut with a flat roof. He came closer, and saw hives made of plaited straw, and bees flying about and humming. The old man was kneeling, busy doing something with a hive. Zhílin stretched to look, and his shackles rattled. The old man turned round, and, giving a yell, snatched a pistol from his belt and shot at Zhílin, who just managed to shelter himself behind the stone wall.

The old man went to Zhílin's master to complain. The master called Zhílin, and said with a laugh, 'Why did you go to the old man's house?'

'I did him no harm,' replied Zhílin. 'I only wanted to see how he lived.'

The master repeated what Zhílin said.

But the old man was in a rage; he hissed and jabbered, showing his tusks, and shaking his fists at Zhílin.

Zhílin could not understand all, but he gathered that the old man was telling Abdul he ought not to keep Russians in the Aoul, but ought to kill them. At last the old man went away.

Zhílin asked the master who the old man was.

'He is a great man!' said the master. 'He was the bravest of our fellows;

he killed many Russians and was at one time very rich. He had three wives and eight sons, and they all lived in one village. Then the Russians came and destroyed the village, and killed seven of his sons. Only one son was left, and he gave himself up to the Russians. The old man also went and gave himself up, and lived among the Russians for three months. At the end of that time he found his son, killed him with his own hands, and then escaped. After that he left off fighting, and went to Mecca to pray to God; that is why he wears a turban. One who has been to Mecca is called "Hadji," and wears a turban. He does not like you fellows. He tells me to kill you. But I can't kill you. I have paid money for you and, besides, I have grown fond of you, Iván. Far from killing you, I would not even let you go if I had not promised.' And he laughed, saying in Russian, 'You, Iván, good; I, Abdul, good!'

IV

Zhílin lived in this way for a month. During the day he sauntered about the Aoul or busied himself with some handicraft, but at night, when all was silent in the Aoul, he dug at the floor of the barn. It was no easy task digging, because of the stones; but he worked away at them with his file, and at last had made a hole under the wall large enough to get through.

'If only I could get to know the lay of the land,' thought he, 'and which way to go! But none of the Tartars will tell me.'

So he chose a day when the master was away from home, and set off after dinner to climb the hill beyond the village, and to look around. But before leaving home the master always gave orders to his son to watch Zhílin, and not to lose sight of him. So the lad ran after Zhílin, shouting: 'Don't go! Father does not allow it. I'll call the neighbours if you won't come back.'

Zhílin tried to persuade him, and said: 'I'm not going far; I only want to climb that hill. I want to find a herb - to cure sick people with. You come with me if you like. How can I run away with these shackles on? To-morrow I'll make a bow and arrows for you.'

So he persuaded the lad, and they went. To look at the hill, it did not seem far to the top; but it was hard walking with shackles on his leg.

Zhílin went on and on, but it was all he could do to reach the top. There he sat down and noted how the land lay. To the south, beyond the barn, was a valley in which a herd of horses was pasturing and at the bottom of the valley one could see another Aoul. Beyond that was a still steeper hill, and another hill beyond that. Between the hills, in the blue distance, were forests, and still further off were mountains, rising higher and higher. The highest of them were covered with snow, white as sugar; and one snowy peak towered above all the rest. To the east and to the west were other such hills, and here and there smoke rose from Aouls in the ravines. 'Ah,' thought he, 'all that is Tartar country.' And he turned towards the Russian side. At his feet he saw a river, and the Aoul he lived in, surrounded by little gardens. He could see women, like tiny dolls, sitting by the river rinsing clothes. Beyond the Aoul was a hill, lower than the one to the south, and beyond it two other hills well wooded; and between these, a smooth bluish plain, and far, far across the plain something that looked like a cloud of smoke. Zhílin tried to remember where the sun used to rise and set when he was living in the fort, and he saw that there was no mistake: the Russian fort must be in that plain. Between those two hills he would have to make his way when he escaped.

The sun was beginning to set. The white, snowy mountains turned red, and the dark hills turned darker; mists rose from the ravine, and the valley, where he supposed the Russian fort to be, seemed on fire with the sunset glow. Zhílin looked carefully. Something seemed to be quivering in the valley like smoke from a chimney, and he felt sure the Russian fortress was there.

It had grown late. The Mullah's cry was heard. The herds were being driven home, the cows were lowing, and the lad kept saying, 'Come home!' But Zhílin did not feel inclined to go away.

At last, however, they went back. 'Well,' thought Zhílin, 'now that I know the way, it is time to escape.' He thought of running away that night. The nights were dark - the moon had waned. But as ill-luck would have it, the Tartars returned home that evening. They generally came back driving cattle before them and in good spirits. But this time they had no cattle. All they brought home was the dead body of a Tartar - the red one's brother - who had been killed. They came back looking sullen, and they all gathered together for the burial. Zhílin also came out to see it.

They wrapped the body in a piece of linen, without any coffin, and carried it out of the village, and laid it on the grass under some plane-trees. The Mullah and the old men came. They wound clothes round their caps, took off their shoes, and squatted on their heels, side by side, near the corpse.

The Mullah was in front: behind him in a row were three old men in turbans, and behind them again the other Tartars. All cast down their eyes and sat in silence. This continued a long time, until the Mullah raised his head and said: 'Allah!' (which means God). He said that one word, and they all cast down their eyes again, and were again silent for a long time. They sat quite still, not moving or making any sound.

Again the Mullah lifted his head and said, 'Allah!' and they all repeated: 'Allah! Allah!' and were again silent.

The dead body lay immovable on the grass, and they sat as still as if they too were dead. Not one of them moved. There was no sound but that of the leaves of the plane-trees stirring in the breeze. Then the Mullah repeated a prayer, and they all rose. They lifted the body and carried it in their arms to a hole in the ground. It was not an ordinary hole, but was hollowed out under the ground like a vault. They took the body under the arms and by the legs, bent it, and let it gently down, pushing it under the earth in a sitting posture, with the hands folded in front.

The Nogáy brought some green rushes, which they stuffed into the hole, and, quickly covering it with earth, they smoothed the ground, and set an upright stone at the head of the grave. Then they trod the earth down, and again sat in a row before the grave, keeping silence for a long time.

At last they rose, said 'Allah! Allah! Allah!' and sighed.

The red-bearded Tartar gave money to the old men; then he too rose, took a whip, struck himself with it three times on the forehead, and went home.

The next morning Zhílin saw the red Tartar, followed by three others, leading a mare out of the village. When they were beyond the village, the red-bearded Tartar took off his tunic and turned up his sleeves, showing his stout arms. Then he drew a dagger and sharpened it on a whetstone. The other Tartars raised the mare's head, and he cut her throat, threw her down and began skinning her, loosening the hide with his big hands.

Women and girls came and began to wash the entrails and the inwards. The mare was cut up, the pieces taken into the hut, and the whole village collected at the red Tartar's hut for a funeral feast.

For three days they went on eating the flesh of the mare, drinking buza, and praying for the dead man. All the Tartars were at home. On the fourth day at dinner-time Zhílin saw them preparing to go away. Horses were brought out, they got ready, and some ten of them (the red one among them) rode away; but Abdul stayed at home. It was new moon, and the nights were still dark.

'Ah!' thought Zhílin, 'to-night is the time to escape.' And he told Kostílin; but Kostílin's heart failed him.

'How can we escape?' he said. 'We don't even know the way.'

'I know the way,' said Zhílin.

'Even if you do" said Kostílin, 'we can't reach the fort in one night.'

'If we can't,' said Zhílin, 'we'll sleep in the forest. See here, I have saved some cheeses. What's the good of sitting and moping here? If they send your ransom - well and good; but suppose they don't manage to collect it? The Tartars are angry now, because the Russians have killed one of their men. They are talking of killing us.'

Kostílin thought it over.

'Well, let's go,' said he.

V

Zhílin crept into the hole, widened it so that Kostílin might also get through, and then they both sat waiting till all should be quiet in the Aoul.

As soon as all was quiet, Zhílin crept under the wall, got out, and whispered to Kostílin, 'Come!' Kostílin crept out, but in so doing he caught a stone with his foot and made a noise. The master had a very vicious watch-dog, a spotted one called Oulyashin. Zhílin had been careful to feed him for some time before. Oulyashin heard the noise and began to bark and jump, and the other dogs did the same. Zhílin gave a slight whistle, and threw him a bit of cheese. Oulyashin knew Zhílin, wagged his tail, and stopped barking.

But the master had heard the dog, and shouted to him from his hut, 'Hayt, hayt, Oulyashin!'

Zhílin, however, scratched Oulyashin behind the ears, and the dog was quiet, and rubbed against his legs, wagging his tail

They sat hidden behind a corner for awhile. All became silent again, only a sheep coughed inside a shed, and the water rippled over the stones in the hollow. It was dark, the stars were high overhead, and the new moon showed red as it set, horns upward, behind the hill. In the valleys the fog was white as milk.

Zhílin rose and said to his companion, 'Well, friend, come along!'

They started; but they had only gone a few steps when they heard the Mullah crying from the roof, 'Allah, Beshmillah! Ilrahman!' That meant that the people would be going to the Mosque. So they sat down again, hiding behind a wall, and waited a long time till the people had passed. At last all was quiet again.

'Now then! May God be with us!' They crossed themselves, and started once more. They passed through a yard and went down the hillside to the river, crossed the river, and went along the valley.

The mist was thick, but only near the ground; overhead the stars shone quite brightly. Zhílin directed their course by the stars. It was cool in the mist, and easy walking, only their boots were uncomfortable, being worn out and trodden down. Zhílin took his off, threw them away, and went barefoot, jumping from stone to stone, and guiding his course by the stars. Kostílin began to lag behind.

'Walk slower,' he said, 'these confounded boots have quite blistered my feet.'

'Take them off!' said Zhílin. 'It will be easier walking without them.'

Kostílin went barefoot, but got on still worse. The stones cut his feet and he kept lagging behind. Zhílin said: 'If your feet get cut, they'll heal again; but if the Tartars catch us and kill us, it will be worse!'

Kostílin did not reply, but went on, groaning all the time.

Their way lay through the valley for a long time. Then, to the right, they heard dogs barking. Zhílin stopped, looked about, and began climbing the hill feeling with his hands.

'Ah!' said he, 'we have gone wrong, and have come too far to the right.

Here is another Aoul, one I saw from the hill. We must turn back and go up that hill to the left. There must be a wood there.'

But Kostílin said: 'Wait a minute! Let me get breath. My feet are all cut and bleeding.'

'Never mind, friend! They'll heal again. You should spring more lightly. Like this!'

And Zhílin ran back and turned to the left up the hill towards the wood.

Kostílin still lagged behind, and groaned. Zhílin only said 'Hush!' and went on and on.

They went up the hill and found a wood as Zhílin had said. They entered the wood and forced their way through the brambles, which tore their clothes. At last they came to a path and followed it.

'Stop!' They heard the tramp of hoofs on the path, and waited, listening. It sounded like the tramping of a horse's feet, but then ceased. They moved on, and again they heard the tramping. When they paused, it also stopped. Zhílin crept nearer to it, and saw something standing on the path where it was not quite so dark. It looked like a horse, and yet not quite like one, and on it was something queer, not like a man. He heard it snorting. 'What can it be?' Zhílin gave a low whistle, and off it dashed from the path into the thicket, and the woods were filled with the noise of crackling, as if a hurricane were sweeping through, breaking the branches.

Kostílin was so frightened that he sank to the ground. But Zhílin laughed and said: 'It's a stag. Don't you hear him breaking the branches with his antlers? We were afraid of him, and he is afraid of us.'

They went on. The Great Bear was already setting. It was near morning, and they did not know whether they were going the right way or not. Zhílin thought it was the way he had been brought by the Tartars, and that they were still some seven miles from the Russian fort; but he had nothing certain to go by, and at night one easily mistakes the way. After a time they came to a clearing. Kostílin sat down and said: 'Do as you like, I can go no farther! My feet won't carry me.'

Zhílin tried to persuade him.

'No I shall never get there, I can't!'

Zhílin grew angry, and spoke roughly to him.

'Well, then, I shall go on alone. Good-bye!'

Kostílin jumped up and followed. They went another three miles. The mist in the wood had settled down still more densely; they could not see a yard before them, and the stars had grown dim.

Suddenly they heard the sound of a horse's hoofs in front of them. They heard its shoes strike the stones. Zhílin lay down flat, and listened with his ear to the ground.

'Yes, so it is! A horseman is coming towards us.'

They ran off the path, crouched among the bushes and waited. Zhílin crept to the road, looked, and saw a Tartar on horseback driving a cow and humming to himself. The Tartar rode past. Zhílin returned to Kostílin.

'God has led him past us; get up and let's go on!'

Kostílin tried to rise, but fell back again.

'I can't; on my word I can't! I have no strength left.'

He was heavy and stout, and had been perspiring freely. Chilled by the mist, and with his feet all bleeding, he had grown quite limp.

Zhílin tried to lift him, when suddenly Kostílin screamed out: 'Oh, how it hurts!'

Zhílin's heart sank.

'What are you shouting for? The Tartar is still near; he'll have heard you!' And he thought to himself, 'He is really quite done up. What am I to do with him? It won't do to desert a comrade.'

'Well, then, get up, and climb up on my back. I'll carry you if you really can't walk.'

He helped Kostílin up, and put his arms under his thighs. Then he went out on to the path, carrying him.

'Only, for the love of heaven,' said Zhílin, 'don't throttle me with your hands! Hold on to my shoulders.'

Zhílin found his load heavy; his feet, too, were bleeding, and he was tired out. Now and then he stooped to balance Kostílin better, jerking him up so that he should sit higher, and then went on again.

The Tartar must, however, really have heard Kostílin scream. Zhílin suddenly heard someone galloping behind and shouting in the Tartar tongue. He darted in among the bushes. The Tartar seized his gun and fired, but did not hit them, shouted in his own language, and galloped off along the road.

'Well, now we are lost, friend!' said Zhílin. 'That dog will gather the Tartars together to hunt us down. Unless we can get a couple of miles away from here we are lost!' And he thought to himself, 'Why the devil did I saddle myself with this block? I should have got away long ago had I been alone.'

'Go on alone,' said Kostílin. 'Why should you perish because of me?'

'No I won't go. It won't do to desert a comrade.'

Again he took Kostílin on his shoulders and staggered on. They went on in that way for another half-mile or more. They were still in the forest, and could not see the end of it. But the mist was already dispersing, and clouds seemed to be gathering, the stars were no longer to be seen. Zhílin was quite done up. They came to a spring walled in with stones by the side of the path. Zhílin stopped and set Kostílin down.

'Let me have a rest and a drink,' said he, 'and let us eat some of the cheese. It can't be much farther now.'

But hardly had he lain down to get a drink, when he heard the sound of horses' feet behind him. Again they darted to the right among the bushes, and lay down under a steep slope.

They heard Tartar voices. The Tartars stopped at the very spot where they had turned off the path. The Tartars talked a bit, and then seemed to be setting a dog on the scent. There was a sound of crackling twigs, and a strange dog appeared from behind the bushes. It stopped, and began to bark.

Then the Tartars, also strangers, came climbing down, seized Zhílin and Kostílin, bound them, put them on horses, and rode away with them.

When they had ridden about two miles, they met Abdul, their owner, with two other Tartars following him. After talking with the strangers, he put Zhílin and Kostílin on two of his own horses and took them back to the Aoul.

Abdul did not laugh now, and did not say a word to them.

They were back at the Aoul by daybreak, and were set down in the street. The children came crowding round, throwing stones, shrieking, and beating them with whips.

The Tartars gathered together in a circle, and the old man from the foot of the hill was also there. They began discussing, and Zhílin heard them considering what should be done with him and Kostílin. Some said they ought to be sent farther into the mountains; but the old man said: 'They must be killed!'

Abdul disputed with him, saying: 'I gave money for them, and I must get ransom for them.' But the old man said: 'They will pay you nothing, but will only bring misfortune. It is a sin to feed Russians. Kill them, and have done with it!'

They dispersed. When they had gone, the master came up to Zhílin and said: 'If the money for your ransom is not sent within a fortnight, I will flog you; and if you try to run away again, I'll kill you like a dog! Write a letter, and write properly!'

Paper was brought to them, and they wrote the letters. Shackles were put on their feet, and they were taken behind the Mosque to a deep pit about twelve feet square, into which they were let down.

VI

Life was now very hard for them. Their shackles were never taken off, and they were not let out into the fresh air. Unbaked dough was thrown to them as if they were dogs, and water was let down in a can.

It was wet and close in the pit, and there was a horrible stench. Kostílin grew quite ill, his body became swollen and he ached all over, and moaned or slept all the time. Zhílin, too, grew downcast; he saw it was a bad look-out, and could think of no way of escape.

He tried to make a tunnel, but there was nowhere to put the earth. His master noticed it, and threatened to kill him.

He was sitting on the floor of the pit one day, thinking of freedom and feeling very downhearted, when suddenly a cake fell into his lap, then another, and then a shower of cherries. He looked up, and there was Dina. She looked at him, laughed, and ran away. And Zhílin thought: 'Might not Dina help me?'

He cleared out a little place in the pit, scraped up some clay, and began modelling toys. He made men, horses, and dogs, thinking, 'When Dina comes I'll throw them up to her.'

But Dina did not come next day. Zhílin heard the tramp of horses; some men rode past, and the Tartars gathered in council near the Mosque. They shouted and argued; the word 'Russians' was repeated several times. He could hear the voice of the old man. Though he could not distinguish what was said, he guessed that Russian troops were somewhere near, and that the Tartars, afraid they might come into the Aoul, did not know what to do with their prisoners.

After talking awhile, they went away. Suddenly he heard a rustling overhead, and saw Dina crouching at the edge of the pit, her knees higher than her head, and bending over so that the coins of her plait dangled above the pit. Her eyes gleamed like stars. She drew two cheeses out of her sleeve and threw them to him. Zhílin took them and said, 'Why did you not come before? I have made some toys for you. Here, catch!' And he began throwing the toys up, one by one.

But she shook her head and would not look at them.

'I don't want any,' she said. She sat silent for awhile, and then went on, 'Iván, they want to kill you!' And she pointed to her own throat.

'Who wants to kill me?'

'Father; the old men say he must. But I am sorry for you!'

Zhílin answered: 'Well, if you are sorry for me, bring me a long pole.'

She shook her head, as much as to say, 'I can't!'

He clasped his hands and prayed her: 'Dina, please do! Dear Dina, I beg of you!'

'I can't!' she said, 'they would see me bringing it. They're all at home.' And she went away.

So when evening came Zhílin still sat looking up now and then, and wondering what would happen. The stars were there, but the moon had not yet risen. The Mullah's voice was heard; then all was silent. Zhílin was beginning to doze, thinking: 'The girl will be afraid to do it!'

Suddenly he felt clay falling on his head. He looked up, and saw a long pole poking into the opposite wall of the pit. It kept poking about for a time, and then it came down, sliding into the pit. Zhílin was glad indeed. He took hold of it and lowered it. It was a strong pole, one that he had seen before on the roof of his master's hut.

He looked up. The stars were shining high in the sky, and just above the pit Dina's eyes gleamed in the dark like a cat's. She stooped with her face close to the edge of the pit, and whispered, 'Iván! Iván!' waving her hand in front of her face to show that he should speak low.

'What?' said Zhílin.

'All but two have gone away.'

Then Zhílin said, 'Well, Kostílin, come; let us have one last try; I'll help you up.'

But Kostílin would not hear of it.

'No,' said he, 'It's clear I can't get away from here. How can I go, when I have hardly strength to turn round?'

'Well, good-bye, then! Don't think ill of me!' and they kissed each other. Zhílin seized the pole, told Dina to hold on, and began to climb. He slipped once or twice; the shackles hindered him. Kostílin helped him, and he managed to get to the top. Dina with her little hands, pulled with all her might at his shirt, laughing.

Zhílin drew out the pole and said, 'Put it back in its place, Dina, or they'll notice, and you will be beaten.'

She dragged the pole away, and Zhílin went down the hill. When he had gone down the steep incline, he took a sharp stone and tried to wrench the lock off the shackles. But it was a strong lock and he could not manage to break it, and besides, it was difficult to get at. Then he heard someone running down the hill, springing lightly. He thought: 'Surely, that's Dina again.'

Dina came, took a stone and said, 'Let me try.'

She knelt down and tried to wrench the lock off, but her little hands were as slender as little twigs, and she had not the strength. She threw the stone away and began to cry. Then Zhílin set to work again at the lock, and Dina squatted beside him with her hand on his shoulder.

Zhílin looked round and saw a red light to the left behind the hill. The moon was just rising. 'Ah!' he thought, 'before the moon has risen I must have passed the valley and be in the forest.' So he rose and threw away the stone. Shackles or no, he must go on.

'Good-bye, Dina dear!' he said. 'I shall never forget you!'

Dina seized hold of him and felt about with her hands for a place to put some cheeses she had brought. He took them from her.

'Thank you, my little one. Who will make dolls for you when I am gone?' And he stroked her head.

Dina burst into tears hiding her face in her hands. Then she ran up the hill like a young goat, the coins in her plait clinking against her back.

Zhílin crossed himself took the lock of his shackles in his hand to prevent its clattering, and went along the road, dragging his shackled leg, and looking towards the place where the moon was about to rise. He now knew the way. If he went straight he would have to walk nearly six miles. If only he could reach the wood before the moon had quite risen! He crossed the river; the light behind the hill was growing whiter. Still looking at it, he went along the valley. The moon was not yet visible. The light became brighter, and one side of the valley was growing lighter and lighter, and shadows were drawing in towards the foot of the hill, creeping nearer and nearer to him.

Zhílin went on, keeping in the shade. He was hurrying, but the moon was moving still faster; the tops of the hills on the right were already lit up. As he got near the wood the white moon appeared from behind the hills, and it became light as day. One could see all the leaves on the trees. It was light on the hill, but silent, as if nothing were alive; no sound could be heard but the gurgling of the river below.

Zhílin reached the wood without meeting any one, chose a dark spot, and sat down to rest.

He rested and ate one of the cheeses. Then he found a stone and set to work again to knock off the shackles. He knocked his hands sore, but could not break the lock. He rose and went along the road. After walking the greater part of a mile he was quite done up, and his feet were aching. He had to stop every ten steps. 'There is nothing else for it,' thought he. 'I must drag on as long as I have any strength left. If I sit down, I shan't be able to rise again. I can't reach the fortress; but when day breaks I'll lie down in the forest, remain there all day, and go on again at night.'

He went on all night. Two Tartars on horseback passed him; but he heard them a long way off, and hid behind a tree.

The moon began to grow paler, the dew to fall. It was getting near dawn, and Zhílin had not reached the end of the forest. 'Well,' thought he, 'I'll walk another thirty steps, and then turn in among the trees and sit down.'

He walked another thirty steps, and saw that he was at the end of the forest. He went to the edge; it was now quite light, and straight before him was the plain and the fortress. To the left, quite close at the foot of the slope, a fire was dying out, and the smoke from it spread round. There were men gathered about the fire.

He looked intently, and saw guns glistening. They were soldiers - Cossacks!

Zhílin was filled with joy. He collected his remaining strength and set off down the hill, saying to himself: 'God forbid that any mounted Tartar should see me now, in the open field! Near as I am, I could not get there in time.'

Hardly had he said this when, a couple of hundred yards off, on a hillock to the left, he saw three Tartars.

They saw him also and made a rush. His heart sank. He waved his hands, and shouted with all his might, 'Brothers, brothers! Help!'

The Cossacks heard him, and a party of them on horseback darted to cut across the Tartars' path. The Cossacks were far and the Tartars were near; but Zhílin, too, made a last effort. Lifting the shackles with his hand, he ran towards the Cossacks, hardly knowing what he was doing, crossing himself and shouting, 'Brothers! Brothers! Brothers!'

There were some fifteen Cossacks. The Tartars were frightened, and stopped before reaching him. Zhilin staggered up to the Cossacks.

They surrounded him and began questioning him. 'Who are you? What are you? Where from?'

But Zhílin was quite beside himself, and could only weep and repeat, 'Brothers! Brothers!'

Then the soldiers came running up and crowded round Zhílin - one giving him bread, another buckwheat, a third vódka: one wrapping a cloak round him, another breaking his shackles.

The officers recognized him, and rode with him to the fortress. The soldiers were glad to see him back, and his comrades all gathered round him.

Zhílin told them all that had happened to him.

'That's the way I went home and got married!' said he. 'No. It seems plain that fate was against it!'

So he went on serving in the Caucasus. A month passed before Kostílin was released, after paying five thousand roubles ransom. He was almost dead when they brought him back.

EVIL ALLURES, BUT GOD ENDURES

There lived in olden times a good and kindly man. He had this world's goods in abundance, and many slaves to serve him. And the slaves prided themselves on their master, saying:

'There is no better lord than ours under the sun. He feeds and clothes us well, and gives us work suited to our strength. He bears no malice and never speaks a harsh word to anyone. He is not like other masters, who treat their slaves worse than cattle: punishing them whether they deserve it or not and never giving them a friendly word. He wishes us well, does good and speaks kindly to us. We do not wish for a better life.'

Thus the slaves praised their lord, and the Devil, seeing it, was vexed that slaves should live in such love and harmony with their master. So getting one of them, whose name was Aleb, into his power, the Devil ordered him to tempt the other slaves. And one day, when they were all sitting together resting and talking of their master's goodness, Aleb raised his voice, and said:

'It is stupid to make so much of our master's goodness. The Devil himself would be kind to you, if you did what he wanted. We serve our master well, and humour him in all things. As soon as he thinks of anything, we do it: foreseeing all his wishes. What can he do but be kind to us? Just try how it will be if, instead of humouring him, we do him some harm instead. He will act like anyone else, and will repay evil for evil, as the worst of masters do.'

The other slaves began denying what Aleb had said and at last bet with him. Aleb undertook to make their master angry. If he failed, he was to lose his holiday garment; but if he succeeded, the other slaves were to give him theirs. Moreover, they promised to defend him against the master, and to set him free if he should be put in chains or imprisoned. Having arranged this bet, Aleb agreed to make his master angry next morning.

Aleb was a shepherd, and had in his charge a number of valuable, pure-bred sheep, of which his master was very fond. Next morning, when the master brought some visitors into the inclosure to show them the valuable sheep, Aleb winked at his companions, as if to say:

'See, now, how angry I will make him.'

All the other slaves assembled, looking in at the gates or over the fence, and the Devil climbed a tree nearby to see how his servant would do his work. The master walked about the inclosure, showing his guests the ewes and lambs, and presently he wished to show them his finest ram.

'All the rams are valuable,' said he, 'but I have one with closely twisted horns, which is priceless. I prize him as the apple of my eye.'

Startled by the strangers, the sheep rushed about the inclosure, so that the visitors could not get a good look at the ram. As soon as it stood still, Aleb startled the sheep as if by accident, and they all got mixed up again. The visitors could not make out which was the priceless ram. At last the master got tired of it.

'Aleb, dear friend,' he said, 'pray catch our best ram for me, the one with the tightly twisted horns. Catch him very carefully, and hold him still for a moment.'

Scarcely had the master said this, when Aleb rushed in among the sheep like a lion, and clutched the priceless ram. Holding him fast by the wool, he seized the left hind leg with one hand, and, before his master's eyes, lifted it and jerked it so that it snapped like a dry branch. He had broken the ram's leg and it fell bleating on to its knees. Then Aleb seized the right hind leg, while the left twisted round and hung quite limp. The visitors and the slaves exclaimed in dismay, and the Devil, sitting up in the tree, rejoiced that Aleb had done his task so cleverly. The master looked as black as thunder, frowned, bent his head, and did not say a word. The visitors and the slaves were silent too, waiting to see what would follow. After remaining silent for a while, the master shook himself as if to throw off some burden. Then he lifted his head, and raising his eyes heavenward, remained so for a short time. Presently the wrinkles passed from his face, and he looked down at Aleb with a smile saying:

'Oh, Aleb, Aleb! Your master bade you anger me; but my master is stronger than yours. I am not angry with you, but I will make your master angry. You are afraid that I shall punish you, and you have been wishing for your freedom. Know, then, Aleb, that I shall not punish you; but, as you wish to be free, here, before my guests, I set you free. Go where you like, and take your holiday garment with you!'

And the kind master returned with his guests to the house; but the Devil, grinding his teeth, fell down from the tree, and sank through the ground.

THE IMP AND THE CRUST

A poor peasant set out early one morning to plough, taking with him for his breakfast a crust of bread. He got his plough ready, wrapped the bread in his coat, put it under a bush, and set to work. After a while when his horse was tired and he was hungry, the peasant fixed the plough, let the horse loose to graze and went to get his coat and his breakfast.

He lifted the coat, but the bread was gone! He looked and looked, turned the coat over, shook it out - but the bread was gone. The peasant could not make this out at all.

'That's strange,' thought he; 'I saw no one, but all the same someone has been here and has taken the bread!'

It was an imp who had stolen the bread while the peasant was ploughing, and at that moment he was sitting behind the bush, waiting to hear the peasant swear and call on the Devil.

The peasant was sorry to lose his breakfast, but 'It can't be helped,' said he. 'After all, I shan't die of hunger! No doubt whoever took the bread needed it. May it do him good!'

And he went to the well, had a drink of water, and rested a bit. Then he caught his horse, harnessed it, and began ploughing again.

The imp was crestfallen at not having made the peasant sin, and he went to report what had happened to the Devil, his master.

He came to the Devil and told how he had taken the peasant's bread, and how the peasant instead of cursing had said, 'May it do him good!'

The Devil was angry, and replied: 'If the man got the better of you, it was your own fault - you don't understand your business! If the peasants, and their wives after them, take to that sort of thing, it will be all up with us. The matter can't be left like that! Go back at once,' said he, 'and put things right. If in three years you don't get the better of that peasant, I'll have you ducked in holy water!'

The imp was frightened. He scampered back to earth, thinking how he could redeem his fault. He thought and thought, and at last hit upon a good plan.

He turned himself into a labouring man, and went and took service with the poor peasant. The first year he advised the peasant to sow corn in a marshy place. The peasant took his advice, and sowed in the marsh. The year turned out a very dry one, and the crops of the other peasants were all scorched by the sun, but the poor peasant's corn grew thick and tall and full-eared. Not only had he grain enough to last him for the whole year, but he had much left over besides.

The next year the imp advised the peasant to sow on the hill; and it turned out a wet summer. Other people's corn was beaten down and rotted and the ears did not fill; but the peasant's crop, up on the hill, was a fine one. He had more grain left over than before, so that he did not know what to do with it all.

Then the imp showed the peasant how he could mash the grain and distil spirit from it; and the peasant made strong drink, and began to drink it himself and to give it to his friends.

So the imp went to the Devil, his master, and boasted that he had made up for his failure. The Devil said that he would come and see for himself how the case stood.

He came to the peasant's house, and saw that the peasant had invited his well-to-do neighbours and was treating them to drink. His wife was offering the drink to the guests, and as she handed it round she tumbled against the table and spilt a glassful.

The peasant was angry, and scolded his wife: 'What do you mean, you slut? Do you think it's ditchwater, you cripple, that you must go pouring good stuff like that over the floor?'

The imp nudged the Devil, his master, with his elbow: 'See,' said he, 'that's the man who did not grudge his last crust!'

The peasant, still railing at his wife, began to carry the drink round himself. Just then a poor peasant returning from work came in uninvited. He greeted the company, sat down, and saw that they were drinking. Tired with his day's work he felt that he too would like a drop. He sat and sat, and his mouth kept watering, but the host instead of offering him any only muttered: 'I can't find drink for everyone who comes along.'

This pleased the Devil; but the imp chuckled and said, 'Wait a bit, there's more to come yet!'

The rich peasants drank, and their host drank too. And they began to make false, oily speeches to one another.

The Devil listened and listened, and praised the imp.

'If,' said he, 'the drink makes them so foxy that they begin to cheat each other, they will soon all be in our hands.'

'Wait for what's coming,' said the imp. 'Let them have another glass all round. Now they are like foxes, wagging their tails and trying to get round one another; but presently you will see them like savage wolves.'

The peasants had another glass each, and their talk became wilder and rougher. Instead of oily speeches they began to abuse and snarl at one another. Soon they took to fighting, and punched one another's noses. And the host joined in the fight, and he too got well beaten.

The Devil looked on and was much pleased at all this. 'This is first-rate!' said he.

But the imp replied: 'Wait a bit - the best is yet to come. Wait till they have had a third glass. Now they are raging like wolves, but let them have one more glass, and they will be like swine.'

The peasants had their third glass, and became quite like brutes. They muttered and shouted, not knowing why, and not listening to one another.

Then the party began to break up. Some went alone, some in twos, and some in threes, all staggering down the street. The host went out to speed his guests, but he fell on his nose into a puddle, smeared himself from top to toe, and lay there grunting like a hog.

This pleased the Devil still more.

'Well,' said he, 'you have hit on a first-rate drink, and have quite made up for your blunder about the bread. But now tell me how this drink is made. You must first have put in fox's blood: that was what made the peasants sly as foxes. Then, I suppose, you added wolf's blood: that is what made them fierce like wolves. And you must have finished off with swine's blood, to make them behave like swine.'

'No,' said the imp, 'that was not the way I did it. All I did was to see that the peasant had more corn than he needed. The blood of the beasts is always in man; but as long as he has only enough corn for his needs, it is kept in bounds. While that was the case, the peasant did not grudge his last crust. But when he had corn left over, he looked for ways of getting pleasure out of it. And I showed him a pleasure - drinking! And when he began to turn God's good gifts into spirits for his own pleasure - the fox's, wolf's and swine's blood in him all came out. If only he goes on drinking, he will always be a beast!'

The Devil praised the imp, forgave him for his former blunder, and advanced him to a post of high honour.

THE KREUTZER SONATA

I

Travellers left and entered our car at every stopping of the train. Three persons, however, remained, bound, like myself, for the farthest station: a lady neither young nor pretty, smoking cigarettes, with a thin face, a cap on her head, and wearing a semi-masculine outer garment; then her companion, a very loquacious gentleman of about forty years, with baggage entirely new and arranged in an orderly manner; then a gentleman who held himself entirely aloof, short in stature, very nervous, of uncertain age, with bright eyes, not pronounced in color, but extremely attractive, - eyes that darted with rapidity from one object to another.

This gentleman, during almost all the journey thus far, had entered into conversation with no fellow-traveller, as if he carefully avoided all acquaintance. When spoken to, he answered curtly and decisively, and began to look out of the car window obstinately.

Yet it seemed to me that the solitude weighed upon him. He seemed to perceive that I understood this, and when our eyes met, as happened frequently, since we were sitting almost opposite each other, he turned away his head, and avoided conversation with me as much as with the others. At nightfall, during a stop at a large station, the gentleman with the fine baggage - a lawyer, as I have since learned - got out with his companion to drink some tea at the restaurant. During their absence several new travellers entered the car, among whom was a tall old man, shaven and wrinkled, evidently a merchant, wearing a large heavily-lined cloak and a big cap. This merchant sat down opposite the empty seats of the lawyer and his companion, and straightway entered into conversation with a young man who seemed like an employee in some commercial house, and who had likewise just boarded the train. At first the clerk had remarked that the seat opposite was occupied, and the old man had answered that he should get out at the first station. Thus their conversation started.

I was sitting not far from these two travellers, and, as the train was not in motion, I could catch bits of their conversation when others were not talking.

They talked first of the prices of goods and the condition of business; they referred to a person whom they both knew; then they plunged into the fair at Nijni Novgorod. The clerk boasted of knowing people who were leading a gay life there, but the old man did not allow him to continue, and, interrupting him, began to describe the festivities of the previous year at Kounavino, in which he had taken part. He was evidently proud of these recollections, and, probably thinking that this would detract nothing from the gravity which his face and manners expressed, he related with pride how, when drunk, he had fired, at Kounavino, such a broadside that he could describe it only in the other's ear.

The clerk began to laugh noisily. The old man laughed too, showing two long yellow teeth. Their conversation not interesting me, I left the car to stretch my legs. At the door I met the lawyer and his lady.

"You have no more time," the lawyer said to me. "The second bell is about to ring."

Indeed I had scarcely reached the rear of the train when the bell sounded. As I entered the car again, the lawyer was talking with his companion in an animated fashion. The merchant, sitting opposite them, was taciturn.

"And then she squarely declared to her husband," said the lawyer with a smile, as I passed by them, "that she neither could nor would live with him, because"...

And he continued, but I did not hear the rest of the sentence, my attention being distracted by the passing of the conductor and a new traveller. When silence was restored, I again heard the lawyer's voice. The conversation had passed from a special case to general considerations.

"And afterward comes discord, financial difficulties, disputes between the two parties, and the couple separate. In the good old days that seldom happened. Is it not so?" asked the lawyer of the two merchants, evidently trying to drag them into the conversation.

Just then the train started, and the old man, without answering, took off his cap, and crossed himself three times while muttering a prayer. When he had finished, he clapped his cap far down on his head, and said:

"Yes, sir, that happened in former times also, but not as often. In the present day it is bound to happen more frequently. People have become too learned."

The lawyer made some reply to the old man, but the train, ever increasing its speed, made such a clatter upon the rails that I could no longer hear distinctly. As I was interested in what the old man was saying, I drew nearer. My neighbor, the nervous gentleman, was evidently interested also, and, without changing his seat, he lent an ear.

"But what harm is there in education?" asked the lady, with a smile that was scarcely perceptible. "Would it be better to marry as in the old days, when the bride and bridegroom did not even see each other before marriage?" she continued, answering, as is the habit of our ladies, not the words that her interlocutor had spoken, but the words she believed he was going to speak. "Women did not know whether they would love or would be loved, and they were married to the first comer, and suffered all their lives. Then you think it was better so?" she continued, evidently addressing the lawyer and myself, and not at all the old man.

"People have become too learned," repeated the last, looking at the lady with contempt, and leaving her question unanswered.

"I should be curious to know how you explain the correlation between education and conjugal differences," said the lawyer, with a slight smile.

The merchant wanted to make some reply, but the lady interrupted him.

"No, those days are past."

The lawyer cut short her words:-

"Let him express his thought."

"Because there is no more fear," replied the old man.

"But how will you marry people who do not love each other? Only animals can be coupled at the will of a proprietor. But people have inclinations, attachments," the lady hastened to say, casting a glance at the lawyer, at me, and even at the clerk, who, standing up and leaning his elbow on the back of a seat, was listening to the conversation with a smile.

"You are wrong to say that, madam," said the old man. "The animals are beasts, but man has received the law."

"But, nevertheless, how is one to live with a man when there is no love?" said the lady, evidently excited by the general sympathy and attention.

"Formerly no such distinctions were made," said the old man, gravely. "Only now have they become a part of our habits. As soon as the least thing happens, the wife says: 'I release you. I am going to leave your house.' Even among the moujiks this fashion has become acclimated. 'There,' she says, 'here are your shirts and drawers. I am going off with Vanka. His hair is curlier than yours.' Just go talk with them. And yet the first rule for the wife should be fear."

The clerk looked at the lawyer, the lady, and myself, evidently repressing a smile, and all ready to deride or approve the merchant's words, according to the attitude of the others.

"What fear?" said the lady.

"This fear, - the wife must fear her husband; that is what fear."

"Oh, that, my little father, that is ended."

"No, madam, that cannot end. As she, Eve, the woman, was taken from man's ribs, so she will remain unto the end of the world," said the old man, shaking his head so triumphantly and so severely that the clerk, deciding that the victory was on his side, burst into a loud laugh.

"Yes, you men think so," replied the lady, without surrendering, and turning toward us. "You have given yourself liberty. As for woman, you wish to keep her in the seraglio. To you, everything is permissible. Is it not so?"

"Oh, man, - that's another affair."

"Then, according to you, to man everything is permissible?"

"No one gives him this permission; only, if the man behaves badly outside, the family is not increased thereby; but the woman, the wife, is a fragile vessel," continued the merchant, severely.

His tone of authority evidently subjugated his hearers. Even the lady felt crushed, but she did not surrender.

"Yes, but you will admit, I think, that woman is a human being, and has feelings like her husband. What should she do if she does not love her husband?"

"If she does not love him!" repeated the old man, stormily, and knitting his brows; "why, she will be made to love him."

This unexpected argument pleased the clerk, and he uttered a murmur of approbation.

"Oh, no, she will not be forced," said the lady. "Where there is no love, one cannot be obliged to love in spite of herself."

"And if the wife deceives her husband, what is to be done?" said the lawyer.

"That should not happen," said the old man. "He must have his eyes about him."

"And if it does happen, all the same? You will admit that it does happen?"

"It happens among the upper classes, not among us," answered the old man. "And if any husband is found who is such a fool as not to rule his wife, he will not have robbed her. But no scandal, nevertheless. Love or not, but do not disturb the household. Every husband can govern his wife. He has the necessary power. It is only the imbecile who does not succeed in doing so."

Everybody was silent. The clerk moved, advanced, and, not wishing to lag behind the others in the conversation, began with his eternal smile:

"Yes, in the house of our employer, a scandal has arisen, and it is very difficult to view the matter clearly. The wife loved to amuse herself, and began to go astray. He is a capable and serious man. First, it was with the book-keeper. The husband tried to bring her back to reason through kindness. She did not change her conduct. She plunged into all sorts of beastliness. She began to steal his money. He beat her, but she grew worse and worse. To an unbaptized, to a pagan, to a Jew (saving your permission), she went in succession for her caresses. What could the employer do? He has dropped her entirely, and now he lives as a bachelor. As for her, she is dragging in the depths."

"He is an imbecile," said the old man. "If from the first he had not allowed her to go in her own fashion, and had kept a firm hand upon her, she would be living honestly, no danger. Liberty must be taken away from the beginning. Do not trust yourself to your horse upon the highway. Do not trust yourself to your wife at home."

At that moment the conductor passed, asking for the tickets for the next station. The old man gave up his.

"Yes, the feminine sex must be dominated in season, else all will perish."

"And you yourselves, at Kounavino, did you not lead a gay life with the pretty girls?" asked the lawyer with a smile.

"Oh, that's another matter," said the merchant, severely. "Good-bye," he added, rising. He wrapped himself in his cloak, lifted his cap, and, taking his bag, left the car.

II

Scarcely had the old man gone when a general conversation began.

"There's a little Old Testament father for you," said the clerk.

"He is a Domostroy," said the lady. "What savage ideas about a woman and marriage!"

"Yes, gentlemen," said the lawyer, "we are still a long way from the European ideas upon marriage. First, the rights of woman, then free marriage, then divorce, as a question not yet solved."

"The main thing, and the thing which such people as he do not understand," rejoined the lady, "is that only love consecrates marriage, and that the real marriage is that which is consecrated by love."

The clerk listened and smiled, with the air of one accustomed to store in his memory all intelligent conversation that he hears, in order to make use of it afterwards.

"But what is this love that consecrates marriage?" said, suddenly, the voice of the nervous and taciturn gentleman, who, unnoticed by us, had approached.

He was standing with his hand on the seat, and evidently agitated. His face was red, a vein in his forehead was swollen, and the muscles of his cheeks quivered.

"What is this love that consecrates marriage?" he repeated.

"What love?" said the lady. "The ordinary love of husband and wife."

"And how, then, can ordinary love consecrate marriage?" continued the nervous gentleman, still excited, and with a displeased air. He seemed to wish to say something disagreeable to the lady. She felt it, and began to grow agitated.

"How? Why, very simply," said she.

The nervous gentleman seized the word as it left her lips.

"No, not simply."

"Madam says," interceded the lawyer indicating his companion, "that marriage should be first the result of an attachment, of a love, if you will, and that, when love exists, and in that case only, marriage represents something sacred. But every marriage which is not based on a natural attachment, on love, has in it nothing that is morally obligatory. Is not that the idea that you intended to convey?" he asked the lady.

The lady, with a nod of her head, expressed her approval of this translation of her thoughts.

"Then," resumed the lawyer, continuing his remarks.

But the nervous gentleman, evidently scarcely able to contain himself, without allowing the lawyer to finish, asked:

"Yes, sir. But what are we to understand by this love that alone consecrates marriage?"

"Everybody knows what love is," said the lady.

"But I don't know, and I should like to know how you define it."

"How? It is very simple," said the lady.

And she seemed thoughtful, and then said:

"Love... love... is a preference for one man or one woman to the exclusion of all others..."

"A preference for how long?... For a month, two days, or half an hour?" said the nervous gentleman, with special irritation.

"No, permit me, you evidently are not talking of the same thing."

"Yes, I am talking absolutely of the same thing. Of the preference for one man or one woman to the exclusion of all others. But I ask: a preference for how long?"

"For how long? For a long time, for a life-time sometimes."

"But that happens only in novels. In life, never. In life this preference for one to the exclusion of all others lasts in rare cases several years, oftener several months, or even weeks, days, hours..."

"Oh, sir. Oh, no, no, permit me," said all three of us at the same time. The clerk himself uttered a monosyllable of disapproval.

"Yes, I know," he said, shouting louder than all of us; "you are talking of what is believed to exist, and I am talking of what is. Every man feels what you call love toward each pretty woman he sees, and very little toward his wife. That is the origin of the proverb, - and it is a true one, - Another's wife is a white swan, and ours is bitter wormwood."

"Ah, but what you say is terrible! There certainly exists among human beings this feeling which is called love, and which lasts, not for months and years, but for life."

"No, that does not exist. Even if it should be admitted that Menelaus had preferred Helen all his life, Helen would have preferred Paris; and so it has been, is, and will be eternally. And it cannot be otherwise, just as it cannot happen that, in a load of chick-peas, two peas marked with a special sign should fall side by side. Further, this is not only an improbability, but it is certain that a feeling of satiety will come to Helen or to Menelaus. The whole difference is that to one it comes sooner, to the other later. It is only in stupid novels that it is written that 'they loved each other all their lives.' And none but children can believe it. To talk of loving a man or woman for life is like saying that a candle can burn forever."

"But you are talking of physical love. Do you not admit a love based upon a conformity of ideals, on a spiritual affinity?"

"Why not? But in that case it is not necessary to procreate together (excuse my brutality). The point is that this conformity of ideals is not met among old people, but among young and pretty persons," said he, and he began to laugh disagreeably.

"Yes, I affirm that love, real love, does not consecrate marriage, as we are in the habit of believing, but that, on the contrary, it ruins it."

"Permit me," said the lawyer. "The facts contradict your words. We see that marriage exists, that all humanity - at least the larger portion - lives conjugally, and that many husbands and wives honestly end a long life together."

The nervous gentleman smiled ill-naturedly.

"And what then? You say that marriage is based upon love, and when I give voice to a doubt as to the existence of any other love than sensual love, you prove to me the existence of love by marriage. But in our day marriage is only a violence and falsehood."

"No, pardon me," said the lawyer. "I say only that marriages have existed and do exist."

"But how and why do they exist? They have existed, and they do exist, for people who have seen, and do see, in marriage something sacramental, a sacrament that is binding before God. For such people marriages exist, but to us they are only hypocrisy and violence. We feel it, and, to clear ourselves, we preach free love; but, really, to preach free love is only a call backward to the promiscuity of the sexes (excuse me, he said to the lady), the haphazard sin of certain raskolniks. The old foundation is shattered; we must build a new one, but we must not preach debauchery."

He grew so warm that all became silent, looking at him in astonishment.

"And yet the transition state is terrible. People feel that haphazard sin is inadmissible. It is necessary in some way or other to regulate the sexual relations; but there exists no other foundation than the old one, in which nobody longer believes? People marry in the old fashion, without believing in what they do, and the result is falsehood, violence. When it is falsehood alone, it is easily endured. The husband and wife simply deceive the world by professing to live monogamically. If they really are polygamous and polyandrous, it is bad, but acceptable. But when, as often happens, the husband and the wife have taken upon themselves the obligation to live together all their lives (they themselves do not know why), and from the second month have already a desire to separate, but continue to live together just the same, then comes that infernal existence in which they resort to drink, in which they fire revolvers, in which they assassinate each other, in which they poison each other."

All were silent, but we felt ill at ease.

"Yes, these critical episodes happen in marital life. For instance, there is the Posdnicheff affair," said the lawyer, wishing to stop the conversation on this embarrassing and too exciting ground. "Have you read how he killed his wife through jealousy?"

The lady said that she had not read it. The nervous gentleman said nothing, and changed color.

"I see that you have divined who I am," said he, suddenly, after a pause.

"No, I have not had that pleasure."

"It is no great pleasure. I am Posdnicheff."

New silence. He blushed, then turned pale again.

"What matters it, however?" said he. "Excuse me, I do not wish to embarrass you."

And he resumed his old seat.

III

I resumed mine, also. The lawyer and the lady whispered together. I was sitting beside Posdnicheff, and I maintained silence. I desired to talk to him, but I did not know how to begin, and thus an hour passed until we reached the next station.

There the lawyer and the lady went out, as well as the clerk. We were left alone, Posdnicheff and I.

"They say it, and they lie, or they do not understand," said Posdnicheff.

"Of what are you talking?"

"Why, still the same thing."

He leaned his elbows upon his knees, and pressed his hands against his temples.

"Love, marriage, family, - all lies, lies, lies."

He rose, lowered the lamp-shade, lay down with his elbows on the cushion, and closed his eyes. He remained thus for a minute.

"Is it disagreeable to you to remain with me, now that you know who I am?"

"Oh, no."

"You have no desire to sleep?"

"Not at all."

"Then do you want me to tell you the story of my life?"

Just then the conductor passed. He followed him with an ill-natured look, and did not begin until he had gone again. Then during all the rest of the story he did not stop once. Even the new travellers as they entered did not stop him.

His face, while he was talking, changed several times so completely that it bore positively no resemblance to itself as it had appeared just before. His eyes, his mouth, his moustache, and even his beard, all were new. Each time it was a beautiful and touching physiognomy, and these transformations were produced suddenly in the penumbra; and for five minutes it was the same face, that could not be compared to that of five minutes before. And then, I know not how, it changed again, and became unrecognizable.

IV

"Well, I am going then to tell you my life, and my whole frightful history, - yes, frightful. And the story itself is more frightful than the outcome."

He became silent for a moment, passed his hands over his eyes, and began:-

"To be understood clearly, the whole must be told from the beginning. It must be told how and why I married, and what I was before my marriage. First, I will tell you who I am. The son of a rich gentleman of the steppes, an old marshal of the nobility, I was a University pupil, a graduate of the law school. I married in my thirtieth year. But before talking to you of my marriage, I must tell you how I lived formerly, and what ideas I had of conjugal life. I led the life of so many other so-called respectable people, - that is, in debauchery. And like the majority, while leading the life of a debauche, I was convinced that I was a man of irreproachable morality.

"The idea that I had of my morality arose from the fact that in my family there was no knowledge of those special debaucheries, so common in the surroundings of land-owners, and also from the fact that my father and my mother did not deceive each other. In consequence of this, I had built from childhood a dream of high and poetical conjugal life. My wife was to be perfection itself, our mutual love was to be incomparable, the purity of our conjugal life stainless. I thought thus, and all the time I marvelled at the nobility of my projects.

"At the same time, I passed ten years of my adult life without hurrying toward marriage, and I led what I called the well-regulated and reasonable life of a bachelor. I was proud of it before my friends, and before all men of my age who abandoned themselves to all sorts of special refinements. I was not a seducer, I had no unnatural tastes, I did not make debauchery the principal object of my life; but I found pleasure within the limits of society's rules, and innocently believed myself a profoundly moral being. The women with whom I had relations did not belong to me alone, and I asked of them nothing but the pleasure of the moment.

"In all this I saw nothing abnormal. On the contrary, from the fact that I did not engage my heart, but paid in cash, I supposed that I was honest. I avoided those women who, by attaching themselves to me, or presenting me with a child, could bind my future. Moreover, perhaps there may have been children or attachments; but I so arranged matters that I could not become aware of them.

"And living thus, I considered myself a perfectly honest man. I did not understand that debauchery does not consist simply in physical acts, that no matter what physical ignominy does not yet constitute debauchery, and that real debauchery consists in freedom from the moral bonds toward a woman with whom one enters into carnal relations, and I regarded THIS FREEDOM as a merit. I remember that I once tortured myself exceedingly for having forgotten to pay a woman who probably had given herself to me through love. I only became tranquil again when, having sent her the money, I had thus shown her that I did not consider myself as in any way bound to her. Oh, do not shake your head as if you were in agreement with me (he cried suddenly with vehemence). I know these tricks. All of you, and you especially, if you are not a rare exception, have the same ideas that I had then. If you are in agreement with me, it is now only. Formerly you did not think so. No more did I; and, if I had been told what I have just told you, that which has happened would not have happened. However, it is all the same. Excuse me (he continued): the truth is that it is frightful, frightful, frightful, this abyss of errors and debaucheries in which we live face to face with the real question of the rights of woman."

"What do you mean by the 'real' question of the rights of woman?"

"The question of the nature of this special being, organized otherwise than man, and how this being and man ought to view the wife..."

V

"Yes: for ten years I lived the most revolting existence, while dreaming of the noblest love, and even in the name of that love. Yes, I want to tell you how I killed my wife, and for that I must tell you how I debauched myself. I killed her before I knew her.

"I killed THE wife when I first tasted sensual joys without love, and then it was that I killed MY wife. Yes, sir: it is only after having suffered, after having tortured myself, that I have come to understand the root of things, that I have come to understand my crimes. Thus you will see where and how began the drama that has led me to misfortune.

"It is necessary to go back to my sixteenth year, when I was still at school, and my elder brother a first-year student. I had not yet known women but, like all the unfortunate children of our society, I was already no longer innocent. I was tortured, as you were, I am sure, and as are tortured ninety-nine one-hundredths of our boys. I lived in a frightful dread, I prayed to God, and I prostrated myself.

"I was already perverted in imagination, but the last steps remained to be taken. I could still escape, when a friend of my brother, a very gay student, one of those who are called good fellows, - that is, the greatest of scamps, - and who had taught us to drink and play cards, took advantage of a night of intoxication to drag us THERE. We started. My brother, as innocent as I, fell that night, and I, a mere lad of sixteen, polluted myself and helped to pollute a sister-woman, without understanding what I did. Never had I heard from my elders that what I thus did was bad. It is true that there are the ten commandments of the Bible; but the commandments are made only to be recited before the priests at examinations, and even then are not as exacting as the commandments in regard to the use of ut in conditional propositions.

"Thus, from my elders, whose opinion I esteemed, I had never heard that this was reprehensible. On the contrary, I had heard people whom I respected say that it was good. I had heard that my struggles and my sufferings would be appeased after this act. I had heard it and read it. I had heard from my elders that it was excellent for the health, and my friends have always seemed to believe that it contained I know not what merit and valor. So nothing is seen in it but what is praiseworthy. As for the danger of disease, it is a foreseen danger. Does not the government guard against it? And even science corrupts us."

"How so, science?" I asked.

"Why, the doctors, the pontiffs of science. Who pervert young people by laying down such rules of hygiene? Who pervert women by devising and teaching them ways by which not to have children?

"Yes: if only a hundredth of the efforts spent in curing diseases were spent in curing debauchery, disease would long ago have ceased to exist, whereas now all efforts are employed, not in extirpating debauchery, but in favoring it, by assuring the harmlessness of the consequences. Besides, it is not a question of that. It is a question of this frightful thing that has happened to me, as it happens to nine-tenths, if not more, not only of the men of our society, but of all societies, even peasants, - this frightful thing that I had fallen, and not because I was subjected to the natural seduction of a certain woman. No, no woman seduced me. I fell because the surroundings in which I found myself saw in this degrading thing only a legitimate function, useful to the health; because others saw in it simply a natural amusement, not only excusable, but even innocent in a young man. I did not understand that it was a fall, and I began to give myself to those pleasures (partly from desire and partly from necessity) which I was led to believe were characteristic of my age, just as I had begun to drink and smoke.

"And yet there was in this first fall something peculiar and touching. I remember that straightway I was filled with such a profound sadness that I had a desire to weep, to weep over the loss forever of my relations with woman. Yes, my relations with woman were lost forever. Pure relations with women, from that time forward, I could no longer have. I had become what is called a voluptuary; and to be a voluptuary is a physical condition like the condition of a victim of the morphine habit, of a drunkard, and of a smoker.

"Just as the victim of the morphine habit, the drunkard, the smoker, is no longer a normal man, so the man who has known several women for his pleasure is no longer normal? He is abnormal forever. He is a voluptuary. Just as the drunkard and the victim of the morphine habit may be recognized by their face and manner, so we may recognize a voluptuary. He may repress himself and struggle, but nevermore will he enjoy simple, pure, and fraternal relations toward woman. By his way of glancing at a young woman one may at once recognize a voluptuary; and I became a voluptuary, and I have remained one."

VI

"Yes, so it is; and that went farther and farther with all sorts of variations. My God! when I remember all my cowardly acts and bad deeds, I am frightened. And I remember that 'me' who, during that period, was still the butt of his comrades' ridicule on account of his innocence.

"And when I hear people talk of the gilded youth, of the officers, of the Parisians, and all these gentlemen, and myself, living wild lives at the age of thirty, and who have on our consciences hundreds of crimes toward women, terrible and varied, when we enter a parlor or a ball-room, washed, shaven, and perfumed, with very white linen, in dress coats or in uniform, as emblems of purity, oh, the disgust! There will surely come a time, an epoch, when all these lives and all this cowardice will be unveiled!

"So, nevertheless, I lived, until the age of thirty, without abandoning for a minute my intention of marrying, and building an elevated conjugal life; and with this in view I watched all young girls who might suit me. I was buried in rottenness, and at the same time I looked for virgins, whose purity was worthy of me! Many of them were rejected: they did not seem to me pure enough!

"Finally I found one that I considered on a level with myself. She was one of two daughters of a landed proprietor of Penza, formerly very rich and since ruined. To tell the truth, without false modesty, they pursued me and finally captured me. The mother (the father was away) laid all sorts of traps, and one of these, a trip in a boat, decided my future.

"I made up my mind at the end of the aforesaid trip one night, by moonlight, on our way home, while I was sitting beside her. I admired her slender body, whose charming shape was moulded by a jersey, and her curling hair, and I suddenly concluded that THIS WAS SHE. It seemed to me on that beautiful evening that she understood all that I thought and felt, and I thought and felt the most elevating things.

"Really, it was only the jersey that was so becoming to her, and her curly hair, and also the fact that I had spent the day beside her, and that I desired a more intimate relation.

"I returned home enthusiastic, and I persuaded myself that she realized the highest perfection, and that for that reason she was worthy to be my wife, and the next day I made to her a proposal of marriage.

"No, say what you will, we live in such an abyss of falsehood, that, unless some event strikes us a blow on the head, as in my case, we cannot awaken. What confusion! Out of the thousands of men who marry, not only among us, but also among the people, scarcely will you find a single one who has not previously married at least ten times. (It is true that there now exist, at least so I have heard, pure young people who feel and know that this is not a joke, but a serious matter. May God come to their aid! But in my time there was not to be found one such in a thousand.)

"And all know it, and pretend not to know it. In all the novels are described down to the smallest details the feelings of the characters, the lakes and brambles around which they walk; but, when it comes to describing their GREAT love, not a word is breathed of what HE, the interesting character, has previously done, not a word about his frequenting of disreputable houses, or his association with nursery-maids, cooks, and the wives of others.

"And if anything is said of these things, such IMPROPER novels are not allowed in the hands of young girls. All men have the air of believing, in presence of maidens, that these corrupt pleasures, in which EVERYBODY takes part, do not exist, or exist only to a very small extent. They pretend it so carefully that they succeed in convincing themselves of it. As for the poor young girls, they believe it quite seriously, just as my poor wife believed it.

"I remember that, being already engaged, I showed her my 'memoirs,' from which she could learn more or less of my past, and especially my last liaison which she might perhaps have discovered through the gossip of some third party. It was for this last reason, for that matter, that I felt the necessity of communicating these memoirs to her. I can still see her fright, her despair, her bewilderment, when she had learned and understood it. She was on the point of breaking the engagement. What a lucky thing it would have been for both of us!"

Posdnicheff was silent for a moment, and then resumed: -

"After all, no! It is better that things happened as they did, better!" he cried. "It was a good thing for me. Besides, it makes no difference. I was saying that in these cases it is the poor young girls who are deceived. As for the mothers, the mothers especially, informed by their husbands, they know all, and, while pretending to believe in the purity of the young man, they act as if they did not believe in it.

"They know what bait must be held out to people for themselves and their daughters. We men sin through ignorance, and a determination not to learn. As for the women, they know very well that the noblest and most poetic love, as we call it, depends, not on moral qualities, but on the physical intimacy, and also on the manner of doing the hair, and the color and shape.

"Ask an experienced coquette, who has undertaken to seduce a man, which she would prefer, - to be convicted, in presence of the man whom she is engaged in conquering, of falsehood, perversity, cruelty, or to appear before him in an ill-fitting dress, or a dress of an unbecoming color. She will prefer the first alternative. She knows very well that we simply lie when we talk of our elevated sentiments, that we seek only the possession of her body, and that because of that we will forgive her every sort of baseness, but will not forgive her a costume of an ugly shade, without taste or fit.

"And these things she knows by reason, where as the maiden knows them only by instinct, like the animal. Hence these abominable jerseys, these artificial humps on the back, these bare shoulders, arms, and throats.

"Women, especially those who have passed through the school of marriage, know very well that conversations upon elevated subjects are only conversations, and that man seeks and desires the body and all that ornaments the body. Consequently, they act accordingly? If we reject conventional explanations, and view the life of our upper and lower classes as it is, with all its shamelessness, it is only a vast perversity. You do not share this opinion? Permit me, I am going to prove it to you (said he, interrupting me).

"You say that the women of our society live for a different interest from that which actuates fallen women. And I say no, and I am going to prove it to you. If beings differ from one another according to the purpose of their life, according to their INNER LIFE, this will necessarily be reflected also in their OUTER LIFE, and their exterior will be very different. Well, then, compare the wretched, the despised, with the women of the highest society: the same dresses, the same fashions, the same perfumeries, the same passion for jewelry, for brilliant and very expensive articles, the same amusements, dances, music, and songs. The former attract by all possible means; so do the latter. No difference, none whatever!

"Yes, and I, too, was captivated by jerseys, bustles, and curly hair."

VII

"And it was very easy to capture me, since I was brought up under artificial conditions, like cucumbers in a hothouse. Our too abundant nourishment, together with complete physical idleness, is nothing but systematic excitement of the imagination. The men of our society are fed and kept like reproductive stallions. It is sufficient to close the valve, - that is, for a young man to live a quiet life for some time, - to produce as an immediate result a restlessness, which, becoming exaggerated by reflection through the prism of our unnatural life, provokes the illusion of love.

"All our idyls and marriage, all, are the result for the most part of our eating. Does that astonish you? For my part, I am astonished that we do not see it. Not far from my estate this spring some moujiks were working on a railway embankment. You know what a peasant's food is, - bread, kvass,* onions. With this frugal nourishment he lives, he is alert, he makes light work in the fields. But on the railway this bill of fare becomes cacha and a pound of meat. Only he restores this meat by sixteen hours of labor pushing loads weighing twelve hundred pounds.

"And we, who eat two pounds of meat and game, we who absorb all sorts of heating drinks and food, how do we expend it? In sensual excesses. If the valve is open, all goes well; but close it, as I had closed it temporarily before my marriage, and immediately there will result an excitement which, deformed by novels, verses, music, by our idle and luxurious life, will give a love of the finest water. I, too, fell in love, as everybody does, and there were transports, emotions, poesy; but really all this passion was prepared by mamma and the dressmakers. If there had been no trips in boats, no well-fitted garments, etc., if my wife had worn some shapeless blouse, and I had seen her thus at her home, I should not have been seduced."

VIII

"And note, also, this falsehood, of which all are guilty; the way in which marriages are made. What could there be more natural? The young girl is marriageable, she should marry. What simpler, provided the young person is not a monster, and men can be found with a desire to marry? Well, no, here begins a new hypocrisy.

"Formerly, when the maiden arrived at a favorable age, her marriage was arranged by her parents. That was done, that is done still, throughout humanity, among the Chinese, the Hindoos, the Mussulmans, and among our common people also. Things are so managed in at least ninety-nine per cent. of the families of the entire human race.

"Only we riotous livers have imagined that this way was bad, and have invented another. And this other, - what is it? It is this. The young girls are seated, and the gentlemen walk up and down before them, as in a bazaar, and make their choice. The maidens wait and think, but do not dare to say: 'Take me, young man, me and not her. Look at these shoulders and the rest.' We males walk up and down, and estimate the merchandise, and then we discourse upon the rights of woman, upon the liberty that she acquires, I know not how, in the theatrical halls."

"But what is to be done?" said I to him. "Shall the woman make the advances?"

"I do not know. But, if it is a question of equality, let the equality be complete. Though it has been found that to contract marriages through the agency of match-makers is humiliating, it is nevertheless a thousand times preferable to our system. There the rights and the chances are equal; here the woman is a slave, exhibited in the market. But as she cannot bend to her condition, or make advances herself, there begins that other and more abominable lie which is sometimes called GOING INTO SOCIETY, sometimes AMUSING ONE'S SELF, and which is really nothing but the hunt for a husband.

"But say to a mother or to her daughter that they are engaged only in a hunt for a husband. God! What an offence! Yet they can do nothing else, and have nothing else to do; and the terrible feature of it all is to see sometimes very young, poor, and innocent maidens haunted solely by such ideas. If only, I repeat, it were done frankly; but it is always accompanied with lies and babble of this sort: -

'Ah, the descent of species! How interesting it is!'

'Oh, Lily is much interested in painting.'

'Shall you go to the Exposition? How charming it is!'

'And the troika, and the plays, and the symphony. Ah, how adorable!'

'My Lise is passionately fond of music.'

'And you, why do you not share these convictions?'

"And through all this verbiage, all have but one single idea: 'Take me, take my Lise. No, me! Only try!' "

IX

"Do you know," suddenly continued Posdnicheff, "that this power of women from which the world suffers arises solely from what I have just spoken of?"

"What do you mean by the power of women?" I said. "Everybody, on the contrary, complains that women have not sufficient rights, that they are in subjection."

"That's it; that's it exactly," said he, vivaciously. "That is just what I mean, and that is the explanation of this extraordinary phenomenon, that on the one hand woman is reduced to the lowest degree of humiliation and on the other hand she reigns over everything. See the Jews: with their power of money, they avenge their subjection, just as the women do. 'Ah! you wish us to be only merchants? All right; remaining merchants, we will get possession of you,' say the Jews. 'Ah! you wish us to be only objects of sensuality? All right; by the aid of sensuality we will bend you beneath our yoke,' say the women.

"The absence of the rights of woman does not consist in the fact that she has not the right to vote, or the right to sit on the bench, but in the fact that in her affectional relations she is not the equal of man, she has not the right to abstain, to choose instead of being chosen. You say that that would be abnormal. Very well! But then do not let man enjoy these rights, while his companion is deprived of them, and finds herself obliged to make use of the coquetry by which she governs, so that the result is that man chooses 'formally,' whereas really it is woman who chooses. As soon as she is in possession of her means, she abuses them, and acquires a terrible supremacy."

"But where do you see this exceptional power?"

"Where? Why, everywhere, in everything. Go see the stores in the large cities. There are millions there, millions. It is impossible to estimate the enormous quantity of labor that is expended there. In nine-tenths of these stores is there anything whatever for the use of men? All the luxury of life is demanded and sustained by woman. Count the factories; the greater part of them are engaged in making feminine ornaments. Millions of men, generations of slaves, die toiling like convicts simply to satisfy the whims of our companions.

"Women, like queens, keep nine-tenths of the human race as prisoners of war, or as prisoners at hard labor. And all this because they have been humiliated, because they have been deprived of rights equal to those which men enjoy. They take revenge for our sensuality; they catch us in their nets.

"Yes, the whole thing is there. Women have made of themselves such a weapon to act upon the senses that a young man, and even an old man, cannot remain tranquil in their presence. Watch a popular festival, or our receptions or ball-rooms. Woman well knows her influence there. You will see it in her triumphant smiles.

"As soon as a young man advances toward a woman, directly he falls under the influence of this opium, and loses his head. Long ago I felt ill at ease when I saw a woman too well adorned, - whether a woman of the people with her red neckerchief and her looped skirt, or a woman of our own society in her ball-room dress. But now it simply terrifies me. I see in it a danger to men, something contrary to the laws; and I feel a desire to call a policeman, to appeal for defence from some quarter, to demand that this dangerous object be removed.

"And this is not a joke, by any means. I am convinced, I am sure, that the time will come - and perhaps it is not far distant - when the world will understand this, and will be astonished that a society could exist in which actions as harmful as those which appeal to sensuality by adorning the body as our companions do were allowed. As well set traps along our public streets, or worse than that."

X

"That, then, was the way in which I was captured. I was in love, as it is called; not only did she appear to me a perfect being, but I considered myself a white blackbird. It is a commonplace fact that there is no one so low in the world that he cannot find someone viler than himself, and consequently puff with pride and self-contentment. I was in that situation. I did not marry for money. Interest was foreign to the affair, unlike the marriages of most of my acquaintances, who married either for money or for relations. First, I was rich, she was poor. Second, I was especially proud of the fact that, while others married with an intention of continuing their polygamic life as bachelors, it was my firm intention to live monogamically after my engagement and the wedding, and my pride swelled immeasurably.

"Yes, I was a wretch, convinced that I was an angel. The period of my engagement did not last long. I cannot remember those days without shame. What an abomination!

"It is generally agreed that love is a moral sentiment, a community of thought rather than of sense. If that is the case, this community of thought ought to find expression in words and conversation. Nothing of the sort. It was extremely difficult for us to talk with each other. What a toil of Sisyphus was our conversation! Scarcely had we thought of something to say, and said it, when we had to resume our silence and try to discover new subjects. Literally, we did not know what to say to each other. All that we could think of concerning the life that was before us and our home was said.

"And then what? If we had been animals, we should have known that we had not to talk. But here, on the contrary, it was necessary to talk, and there were no resources! For that which occupied our minds was not a thing to be expressed in words.

"And then that silly custom of eating bon-bons, that brutal gluttony for sweetmeats, those abominable preparations for the wedding, those discussions with mamma upon the apartments, upon the sleeping-rooms, upon the bedding, upon the morning-gowns, upon the wrappers, the linen, the costumes! Understand that if people married according to the old fashion, as this old man said just now, then these eiderdown coverlets and this bedding would all be sacred details; but with us, out of ten married people there is scarcely to be found one who, I do not say believes in sacraments (whether he believes or not is a matter of indifference to us), but believes in what he promises. Out of a hundred men, there is scarcely one who has not married before, and out of fifty scarcely one who has not made up his mind to deceive his wife.

"The great majority look upon this journey to the church as a condition necessary to the possession of a certain woman. Think then of the supreme significance which material details must take on. Is it not a sort of sale, in which a maiden is given over to a debauche, the sale being surrounded with the most agreeable details?"

XI

"All marry in this way. And I did like the rest. If the young people who dream of the honeymoon only knew what a disillusion it is, and always a disillusion! I really do not know why all think it necessary to conceal it.

"One day I was walking among the shows in Paris, when, attracted by a sign, I entered an establishment to see a bearded woman and a water-dog. The woman was a man in disguise, and the dog was an ordinary dog, covered with a sealskin, and swimming in a bath. It was not in the least interesting, but the Barnum accompanied me to the exit very courteously, and, in addressing the people who were coming in, made an appeal to my testimony. 'Ask the gentleman if it is not worth seeing! Come in, come in! It only costs a franc!' And in my confusion I did not dare to answer that there was nothing curious to be seen, and it was upon my false shame that the Barnum must have counted.

"It must be the same with the persons who have passed through the abominations of the honeymoon. They do not dare to undeceive their neighbor. And I did the same.

"The felicities of the honeymoon do not exist. On the contrary, it is a period of uneasiness, of shame, of pity, and, above all, of ennui, - of ferocious ennui. It is something like the feeling of a youth when he is beginning to smoke. He desires to vomit; he drivels, and swallows his drivel, pretending to enjoy this little amusement. The vice of marriage..."

"What! Vice?" I said. "But you are talking of one of the most natural things."

"Natural!" said he. "Natural! No, I consider on the contrary that it is against nature, and it is I, a perverted man, who have reached this conviction. What would it be, then, if I had not known corruption? To a young girl, to every unperverted young girl, it is an act extremely unnatural, just as it is to children. My sister married, when very young, a man twice her own age, and who was utterly corrupt. I remember how astonished we were the night of her wedding, when, pale and covered with tears, she fled from her husband, her whole body trembling, saying that for nothing in the world would she tell what he wanted of her.

"You say natural? It is natural to eat; that is a pleasant, agreeable function, which no one is ashamed to perform from the time of his birth. No, it is not natural. A pure young girl wants one thing, - children. Children, yes, not a lover."

"But," said I, with astonishment, "how would the human race continue?"

"But what is the use of its continuing?" he rejoined, vehemently.

"What! What is the use? But then we should not exist."

"And why is it necessary that we should exist?"

"Why, to live, to be sure."

"And why live? The Schopenhauers, the Hartmanns, and all the Buddhists, say that the greatest happiness is Nirvana, Non-Life; and they are right in this sense, - that human happiness is coincident with the annihilation of 'Self.' Only they do not express themselves well. They say that Humanity should annihilate itself to avoid its sufferings, that its object should be to destroy itself. Now the object of Humanity cannot be to avoid sufferings by annihilation, since suffering is the result of activity. The object of activity cannot consist in suppressing its consequences. The object of Man, as of Humanity, is happiness, and, to attain it, Humanity has a law which it must carry out. This law consists in the union of beings. This union is thwarted by the passions. And that is why, if the passions disappear, the union will be accomplished. Humanity then will have carried out the law, and will have no further reason to exist."

"And before Humanity carries out the law?"

"In the meantime it will have the sign of the unfulfilled law, and the existence of physical love. As long as this love shall exist, and because of it, generations will be born, one of which will finally fulfil the law. When at last the law shall be fulfilled, the Human Race will be annihilated. At least it is impossible for us to conceive of Life in the perfect union of people."

XII

"Strange theory!" cried I.

"Strange in what? According to all the doctrines of the Church, the world will have an end. Science teaches the same fatal conclusions. Why, then, is it strange that the same thing should result from moral Doctrine? 'Let those who can, contain,' said Christ. And I take this passage literally, as it is written. That morality may exist between people in their worldly relations, they must make complete chastity their object. In tending toward this end, man humiliates himself. When he shall reach the last degree of humiliation, we shall have moral marriage.

"But if man, as in our society, tends only toward physical love, though he may clothe it with pretexts and the false forms of marriage, he will have only permissible debauchery, he will know only the same immoral life in which I fell and caused my wife to fall, a life which we call the honest life of the family. Think what a perversion of ideas must arise when the happiest situation of man, liberty, chastity, is looked upon as something wretched and ridiculous. The highest ideal, the best situation of woman, to be pure, to be a vestal, a virgin, excites fear and laughter in our society. How many, how many young girls sacrifice their purity to this Moloch of opinion by marrying rascals that they may not remain virgins, - that is, superiors! Through fear of finding themselves in that ideal state, they ruin themselves.

"But I did not understand formerly, I did not understand that the words of the Gospel, that 'he who looks upon a woman to lust after her has already committed adultery,' do not apply to the wives of others, but notably and especially to our own wives. I did not understand this, and I thought that the honeymoon and all of my acts during that period were virtuous, and that to satisfy one's desires with his wife is an eminently chaste thing. Know, then, that I consider these departures, these isolations, which young married couples arrange with the permission of their parents, as nothing else than a license to engage in debauchery.

"I saw, then, in this nothing bad or shameful, and, hoping for great joys, I began to live the honeymoon. And very certainly none of these joys followed. But I had faith, and was determined to have them, cost what they might. But the more I tried to secure them, the less I succeeded. All this time I felt anxious, ashamed, and weary. Soon I began to suffer. I believe that on the third or fourth day I found my wife sad and asked her the reason. I began to embrace her, which in my opinion was all that she could desire. She put me away with her hand, and began to weep.

"At what? She could not tell me. She was filled with sorrow, with anguish. Probably her tortured nerves had suggested to her the truth about the baseness of our relations, but she found no words in which to say it. I began to question her; she answered that she missed her absent mother. It seemed to me that she was not telling the truth. I sought to console her by maintaining silence in regard to her parents. I did not imagine that she felt herself simply overwhelmed, and that her parents had nothing to do with her sorrow. She did not listen to me, and I accused her of caprice. I began to laugh at her gently. She dried her tears, and began to reproach me, in hard and wounding terms, for my selfishness and cruelty.

"I looked at her. Her whole face expressed hatred, and hatred of me. I cannot describe to you the fright which this sight gave me. 'How? What?' thought I, 'love is the unity of souls, and here she hates me? Me? Why? But it is impossible! It is no longer she!'

"I tried to calm her. I came in conflict with an immovable and cold hostility, so that, having no time to reflect, I was seized with keen irritation. We exchanged disagreeable remarks. The impression of this first quarrel was terrible. I say quarrel, but the term is inexact. It was the sudden discovery of the abyss that had been dug between us. Love was exhausted with the satisfaction of sensuality. We stood face to face in our true light, like two egoists trying to procure the greatest possible enjoyment, like two individuals trying to mutually exploit each other.

"So what I called our quarrel was our actual situation as it appeared after the satisfaction of sensual desire. I did not realize that this cold hostility was our normal state, and that this first quarrel would soon be drowned under a new flood of the intensest sensuality. I thought that we had disputed with each other, and had become reconciled, and that it would not happen again. But in this same honeymoon there came a period of satiety, in which we ceased to be necessary to each other, and a new quarrel broke out.

"It became evident that the first was not a matter of chance. 'It was inevitable,' I thought. This second quarrel stupefied me the more, because it was based on an extremely unjust cause. It was something like a question of money, - and never had I haggled on that score; it was even impossible that I should do so in relation to her. I only remember that, in answer to some remark that I made, she insinuated that it was my intention to rule her by means of money, and that it was upon money that I based my sole right over her. In short, something extraordinarily stupid and base, which was neither in my character nor in hers.

"I was beside myself. I accused her of indelicacy. She made the same accusation against me, and the dispute broke out. In her words, in the expression of her face, of her eyes, I noticed again the hatred that had so astonished me before. With a brother, friends, my father, I had occasionally quarrelled, but never had there been between us this fierce spite. Some time passed. Our mutual hatred was again concealed beneath an access of sensual desire, and I again consoled myself with the reflection that these scenes were reparable faults.

"But when they were repeated a third and a fourth time, I understood that they were not simply faults, but a fatality that must happen again. I was no longer frightened, I was simply astonished that I should be precisely the one to live so uncomfortably with my wife, and that the same thing did not happen in other households. I did not know that in all households the same sudden changes take place, but that all, like myself, imagine that it is a misfortune exclusively reserved for themselves alone, which they carefully conceal as shameful, not only to others, but to themselves, like a bad disease.

"That was what happened to me. Begun in the early days, it continued and increased with characteristics of fury that were ever more pronounced. At the bottom of my soul, from the first weeks, I felt that I was in a trap, that I had what I did not expect, and that marriage is not a joy, but a painful trial. Like everybody else, I refused to confess it (I should not have confessed it even now but for the outcome). Now I am astonished to think that I did not see my real situation. It was so easy to perceive it, in view of those quarrels, begun for reasons so trivial that afterwards one could not recall them.

"Just as it often happens among gay young people that, in the absence of jokes, they laugh at their own laughter, so we found no reasons for our hatred, and we hated each other because hatred was naturally boiling up in us. More extraordinary still was the absence of causes for reconciliation.

"Sometimes words, explanations, or even tears, but sometimes, I remember, after insulting words, there tacitly followed embraces and declarations. Abomination! Why is it that I did not then perceive this baseness?"

XIII

"All of us, men and women, are brought up in these aberrations of feeling that we call love. I from childhood had prepared myself for this thing, and I loved, and I loved during all my youth, and I was joyous in loving. It had been put into my head that it was the noblest and highest occupation in the world. But when this expected feeling came at last, and I, a man, abandoned myself to it, the lie was pierced through and through. Theoretically a lofty love is conceivable; practically it is an ignoble and degrading thing, which it is equally disgusting to talk about and to remember. It is not in vain that nature has made ceremonies, but people pretend that the ignoble and the shameful is beautiful and lofty.

"I will tell you brutally and briefly what were the first signs of my love. I abandoned myself to beastly excesses, not only not ashamed of them, but proud of them, giving no thought to the intellectual life of my wife. And not only did I not think of her intellectual life, I did not even consider her physical life.

"I was astonished at the origin of our hostility, and yet how clear it was! This hostility is nothing but a protest of human nature against the beast that enslaves it. It could not be otherwise. This hatred was the hatred of accomplices in a crime. Was it not a crime that, this poor woman having become pregnant in the first month, our liaison should have continued just the same?

"You imagine that I am wandering from my story. Not at all. I am always giving you an account of the events that led to the murder of my wife. The imbeciles! They think that I killed my wife on the 5th of October. It was long before that that I immolated her, just as they all kill now. Understand well that in our society there is an idea shared by all that woman procures man pleasure (and vice versa, probably, but I know nothing of that, I only know my own case). Wein, Weiber und Gesang. So say the poets in their verses: Wine, women, and song!

"If it were only that! Take all the poetry, the painting, the sculpture, beginning with Pouschkine's 'Little Feet,' with 'Venus and Phryne,' and you will see that woman is only a means of enjoyment. That is what she is at Trouba, at Gratchevka, and in a court ball-room. And think of this diabolical trick: if she were a thing without moral value, it might be said that woman is a fine morsel; but, in the first place, these knights assure us that they adore woman (they adore her and look upon her, however, as a means of enjoyment), then all assure us that they esteem woman. Some give up their seats to her, pick up her handkerchief; others recognize in her a right to fill all offices, participate in government, etc., but, in spite of all that, the essential point remains the same. She is, she remains, an object of sensual desire, and she knows it. It is slavery, for slavery is nothing else than the utilization of the labor of some for the enjoyment of others. That slavery may not exist people must refuse to enjoy the labor of others, and look upon it as a shameful act and as a sin.

"Actually, this is what happens. They abolish the external form, they suppress the formal sales of slaves, and then they imagine and assure others that slavery is abolished. They are unwilling to see that it still exists, since people, as before, like to profit by the labor of others, and think it good and just. This being given, there will always be found beings stronger or more cunning than others to profit thereby. The same thing happens in the emancipation of woman. At bottom feminine servitude consists entirely in her assimilation with a means of pleasure. They excite woman, they give her all sorts of rights equal to those of men, but they continue to look upon her as an object of sensual desire, and thus they bring her up from infancy and in public opinion.

"She is always the humiliated and corrupt serf, and man remains always the debauched Master. Yes, to abolish slavery, public opinion must admit that it is shameful to exploit one's neighbor, and, to make woman free, public opinion must admit that it is shameful to consider woman as an instrument of pleasure.

"The emancipation of woman is not to be effected in the public courts or in the chamber of deputies, but in the sleeping chamber. Prostitution is to be combated, not in the houses of ill-fame, but in the family. They free woman in the public courts and in the chamber of deputies, but she remains an instrument. Teach her, as she is taught among us, to look upon herself as such, and she will always remain an inferior being. Either, with the aid of the rascally doctors, she will try to prevent conception, and descend, not to the level of an animal, but to the level of a thing; or she will be what she is in the great majority of cases, - sick, hysterical, wretched, without hope of spiritual progress."

"But why that?" I asked.

"Oh! the most astonishing thing is that no one is willing to see this thing, evident as it is, which the doctors must understand, but which they take good care not to do. Man does not wish to know the law of nature, - children. But children are born and become an embarrassment. Then man devises means of avoiding this embarrassment. We have not yet reached the low level of Europe, nor Paris, nor the 'system of two children,' nor Mahomet. We have discovered nothing, because we have given it no thought. We feel that there is something bad in the two first means; but we wish to preserve the family, and our view of woman is still worse.

"With us woman must be at the same time mistress and nurse, and her strength is not sufficient. That is why we have hysteria, nervous attacks, and, among the peasants, witchcraft. Note that among the young girls of the peasantry this state of things does not exist, but only among the wives, and the wives who live with their husbands. The reason is clear, and this is the cause of the intellectual and moral decline of woman, and of her abasement.

"If they would only reflect what a grand work for the wife is the period of gestation! In her is forming the being who continues us, and this holy work is thwarted and rendered painful... by what? It is frightful to think of it! And after that they talk of the liberties and the rights of woman! It is like the cannibals fattening their prisoners in order to devour them, and assuring these unfortunates at the same time that their rights and their liberties are guarded!"

All this was new to me, and astonished me very much.

"But if this is so," said I, "it follows that one may love his wife only once every two years; and as man..."

"And as man has need of her, you are going to say. At least, so the priests of science assure us. I would force these priests to fulfil the function of these women, who, in their opinion, are necessary to man. I wonder what song they would sing then. Assure man that he needs brandy, tobacco, opium, and he will believe those poisons necessary. It follows that God did not know how to arrange matters properly, since, without asking the opinions of the priests, he has combined things as they are. Man needs, so they have decided, to satisfy his sensual desire, and here this function is disturbed by the birth and the nursing of children.

"What, then, is to be done? Why, apply to the priests; they will arrange everything, and they have really discovered a way. When, then, will these rascals with their lies be uncrowned! It is high time. We have had enough of them. People go mad, and shoot each other with revolvers, and always because of that! And how could it be otherwise?

"One would say that the animals know that descent continues their race, and that they follow a certain law in regard thereto. Only man does not know this, and is unwilling to know it. He cares only to have as much sensual enjoyment as possible. The king of nature, - man! In the name of his love he kills half the human race. Of woman, who ought to be his aid in the movement of humanity toward liberty, he makes, in the name of his pleasures, not an aid, but an enemy. Who is it that everywhere puts a check upon the progressive movement of humanity? Woman. Why is it so?

"For the reason that I have given, and for that reason only."

XIV

"Yes, much worse than the animal is man when he does not live as a man. Thus was I. The horrible part is that I believed, inasmuch as I did not allow myself to be seduced by other women that I was leading an honest family life, that I was a very mortal being, and that if we had quarrels, the fault was in my wife, and in her character.

"But it is evident that the fault was not in her. She was like everybody else, like the majority. She was brought up according to the principles exacted by the situation of our society, - that is, as all the young girls of our wealthy classes, without exception, are brought up, and as they cannot fail to be brought up. How many times we hear or read of reflections upon the abnormal condition of women, and upon what they ought to be. But these are only vain words. The education of women results from the real and not imaginary view which the world entertains of women's vocation. According to this view, the condition of women consists in procuring pleasure and it is to that end that her education is directed. From her infancy she is taught only those things that are calculated to increase her charm. Every young girl is accustomed to think only of that.

"As the serfs were brought up solely to please their masters, so woman is brought up to attract men. It cannot be otherwise. But you will say, perhaps, that that applies only to young girls who are badly brought up, but that there is another education, an education that is serious, in the schools, an education in the dead languages, an education in the institutions of midwifery, an education in medical courses, and in other courses. It is false.

"Every sort of feminine education has for its sole object the attraction of men.

"Some attract by music or curly hair, others by science or by civic virtue. The object is the same, and cannot be otherwise (since no other object exists), - to seduce man in order to possess him. Imagine courses of instruction for women and feminine science without men, - that is, learned women, and men not KNOWING them as learned. Oh, no! No education, no instruction can change woman as long as her highest ideal shall be marriage and not virginity, freedom from sensuality. Until that time she will remain a serf. One need only imagine, forgetting the universality of the case, the conditions in which our young girls are brought up, to avoid astonishment at the debauchery of the women of our upper classes. It is the opposite that would cause astonishment.

"Follow my reasoning. From infancy garments, ornaments, cleanliness, grace, dances, music, reading of poetry, novels, singing, the theatre, the concert, for use within and without, according as women listen, or practice themselves. With that, complete physical idleness, an excessive care of the body, a vast consumption of sweetmeats; and God knows how the poor maidens suffer from their own sensuality, excited by all these things. Nine out of ten are tortured intolerably during the first period of maturity, and afterward provided they do not marry at the age of twenty. That is what we are unwilling to see, but those who have eyes see it all the same. And even the majority of these unfortunate creatures are so excited by a hidden sensuality (and it is lucky if it is hidden) that they are fit for nothing. They become animated only in the presence of men. Their whole life is spent in preparations for coquetry, or in coquetry itself. In the presence of men they become too animated; they begin to live by sensual energy. But the moment the man goes away, the life stops.

"And that, not in the presence of a certain man, but in the presence of any man, provided he is not utterly hideous. You will say that this is an exception. No, it is a rule. Only in some it is made very evident, in other less so. But no one lives by her own life; they are all dependent upon man. They cannot be otherwise, since to them the attraction of the greatest number of men is the ideal of life (young girls and married women), and it is for this reason that they have no feeling stronger than that of the animal need of every female who tries to attract the largest number of males in order to increase the opportunities for choice. So it is in the life of young girls, and so it continues during marriage. In the life of young girls it is necessary in order to selection, and in marriage it is necessary in order to rule the husband. Only one thing suppresses or interrupts these tendencies for a time, - namely, children, - and then only when the woman is not a monster, - that is, when she nurses her own children. Here again the doctor interferes.

"With my wife, who desired to nurse her own children, and who did nurse six of them, it happened that the first child was sickly. The doctors, who cynically undressed her and felt of her everywhere, and whom I had to thank and pay for these acts, - these dear doctors decided that she ought not to nurse her child, and she was temporarily deprived of the only remedy for coquetry. A nurse finished the nursing of this first-born, - that is to say, we profited by the poverty and ignorance of a woman to steal her from her own little one in favor of ours, and for that purpose we dressed her in a kakoschnik trimmed with gold lace. Nevertheless, that is not the question; but there was again awakened in my wife that coquetry which had been sleeping during the nursing period. Thanks to that, she reawakened in me the torments of jealousy which I had formerly known, though in a much slighter degree."

XV

"Yes, jealousy, that is another of the secrets of marriage known to all and concealed by all. Besides the general cause of the mutual hatred of husbands and wives resulting from complicity in the pollution of a human being, and also from other causes, the inexhaustible source of marital wounds is jealousy. But by tacit consent it is determined to conceal them from all, and we conceal them. Knowing them, each one supposes in himself that it is an unfortunate peculiarity, and not a common destiny. So it was with me, and it had to be so. There cannot fail to be jealousy between husbands and wives who live immorally. If they cannot sacrifice their pleasures for the welfare of their child, they conclude therefrom, and truly, that they will not sacrifice their pleasures for, I will not say happiness and tranquillity (since one may sin in secret), but even for the sake of conscience. Each one knows very well that neither admits any high moral reasons for not betraying the other, since in their mutual relations they fail in the requirements of morality, and from that time distrust and watch each other.

"Oh, what a frightful feeling of jealousy! I do not speak of that real jealousy which has foundations (it is tormenting, but it promises an issue), but of that unconscious jealousy which inevitably accompanies every immoral marriage, and which, having no cause, has no end. This jealousy is frightful. Frightful, that is the word.

"And this is it. A young man speaks to my wife. He looks at her with a smile, and, as it seems to me, he surveys her body. How does he dare to think of her, to think of the possibility of a romance with her? And how can she, seeing this, tolerate him? Not only does she tolerate him, but she seems pleased. I even see that she puts herself to trouble on his account. And in my soul there rises such a hatred for her that each of her words, each gesture, disgusts me. She notices it, she knows not what to do, and how assume an air of indifferent animation? Ah! I suffer! That makes her gay, she is content. And my hatred increases tenfold, but I do not dare to give it free force, because at the bottom of my soul I know that there are no real reasons for it, and I remain in my seat, feigning indifference, and exaggerating my attention and courtesy to HIM.

"Then I get angry with myself. I desire to leave the room, to leave them alone, and I do, in fact, go out; but scarcely am I outside when I am invaded by a fear of what is taking place within my absence. I go in again, inventing some pretext. Or sometimes I do not go in; I remain near the door, and listen. How can she humiliate herself and humiliate me by placing me in this cowardly situation of suspicion and espionage? Oh, abomination! Oh, the wicked animal! And he too, what does he think of you? But he is like all men. He is what I was before my marriage. It gives him pleasure. He even smiles when he looks at me, as much as to say: 'What have you to do with this? It is my turn now.'

"This feeling is horrible. Its burn is unendurable. To entertain this feeling toward any one, to once suspect a man of lusting after my wife, was enough to spoil this man forever in my eyes, as if he had been sprinkled with vitriol. Let me once become jealous of a being, and nevermore could I re-establish with him simple human relations, and my eyes flashed when I looked at him.

"As for my wife, so many times had I enveloped her with this moral vitriol, with this jealous hatred, that she was degraded thereby. In the periods of this causeless hatred I gradually uncrowned her. I covered her with shame in my imagination.

"I invented impossible knaveries. I suspected, I am ashamed to say, that she, this queen of 'The Thousand and One Nights,' deceived me with my serf, under my very eyes, and laughing at me.

"Thus, with each new access of jealousy (I speak always of causeless jealousy), I entered into the furrow dug formerly by my filthy suspicions, and I continually deepened it. She did the same thing. If I have reasons to be jealous, she who knew my past had a thousand times more. And she was more ill-natured in her jealousy than I. And the sufferings that I felt from her jealousy were different, and likewise very painful.

"The situation may be described thus. We are living more or less tranquilly. I am even gay and contented. Suddenly we start a conversation on some most commonplace subject, and directly she finds herself disagreeing with me upon matters concerning which we have been generally in accord. And furthermore I see that, without any necessity therefor, she is becoming irritated. I think that she has a nervous attack, or else that the subject of conversation is really disagreeable to her. We talk of something else, and that begins again. Again she torments me, and becomes irritated. I am astonished and look for a reason. Why? For what? She keeps silence, answers me with monosyllables, evidently making allusions to something. I begin to divine that the reason of all this is that I have taken a few walks in the garden with her cousin, to whom I did not give even a thought. I begin to divine, but I cannot say so. If I say so, I confirm her suspicions. I interrogate her, I question her. She does not answer, but she sees that I understand, and that confirms her suspicions.

'What is the matter with you?' I ask.

'Nothing, I am as well as usual,' she answers.

"And at the same time, like a crazy woman, she gives utterance to the silliest remarks, to the most inexplicable explosions of spite.

"Sometimes I am patient, but at other times I break out with anger. Then her own irritation is launched forth in a flood of insults, in charges of imaginary crimes and all carried to the highest degree by sobs, tears, and retreats through the house to the most improbable spots. I go to look for her. I am ashamed before people, before the children, but there is nothing to be done. She is in a condition where I feel that she is ready for anything. I run, and finally find her. Nights of torture follow, in which both of us, with exhausted nerves, appease each other, after the most cruel words and accusations.

"Yes, jealousy, causeless jealousy, is the condition of our debauched conjugal life. And throughout my marriage never did I cease to feel it and to suffer from it. There were two periods in which I suffered most intensely. The first time was after the birth of our first child, when the doctors had forbidden my wife to nurse it. I was particularly jealous, in the first place, because my wife felt that restlessness peculiar to animal matter when the regular course of life is interrupted without occasion. But especially was I jealous because, having seen with what facility she had thrown off her moral duties as a mother, I concluded rightly, though unconsciously, that she would throw off as easily her conjugal duties, feeling all the surer of this because she was in perfect health, as was shown by the fact that, in spite of the prohibition of the dear doctors, she nursed her following children, and even very well."

"I see that you have no love for the doctors," said I, having noticed Posdnicheff's extraordinarily spiteful expression of face and tone of voice whenever he spoke of them.

"It is not a question of loving them or of not loving them. They have ruined my life, as they have ruined the lives of thousands of beings before me, and I cannot help connecting the consequence with the cause. I conceive that they desire, like the lawyers and the rest, to make money. I would willingly have given them half of my income - and any one would have done it in my place, understanding what they do - if they had consented not to meddle in my conjugal life, and to keep themselves at a distance. I have compiled no statistics, but I know scores of cases - in reality, they are innumerable - where they have killed, now a child in its mother's womb, asserting positively that the mother could not give birth to it (when the mother could give birth to it very well), now mothers, under the pretext of a so-called operation. No one has counted these murders, just as no one counted the murders of the Inquisition, because it was supposed that they were committed for the benefit of humanity. Innumerable are the crimes of the doctors! But all these crimes are nothing compared with the materialistic demoralization which they introduce into the world through women. I say nothing of the fact that, if it were to follow their advice, - thanks to the microbe which they see everywhere, - humanity, instead of tending to union, would proceed straight to complete disunion. Everybody, according to their doctrine, should isolate himself, and never remove from his mouth a syringe filled with phenic acid (moreover, they have found out now that it does no good). But I would pass over all these things. The supreme poison is the perversion of people, especially of women. One can no longer say now: 'You live badly, live better.' One can no longer say it either to himself or to others, for, if you live badly (say the doctors), the cause is in the nervous system or in something similar, and it is necessary to go to consult them, and they will prescribe for you thirty-five copecks' worth of remedies to be bought at the drug-store, and you must swallow them. Your condition grows worse? Again to the doctors, and more remedies! An excellent business!

"But to return to our subject. I was saying that my wife nursed her children well, that the nursing and the gestation of the children, and the children in general, quieted my tortures of jealousy, but that, on the other hand, they provoked torments of a different sort."

XVI

"The children came rapidly, one after another, and there happened what happens in our society with children and doctors. Yes, children, maternal love, it is a painful thing. Children, to a woman of our society, are not a joy, a pride, nor a fulfilment of her vocation, but a cause of fear, anxiety, and interminable suffering, torture. Women say it, they think it, and they feel it too. Children to them are really a torture, not because they do not wish to give birth to them, nurse them, and care for them (women with a strong maternal instinct - and such was my wife - are ready to do that), but because the children may fall sick and die. They do not wish to give birth to them, and then not love them; and when they love, they do not wish to feel fear for the child's health and life. That is why they do not wish to nurse them. 'If I nurse it,' they say, 'I shall become too fond of it.' One would think that they preferred india-rubber children, which could neither be sick nor die, and could always be repaired. What an entanglement in the brains of these poor women! Why such abominations to avoid pregnancy, and to avoid the love of the little ones?

"Love, the most joyous condition of the soul, is represented as a danger. And why? Because, when a man does not live as a man, he is worse than a beast. A woman cannot look upon a child otherwise than as a pleasure. It is true that it is painful to give birth to it, but what little hands!... Oh, the little hands! Oh, the little feet! Oh, its smile! Oh, its little body! Oh, its prattle! Oh, its hiccough! In a word, it is a feeling of animal, sensual maternity. But as for any idea as to the mysterious significance of the appearance of a new human being to replace us, there is scarcely a sign of it.

"Nothing of it appears in all that is said and done. No one has any faith now in a baptism of the child, and yet that was nothing but a reminder of the human significance of the newborn babe.

"They have rejected all that, but they have not replaced it, and there remain only the dresses, the laces, the little hands, the little feet, and whatever exists in the animal. But the animal has neither imagination, nor foresight, nor reason, nor a doctor.

"No! not even a doctor! The chicken droops its head, overwhelmed, or the calf dies; the hen clucks and the cow lows for a time, and then these beasts continue to live, forgetting what has happened.

"With us, if the child falls sick, what is to be done, how to care for it, what doctor to call, where to go? If it dies, there will be no more little hands or little feet, and then what is the use of the sufferings endured? The cow does not ask all that, and this is why children are a source of misery. The cow has no imagination, and for that reason cannot think how it might have saved the child if it had done this or that, and its grief, founded in its physical being, lasts but a very short time. It is only a condition, and not that sorrow which becomes exaggerated to the point of despair, thanks to idleness and satiety. The cow has not that reasoning faculty which woul't enable it to ask the why. Why endure all these tortures? What was the use of so much love, if the little ones were to die? The cow has no logic which tells it to have no more children, and, if any come accidentally, to neither love nor nurse them, that it may not suffer. But our wives reason, and reason in this way, and that is why I said that, when a man does not live as a man, he is beneath the animal."

"But then, how is it necessary to act, in your opinion, in order to treat children humanly?" I asked.

"How? Why, love them humanly."

"Well, do not mothers love their children?"

"They do not love them humanly, or very seldom do, and that is why they do not love them even as dogs. Mark this, a hen, a goose, a wolf, will always remain to woman inaccessible ideals of animal love. It is a rare thing for a woman to throw herself, at the peril of her life, upon an elephant to snatch her child away, whereas a hen or a sparrow will not fail to fly at a dog and sacrifice itself utterly for its children. Observe this, also. Woman has the power to limit her physical love for her children, which an animal cannot do. Does that mean that, because of this, woman is inferior to the animal? No. She is superior (and even to say superior is unjust, she is not superior, she is different), but she has other duties, human duties. She can restrain herself in the matter of animal love, and transfer her love to the soul of the child. That is what woman's role should be, and that is precisely what we do not see in our society. We read of the heroic acts of mothers who sacrifice their children in the name of a superior idea, and these things seem to us like tales of the ancient world, which do not concern us. And yet I believe that, if the mother has not some ideal, in the name of which she can sacrifice the animal feeling, and if this force finds no employment, she will transfer it to chimerical attempts to physically preserve her child, aided in this task by the doctor, and she will suffer as she does suffer.

"So it was with my wife. Whether there was one child or five, the feeling remained the same. In fact, it was a little better when there had been five. Life was always poisoned with fear for the children, not only from their real or imaginary diseases, but even by their simple presence. For my part, at least, throughout my conjugal life, all my interests and all my happiness depended upon the health of my children, their condition, their studies. Children, it is needless to say, are a serious consideration; but all ought to live, and in our days parents can no longer live. Regular life does not exist for them. The whole life of the family hangs by a hair. What a terrible thing it is to suddenly receive the news that little Basile is vomiting, or that Lise has a cramp in the stomach! Immediately you abandon everything, you forget everything, everything becomes nothing. The essential thing is the doctor, the enema, the temperature. You cannot begin a conversation but little Pierre comes running in with an anxious air to ask if he may eat an apple, or what jacket he shall put on, or else it is the servant who enters with a screaming baby.

"Regular, steady family life does not exist. Where you live, and consequently what you do, depends upon the health of the little ones, the health of the little ones depends upon nobody, and, thanks to the doctors, who pretend to aid health, your entire life is disturbed. It is a perpetual peril. Scarcely do we believe ourselves out of it when a new danger comes: more attempts to save. Always the situation of sailors on a foundering vessel. Sometimes it seemed to me that this was done on purpose, that my wife feigned anxiety in order to conquer me, since that solved the question so simply for her benefit. It seemed to me that all that she did at those times was done for its effect upon me, but now I see that she herself, my wife, suffered and was tortured on account of the little ones, their health, and their diseases.

"A torture to both of us, but to her the children were also a means of forgetting herself, like an intoxication. I often noticed, when she was very sad, that she was relieved, when a child fell sick, at being able to take refuge in this intoxication. It was involuntary intoxication, because as yet there was nothing else. On every side we heard that Mrs. So-and-so had lost children, that Dr. So-and-so had saved the child of Mrs. So-and-so, and that in a certain family all had moved from the house in which they were living, and thereby saved the little ones. And the doctors, with a serious air, confirmed this, sustaining my wife in her opinions. She was not prone to fear, but the doctor dropped some word, like corruption of the blood, scarlatina, or else - heaven help us - diphtheria, and off she went.

"It was impossible for it to be otherwise. Women in the old days had the belief that 'God has given, God has taken away,' that the soul of the little angel is going to heaven, and that it is better to die innocent than to die in sin. If the women of to-day had something like this faith, they could endure more peacefully the sickness of their children. But of all that there does not remain even a trace. And yet it is necessary to believe in something; consequently they stupidly believe in medicine, and not even in medicine, but in the doctor. One believes in X, another in Z, and, like all believers, they do not see the idiocy of their beliefs. They believe quia absurdum, because, in reality, if they did not believe in a stupid way, they would see the vanity of all that these brigands prescribe for them. Scarlatina is a contagious disease; so, when one lives in a large city, half the family has to move away from its residence (we did it twice), and yet every man in the city is a centre through which pass innumerable diameters, carrying threads of all sorts of contagions. There is no obstacle: the baker, the tailor, the coachman, the laundresses.

"And I would undertake, for every man who moves on account of contagion, to find in his new dwelling-place another contagion similar, if not the same.

"But that is not all. Everyone knows rich people who, after a case of diphtheria, destroy everything in their residences, and then fall sick in houses newly built and furnished. Everyone knows, likewise, numbers of men who come in contact with sick people and do not get infected. Our anxieties are due to the people who circulate tall stories. One woman says that she has an excellent doctor. 'Pardon me,' answers the other, 'he killed such a one,' or such a one. And vice versa. Bring her another, who knows no more, who learned from the same books, who treats according to the same formulas, but who goes about in a carriage, and asks a hundred roubles a visit, and she will have faith in him.

"It all lies in the fact that our women are savages. They have no belief in God, but some of them believe in the evil eye, and the others in doctors who charge high fees. If they had faith they would know that scarlatina, diphtheria, etc., are not so terrible, since they cannot disturb that which man can and should love, - the soul. There can result from them only that which none of us can avoid, - disease and death. Without faith in God, they love only physically, and all their energy is concentrated upon the preservation of life, which cannot be preserved, and which the doctors promise the fools of both sexes to save. And from that time there is nothing to be done; the doctors must be summoned.

"Thus the presence of the children not only did not improve our relations as husband and wife, but, on the contrary, disunited us. The children became an additional cause of dispute, and the larger they grew, the more they became an instrument of struggle.

"One would have said that we used them as weapons with which to combat each other. Each of us had his favorite. I made use of little Basile (the eldest), she of Lise. Further, when the children reached an age where their characters began to be defined, they became allies, which we drew each in his or her own direction. They suffered horribly from this, the poor things, but we, in our perpetual hubbub, were not clear-headed enough to think of them. The little girl was devoted to me, but the eldest boy, who resembled my wife, his favorite, often inspired me with dislike."

XVII

"We lived at first in the country, then in the city, and, if the final misfortune had not happened, I should have lived thus until my old age and should then have believed that I had had a good life, - not too good, but, on the other hand, not bad, - an existence such as other people lead. I should not have understood the abyss of misfortune and ignoble falsehood in which I floundered about, feeling that something was not right. I felt, in the first place, that I, a man, who, according to my ideas, ought to be the master, wore the petticoats, and that I could not get rid of them. The principal cause of my subjection was the children. I should have liked to free myself, but I could not. Bringing up the children, and resting upon them, my wife ruled. I did not then realize that she could not help ruling, especially because, in marrying, she was morally superior to me, as every young girl is incomparably superior to the man, since she is incomparably purer. Strange thing! The ordinary wife in our society is a very commonplace person or worse, selfish, gossiping, whimsical, whereas the ordinary young girl, until the age of twenty, is a charming being, ready for everything that is beautiful and lofty. Why is this so? Evidently because husbands pervert them, and lower them to their own level.

"In truth, if boys and girls are born equal, the little girls find themselves in a better situation. In the first place, the young girl is not subjected to the perverting conditions to which we are subjected. She has neither cigarettes, nor wine, nor cards, nor comrades, nor public houses, nor public functions. And then the chief thing is that she is physically pure, and that is why, in marrying, she is superior to her husband. She is superior to man as a young girl, and when she becomes a wife in our society, where there is no need to work in order to live, she becomes superior, also, by the gravity of the acts of generation, birth, and nursing.

"Woman, in bringing a child into the world, and giving it her bosom, sees clearly that her affair is more serious than the affair of man, who sits in the Zemstvo, in the court. She knows that in these functions the main thing is money, and money can be made in different ways, and for that very reason money is not inevitably necessary, like nursing a child. Consequently woman is necessarily superior to man, and must rule. But man, in our society, not only does not recognize this, but, on the contrary, always looks upon her from the height of his grandeur, despising what she does.

"Thus my wife despised me for my work at the Zemstvo, because she gave birth to children and nursed them. I, in turn, thought that woman's labor was most contemptible, which one might and should laugh at.

"Apart from the other motives, we were also separated by a mutual contempt. Our relations grew ever more hostile, and we arrived at that period when, not only did dissent provoke hostility, but hostility provoked dissent. Whatever she might say, I was sure in advance to hold a contrary opinion; and she the same. Toward the fourth year of our marriage it was tacitly decided between us that no intellectual community was possible, and we made no further attempts at it. As to the simplest objects, we each held obstinately to our own opinions. With strangers we talked upon the most varied and most intimate matters, but not with each other. Sometimes, in listening to my wife talk with others in my presence, I said to myself: 'What a woman! Everything that she says is a lie!' And I was astonished that the person with whom she was conversing did not see that she was lying. When we were together; we were condemned to silence, or to conversations which, I am sure, might have been carried on by animals.

"What time is it? It is bed-time. What is there for dinner to-day? Where shall we go? What is there in the newspaper? The doctor must be sent for, Lise has a sore throat."

"Unless we kept within the extremely narrow limits of such conversation, irritation was sure to ensue. The presence of a third person relieved us, for through an intermediary we could still communicate. She probably believed that she was always right. As for me, in my own eyes, I was a saint beside her.

"The periods of what we call love arrived as often as formerly. They were more brutal, without refinement, without ornament; but they were short, and generally followed by periods of irritation without cause, irritation fed by the most trivial pretexts. We hàd spats about the coffee, the table-cloth, the carriage, games of cards, - trifles, in short, which could not be of the least importance to either of us. As for me, a terrible execration was continually boiling up within me. I watched her pour the tea, swing her foot, lift her spoon to her mouth, and blow upon hot liquids or sip them, and I detested her as if these had been so many crimes.

"I did not notice that these periods of irritation depended very regularly upon the periods of love. Each of the latter was followed by one of the former. A period of intense love was followed by a long period of anger; a period of mild love induced a mild irritation. We did not understand that this love and this hatred were two opposite faces of the same animal feeling. To live thus would be terrible, if one understood the philosophy of it. But we did not perceive this, we did not analyze it. It is at once the torture and the relief of man that, when he lives irregularly, he can cherish illusions as to the miseries of his situation. So did we. She tried to forget herself in sudden and absorbing occupations, in household duties, the care of the furniture, her dress and that of her children, in the education of the latter, and in looking after their health. These were occupations that did not arise from any immediate necessity, but she accomplished them as if her life and that of her children depended on whether the pastry was allowed to burn, whether a curtain was hanging properly, whether a dress was a success, whether a lesson was well learned, or whether a medicine was swallowed.

"I saw clearly that to her all this was, more than anything else, a means of forgetting, an intoxication, just as hunting, card-playing, and my functions at the Zemstvo served the same purpose for me. It is true that in addition I had an intoxication literally speaking, - tobacco, which I smoked in large quantities, and wine, upon which I did not get drunk, but of which I took too much. Vodka before meals, and during meals two glasses of wine, so that a perpetual mist concealed the turmoil of existence.

"These new theories of hypnotism, of mental maladies, of hysteria are not simple stupidities, but dangerous or evil stupidities. Charcot, I am sure, would have said that my wife was hysterical, and of me he would have said that I was an abnormal being, and he would have wanted to treat me. But in us there was nothing requiring treatment. All this mental malady was the simple result of the fact that we were living immorally. Thanks to this immoral life, we suffered, and, to stifle our sufferings, we tried abnormal means, which the doctors call the 'symptoms' of a mental malady, - hysteria.

"There was no occasion in all this to apply for treatment to Charcot or to anybody else. Neither suggestion nor bromide would have been effective in working our cure. The needful thing was an examination of the origin of the evil. It is as when one is sitting on a nail; if you see the nail, you see that which is irregular in your life, and you avoid it. Then the pain stops, without any necessity of stifling it. Our pain arose from the irregularity of our life, and also my jealousy, my irritability, and the necessity of keeping myself in a state of perpetual semi-intoxication by hunting, card-playing, and, above all, the use of wine and tobacco. It was because of this irregularity that my wife so passionately pursued her occupations. The sudden changes of her disposition, from extreme sadness to extreme gayety, and her babble, arose from the need of forgetting herself, of forgetting her life, in the continual intoxication of varied and very brief occupations.

"Thus we lived in a perpetual fog, in which we did not distinguish our condition. We were like two galley-slaves fastened to the same ball, cursing each other, poisoning each other's existence, and trying to shake each other off. I was still unaware that ninety-nine families out of every hundred live in the same hell, and that it cannot be otherwise. I had not learned this fact from others or from myself. The coincidences that are met in regular, and even in irregular life, are surprising. At the very period when the life of parents becomes impossible, it becomes indispensable that they go to the city to live, in order to educate their children. That is what we did."

Posdnicheff became silent, and twice there escaped him, in the half-darkness, sighs, which at that moment seemed to me like suppressed sobs. Then he continued.

XVIII

"So we lived in the city. In the city the wretched feel less sad. One can live there a hundred years without being noticed, and be dead a long time before anybody will notice it. People have no time to inquire into your life. All are absorbed. Business, social relations, art, the health of children, their education. And there are visits that must be received and made; it is necessary to see this one, it is necessary to hear that one or the other one. In the city there are always one, two, or three celebrities that it is indispensable that one should visit.

"Now one must care for himself, or care for such or such a little one, now it is the professor, the private tutor, the governesses... and life is absolutely empty. In this activity we were less conscious of the sufferings of our cohabitation. Moreover, in the first of it, we had a superb occupation, - the arrangement of the new dwelling, and then, too, the moving from the city to the country, and from the country to the city.

"Thus we spent a winter. The following winter an incident happened to us which passed unnoticed, but which was the fundamental cause of all that happened later. My wife was suffering, and the rascals (the doctors) would not permit her to conceive a child, and taught her how to avoid it. I was profoundly disgusted. I struggled vainly against it, but she insisted frivolously and obstinately, and I surrendered. The last justification of our life as wretches was thereby suppressed, and life became baser than ever.

"The peasant and the workingman need children, and hence their conjugal relations have a justification. But we, when we have a few children, have no need of any more. They make a superfluous confusion of expenses and joint heirs, and are an embarrassment. Consequently we have no excuses for our existence as wretches, but we are so deeply degraded that we do not see the necessity of a justification. The majority of people in contemporary society give themselves up to this debauchery without the slightest remorse. We have no conscience left, except, so to speak, the conscience of public opinion and of the criminal code. But in this matter neither of these consciences is struck. There is not a being in society who blushes at it. Each one practices it, - X, Y, Z, etc. What is the use of multiplying beggars, and depriving ourselves of the joys of social life? There is no necessity of having conscience before the criminal code, or of fearing it: low girls, soldiers' wives who throw their children into ponds or wells, these certainly must be put in prison. But with us the suppression is effected opportunely and properly.

"Thus we passed two years more. The method prescribed by the rascals had evidently succeeded. My wife had grown stouter and handsomer. It was the beauty of the end of summer. She felt it, and paid much attention to her person. She had acquired that provoking beauty that stirs men. She was in all the brilliancy of the wife of thirty years, who conceives no children, eats heartily, and is excited. The very sight of her was enough to frighten one. She was like a spirited carriage-horse that has long been idle, and suddenly finds itself without a bridle. As for my wife, she had no bridle, as for that matter, ninety-nine hundredths of our women have none."

XIX

Posdnicheff's face had become transformed; his eyes were pitiable; their expression seemed strange, like that of another being than himself; his moustache and beard turned up toward the top of his face; his nose was diminished, and his mouth enlarged, immense, frightful.

"Yes," he resumed "she had grown stouter since ceasing to conceive, and her anxieties about her children began to disappear. Not even to disappear. One would have said that she was waking from a long intoxication, that on coming to herself she had perceived the entire universe with its joys, a whole world in which she had not learned to live, and which she did not understand.

"If only this world shall not vanish! When time is past, when old age comes, one cannot recover it.' Thus, I believe, she thought, or rather felt. Moreover, she could neither think nor feel otherwise. She had been brought up in this idea that there is in the world but one thing worthy of attention, - love. In marrying, she had known something of this love, but very far from everything that she had understood as promised her, everything that she expected. How many disillusions! How much suffering! And an unexpected torture, - the children! This torture had told upon her, and then, thanks to the obliging doctor, she had learned that it is possible to avoid having children. That had made her glad. She had tried, and she was now revived for the only thing that she knew, - for love. But love with a husband polluted by jealousy and ill-nature was no longer her ideal. She began to think of some other tenderness; at least, that is what I thought. She looked about her as if expecting some event or some being. I noticed it, and I could not help being anxious.

"Always, now, it happened that, in talking with me through a third party (that is, in talking with others, but with the intention that I should hear), she boldly expressed, - not thinking that an hour before she had said the opposite, - half joking, half seriously, this idea that maternal anxieties are a delusion; that it is not worthwhile to sacrifice one's life to children. When one is young, it is necessary to enjoy life. So she occupied herself less with the children, not with the same intensity as formerly, and paid more and more attention to herself, to her face, - although she concealed it, - to her pleasures, and even to her perfection from the worldly point of view. She began to devote herself passionately to the piano, which had formerly stood forgotten in the corner. There, at the piano, began the adventure.

"The MAN appeared."

Posdnicheff seemed embarrassed, and twice again there escaped him that nasal sound of which I spoke above. I thought that it gave him pain to refer to the MAN, and to remember him. He made an effort, as if to break down the obstacle that embarrassed him, and continued with determination.

"He was a bad man in my eyes, and not because he has played such an important role in my life, but because he was really such. For the rest, from the fact that he was bad, we must conclude that he was irresponsible. He was a musician, a violinist. Not a professional musician, but half man of the world, half artist. His father, a country proprietor, was a neighbor of my father's. The father had become ruined, and the children, three boys, were all sent away. Our man, the youngest, was sent to his godmother at Paris. There they placed him in the Conservatory, for he showed a taste for music. He came out a violinist, and played in concerts."

On the point of speaking evil of the other, Posdnicheff checked himself, stopped, and said suddenly:

"In truth, I know not how he lived. I only know that that year he came to Russia, and came to see me. Moist eyes of almond shape, smiling red lips, a little moustache well waxed, hair brushed in the latest fashion, a vulgarly pretty face, - what the women call 'not bad,' - feebly built physically, but with no deformity; with hips as broad as a woman's; correct, and insinuating himself into the familiarity of people as far as possible, but having that keen sense that quickly detects a false step and retires in reason, - a man, in short, observant of the external rules of dignity, with that special Parisianism that is revealed in buttoned boots, a gaudy cravat, and that something which foreigners pick up in Paris, and which, in its peculiarity and novelty, always has an influence on our women. In his manners an external and artificial gayety, a way, you know, of referring to everything by hints, by unfinished fragments, as if everything that one says you knew already, recalled it, and could supply the omissions. Well, he, with his music, was the cause of all.

"At the trial the affair was so represented that everything seemed attributable to jealousy. It is false, - that is, not quite false, but there was something else. The verdict was rendered that I was a deceived husband, that I had killed in defence of my sullied honor (that is the way they put it in their language), and thus I was acquitted. I tried to explain the affair from my own point of view, but they concluded that I simply wanted to rehabilitate the memory of my wife. Her relations with the musician, whatever they may have been, are now of no importance to me or to her. The important part is what I have told you. The whole tragedy was due to the fact that this man came into our house at a time when an immense abyss had already been dug between us, that frightful tension of mutual hatred, in which the slightest motive sufficed to precipitate the crisis. Our quarrels in the last days were something terrible, and the more astonishing because they were followed by a brutal passion extremely strained. If it had not been he, some other would have come. If the pretext had not been jealousy, I should have discovered another. I insist upon this point, - that all husbands who live the married life that I lived must either resort to outside debauchery, or separate from their wives, or kill themselves, or kill their wives as I did. If there is any one in my case to whom this does not happen, he is a very rare exception, for, before ending as I ended, I was several times on the point of suicide, and my wife made several attempts to poison herself."

XX

"In order that you may understand me, I must tell you how this happened. We were living along, and all seemed well. Suddenly we began to talk of the children's education. I do not remember what words either of us uttered, but a discussion began, reproaches, leaps from one subject to another. 'Yes, I know it. It has been so for a long time'... 'You said that'... 'No, I did not say that'... 'Then I lie?' etc.

"And I felt that the frightful crisis was approaching when I should desire to kill her or else myself. I knew that it was approaching; I was afraid of it as of fire; I wanted to restrain myself. But rage took possession of my whole being. My wife found herself in the same condition, perhaps worse. She knew that she intentionally distorted each of my words, and each of her words was saturated with venom. All that was dear to me she disparaged and profaned. The farther the quarrel went, the more furious it became. I cried, 'Be silent,' or something like that.

"She bounded out of the room and ran toward the children. I tried to hold her back to finish my insults. I grasped her by the arm, and hurt her. She cried: 'Children, your father is beating me.' I cried: 'Don't lie.' She continued to utter falsehoods for the simple purpose of irritating me further. 'Ah, it is not the first time,' or something of that sort. The children rushed toward her and tried to quiet her. I said: 'Don't sham.' She said: 'You look upon everything as a sham. You would kill a person and say he was shamming. Now I understand you. That is what you want to do.' 'Oh, if you were only dead!' I cried.

"I remember how that terrible phrase frightened me. Never had I thought that I could utter words so brutal, so frightful, and I was stupefied at what had just escaped my lips. I fled into my private apartment. I sat down and began to smoke. I heard her go into the hall and prepare to go out. I asked her: 'Where are you going?' She did not answer. 'Well, may the devil take you!' said I to myself, going back into my private room, where I lay down again and began smoking afresh. Thousands of plans of vengeance, of ways of getting rid of her, and how to arrange this, and act as if nothing had happened, - all this passed through my head. I thought of these things, and I smoked, and smoked, and smoked. I thought of running away, of making my escape, of going to America. I went so far as to dream how beautiful it would be, after getting rid of her, to love another woman, entirely different from her. I should be rid of her if she should die or if I should get a divorce, and I tried to think how that could be managed. I saw that I was getting confused, but, in order not to see that I was not thinking rightly, I kept on smoking.

"And the life of the house went on as usual. The children's teacher came and asked: 'Where is Madame? When will she return?'

"The servants asked if they should serve the tea. I entered the dining-room. The children, Lise, the eldest girl, looked at me with fright, as if to question me, and she did not come. The whole evening passed, and still she did not come. Two sentiments kept succeeding each other in my soul, - hatred of her, since she tortured myself and the children by her absence, but would finally return just the same, and fear lest she might return and make some attempt upon herself. But where should I look for her? At her sister's? It seemed so stupid to go to ask where one's wife is. Moreover, may God forbid, I hoped, that she should be at her sister's! If she wishes to torment any one, let her torment herself first. And suppose she were not at her sister's.

"Suppose she were to do, or had already done, something.

"Eleven o'clock, midnight, one o'clock... I did not sleep. I did not go to my chamber. It is stupid to lie stretched out all alone, and to wait. But in my study I did not rest. I tried to busy myself, to write letters, to read. Impossible! I was alone, tortured, wicked, and I listened. Toward daylight I went to sleep. I awoke. She had not returned. Everything in the house went on as usual, and all looked at me in astonishment, questioningly. The children's eyes were full of reproach for me.

"And always the same feeling of anxiety about her, and of hatred because of this anxiety.

"Toward eleven o'clock in the morning came her sister, her ambassadress. Then began the usual phrases: 'She is in a terrible state. What is the matter?' 'Why, nothing has happened.' I spoke of her asperity of character, and I added that I had done nothing, and that I would not take the first step. If she wants a divorce, so much the better! My sister-in-law would not listen to this idea, and went away without having gained anything. I was obstinate, and I said boldly and determinedly, in talking to her, that I would not take the first step. Immediately she had gone I went into the other room, and saw the children in a frightened and pitiful state, and there I found myself already inclined to take this first step. But I was bound by my word. Again I walked up and down, always smoking. At breakfast I drank brandy and wine, and I reached the point which I unconsciously desired, the point where I no longer saw the stupidity and baseness of my situation.

"Toward three o'clock she came. I thought that she was appeased, or admitted her defeat. I began to tell her that I was provoked by her reproaches. She answered me, with the same severe and terribly downcast face, that she had not come for explanations, but to take the children, that we could not live together. I answered that it was not my fault, that she had put me beside myself. She looked at me with a severe and solemn air, and said: 'Say no more. You will repent it.' I said that I could not tolerate comedies. Then she cried out something that I did not understand, and rushed toward her room. The key turned in the lock, and she shut herself up. I pushed at the door. There was no response. Furious, I went away.

"A half hour later Lise came running all in tears. 'What! Has anything happened? We cannot hear Mamma!' We went toward my wife's room. I pushed the door with all my might. The bolt was scarcely drawn, and the door opened. In a skirt, with high boots, my wife lay awkwardly on the bed. On the table an empty opium phial. We restored her to life. Tears and then reconciliation! Not reconciliation; internally each kept the hatred for the other, but it was absolutely necessary for the moment to end the scene in some way, and life began again as before. These scenes, and even worse, came now once a week, now every month, now every day. And invariably the same incidents. Once I was absolutely resolved to fly, but through some inconceivable weakness I remained.

"Such were the circumstances in which we were living when the MAN came. The man was bad, it is true. But what! No worse than we were."

XXI

"When we moved to Moscow, this gentleman - his name was Troukhatchevsky - came to my house. It was in the morning. I received him. In former times we had been very familiar. He tried, by various advances, to re-establish the familiarity, but I was determined to keep him at a distance, and soon he gave it up. He displeased me extremely. At the first glance I saw that he was a filthy debauche. I was jealous of him, even before he had seen my wife. But, strange thing! some occult fatal power kept me from repulsing him and sending him away, and, on the contrary, induced me to suffer this approach. What could have been simpler than to talk with him a few minutes, and then dismiss him coldly without introducing him to my wife? But no, as if on purpose, I turned the conversation upon his skill as a violinist, and he answered that, contrary to what I had heard, he now played the violin more than formerly. He remembered that I used to play. I answered that I had abandoned music, but that my wife played very well.

"Singular thing! Why, in the important events of our life, in those in which a man's fate is decided, - as mine was decided in that moment, - why in these events is there neither a past nor a future? My relations with Troukhatchevsky the first day, at the first hour, were such as they might still have been after all that has happened. I was conscious that some frightful misfortune must result from the presence of this man, and, in spite of that, I could not help being amiable to him. I introduced him to my wife. She was pleased with him. In the beginning, I suppose, because of the pleasure of the violin playing, which she adored. She had even hired for that purpose a violinist from the theatre. But when she cast a glance at me, she understood my feelings, and concealed her impression. Then began the mutual trickery and deceit. I smiled agreeably, pretending that all this pleased me extremely. He, looking at my wife, as all debauches look at beautiful women, with an air of being interested solely in the subject of conversation, - that is, in that which did not interest him at all.

"She tried to seem indifferent. But my expression, my jealous or false smile, which she knew so well, and the voluptuous glances of the musician, evidently excited her. I saw that, after the first interview, her eyes were already glittering, glittering strangely, and that, thanks to my jealousy, between him and her had been immediately established that sort of electric current which is provoked by an identity of expression in the smile and in the eyes.

"We talked, at the first interview, of music, of Paris, and of all sorts of trivialities. He rose to go. Pressing his hat against his swaying hip, he stood erect, looking now at her and now at me, as if waiting to see what she would do. I remember that minute, precisely because it was in my power not to invite him. I need not have invited him, and then nothing would have happened. But I cast a glance first at him, then at her. 'Don't flatter yourself that I can be jealous of you,' I thought, addressing myself to her mentally, and I invited the other to bring his violin that very evening, and to play with my wife. She raised her eyes toward me with astonishment, and her face turned purple, as if she were seized with a sudden fear. She began to excuse herself, saying that she did not play well enough. This refusal only excited me the more. I remember the strange feeling with which I looked at his neck, his white neck, in contrast with his black hair, separated by a parting, when, with his skipping gait, like that of a bird, he left my house. I could not help confessing to myself that this man's presence caused me suffering. 'It is in my power,' thought I, 'to so arrange things that I shall never see him again. But can it be that I, I, fear him? No, I do not fear him. It would be too humiliating!'

"And there in the hall, knowing that my wife heard me, I insisted that he should come that very evening with his violin. He promised me, and went away. In the evening he arrived with his violin, and they played together. But for a long time things did not go well; we had not the necessary music, and that which we had my wife could not play at sight. I amused myself with their difficulties. I aided them, I made proposals, and they finally executed a few pieces, - songs without words, and a little sonata by Mozart. He played in a marvellous manner. He had what is called the energetic and tender tone. As for difficulties, there were none for him. Scarcely had he begun to play, when his face changed. He became serious, and much more sympathetic. He was, it is needless to say, much stronger than my wife. He helped her, he advised her simply and naturally, and at the same time played his game with courtesy. My wife seemed interested only in the music. She was very simple and agreeable. Throughout the evening I feigned, not only for the others, but for myself, an interest solely in the music. Really, I was continually tortured by jealousy. From the first minute that the musician's eyes met those of my wife, I saw that he did not regard her as a disagreeable woman, with whom on occasion it would be unpleasant to enter into intimate relations.

"If I had been pure, I should not have dreamed of what he might think of her. But I looked at women, and that is why I understood him and was in torture. I was in torture, especially because I was sure that toward me she had no other feeling than of perpetual irritation, sometimes interrupted by the customary sensuality, and that this man, - thanks to his external elegance and his novelty, and, above all, thanks to his unquestionably remarkable talent, thanks to the attraction exercised under the influence of music, thanks to the impression that music produces upon nervous natures, - this man would not only please, but would inevitably, and without difficulty, subjugate and conquer her, and do with her as he liked.

"I could not help seeing this. I could not help suffering, or keep from being jealous. And I was jealous, and I suffered, and in spite of that, and perhaps even because of that, an unknown force, in spite of my will, impelled me to be not only polite, but more than polite, amiable. I cannot say whether I did it for my wife, or to show him that I did not fear HIM, or to deceive myself; but from my first relations with him I could not be at my ease. I was obliged, that I might not give way to a desire to kill him immediately, to 'caress' him. I filled his glass at the table, I grew enthusiastic over his playing, I talked to him with an extremely amiable smile, and I invited him to dinner the following Sunday, and to play again. I told him that I would invite some of my acquaintances, lovers of his art, to hear him.

"Two or three days later I was entering my house, in conversation with a friend, when in the hall I suddenly felt something as heavy as a stone weighing on my heart, and I could not account for it. And it was this, it was this: in passing through the hall, I had noticed something which reminded me of HIM. Not until I reached my study did I realize what it was, and I returned to the hall to verify my conjecture. Yes, I was not mistaken. It was his overcoat (everything that belonged to him, I, without realizing it, had observed with extraordinary attention). I questioned the servant. That was it. He had come.

"I passed near the parlor, through my children's study-room. Lise, my daughter, was sitting before a book, and the old nurse, with my youngest child, was beside the table, turning the cover of something or other. In the parlor I heard a slow arpeggio, and his voice, deadened, and a denial from her. She said: 'No, no! There is something else!' And it seemed to me that someone was purposely deadening the words by the aid of the piano.

"My God! How my heart leaped! What were my imaginations! When I remember the beast that lived in me at that moment, I am seized with fright. My heart was first compressed, then stopped, and then began to beat like a hammer. The principal feeling, as in every bad feeling, was pity for myself. 'Before the children, before the old nurse,' thought I, 'she dishonors me. I will go away. I can endure it no longer. God knows what I should do if... But I must go in.'

"The old nurse raised her eyes to mine, as if she understood, and advised me to keep a sharp watch. 'I must go in,' I said to myself, and, without knowing what I did, I opened the door. He was sitting at the piano and making arpeggios with his long, white, curved fingers. She was standing in the angle of the grand piano, before the open score. She saw or heard me first, and raised her eyes to mine. Was she stunned, was she pretending not to be frightened, or was she really not frightened at all? In any case, she did not tremble, she did not stir. She blushed, but only a little later.

'How glad I am that you have come! We have not decided what we will play Sunday,' said she, in a tone that she would not have had if she had been alone with me.

"This tone, and the way in which she said 'we' in speaking of herself and of him, revolted me. I saluted him silently. He shook hands with me directly, with a smile that seemed to me full of mockery. He explained to me that he had brought some scores, in order to prepare for the Sunday concert, and that they were not in accord as to the piece to choose, - whether difficult, classic things, notably a sonata by Beethoven, or lighter pieces.

"And as he spoke, he looked at me. It was all so natural, so simple, that there was absolutely nothing to be said against it. And at the same time I saw, I was sure, that it was false, that they were in a conspiracy to deceive me.

"One of the most torturing situations for the jealous (and in our social life everybody is jealous) are those social conditions which allow a very great and dangerous intimacy between a man and a woman under certain pretexts. One must make himself the laughing stock of everybody, if he desires to prevent associations in the ball-room, the intimacy of doctors with their patients, the familiarity of art occupations, and especially of music. In order that people may occupy themselves together with the noblest art, music, a certain intimacy is necessary, in which there is nothing blameworthy. Only a jealous fool of a husband can have anything to say against it. A husband should not have such thoughts, and especially should not thrust his nose into these affairs, or prevent them. And yet, everybody knows that precisely in these occupations, especially in music, many adulteries originate in our society.

"I had evidently embarrassed them, because for some time I was unable to say anything. I was like a bottle suddenly turned upside down, from which the water does not run because it is too full. I wanted to insult the man, and to drive him away, but I could do nothing of the kind. On the contrary, I felt that I was disturbing them, and that it was my fault. I made a presence of approving everything, this time also, thanks to that strange feeling that forced me to treat him the more amiably in proportion as his presence was more painful to me. I said that I trusted to his taste, and I advised my wife to do the same. He remained just as long as it was necessary in order to efface the unpleasant impression of my abrupt entrance with a frightened face. He went away with an air of satisfaction at the conclusions arrived at. As for me, I was perfectly sure that, in comparison with that which preoccupied them, the question of music was indifferent to them. I accompanied him with especial courtesy to the hall (how can one help accompanying a man who has come to disturb your tranquillity and ruin the happiness of the entire family?), and I shook his white, soft hand with fervent amiability."

XXII

"All that day I did not speak to my wife. I could not. Her proximity excited such hatred that I feared myself. At the table she asked me, in presence of the children, when I was to start upon a journey. I was to go the following week to an assembly of the Zemstvo, in a neighboring locality. I named the date. She asked me if I would need anything for the journey. I did not answer. I sat silent at the table, and silently I retired to my study. In those last days she never entered my study, especially at that hour. Suddenly I heard her steps, her walk, and then a terribly base idea entered my head that, like the wife of Uri, she wished to conceal a fault already committed, and that it was for this reason that she came to see me at this unseasonable hour. 'Is it possible,' thought I, 'that she is coming to see me?' On hearing her step as it approached: 'If it is to see me that she is coming, then I am right.'

"An inexpressible hatred invaded my soul. The steps drew nearer, and nearer, and nearer yet. Would she pass by and go on to the other room? No, the hinges creaked, and at the door her tall, graceful, languid figure appeared. In her face, in her eyes, a timidity, an insinuating expression, which she tried to hide, but which I saw, and of which I understood the meaning. I came near suffocating, such were my efforts to hold my breath, and, continuing to look at her, I took my cigarette, and lighted it.

'What does this mean? One comes to talk with you, and you go to smoking.'

"And she sat down beside me on the sofa, resting against my shoulder. I recoiled, that I might not touch her.

'I see that you are displeased with what I wish to play on Sunday,' said she.

'I am not at all displeased,' said I.

'Can I not see?'

'Well, I congratulate you on your clairvoyance. Only to you every baseness is agreeable, and I abhor it.'

'If you are going to swear like a trooper, I am going away.'

'Then go away. Only know that, if the honor of the family is nothing to you, to me it is dear. As for you, the devil take you!'

'What! What is the matter?'

'Go away, in the name of God.'

"But she did not go away. Was she pretending not to understand, or did she really not understand what I meant? But she was offended and became angry.

'You have become absolutely impossible,' she began, or some such phrase as that regarding my character, trying, as usual, to give me as much pain as possible. 'After what you have done to my sister (she referred to an incident with her sister, in which, beside myself, I had uttered brutalities; she knew that that tortured me, and tried to touch me in that tender spot) nothing will astonish me.'

'Yes, offended, humiliated, and dishonored, and after that to hold me still responsible,' thought I, and suddenly a rage, such a hatred invaded me as I do not remember to have ever felt before. For the first time I desired to express this hatred physically. I leaped upon her, but at the same moment I understood my condition, and I asked myself whether it would be well for me to abandon myself to my fury. And I answered myself that it would be well, that it would frighten her, and, instead of resisting, I lashed and spurred myself on, and was glad to feel my anger boiling more and more fiercely.

'Go away, or I will kill you!' I cried, purposely, with a frightful voice, and I grasped her by the arm. She did not go away. Then I twisted her arm, and pushed her away violently.

'What is the matter with you? Come to your senses!' she shrieked.

'Go away,' roared I, louder than ever, rolling my eyes wildly. 'It takes you to put me in such a fury. I do not answer for myself! Go away!'

"In abandoning myself to my anger, I became steeped in it, and I wanted to commit some violent act to show the force of my fury. I felt a terrible desire to beat her, to kill her, but I realized that that could not be, and I restrained myself. I drew back from her, rushed to the table, grasped the paper-weight, and threw it on the floor by her side. I took care to aim a little to one side, and, before she disappeared (I did it so that she could see it), I grasped a candlestick, which I also hurled, and then took down the barometer, continuing to shout:

'Go away! I do not answer for myself!'

"She disappeared, and I immediately ceased my demonstrations. An hour later the old servant came to me and said that my wife was in a fit of hysterics. I went to see her. She sobbed and laughed, incapable of expressing anything, her whole body in a tremble. She was not shamming, she was really sick. We sent for the doctor, and all night long I cared for her. Toward daylight she grew calmer, and we became reconciled under the influence of that feeling which we called 'love.' The next morning, when, after the reconciliation, I confessed to her that I was jealous of Troukhatchevsky, she was not at all embarrassed, and began to laugh in the most natural way, so strange did the possibility of being led astray by such a man appear to her.

'With such a man can an honest woman entertain any feeling beyond the pleasure of enjoying music with him? But if you like, I am ready to never see him again, even on Sunday, although everybody has been invited. Write him that I am indisposed, and that will end the matter. Only one thing annoys me, - that anyone could have thought him dangerous. I am too proud not to detest such thoughts.'

"And she did not lie. She believed what she said. She hoped by her words to provoke in herself a contempt for him, and thereby to defend herself. But she did not succeed. Everything was directed against her, especially that abominable music. So ended the quarrel, and on Sunday our guests came, and Troukhatchevsky and my wife again played together."

XXIII

"I think that it is superfluous to say that I was very vain. If one has no vanity in this life of ours, there is no sufficient reason for living. So for that Sunday I had busied myself in tastefully arranging things for the dinner and the musical soiree. I had purchased myself numerous things for the dinner, and had chosen the guests. Toward six o'clock they arrived, and after them Troukhatchevsky, in his dress-coat, with diamond shirt-studs, in bad taste. He bore himself with ease. To all questions he responded promptly, with a smile of contentment and understanding, and that peculiar expression which was intended to mean: 'All that you may do and say will be exactly what I expected.' Everything about him that was not correct I now noticed with especial pleasure, for it all tended to tranquillize me, and prove to me that to my wife he stood in such a degree of inferiority that, as she had told me, she could not stoop to his level. Less because of my wife's assurances than because of the atrocious sufferings which I felt in jealousy, I no longer allowed myself to be jealous.

"In spite of that, I was not at ease with the musician or with her during dinner-time and the time that elapsed before the beginning of the music. Involuntarily I followed each of their gestures and looks. The dinner, like all dinners, was tiresome and conventional. Not long afterward the music began. He went to get his violin; my wife advanced to the piano, and rummaged among the scores. Oh, how well I remember all the details of that evening! I remember how he brought the violin, how he opened the box, took off the serge embroidered by a lady's hand, and began to tune the instrument. I can still see my wife sit down, with a false air of indifference, under which it was plain that she hid a great timidity, a timidity that was especially due to her comparative lack of musical knowledge. She sat down with that false air in front of the piano, and then began the usual preliminaries, - the pizzicati of the violin and the arrangement of the scores. I remember then how they looked at each other, and cast a glance at their auditors who were taking their seats. They said a few words to each other, and the music began. They played Beethoven's 'Kreutzer Sonata.' Do you know the first presto? Do you know it? Ah!"...

Posdnicheff heaved a sigh, and was silent for a long time.

"A terrible thing is that sonata, especially the presto! And a terrible thing is music in general. What is it? Why does it do what it does? They say that music stirs the soul. Stupidity! A lie! It acts, it acts frightfully (I speak for myself), but not in an ennobling way. It acts neither in an ennobling nor a debasing way, but in an irritating way. How shall I say it? Music makes me forget my real situation. It transports me into a state which is not my own. Under the influence of music I really seem to feel what I do not feel, to understand what I do not understand, to have powers which I cannot have. Music seems to me to act like yawning or laughter; I have no desire to sleep, but I yawn when I see others yawn; with no reason to laugh, I laugh when I hear others laugh. And music transports me immediately into the condition of soul in which he who wrote the music found himself at that time. I become confounded with his soul, and with him I pass from one condition to another. But why that? I know nothing about it? But he who wrote Beethoven's 'Kreutzer Sonata' knew well why he found himself in a certain condition. That condition led him to certain actions, and for that reason to him had a meaning, but to me none, none whatever. And that is why music provokes an excitement which it does not bring to a conclusion. For instance, a military march is played; the soldier passes to the sound of this march, and the music is finished. A dance is played; I have finished dancing, and the music is finished. A mass is sung; I receive the sacrament, and again the music is finished. But any other music provokes an excitement, and this excitement is not accompanied by the thing that needs properly to be done, and that is why music is so dangerous, and sometimes acts so frightfully.

"In China music is under the control of the State, and that is the way it ought to be. Is it admissible that the first comer should hypnotize one or more persons, and then do with them as he likes? And especially that the hypnotizer should be the first immoral individual who happens to come along? It is a frightful power in the hands of any one, no matter whom. For instance, should they be allowed to play this 'Kreutzer Sonata,' the first presto, - and there are many like it, - in parlors, among ladies wearing low necked dresses, or in concerts, then finish the piece, receive the applause, and then begin another piece? These things should be played under certain circumstances, only in cases where it is necessary to incite certain actions corresponding to the music. But to incite an energy of feeling which corresponds to neither the time nor the place, and is expended in nothing, cannot fail to act dangerously. On me in particular this piece acted in a frightful manner. One would have said that new sentiments, new virtualities, of which I was formerly ignorant, had developed in me. 'Ah, yes, that's it! Not at all as I lived and thought before! This is the right way to live!'

"Thus I spoke to my soul as I listened to that music. What was this new thing that I thus learned? That I did not realize, but the consciousness of this indefinite state filled me with joy. In that state there was no room for jealousy. The same faces, and among them HE and my wife, I saw in a different light. This music transported me into an unknown world, where there was no room for jealousy. Jealousy and the feelings that provoke it seemed to me trivialities, nor worth thinking of.

"After the presto followed the andante, not very new, with commonplace variations, and the feeble finale. Then they played more, at the request of the guests, - first an elegy by Ernst, and then various other pieces. They were all very well, but did not produce upon me a tenth part of the impression that the opening piece did. I felt light and gay throughout the evening. As for my wife, never had I seen her as she was that night. Those brilliant eyes, that severity and majestic expression while she was playing, and then that utter languor, that weak, pitiable, and happy smile after she had finished, - I saw them all and attached no importance to them, believing that she felt as I did, that to her, as to me, new sentiments had been revealed, as through a fog. During almost the whole evening I was not jealous.

"Two days later I was to start for the assembly of the Zemstvo, and for that reason, on taking leave of me and carrying all his scores with him, Troukhatchevsky asked me when I should return. I inferred from that that he believed it impossible to come to my house during my absence, and that was agreeable to me. Now I was not to return before his departure from the city. So we bade each other a definite farewell. For the first time I shook his hand with pleasure, and thanked him for the satisfaction that he had given me. He likewise took leave of my wife, and their parting seemed to me very natural and proper. All went marvellously. My wife and I retired, weil satisfied with the evening. We talked of our impressions in a general way, and we were nearer together and more friendly than we had been for a long time."

XXIV

"Two days later I started for the assembly, having bid farewell to my wife in an excellent and tranquil state of mind. In the district there was always much to be done. It was a world and a life apart. During two days I spent ten hours at the sessions. The evening of the second day, on returning to my district lodgings, I found a letter from my wife, telling me of the children, of their uncle, of the servants, and, among other things, as if it were perfectly natural, that Troukhatchevsky had been at the house, and had brought her the promised scores. He had also proposed that they play again, but she had refused.

"For my part, I did not remember at all that he had promised any score. It had seemed to me on Sunday evening that he took a definite leave, and for this reason the news gave me a disagreeable surprise. I read the letter again. There was something tender and timid about it. It produced an extremely painful impression upon me. My heart swelled, and the mad beast of jealousy began to roar in his lair, and seemed to want to leap upon his prey. But I was afraid of this beast, and I imposed silence upon it.

"What an abominable sentiment is jealousy! 'What could be more natural than what she has written?' said I to myself. I went to bed, thinking myself tranquil again. I thought of the business that remained to be done, and I went to sleep without thinking of her.

"During these assemblies of the Zemstvo I always slept badly in my strange quarters. That night I went to sleep directly, but, as sometimes happens, a sort of sudden shock awoke me. I thought immediately of her, of my physical love for her, of Troukhatchevsky, and that between them everything had happened. And a feeling of rage compressed my heart, and I tried to quiet myself.

'How stupid!' said I to myself; 'there is no reason, none at all. And why humiliate ourselves, herself and myself, and especially myself, by supposing such horrors? This mercenary violinist, known as a bad man, - shall I think of him in connection with a respectable woman, the mother of a family, MY wife? How silly!' But on the other hand, I said to myself: 'Why should it not happen?'

"Why? Was it not the same simple and intelligible feeling in the name of which I married, in the name of which I was living with her, the only thing I wanted of her, and that which, consequently, others desired, this musician among the rest? He was not married, was in good health (I remember how his teeth ground the gristle of the cutlets, and how eagerly he emptied the glass of wine with his red lips), was careful of his person, well fed, and not only without principles, but evidently with the principle that one should take advantage of the pleasure that offers itself. There was a bond between them, music, - the most refined form of sensual voluptuousness. What was there to restrair them? Nothing. Everything, on the contrary, attracted them. And she, she had been and had remained a mystery. I did not know her. I knew her only as an animal, and an animal nothing can or should restrain. And now I remember their faces on Sunday evening, when, after the 'Kreutzer Sonata,' they played a passionate piece, written I know not by whom, but a piece passionate to the point of obscenity.

'How could I have gone away?' said I to myself, as I recalled their faces. 'Was it not clear that between them everything was done that evening? Was it not clear that between them not only there were no more obstacles, but that both - especially she - felt a certain shame after what had happened at the piano? How weakly, pitiably, happily she smiled, as she wiped the perspiration from her reddened face! They already avoided each other's eyes, and only at the supper, when she poured some water for him, did they look at each other and smile imperceptibly.'

"Now I remember with fright that look and that scarcely perceptible smile. 'Yes, everything has happened,' a voice said to me, and directly another said the opposite. 'Are you mad? It is impossible!' said the second voice.

"It was too painful to me to remain thus stretched in the darkness. I struck a match, and the little yellow-papered room frightened me. I lighted a cigarette, and, as always happens, when one turns in a circle of inextricable contradiction, I began to smoke. I smoked cigarette after cigarette to dull my senses, that I might not see my contradictions. All night I did not sleep, and at five o'clock, when it was not yet light, I decided that I could stand this strain no longer, and that I would leave directly. There was a train at eight o'clock. I awakened the keeper who was acting as my servant, and sent him to look for horses. To the assembly of Zemstvo I sent a message that I was called back to Moscow by pressing business, and that I begged them to substitute for me a member of the Committee. At eight o'clock I got into a tarantass and started off."

XXV

"I had to go twenty-five versts by carriage and eight hours by train. By carriage it was a very pleasant journey. The coolness of autumn was accompanied by a brilliant sun. You know the weather when the wheels imprint themselves upon the dirty road. The road was level, and the light strong, and the air strengthening. The tarantass was comfortable. As I looked at the horses, the fields, and the people whom we passed, I forgot where I was going. Sometimes it seemed to me that I was travelling without an object, - simply promenading, - and that I should go on thus to the end of the world. And I was happy when I so forgot myself. But when I remembered where I was going, I said to myself: 'I shall see later. Don't think about it.'

"When half way, an incident happened to distract me still further. The tarantass, though new, broke down, and had to be repaired. The delays in looking for a telegue, the repairs, the payment, the tea in the inn, the conversation with the dvornik, all served to amuse me. Toward nightfall all was ready, and I started off again. By night the journey was still pleasanter than by day. The moon in its first quarter, a slight frost, the road still in good condition, the horses, the sprightly coachman, all served to put me in good spirits. I scarcely thought of what awaited me, and was gay perhaps because of the very thing that awaited me, and because I was about to say farewell to the joys of life.

"But this tranquil state, the power of conquering my preoccupation, all ended with the carriage drive. Scarcely had I entered the cars, when the other thing began. Those eight hours on the rail were so terrible to me that I shall never forget them in my life. Was it because on entering the car I had a vivid imagination of having already arrived, or because the railway acts upon people in such an exciting fashion? At any rate, after boarding the train I could no longer control my imagination, which incessantly, with extraordinary vivacity, drew pictures before my eyes, each more cynical than its predecessor, which kindled my jealousy. And always the same things about what was happening at home during my absence. I burned with indignation, with rage, and with a peculiar feeling which steeped me in humiliation, as I contemplated these pictures. And I could not tear myself out of this condition. I could not help looking at them, I could not efface them, I could not keep from evoking them.

"The more I looked at these imaginary pictures, the more I believed in their reality, forgetting that they had no serious foundation. The vivacity of these images seemed to prove to me that my imaginations were a reality. One would have said that a demon, against my will, was inventing and breathing into me the most terrible fictions. A conversation which dated a long time back, with the brother of Troukhatchevsky, I remembered at that moment, in a sort of ecstasy, and it tore my heart as I connected it with the musician and my wife. Yes, it was very long ago. The brother of Troukhatchevsky, answering my questions as to whether he frequented disreputable houses, said that a respectable man does not go where he may contract a disease, in a low and unclean spot, when one can find an honest woman. And here he, his brother, the musician, had found the honest woman. 'It is true that she is no longer in her early youth. She has lost a tooth on one side, and her face is slightly bloated,' thought I for Troukhatchevsky. 'But what is to be done? One must profit by what one has.'

'Yes, he is bound to take her for his mistress,' said I to myself again; 'and besides, she is not dangerous.'

'No, it is not possible' I rejoined in fright. 'Nothing, nothing of the kind has happened, and there is no reason to suppose there has. Did she not tell me that the very idea that I could be jealous of her because of him was humiliating to her?' 'Yes, but she lied,' I cried, and all began over again.

"There were only two travellers in my compartment: an old woman with her husband, neither of them very talkative; and even they got out at one of the stations, leaving me all alone. I was like a beast in a cage. Now I jumped up and approached the window, now I began to walk back and forth, staggering as if I hoped to make the train go faster by my efforts, and the car with its seats and its windows trembled continually, as ours does now."

And Posdnicheff rose abruptly, took a few steps, and sat down again.

"Oh, I am afraid, I am afraid of railway carriages. Fear seizes me. I sat down again, and I said to myself: 'I must think of something else. For instance, of the inn keeper at whose house I took tea.' And then, in my imagination arose the dvornik, with his long beard, and his grandson, a little fellow of the same age as my little Basile. My little Basile! My little Basile! He will see the musician kiss his mother! What thoughts will pass through his poor soul! But what does that matter to her! She loves.

"And again it all began, the circle of the same thoughts. I suffered so much that at last I did not know what to do with myself, and an idea passed through my head that pleased me much, - to get out upon the rails, throw myself under the cars, and thus finish everything. One thing prevented me from doing so. It was pity! It was pity for myself, evoking at the same time a hatred for her, for him, but not so much for him. Toward him I felt a strange sentiment of my humiliation and his victory, but toward her a terrible hatred.

'But I cannot kill myself and leave her free. She must suffer, she must understand at least that I have suffered,' said I to myself.

"At a station I saw people drinking at the lunch counter, and directly I went to swallow a glass of vodki. Beside me stood a Jew, drinking also. He began to talk to me, and I, in order not to be left alone in my compartment, went with him into his third-class, dirty, full of smoke, and covered with peelings and sunflower seeds. There I sat down beside the Jew, and, as it seemed, he told many anecdotes.

"First I listened to him, but I did not understand what he said. He noticed it, and exacted my attention to his person. Then I rose and entered my own compartment.

'I must consider,' said I to myself, 'whether what I think is true, whether there is any reason to torment myself.' I sat down, wishing to reflect quietly; but directly, instead of the peaceful reflections, the same thing began again. Instead of the reasoning, the pictures.

'How many times have I tormented myself in this way,' I thought (I recalled previous and similar fits of jealousy), 'and then seen it end in nothing at all? It is the same now. Perhaps, yes, surely, I shall find her quietly sleeping. She will awaken, she will be glad, and in her words and looks I shall see that nothing has happened, that all this is vain. Ah, if it would only so turn out!' 'But no, that has happened too often! Now the end has come,' a voice said to me.

"And again it all began. Ah, what torture! It is not to a hospital filled with syphilitic patients that I would take a young man to deprive him of the desire for women, but into my soul, to show him the demon which tore it. The frightful part was that I recognized in myself an indisputable right to the body of my wife, as if her body were entirely mine. And at the same time I felt that I could not possess this body, that it was not mine, that she could do with it as she liked, and that she liked to do with it as I did not like. And I was powerless against him and against her. He, like the Vanka of the song, would sing, before mounting the gallows, how he would kiss her sweet lips, etc., and he would even have the best of it before death. With her it was still worse. If she HAD NOT DONE IT, she had the desire, she wished to do it, and I knew that she did. That was worse yet. It would be better if she had already done it, to relieve me of my uncertainty.

"In short, I could not say what I desired. I desired that she might not want what she MUST want. It was complete madness."

XXVI

"At the station before the last, when the conductor came to take the tickets, I took my baggage and went out on the car platform, and the consciousness that the climax was near at hand only added to my agitation. I was cold, my jaw trembled so that my teeth chattered. Mechanically I left the station with the crowd, I took a tchik, and I started. I looked at the few people passing in the streets and at the dvorniks. I read the signs, without thinking of anything. After going half a verst my feet began to feel cold, and I remembered that in the car I had taken off my woollen socks, and had put them in my travelling bag. Where had I put the bag? Was it with me? Yes, and the basket?

"I bethought myself that I had totally forgotten my baggage. I took out my check, and then decided it was not worthwhile to return. I continued on my way. In spite of all my efforts to remember, I cannot at this moment make out why I was in such a hurry. I know only that I was conscious that a serious and menacing event was approaching in my life. It was a case of real auto-suggestion. Was it so serious because I thought it so? Or had I a presentiment? I do not know. Perhaps, too, after what has happened, all previous events have taken on a lugubrious tint in my memory.

"I arrived at the steps. It was an hour past midnight. A few isvotchiks were before the door, awaiting customers, attracted by the lighted windows (the lighted windows were those of our parlor and reception room). Without trying to account for this late illumination, I went up the steps, always with the same expectation of something terrible, and I rang. The servant, a good, industrious, and very stupid being, named Gregor, opened the door. The first thing that leaped to my eyes in the hall, on the hat-stand, among other garments, was an overcoat. I ought to have been astonished, but I was not astonished. I expected it. 'That's it!' I said to myself.

"When I had asked Gregor who was there, and he had named Troukhatchevsky, I inquired whether there were other visitors. He answered: 'Nobody.' I remember the air with which he said that, with a tone that was intended to give me pleasure, and dissipate my doubts. 'That's it! that's it!' I had the air of saying to myself. 'And the children?'

'Thank God, they are very well. They went to sleep long ago.'

"I scarcely breathed, and I could not keep my jaw from trembling.

"Then it was not as I thought. I had often before returned home with the thought that a misfortune had awaited me, but had been mistaken, and everything was going on as usual. But now things were not going on as usual. All that I had imagined, all that I believed to be chimeras, all really existed. Here was the truth.

"I was on the point of sobbing, but straightway the demon whispered in my ear: 'Weep and be sentimental, and they will separate quietly, and there will be no proofs, and all your life you will doubt and suffer.' And pity for myself vanished, and there remained only the bestial need of some adroit, cunning, and energetic action. I became a beast, an intelligent beast.

'No, no,' said I to Gregor, who was about to announce my arrival. 'Do this, take a carriage, and go at once for my baggage. Here is the check. Start.'

"He went along the hall to get his overcoat. Fearing lest he might frighten them, I accompanied him to his little room, and waited for him to put on his things. In the dining-room could be heard the sound of conversation and the rattling of knives and plates. They were eating. They had not heard the ring. 'Now if they only do not go out,' I thought.

"Gregor put on his fur-collared coat and went out. I closed the door after him. I felt anxious when I was alone, thinking that directly I should have to act. How? I did not yet know. I knew only that all was ended, that there could be no doubt of his innocence, and that in an instant my relations with her were going to be terminated. Before, I had still doubts. I said to myself: 'Perhaps this is not true. Perhaps I am mistaken.' Now all doubt had disappeared. All was decided irrevocably. Secretly, all alone with him, at night! It is a violation of all duties! Or, worse yet, she may make a show of that audacity, of that insolence in crime, which, by its excess, tends to prove innocence. All is clear. No doubt. I feared but one thing, - that they might run in different directions, that they might invent some new lie, and thus deprive me of material proof, and of the sorrowful joy of punishing, yes, of executing them.

"And to surprise them more quickly, I started on tiptoe for the dining-room, not through the parlor, but through the hall and the children's rooms. In the first room slept the little boy. In the second, the old nurse moved in her bed, and seemed on the point of waking, and I wondered what she would think when she knew all. And pity for myself gave me such a pang that I could not keep the tears back. Not to wake the children, I ran lightly through the hall into my study. I dropped upon the sofa, and sobbed. 'I, an honest man, I, the son of my parents, who all my life long have dreamed of family happiness, I who have never betrayed!... And here my five children, and she embracing a musician because he has red lips! No, she is not a woman! She is a bitch, a dirty bitch! Beside the chamber of the children, whom she had pretended to love all her life! And then to think of what she wrote me! And how do I know? Perhaps it has always been thus. Perhaps all these children, supposed to be mine, are the children of my servants. And if I had arrived tomorrow, she would have come to meet me with her coiffure, with her corsage, her indolent and graceful movements (and I see her attractive and ignoble features), and this jealous animal would have remained forever in my heart, tearing it. What will the old nurse say? And Gregor? And the poor little Lise? She already understands things. And this impudence, this falsehood, this bestial sensuality, that I know so well,' I said to myself.

"I tried to rise. I could not. My heart was beating so violently that I could not hold myself upon my legs. 'Yes, I shall die of a rush of blood. She will kill me. That is what she wants. What is it to her to kill? But that would be too agreeable to him, and I will not allow him to have this pleasure.'

"Yes, here I am, and there they are. They are laughing, they... Yes, in spite of the fact that she is no longer in her early youth, he has not disdained her. 'At any rate, she is by no means ugly, and above all, not dangerous to his dear health, to him. Why did I not stifle her then?' said I to myself, as I remembered that other scene of the previous week, when I drove her from my study, and broke the furniture.

"And I recalled the state in which I was then. Not only did I recall it, but I again entered into the same bestial state. And suddenly there came to me a desire to act, and all reasoning, except such as was necessary to action, vanished from my brain, and I was in the condition of a beast, and of a man under the influence of physical excitement pending a danger, who acts imperturbably, without haste, and yet without losing a minute, pursuing a definite object.

"The first thing that I did was to take off my boots, and now, having only stockings on, I advanced toward the wall, over the sofa, where firearms and daggers were hanging, and I took down a curved Damascus blade, which I had never used, and which was very sharp. I took it from its sheath. I remember that the sheath fell upon the sofa, and that I said to myself: 'I must look for it later; it must not be lost.'

"Then I took off my overcoat, which I had kept on all the time, and with wolf-like tread started for THE ROOM. I do not remember how I proceeded, whether I ran or went slowly, through what chambers I passed, how I approached the dining-room, how I opened the door, how I entered. I remember nothing about it."

XXVII

"I Remember only the expression of their faces when I opened the door. I remember that, because it awakened in me a feeling of sorrowful joy. It was an expression of terror, such as I desired. Never shall I forget that desperate and sudden fright that appeared on their faces when they saw me. He, I believe, was at the table, and, when he saw or heard me, he started, jumped to his feet, and retreated to the sideboard. Fear was the only sentiment that could be read with certainty in his face. In hers, too, fear was to be read, but accompanied by other impressions. And yet, if her face had expressed only fear, perhaps that which happened would not have happened. But in the expression of her face there was at the first moment - at least, I thought I saw it - a feeling of ennui, of discontent, at this disturbance of her love and happiness. One would have said that her sole desire was not to be disturbed IN THE MOMENT OF HER HAPPINESS. But these expressions appeared upon their faces only for a moment. Terror almost immediately gave place to interrogation. Would they lie or not? If yes, they must begin. If not, something else was going to happen. But what?

"He gave her a questioning glance. On her face the expression of anguish and ennui changed, it seemed to me, when she looked at him, into an expression of anxiety for HIM. For a moment I stood in the doorway, holding the dagger hidden behind my back. Suddenly he smiled, and in a voice that was indifferent almost to the point of ridicule, he said:

'We were having some music.'

'I did not expect' - she began at the same time, chiming in with the tone of the other.

"But neither he nor she finished their remarks. The same rage that I had felt the previous week took possession of me. I felt the need of giving free course to my violence and 'the joy of wrath.'

"No, they did not finish. That other thing was going to begin, of which he was afraid, and was going to annihilate what they wanted to say. I threw myself upon her, still hiding the dagger, that he might not prevent me from striking where I desired, in her bosom, under the breast. At that moment he saw... and, what I did not expect on his part, he quickly seized my hand, and cried:

'Come to your senses! What are you doing? Help! Help!'

"I tore my hands from his grasp, and leaped upon him. I must have been very terrible, for he turned as white as a sheet, to his lips. His eyes scintillated singularly, and - again what I did not expect of him - he scrambled under the piano, toward the other room. I tried to follow him, but a very heavy weight fell upon my left arm. It was she.

"I made an effort to clear myself. She clung more heavily than ever, refusing to let go. This unexpected obstacle, this burden, and this repugnant touch only irritated me the more. I perceived that I was completely mad, that I must be frightful, and I was glad of it. With a sudden impulse, and with all my strength, I dealt her, with my left elbow, a blow squarely in the face.

"She uttered a cry and let go my arm. I wanted to follow the other, but I felt that it would be ridiculous to pursue in my stockings the lover of my wife, and I did not wish to be grotesque, I wished to be terrible. In spite of my extreme rage, I was all the time conscious of the impression that I was making upon others, and even this impression partially guided me.

"I turned toward her. She had fallen on the long easy chair, and covering her face at the spot where I had struck her, she looked at me. Her features exhibited fear and hatred toward me, her enemy, such as the rat exhibits when one lifts the rat-trap. At least, I saw nothing in her but that fear and hatred, the fear and hatred which love for another had provoked. Perhaps I still should have restrained myself, and should not have gone to the last extremity, if she had maintained silence. But suddenly she began to speak; she grasped my hand that held the dagger.

'Come to your senses! What are you doing? What is the matter with you? Nothing has happened, nothing, nothing! I swear it to you!'

"I might have delayed longer, but these last words, from which I inferred the contrary of what they affirmed, - that is, that EVERYTHING had happened, - these words called for a reply. And the reply must correspond to the condition into which I had lashed myself, and which was increasing and must continue to increase. Rage has its laws.

'Do not lie, wretch. Do not lie!' I roared.

"With my left hand I seized her hands. She disengaged herself. Then, without dropping my dagger, I seized her by the throat, forced her to the floor, and began to strangle her. With her two hands she clutched mine, tearing them from her throat, stifling. Then I struck her a blow with the dagger, in the left side, between the lower ribs.

"When people say that they do not remember what they do in a fit of fury, they talk nonsense. It is false. I remember everything.

"I did not lose my consciousness for a single moment. The more I lashed myself to fury, the clearer my mind became, and I could not help seeing what I did. I cannot say that I knew in advance what I would do, but at the moment when I acted, and it seems to me even a little before, I knew what I was doing, as if to make it possible to repent, and to be able to say later that I could have stopped.

"I knew that I struck the blow between the ribs, and that the dagger entered.

"At the second when I did it, I knew that I was performing a horrible act, such as I had never performed, - an act that would have frightful consequences. My thought was as quick as lightning, and the deed followed immediately. The act, to my inner sense, had an extraordinary clearness. I perceived the resistance of the corset and then something else, and then the sinking of the knife into a soft substance. She clutched at the dagger with her hands, and cut herself with it, but could not restrain the blow.

"Long afterward, in prison when the moral revolution had been effected within me, I thought of that minute, I remembered it as far as I could, and I co-ordinated all the sudden changes. I remembered the terrible consciousness which I felt, - that I was killing a wife, MY wife.

"I well remember the horror of that consciousness and I know vaguely that, having plunged in the dagger, I drew it out again immediately, wishing to repair and arrest my action. She straightened up and cried:

'Nurse, he has killed me!'

"The old nurse, who had heard the noise, was standing in the doorway. I was still erect, waiting, and not believing myself in what had happened. But at that moment, from under her corset, the blood gushed forth. Then only did I understand that all reparation was impossible, and promptly I decided that it was not even necessary, that all had happened in accordance with my wish, and that I had fulfilled my desire. I waited until she fell, and until the nurse, exclaiming, 'Oh, my God!' ran to her; then only I threw away the dagger and went out of the room.

'I must not be agitated. I must be conscious of what I am doing,' I said to myself, looking neither at her nor at the old nurse. The latter cried and called the maid. I passed through the hall, and, after having sent the maid, started for my study.

'What shall I do now?' I asked myself.

"And immediately I understood what I should do. Directly after entering the study, I went straight to the wall, took down the revolver, and examined it attentively. It was loaded. Then I placed it on the table. Next I picked up the sheath of the dagger, which had dropped down behind the sofa, and then I sat down. I remained thus for a long time. I thought of nothing, I did not try to remember anything. I heard a stifled noise of steps, a movement of objects and of tapestries, then the arrival of a person, and then the arrival of another person. Then I saw Gregor bring into my room the baggage from the railway; as if any one needed it!

'Have you heard what has happened?' I asked him. 'Have you told the dvornik to inform the police?'

"He made no answer, and went out. I rose, closed the door, took the cigarettes and the matches, and began to smoke. I had not finished one cigarette, when a drowsy feeling came over me and sent me into a deep sleep. I surely slept two hours. I remember having dreamed that I was on good terms with her, that after a quarrel we were in the act of making up, that something prevented us, but that we were friends all the same.

"A knock at the door awoke me.

'It is the police,' thought I, as I opened my eyes. 'I have killed, I believe. But perhaps it is SHE; perhaps nothing has happened.'

"Another knock. I did not answer. I was solving the question: 'Has it happened or not? Yes, it has happened.'

"I remembered the resistance of the corset, and then... 'Yes, it has happened. Yes, it has happened. Yes, now I must execute myself,' said I to myself.

"I said it, but I knew well that I should not kill myself. Nevertheless, I rose and took the revolver, but, strange thing, I remembered that formerly I had very often had suicidal ideas, that that very night, on the cars, it had seemed to me easy, especially easy because I thought how it would stupefy her. Now I not only could not kill myself, but I could not even think of it.

'Why do it?' I asked myself, without answering.

"Another knock at the door.

'Yes, but I must first know who is knocking. I have time enough.'

"I put the revolver back on the table, and hid it under my newspaper. I went to the door and drew back the bolt.

"It was my wife's sister, - a good and stupid widow.

'Basile, what does this mean?' said she, and her tears, always ready, began to flow.

'What do you want?' I asked roughly.

"I saw clearly that there was no necessity of being rough with her, but I could not speak in any other tone.

'Basile, she is dying. Ivan Fedorowitch says so.'

"Ivan Fedorowitch was the doctor, HER doctor, her counsellor.

'Is he here?' I inquired.

"And all my hatred of her arose anew.

"Well, what?

'Basile, go to her! Ah! how terrible it is!' said she.

'Go to her?' I asked myself; and immediately I made answer to myself that I ought to go, that probably that was the thing that is usually done when a husband like myself kills his wife, that it was absolutely necessary that I should go and see her.

'If that is the proper thing, I must go,' I repeated to myself. 'Yes, if it is necessary, I shall still have time,' said I to myself, thinking of my intention of blowing my brains out.

"And I followed my sister-in-law. 'Now there are going to be phrases and grimaces, but I will not yield,' I declared to myself.

'Wait,' said I to my sister-in-law, 'it is stupid to be without boots. Let me at least put on my slippers'. "

XXVIII

"Strange thing! Again, when I had left my study, and was passing through the familiar rooms, again the hope came to me that nothing had happened. But the odor of the drugs, iodoform and phenic acid, brought me back to a sense of reality.

'No, everything has happened.'

"In passing through the hall, beside the children's chamber, I saw little Lise. She was looking at me, with eyes that were full of fear. I even thought that all the children were looking at me. As I approached the door of our sleeping-room, a servant opened it from within, and came out. The first thing that I noticed was HER light gray dress upon a chair, all dark with blood. On our common bed she was stretched, with knees drawn up.

"She lay very high, upon pillows, with her chemise half open. Linen had been placed upon the wound. A heavy smell of iodoform filled the room. Before, and more than anything else, I was astonished at her face, which was swollen and bruised under the eyes and over a part of the nose. This was the result of the blow that I had struck her with my elbow, when she had tried to hold me back. Of beauty there was no trace left. I saw something hideous in her. I stopped upon the threshold.

'Approach, approach her,' said her sister.

'Yes, probably she repents,' thought I; 'shall I forgive her? Yes, she is dying, I must forgive her,' I added, trying to be generous.

"I approached the bedside. With difficulty she raised her eyes, one of which was swollen, and uttered these words haltingly:

'You have accomplished what you desired. You have killed me.'

"And in her face, through the physical sufferings, in spite of the approach of death, was expressed the same old hatred, so familiar to me.

'The children... I will not give them to you... all the same... She (her sister) shall take them.'

"But of that which I considered essential, of her fault, of her treason, one would have said that she did not think it necessary to say even a word.

'Yes, revel in what you have done.'

"And she sobbed.

"At the door stood her sister with the children.

'Yes, see what you have done!'

"I cast a glance at the children, and then at her bruised and swollen face, and for the first time I forgot myself (my rights, my pride), and for the first time I saw in her a human being, a sister.

"And all that which a moment before had been so offensive to me now seemed to me so petty, - all this jealousy, - and, on the contrary, what I had done seemed to me so important that I felt like bending over, approaching my face to her hand, and saying:

'Forgive me!'

"But I did not dare. She was silent, with eyelids lowered, evidently having no strength to speak further. Then her deformed face began to tremble and shrivel, and she feebly pushed me back.

'Why has all this happened? Why?'

'Forgive me,' said I.

'Yes, if you had not killed me,' she cried suddenly, and her eyes shone feverishly. 'Forgiveness - that is nothing... If I only do not die! Ah, you have accomplished what you desired! I hate you!'

"Then she grew delirious. She was frightened, and cried:

'Fire, I do not fear... but strike them all... He has gone... He has gone...'

"The delirium continued. She no longer recognized the children, not even little Lise, who had approached. Toward noon she died. As for me, I was arrested before her death, at eight o'clock in the morning. They took me to the police station, and then to prison, and there, during eleven months, awaiting the verdict, I reflected upon myself, and upon my past, and I understood it. Yes, I began to understand from the third day. The third day they took me to the house."

Posdnicheff seemed to wish to add something, but, no longer having the strength to repress his sobs, he stopped. After a few minutes, having recovered his calmness, he resumed:

"I began to understand only when I saw her in the coffin."

He uttered a sob, and then immediately continued, with haste:

"Then only, when I saw her dead face, did I understand all that I had done. I understood that it was I, I, who had killed her. I understood that I was the cause of the fact that she, who had been a moving, living, palpitating being, had now become motionless and cold, and that there was no way of repairing this thing. He who has not lived through that cannot understand it."

We remained silent a long time. Posdnicheff sobbed and trembled before me. His face had become delicate and long, and his mouth had grown larger.

"Yes," said he suddenly, "if I had known what I now know, I should never have married her, never, not for anything."

Again we remained silent for a long time.

"Yes, that is what I have done, that is my experience, We must understand the real meaning of the words of the Gospel, - Matthew, V. 28, - 'that whosoever looketh on a woman to lust after her hath committed adultery'; and these words relate to the wife, to the sister, and not only to the wife of another, but especially to one's own wife."

THE COFFEE HOUSE OF SURAT

(AFTER BERNARDIN DE SENT-PIERRE.)

In the town of Surat, in India, was a coffee-house where many travellers and foreigners from all parts of the world met and conversed.

One day a learned Persian theologian visited this coffee-house. He was a man who had spent his life studying the nature of the Deity, and reading and writing books upon the subject. He had thought, read, and written so much about God, that eventually he lost his wits became quite confused, and ceased even to believe in the existence of a God. The Shah, hearing of this, had banished him from Persia.

After having argued all his life about the First Cause, this unfortunate theologian had ended by quite perplexing himself, and instead of understanding that he had lost his own reason, he began to think that there was no higher Reason controlling the universe.

This man had an African slave who followed him everywhere. When the theologian entered the coffeehouse, the slave remained outside, near the door sitting on a stone in the glare of the sun, and driving away the flies that buzzed around him. The Persian having settled down on a divan in the coffee-house, ordered himself a cup of opium. When he had drunk it and the opium had begun to quicken the workings of his brain, he addressed his slave through the open door:

'Tell me, wretched slave,' said he, 'do you think there is a God, or not?'

'Of course there is,' said the slave, and immediately drew from under his girdle a small idol of wood.

'There,' said he, 'that is the God who has guarded me from the day of my birth. Everyone in our country worships the fetish tree, from the wood of which this God was made.'

This conversation between the theologian and his slave was listened to with surprise by the other guests in the coffee-house. They were astonished at the master's question, and yet more so at the slave's reply.

One of them, a Brahmin, on hearing the words spoken by the slave, turned to him and said:

'Miserable fool! Is it possible you believe that God can be carried under a man's girdle? There is one God - Brahma, and he is greater than the whole world, for he created it. Brahma is the One, the mighty God, and in His honour are built the temples on the Ganges' banks, where his true priests, the Brahmins, worship him. They know the true God, and none but they. A thousand score of years have passed, and yet through revolution after revolution these priests have held their sway, because Brahma, the one true God, has protected them.'

So spoke the Brahmin, thinking to convince everyone; but a Jewish broker who was present replied to him, and said:

'No! the temple of the true God is not in India. Neither does God protect the Brahmin caste. The true God is not the God of the Brahmins, but of Abraham, Isaac, and Jacob. None does He protect but His chosen people, the Israelites. From the commencement of the world, our nation has been beloved of Him, and ours alone. If we are now scattered over the whole earth, it is but to try us; for God has promised that He will one day gather His people together in Jerusalem. Then, with the Temple of Jerusalem - the wonder of the ancient world - restored to its splendor, shall Israel be established a ruler over all nations.'

So spoke the Jew, and burst into tears. He wished to say more, but an Italian missionary who was there interrupted him.

'What you are saying is untrue,' said he to the Jew. 'You attribute injustice to God. He cannot love your nation above the rest. Nay rather, even if it be true that of old He favored the Israelites, it is now nineteen hundred years since they angered Him, and caused Him to destroy their nation and scatter them over the earth, so that their faith makes no converts and has died out except here and there. God shows preference to no nation, but calls all who wish to be saved to the bosom of the Catholic Church of Rome, the one outside whose borders no salvation can be found.'

So spoke the Italian. But a Protestant minister, who happened to be present, growing pale, turned to the Catholic missionary and exclaimed:

'How can you say that salvation belongs to your religion? Those only will be saved, who serve God according to the Gospel, in spirit and in truth, as bidden by the word of Christ.'

Then a Turk, an office-holder in the custom-house at Surat, who was sitting in the coffee-house smoking a pipe, turned with an air of superiority to both the Christians.

'Your belief in your Roman religion is vain,' said he. 'It was superseded twelve hundred years ago by the true faith: that of Mohammed! You cannot but observe how the true Mohammed faith continues to spread both in Europe and Asia, and even in the enlightened country of China. You say yourselves that God has rejected the Jews; and, as a proof, you quote the fact that the Jews are humiliated and their faith does not spread. Confess then the truth of Mohammedanism, for it is triumphant and spreads far and wide. None will be saved but the followers of Mohammed, God's latest prophet; and of them, only the followers of Omar, and not of Ali, for the latter are false to the faith.'

To this the Persian theologian, who was of the sect of Ali, wished to reply; but by this time a great dispute had arisen among all the strangers of different faiths and creeds present. There were Abyssinian Christians, Llamas from Thibet, Ismailians and Fireworshippers. They all argued about the nature of God, and how He should be worshipped. Each of them asserted that in his country alone was the true God known and rightly worshipped.

Every one argued and shouted, except a Chinaman, a student of Confucius, who sat quietly in one corner of the coffee-house, not joining in the dispute. He sat there drinking tea and listening to what the others said, but did not speak himself.

The Turk noticed him sitting there, and appealed to him, saying:

'You can confirm what I say, my good Chinaman. You hold your peace, but if you spoke I know you would uphold my opinion. Traders from your country, who come to me for assistance, tell me that though many religions have been introduced into China, you Chinese consider Mohammedanism the best of all, and adopt it willingly. Confirm, then, my words, and tell us your opinion of the true God and of His prophet.'

'Yes, yes,' said the rest, turning to the Chinaman, 'let us hear what you think on the subject.'

The Chinaman, the student of Confucius, closed his eyes, and thought a while. Then he opened them again, and drawing his hands out of the wide sleeves of his garment, and folding them on his breast, he spoke as follows, in a calm and quiet voice.

Sirs, it seems to me that it is chiefly pride that prevents men agreeing with one another on matters of faith. If you care to listen to me, I will tell you a story which will explain this by an example.

I came here from China on an English steamer which had been round the world. We stopped for fresh water, and landed on the east coast of the island of Sumatra. It was midday, and some of us, having landed, sat in the shade of some coconut palms by the seashore, not far from a native village. We were a party of men of different nationalities.

As we sat there, a blind man approached us. We learned afterwards that he had gone blind from gazing too long and too persistently at the sun, trying to find out what it is, in order to seize its light.

He strove a long time to accomplish this, constantly looking at the sun; but the only result was that his eyes were injured by its brightness, and he became blind.

Then he said to himself:

'The light of the sun is not a liquid; for if it were a liquid it would be possible to pour it from one vessel into another, and it would be moved, like water, by the wind. Neither is it fire; for if it were fire, water would extinguish it. Neither is light a spirit, for it is seen by the eye; nor is it matter, for it cannot be moved. Therefore, as the light of the sun is neither liquid, nor fire, nor spirit, nor matter, it is - nothing!'

So he argued, and, as a result of always looking at the sun and always thinking about it, he lost both his sight and his reason. And when he went quite blind, he became fully convinced that the sun did not exist.

With this blind man came a slave, who after placing his master in the shade of a coconut tree, picked up a coconut from the ground, and began making it into a night-light. He twisted a wick from the fibre of the coconut: squeezed oil from the nut in the shell, and soaked the wick in it.

As the slave sat doing this, the blind man sighed and said to him:

'Well, slave, was I not right when I told you there is no sun? Do you not see how dark it is? Yet people say there is a sun... But if so, what is it?'

'I do not know what the sun is,' said the slave. 'That is no business of mine. But I know what light is. Here I have made a night-light, by the help of which I can serve you and find anything I want in the hut.'

And the slave picked up the coconut shell, saying:

'This is my sun.'

A lame man with crutches, who was sitting nearby, heard these words, and laughed:

'You have evidently been blind all your life,' said he to the blind man, 'not to know what the sun is. I will tell you what it is. The sun is a ball of fire, which rises every morning out of the sea and goes down again among the mountains of our island each evening. We have all seen this, and if you had had your eyesight you too would have seen it.'

A fisherman, who had been listening to the conversation said:

'It is plain enough that you have never been beyond your own island. If you were not lame, and if you had been out as I have in a fishing-boat, you would know that the sun does not set among the mountains of our island, but as it rises from the ocean every morning so it sets again in the sea every night. What I am telling you is true, for I see it every day with my own eyes.'

Then an Indian who was of our party, interrupted him by saying:

'I am astonished that a reasonable man should talk such nonsense. How can a ball of fire possibly descend into the water and not be extinguished? The sun is not a ball of fire at all, it is the Deity named Deva, who rides for ever in a chariot round the golden mountain, Meru. Sometimes the evil serpents Ragu and Ketu attack Deva and swallow him: and then the earth is dark. But our priests pray that the Deity may be released, and then he is set free. Only such ignorant men as you, who have never been beyond their own island, can imagine that the sun shines for their country alone.'

Then the master of an Egyptian vessel, who was present, spoke in his turn.

'No,' said he, 'you also are wrong. The sun is not a Deity, and does not move only round India and its golden mountain. I have sailed much on the Black Sea, and along the coasts of Arabia, and have been to Madagascar and to the Philippines. The sun lights the whole earth, and not India alone. It does not circle round one mountain, but rises far in the East, beyond the Isles of Japan, and sets far, far away in the West, beyond the islands of England. That is why the Japanese call their country 'Nippon,' that is, 'the birth of the sun.' I know this well, for I have myself seen much, and heard more from my grandfather, who sailed to the very ends of the sea.'

He would have gone on, but an English sailor from our ship interrupted him.

'There is no country,' he said 'where people know so much about the sun's movements as in England. The sun, as everyone in England knows, rises nowhere and sets nowhere. It is always moving round the earth. We can be sure of this for we have just been round the world ourselves, and nowhere knocked up against the sun. Wherever we went, the sun showed itself in the morning and hid itself at night, just as it does here.'

And the Englishman took a stick and, drawing circles on the sand, tried to explain how the sun moves in the heavens and goes round the world. But he was unable to explain it clearly, and pointing to the ship's pilot said:

'This man knows more about it than I do. He can explain it properly.'

The pilot, who was an intelligent man, had listened in silence to the talk till he was asked to speak. Now everyone turned to him, and he said:

'You are all misleading one another, and are yourselves deceived. The sun does not go round the earth, but the earth goes round the sun, revolving as it goes, and turning towards the sun in the course of each twenty-four hours, not only Japan, and the Philippines, and Sumatra where we now are, but Africa, and Europe, and America, and many lands besides. The sun does not shine for some one mountain, or for some one island, or for some one sea, nor even for one earth alone, but for other planets as well as our earth. If you would only look up at the heavens, instead of at the ground beneath your own feet, you might all understand this, and would then no longer suppose that the sun shines for you or for your country alone.'

Thus spoke the wise pilot, who had voyaged much about the world, and had gazed much upon the heavens above.

'So on matters of faith,' continued the Chinaman, the student of Confucius, 'it is pride that causes error and discord among men. As with the sun, so it is with God. Each man wants to have a special God of his own or at least a special God for his native land. Each nation wishes to confine in its own temples Him, whom the world cannot contain.

"Can any temple compare with that which God Himself has built to unite all men in one faith and one religion?

"All human temples are built on the model of this temple, which is God's own world. Every temple has its fonts, its vaulted roof, its lamps, its pictures or sculptures, its inscriptions, its books of the law, its offerings, its altars and its priests. But in what temple is there such a font as the ocean; such a vault as that of the heavens; such lamps as the sun, moon, and stars; or any figures to be compared with living, loving, mutually-helpful men? Where are there any records of God's goodness so easy to understand as the blessings which God has strewn abroad for man's happiness? Where is there any book of the law so clear to each man as that written in his heart? What sacrifices equal the self-denials which loving men and women make for one another? And what altar can be compared with the heart of a good man, on which God Himself accepts the sacrifice?

"The higher a man's conception of God, the better will he know Him. And the better he knows God, the nearer will he draw to Him, imitating His goodness, His mercy, and His love of man.

'Therefore, let him who sees the sun's whole light filling the world, refrain from blaming or despising the superstitious man, who in his own idol sees one ray of that same light. Let him not despise even the unbeliever who is blind and cannot see the sun at all.'

So spoke the Chinaman, the student of Confucius; and all who were present in the coffee-house were silent, and disputed no more as to whose faith was the best.

WHAT MEN LIVE BY

∞

"We know that we have passed out of death into life, because we love the brethren. He that loveth not abideth in death." - I Epistle St. John - iii. 14.

"Whoso hath the world's goods, and beholdeth his brother in need, and shutteth up his compassion from him, how doth the love of God abide in him? My little children, let us not love in word, neither with the tongue; but in deed and truth." -iii. 17-18.

"Love is of God; and every one that loveth is begotten of God, and knoweth God. He that loveth not knoweth not God; for God is love." - iv. 7-8.

"No man hath beheld God at any time; if we love one another, God abideth in us." - iv. 12.

"God is love; and he that abideth in love abideth in God, and God abideth in him." - iv. 16.

"If a man say, I love God, and hateth his brother, he is a liar; for he that loveth not his brother whom he hath seen, how can he love God whom he hath not seen?" - iv. 20.

I

A shoemaker named Simon, who had neither house nor land of his own, lived with his wife and children in a peasant's hut, and earned his living by his work. Work was cheap, but bread was dear, and what he earned he spent for food. The man and his wife had but one sheepskin coat between them for winter wear, and even that was torn to tatters, and this was the second year he had been wanting to buy sheep-skins for a new coat. Before winter Simon saved up a little money: a three-rouble note lay hidden in his wife's box, and five roubles and twenty kopeks were owed him by customers in the village.

So one morning he prepared to go to the village to buy the sheep-skins. He put on over his shirt his wife's wadded nankeen jacket, and over that he put his own cloth coat. He took the three - rouble note in his pocket, cut himself a stick to serve as a staff, and started off after breakfast. "I'll collect the five roubles that are due to me," thought he, "add the three I have got, and that will be enough to buy sheep-skins for the winter coat."

He came to the village and called at a peasant's hut, but the man was not at home. The peasant's wife promised that the money should be paid next week, but she would not pay it herself. Then Simon called on another peasant, but this one swore he had no money, and would only pay twenty kopeks which he owed for a pair of boots Simon had mended. Simon then tried to buy the sheep-skins on credit, but the dealer would not trust him.

"Bring your money," said he, "then you may have your pick of the skins. We know what debt-collecting is like." So all the business the shoemaker did was to get the twenty kopeks for boots he had mended, and to take a pair of felt boots a peasant gave him to sole with leather.

Simon felt downhearted. He spent the twenty kopeks on vodka, and started homewards without having bought any skins. In the morning he had felt the frost; but now, after drinking the vodka, he felt warm, even without a sheep-skin coat. He trudged along, striking his stick on the frozen earth with one hand, swinging the felt boots with the other, and talking to himself.

"I'm quite warm," said he, "though I have no sheep-skin coat. I've had a drop, and it runs through all my veins. I need no sheep-skins. I go along and don't worry about anything. That's the sort of man I am! What do I care? I can live without sheep-skins. I don't need them. My wife will fret, to be sure. And, true enough, it is a shame; one works all day long, and then does not get paid. Stop a bit! If you don't bring that money along, sure enough I'll skin you, blessed if I don't. How's that? He pays twenty kopeks at a time! What can I do with twenty kopeks? Drink it-that's all one can do! Hard up, he says he is! So he may be - but what about me? You have a house, and cattle, and everything; I've only what I stand up in! You have corn of your own growing; I have to buy every grain. Do what I will, I must spend three roubles every week for bread alone. I come home and find the bread all used up, and I have to fork out another rouble and a half. So just pay up what you owe, and no nonsense about it!"

By this time he had nearly reached the shrine at the bend of the road. Looking up, he saw something whitish behind the shrine. The daylight was fading, and the shoemaker peered at the thing without being able to make out what it was. "There was no white stone here before. Can it be an ox? It's not like an ox. It has a head like a man, but it's too white; and what could a man be doing there?"

He came closer, so that it was clearly visible. To his surprise it really was a man, alive or dead, sitting naked, leaning motionless against the shrine. Terror seized the shoemaker, and he thought, "Someone has killed him, stripped him, and left him there. If I meddle I shall surely get into trouble."

So the shoemaker went on. He passed in front of the shrine so that he could not see the man. When he had gone some way, he looked back, and saw that the man was no longer leaning against the shrine, but was moving as if looking towards him. The shoemaker felt more frightened than before, and thought, "Shall I go back to him, or shall I go on? If I go near him something dreadful may happen. Who knows who the fellow is? He has not come here for any good. If I go near him he may jump up and throttle me, and there will be no getting away. Or if not, he'd still be a burden on one's hands. What could I do with a naked man? I couldn't give him my last clothes. Heaven only help me to get away!"

So the shoemaker hurried on, leaving the shrine behind him - when suddenly his conscience smote him, and he stopped in the road.

"What are you doing, Simon?" said he to himself. "The man may be dying of want, and you slip past afraid. Have you grown so rich as to be afraid of robbers? Ah, Simon, shame on you!"

So he turned back and went up to the man.

II

Simon approached the stranger, looked at him, and saw that he was a young man, fit, with no bruises on his body, only evidently freezing and frightened, and he sat there leaning back without looking up at Simon, as if too faint to lift his eyes. Simon went close to him, and then the man seemed to wake up. Turning his head, he opened his eyes and looked into

Simon's face. That one look was enough to make Simon fond of the man. He threw the felt boots on the ground, undid his sash, laid it on the boots, and took off his cloth coat.

"It's not a time for talking," said he. "Come, put this coat on at once!" And Simon took the man by the elbows and helped him to rise. As he stood there, Simon saw that his body was clean and in good condition, his hands and feet shapely, and his face good and kind. He threw his coat over the man's shoulders, but the latter could not find the sleeves. Simon guided his arms into them, and drawing the coat well on, wrapped it closely about him, tying the sash round the man's waist.

Simon even took off his torn cap to put it on the man's head, but then his own head felt cold, and he thought: "I'm quite bald, while he has long curly hair." So he put his cap on his own head again. "It will be better to give him something for his feet," thought he; and he made the man sit down, and helped him to put on the felt boots, saying, "There, friend, now move about and warm yourself. Other matters can be settled later on. Can you walk?"

The man stood up and looked kindly at Simon, but could not say a word.

"Why don't you speak?" said Simon. "It's too cold to stay here, we must be getting home. There now, take my stick, and if you're feeling weak, lean on that. Now step out!"

The man started walking, and moved easily, not lagging behind.

As they went along, Simon asked him, "And where do you belong to?" "I'm not from these parts."

"I thought as much. I know the folks hereabouts. But, how did you come to be there by the shrine ?"

"I cannot tell."

"Has someone been ill-treating you?"

"No one has ill-treated me. God has punished me."

"Of course God rules all. Still, you'll have to find food and shelter somewhere. Where do you want to go to?"

"It is all the same to me."

Simon was amazed. The man did not look like a rogue, and he spoke gently, but yet he gave no account of himself. Still Simon thought, "Who knows what may have happened?" And he said to the stranger: "Well then, come home with me, and at least warm yourself awhile."

So Simon walked towards his home, and the stranger kept up with him, walking at his side. The wind had risen and Simon felt it cold under his shirt. He was getting over his tipsiness by now, and began to feel the frost. He went along sniffling and wrapping his wife's coat round him, and he thought to himself: "There now - talk about sheep-skins! I went out for sheep-skins and come home without even a coat to my back and what is more, I'm bringing a naked man along with me. Matryona won't be pleased!" And when he thought of his wife he felt sad; but when he looked at the stranger and remembered how he had looked up at him at the shrine, his heart was glad.

III

Simon's wife had everything ready early that day. She had cut wood, brought water, fed the children, eaten her own meal, and now she sat thinking. She wondered when she ought to make bread: now or tomorrow? There was still a large piece left.

"If Simon has had some dinner in town," thought she, "and does not eat much for supper, the bread will last out another day."

She weighed the piece of bread in her hand again and again, and thought: "I won't make any more today. We have only enough flour left to bake one batch; We can manage to make this last out till Friday."

So Matryona put away the bread, and sat down at the table to patch her husband's shirt. While she worked she thought how her husband was buying skins for a winter coat.

"If only the dealer does not cheat him. My good man is much too simple; he cheats nobody, but any child can take him in. Eight roubles is a lot of money - he should get a good coat at that price. Not tanned skins, but still a proper winter coat. How difficult it was last winter to get on without a warm coat. I could neither get down to the river, nor go out anywhere. When he went out he put on all we had, and there was nothing left for me. He did not start very early today, but still it's time he was back. I only hope he has not gone on the spree!"

Hardly had Matryona thought this, when steps were heard on the threshold, and someone entered. Matryona stuck her needle into her work and went out into the passage. There she saw two men: Simon, and with him a man without a hat, and wearing felt boots.

Matryona noticed at once that her husband smelt of spirits. "There now, he has been drinking," thought she. And when she saw that he was coatless, had only her jacket on, brought no parcel, stood there silent, and seemed ashamed, her heart was ready to break with disappointment. "He has drunk the money," thought she, "and has been on the spree with some good-for-nothing fellow whom he has brought home with him."

Matryona let them pass into the hut, followed them in, and saw that the stranger was a young, slight man,. wearing her husband's coat. There was no shirt to be seen under it, and he had no hat. Having entered, he stood, neither moving, nor raising his eyes, and Matryona thought: "He must be a bad man - he's afraid."

Matryona frowned, and stood beside the oven looking to see what they would do.

Simon took off his cap and sat down on the bench as if things were all right.

"Come, Matryona; if supper is ready, let us have some."

Matryona muttered something to herself and did not move, but stayed where she was, by the oven. She looked first at the one and then at the other of them, and only shook her head. Simon saw that his wife was annoyed, but tried to pass it off. Pretending not to notice anything, he took the stranger by the arm.

"Sit down, friend," said he, "and let us have some supper."

The stranger sat down on the bench.

"Haven't you cooked anything for us?" said Simon.

Matryona's anger boiled over. "I've cooked, but not for you. It seems to me you have drunk your wits away. You went to buy a sheep-skin coat, but come home without so much as the coat you had on, and bring a naked vagabond home with you. I have no supper for drunkards like you."

"That's enough, Matryona. Don't wag your tongue without reason. You had better ask what sort of man-"

"And you tell me what you've done with the money?"

Simon found the pocket of the jacket, drew out the three-rouble note, and unfolded it.

"Here is the money. Trifonof did not pay, but promises to pay soon."

Matryona got still more angry; he had bought no sheep-skins, but had put his only coat on some naked fellow and had even brought him to their house.

She snatched up the note from the table, took it to put away in safety, and said: "I have no supper for you. We can't feed all the naked drunkards in the world."

"There now, Matryona, hold your tongue a bit. First hear what a man has to say-"

"Much wisdom I shall hear from a drunken fool. I was right in not wanting to marry you-a drunkard. The linen my mother gave me you drank; and now you've been to buy a coat-and have drunk it, too!"

Simon tried to explain to his wife that he had only spent twenty kopeks; tried to tell how he had found the man - but Matryona would not let him get a word in. She talked nineteen to the dozen, and dragged in things that had happened ten years before.

Matryona talked and talked, and at last she flew at Simon and seized him by the sleeve.

"Give me my jacket. It is the only one I have, and you must needs take it from me and wear it yourself. Give it here, you mangy dog, and may the devil take you."

Simon began to pull off the jacket, and turned a sleeve of it inside out; Matryona seized the jacket and it burst its seams, She snatched it up, threw it over her head and went to the door. She meant to go out, but stopped undecided - she wanted to work off her anger, but she also wanted to learn what sort of a man the stranger was.

IV

Matryona stopped and said: "If he were a good man he would not be naked. Why, he hasn't even a shirt on him. If he were all right, you would say where you came across the fellow."

"That's just what I am trying to tell you," said Simon. "As I came to the shrine I saw him sitting all naked and frozen. It isn't quite the weather to sit about naked! God sent me to him, or he would have perished. What was I to do? How do we know what may have happened to him? So I took him, clothed him, and brought him along. Don't be so angry, Matryona. It is a sin. Remember, we all must die one day."

Angry words rose to Matryona's lips, but she looked at the stranger and was silent. He sat on the edge of the bench, motionless, his hands folded on his knees, his head drooping on his breast, his eyes closed, and his brows knit as if in pain. Matryona was silent: and Simon said: "Matryona, have you no love of God?"

Matryona heard these words, and as she looked at the stranger, suddenly her heart softened towards him. She came back from the door, and going to the oven she got out the supper. Setting a cup on the table, she poured out some kvas. Then she brought out the last piece of bread, and set out a knife and spoons.

"Eat, if you want to," said she.

Simon drew the stranger to the table.

"Take your place, young man," said he.

Simon cut the bread, crumbled it into the broth, and they began to eat. Matryona sat at the corner of the table resting her head on her hand and looking at the stranger.

And Matryona was touched with pity for the stranger, and began to feel fond of him. And at once the stranger's face lit up; his brows were no longer bent, he raised his eyes and smiled at Matryona.

When they had finished supper, the woman cleared away the things and began questioning the stranger. "Where are you from?" said she.

"I am not from these parts."

"But how did you come to be on the road?"

"I may not tell."

"Did someone rob you?"

"God punished me."

"And you were lying there naked?"

"Yes, naked and freezing. Simon saw me and had pity on me. He took off his coat, put it on me and brought me here. And you have fed me, given me drink, and shown pity on me. God will reward you!"

Matryona rose, took from the window Simon's old shirt she had been patching, and gave it to the stranger. She also brought out a pair of trousers for him.

"There," said she, "I see you have no shirt. Put this on, and lie down where you please, in the loft or on the oven."

The stranger took off the coat, put on the shirt, and lay down in the loft. Matryona put out the candle, took the coat, and climbed to where her husband lay.

Matryona drew the skirts of the coat over her and lay down, but could not sleep; she could not get the stranger out of her mind.

When she remembered that he had eaten their last piece of bread and that there was none for tomorrow, and thought of the shirt and trousers she had given away, she felt grieved; but when she remembered how he had smiled, her heart was glad.

Long did Matryona lie awake, and she noticed that Simon also was awake - he drew the coat towards him.

"Simon!"

"Well?"

"You have had the last of the bread, and I have not put any to rise. I don't know what we shall do tomorrow. Perhaps I can borrow some of neighbor Martha."

"If we're alive we shall find something to eat."

The woman lay still awhile, and then said, "He seems a good man, but why does he not tell us who he is?"

"I suppose he has his reasons."

"Simon!"

"Well?"

"We give; but why does nobody give us anything?"

Simon did not know what to say; so he only said, "Let us stop talking," and turned over and went to sleep.

V

In the morning Simon awoke. The children were still asleep; his wife had gone to the neighbor's to borrow some bread. The stranger alone was sitting on the bench, dressed in the old shirt and trousers, and looking upwards. His face was brighter than it had been the day before.

Simon said to him, "Well, friend; the belly wants bread, and the naked body clothes. One has to work for a living What work do you know?"

"I do not know any."

This surprised Simon, but he said, "Men who want to learn can learn anything."

"Men work, and I will work also."

"What is your name?"

"Michael."

"Well, Michael, if you don't wish to talk about yourself, that is your own affair; but you'll have to earn a living for yourself. If you will work as I tell you, I will give you food and shelter."

"May God reward you! I will learn. Show me what to do."

Simon took yarn, put it round his thumb and began to twist it.

"It is easy enough - see!"

Michael watched him, put some yarn round his own thumb in the same way, caught the knack, and twisted the yarn also.

Then Simon showed him how to wax the thread. This also Michael mastered. Next Simon showed him how to twist the bristle in, and how to sew, and this, too, Michael learned at once.

Whatever Simon showed him he understood at once, and after three days he worked as if he had sewn boots all his life. He worked without stopping, and ate little. When work was over he sat silently, looking upwards. He hardly went into the street, spoke only when necessary, and neither joked nor laughed. They never saw him smile, except that first evening when Matryona gave them supper.

VI

Day by day and week by week the year went round. Michael lived and worked with Simon. His fame spread till people said that no one sewed boots so neatly and strongly as Simon's workman, Michael; and from all the district round people came to Simon for their boots, and he began to be well off.

One winter day, as Simon and Michael sat working, a carriage on sledge-runners, with three horses and with bells, drove up to the hut. They looked out of the window; the carriage stopped at their door, a fine servant jumped down from the box and opened the door. A gentleman in a fur coat got out and walked up to Simon's hut. Up jumped Matryona and opened the door wide. The gentleman stooped to enter the hut, and when he drew himself up again his head nearly reached the ceiling, and he seemed quite to fill his end of the room.

Simon rose, bowed, and looked at the gentleman with astonishment. He had never seen anyone like him. Simon himself was lean, Michael was thin, and Matryona was dry as a bone, but this man was like someone from another world: red-faced, burly, with a neck like a bull's, and looking altogether as if he were cast in iron.

The gentleman puffed, threw off his fur coat, sat down on the bench, and said, "Which of you is the master bootmaker?"

"I am, your Excellency," said Simon, coming forward.

Then the gentleman shouted to his lad, "Hey, Fedka, bring the leather!"

The servant ran in, bringing a parcel. The gentleman took the parcel and put it on the table.

"Untie it," said he. The lad untied it.

The gentleman pointed to the leather.

"Look here, shoemaker," said he, "do you see this leather?"

"Yes, your honor."

"But do you know what sort of leather it is?"

Simon felt the leather and said, "It is good leather."

"Good, indeed! Why, you fool, you never saw such leather before in your life. It's German, and cost twenty roubles."

Simon was frightened, and said, "Where should I ever see leather like that?"

"Just so! Now, can you make it into boots for me?"

"Yes, your Excellency, I can."

Then the gentleman shouted at him: "You can, can you? Well, remember whom you are to make them for, and what the leather is. You must make me boots that will wear for a year, neither losing shape nor coming unsown. If you can do it, take the leather and cut it up; but if you can't, say so. I warn you now if your boots become unsewn or lose shape within a year, I will have you put in prison. If they don't burst or lose shape for a year I will pay you ten roubles for your work."

Simon was frightened, and did not know what to say. He glanced at Michael and nudging him with his elbow, whispered: "Shall I take the work?"

Michael nodded his head as if to say, "Yes, take it."

Simon did as Michael advised, and undertook to make boots that would not lose shape or split for a whole year.

Calling his servant, the gentleman told him to pull the boot off his left leg, which he stretched out.

"Take my measure!" said he.

Simon stitched a paper measure seventeen inches long, smoothed it out, knelt down, wiped his hand well on his apron so as not to soil the gentleman's sock, and began to measure. He measured the sole, and round the instep, and began to measure the calf of the leg, but the paper was too short. The calf of the leg was as thick as a beam.

"Mind you don't make it too tight in the leg."

Simon stitched on another strip of paper. The gentleman twitched his toes about in his sock, looking round at those in the hut, and as he did so he noticed Michael.

"Whom have you there?" asked he.

"That is my workman. He will sew the boots."

"Mind," said the gentleman to Michael, "remember to make them so that they will last me a year."

Simon also looked at Michael, and saw that Michael was not looking at the gentleman, but was gazing into the corner behind the gentleman, as if he saw someone there. Michael looked and looked, and suddenly he smiled, and his face became brighter.

"What are you grinning at, you fool?" thundered the gentleman. "You had better look to it that the boots are ready in time."

"They shall be ready in good time," said Michael.

"Mind it is so," said the gentleman, and he put on his boots and his fur coat, wrapped the latter round him, and went to the door. But he forgot to stoop, and struck his head against the lintel.

He swore and rubbed his head. Then he took his seat in the carriage and drove away.

When he had gone, Simon said: "There's a figure of a man for you! You could not kill him with a mallet. He almost knocked out the lintel, but little harm it did him."

And Matryona said: "Living as he does, how should he not grow strong? Death itself can't touch such a rock as that."

VII

Then Simon said to Michael: "Well, we have taken the work, but we must see we don't get into trouble over it. The leather is dear, and the gentleman hot-tempered. We must make no mistakes. Come, your eye is truer and your hands have become nimbler than mine, so you take this measure and cut out the boots. I will finish off the sewing of the vamps."

Michael did as he was told. He took the leather, spread it out on the table, folded it in two, took a knife and began to cut out.

Matryona came and watched him cutting, and was surprised to see how he was doing it. Matryona was accustomed to seeing boots made, and she looked and saw that Michael was not cutting the leather for boots, but was cutting it round.

She wished to say something, but she thought to herself: "Perhaps I do not understand how gentleman's boots should be made. I suppose Michael knows more about it and I won't interfere."

When Michael had cut up the leather, he took a thread and began to sew not with two ends, as boots are sewn, but with a single end, as for soft slippers.

Again Matryona wondered, but again she did not interfere. Michael sewed on steadily till noon. Then Simon rose for dinner, looked around, and saw that Michael had made slippers out of the gentleman's leather.

"Ah," groaned Simon, and he thought, "How is it that Michael, who has been with me a whole year and never made a mistake before, should do such a dreadful thing? The gentleman ordered high boots, welted, with whole fronts, and Michael has made soft slippers with single soles, and has wasted the leather. What am I to say to the gentleman? I can never replace leather such as this."

And he said to Michael, "What are you doing, friend? You have ruined me! You know the gentleman ordered high boots, but see what you have made!"

Hardly had he begun to rebuke Michael, when "rat-tat" went the iron ring that hung at the door. Someone was knocking. They looked out of the window; a man had come on horseback, and was fastening his horse. They opened the door, and the servant who had been with the gentleman came in.

"Good day," said he.

"Good day," replied Simon. "What can we do for you?"

"My mistress has sent me about the boots."

"What about the boots?"

"Why, my master no longer needs them. He is dead."

"Is it possible?"

"He did not live to get home after leaving you, but died in the carriage. When we reached home and the servants came to help him alight, he rolled over like a sack. He was dead already, and so stiff that he could hardly be got out of the carriage. My mistress sent me here, saying: 'Tell the bootmaker that the gentleman who ordered boots of him and left the leather for them no longer needs the boots, but that he must quickly make soft slippers for the corpse. Wait till they are ready, and bring them back with you.' That is why I have come."

Michael gathered up the remnants of the leather; rolled them up, took the soft slippers he had made, slapped them together, wiped them down with his apron, and handed them and the roll of leather to the servant, who took them and said: "Good-bye, masters, and good day to you!"

VIII

Another year passed, and another, and Michael was now living his sixth year with Simon. He lived as before. He went nowhere, only spoke when necessary, and had only smiled twice in all those years - once when Matryona gave him food, and a second time when the gentleman was in their hut. Simon was more than pleased with his workman. He never now asked him where he came from, and only feared lest Michael should go away.

They were all at home one day. Matryona was putting iron pots in the oven; the children were running along the benches and looking out of the window; Simon was sewing at one window, and Michael was fastening on a heel at the other.

One of the boys ran along the bench to Michael, leant on his shoulder, and looked out of the window.

"Look, Uncle Michael! There is a lady with little girls! She seems to be coming here. And one of the girls is lame."

When the boy said that, Michael dropped his work, turned to the window, and looked out into the street.

Simon was surprised. Michael never used to look out into the street, but now he pressed against the window, staring at something. Simon also looked out, and saw that a well-dressed woman was really coming to his hut, leading by the hand two little girls in fur coats and woolen shawls. The girls could hardly be told one from the other, except that one of them was crippled in her left leg and walked with a limp.

The woman stepped into the porch and entered the passage. Feeling about for the entrance she found the latch, which she lifted, and opened the door. She let the two girls go in first, and followed them into the hut.

"Good day, good folk!"

"Pray come in," said Simon. "What can we do for you?"

The woman sat down by the table. The two little girls pressed close to her knees, afraid of the people in the hut.

"I want leather shoes made for these two little girls for spring."

"We can do that. We never have made such small shoes, but we can make them; either welted or turnover shoes, linen lined. My man, Michael, is a master at the work."

Simon glanced at Michael and saw that he had left his work and was sitting with his eyes fixed on the little girls. Simon was surprised. It was true the girls were pretty, with black eyes, plump, and rosy-cheeked, and they wore nice kerchiefs and fur coats, but still Simon could not understand why Michael should look at them like that - just as if he had known them before. He was puzzled, but went on talking with the woman, and arranging the price. Having fixed it, he prepared the measure. The woman lifted the lame girl on to her lap and said: "Take two measures from this little girl. Make one shoe for the lame foot and three for the sound one. They both have the same size feet. They are twins."

Simon took the measure and, speaking of the lame girl, said: "How did it happen to her? She is such a pretty girl. Was she born so?"

"No, her mother crushed her leg."

Then Matryona joined in. She wondered who this woman was, and whose the children were, so she said: "Are not you their mother then?"

"No, my good woman; I am neither their mother nor any relation to them. They were quite strangers to me, but I adopted them."

"They are not your children and yet you are so fond of them?"

"How can I help being fond of them? I fed them both at my own breasts. I had a child of my own, but God took him. I was not so fond of him as I now am of them."

"Then whose children are they?"

IX

The woman, having begun talking, told them the whole story.

"It is about six years since their parents died, both in one week: their father was buried on the Tuesday, and their mother died on the Friday. These orphans were born three days after their father's death, and their mother did not live another day. My husband and I were then living as peasants in the village. We were neighbors of theirs, our yard being next to theirs. Their father was a lonely man; a wood-cutter in the forest. When felling trees one day, they let one fall on him. It fell across his body and crushed his bowels out. They hardly got him home before his soul went to God; and that same week his wife gave birth to twins - these little girls. She was poor and alone; she had no one, young or old, with her. Alone she gave them birth, and alone she met her death."

"The next morning I went to see her, but when I entered the hut, she, poor thing, was already stark and cold. In dying she had rolled on to this child and crushed her leg. The village folk came to the hut, washed the body, laid her out, made a coffin, and buried her. They were good folk. The babies were left alone. What was to be done with them? I was the only woman there who had a baby at the time. I was nursing my first-born -

eight weeks old. So I took them for a time. The peasants came together, and thought and thought what to do with them; and at last they said to me: "For the present, Mary, you had better keep the girls, and later on we will arrange what to do for them." So I nursed the sound one at my breast, but at first I did not feed this crippled one. I did not suppose she would live. But then I thought to myself, why should the poor innocent suffer? I pitied her, and began to feed her. And so I fed my own boy and these two - the three of them - at my own breast. I was young and strong, and had good food, and God gave me so much milk that at times it even overflowed. I used sometimes to feed two at a time, while the third was waiting. When one had enough I nursed the third. And God so ordered it that these grew up, while my own was buried before he was two years old. And I had no more children, though we prospered. Now my husband is working for the corn merchant at the mill. The pay is good, and we are well off. But I have no children of my own, and how lonely I should be without these little girls! How can I help loving them! They are the joy of my life!"

She pressed the lame little girl to her with one hand, while with the other she wiped the tears from her cheeks.

And Matryona sighed, and said: "The proverb is true that says, 'One may live without father or mother, but one cannot live without God.'"

So they talked together, when suddenly the whole hut was lighted up as though by summer lightning from the corner where Michael sat. They all looked towards him and saw him sitting, his hands folded on his knees, gazing upwards and smiling.

X

The woman went away with the girls. Michael rose from the bench, put down his work, and took off his apron. Then, bowing low to Simon and his wife, he said: "Farewell, masters. God has forgiven me. I ask your forgiveness, too, for anything done amiss."

And they saw that a light shone from Michael. And Simon rose, bowed down to Michael, and said: "I see, Michael, that you are no common man, and I can neither keep you nor question you. Only tell me this: how is it that when I found you and brought you home, you were gloomy, and when my wife gave you food you smiled at her and became brighter? Then when the gentleman came to order the boots, you smiled again and became brighter still? And now, when this woman brought the little girls, you smiled a third time, and have become as bright as day? Tell me, Michael, why does your face shine so, and why did you smile those three times?"

And Michael answered: "Light shines from me because I have been punished, but now God has pardoned me. And I smiled three times, because God sent me to learn three truths, and I have learnt them. One I learnt when your wife pitied me, and that is why I smiled the first time. The second I learnt when the rich man ordered the boots, and then I smiled again. And now, when I saw those little girls, I learn the third and last truth, and I smiled the third time."

And Simon said, "Tell me, Michael, what did God punish you for? and what were the three truths? that I, too, may know them."

And Michael answered: "God punished me for disobeying Him. I was an angel in heaven and disobeyed God. God sent me to fetch a woman's soul. I flew to earth, and saw a sick woman lying alone, who had just given birth to twin girls. They moved feebly at their mother's side, but she could not lift them to her breast. When she saw me, she understood that God had sent for her soul, and she wept and said: 'Angel of God! My husband has just been buried, killed by a falling tree. I have neither sister, nor aunt, nor mother: no one to care for my orphans. Do not take my soul! Let me nurse my babes, feed them, and set them on their feet before I die. Children cannot live without father or mother.' And I hearkened to her. I placed one child at her breast and gave the other into her arms, and returned to the Lord in heaven. I flew to the Lord, and said: 'I could not take the soul of the mother. Her husband was killed by a tree; the woman has twins, and prays that her soul may not be taken. She says: "Let me nurse and feed my children, and set them on their feet. Children cannot live without father or mother." I have not taken her soul.' And God said: 'Go-take the mother's soul, and learn three truths: Learn What dwells in man, What is not given to man, and What men live by. When thou has learnt these things, thou shalt return to heaven.' So I flew again to earth and took the mother's soul. The babes dropped from her breasts. Her body rolled over on the bed and crushed one babe, twisting its leg. I rose above the village, wishing to take her soul to God; but a wind seized me, and my wings drooped and dropped off. Her soul rose alone to God, while I fell to earth by the roadside."

XI

And Simon and Matryona understood who it was that had lived with them, and whom they had clothed and fed. And they wept with awe and with joy. And the angel said: "I was alone in the field, naked. I had never known human needs, cold and hunger, till I became a man. I was famished, frozen, and did not know what to do. I saw, near the field I was in, a shrine built for God, and I went to it hoping to find shelter. But the shrine was locked, and I could not enter. So I sat down behind the shrine to shelter myself at least from the wind. Evening drew on. I was hungry, frozen, and in pain. Suddenly I heard a man coming along the road. He carried a pair of boots, and was talking to himself. For the first time since I became a man I saw the mortal face of a man, and his face seemed terrible to me and I turned from it. And I heard the man talking to himself of how to cover his body from the cold in winter, and how to feed wife and children. And I thought: "I am perishing of cold and hunger, and here is a man thinking only of how to clothe himself and his wife, and how to get bread for themselves. He cannot help me. When the man saw me he frowned and became still more terrible, and passed me by on the other side. I despaired; but suddenly I heard him coming back. I looked up, and did not recognize the same man; before, I had seen death in his face; but now he was alive, and I recognized in him the presence of God. He came up to me, clothed me, took me with him, and brought me to his home. I entered the house; a woman came to meet us and began to speak. The woman was still more terrible than the man had been; the spirit of death came from her mouth; I could not breathe for the stench of death that spread around her. She wished to drive me out into the cold, and I knew that if she did so she would die. Suddenly her husband spoke to her of God, and the woman changed at once. And when she brought me food and looked at me, I glanced at her and saw that death no longer dwelt in her; she had become alive, and in her, too, I saw God.

"Then I remembered the first lesson God had set me: 'Learn what dwells in man.' And I understood that in man dwells Love! I was glad that God had already begun to show me what He had promised, and I smiled for the first time. But I had not yet learnt all. I did not yet know What is not given to man, and What men live by.

"I lived with you, and a year passed. A man came to order boots that should wear for a year without losing shape or cracking. I looked at him, and suddenly, behind his shoulder, I saw my comrade - the angel of death. None but me saw that angel; but I knew him, and knew that before the sun set he would take that rich man's soul. And I thought to myself, 'The man is making preparations for a year, and does not know that he will die before evening.' And I remembered God's second saying, 'Learn what is not given to man.'

"What dwells in man I already knew. Now I learnt what is not given him. It is not given to man to know his own needs. And I smiled for the second time. I was glad to have seen my comrade angel - glad also that God had revealed to me the second saying.

"But I still did not know all. I did not know What men live by. And I lived on, waiting till God should reveal to me the last lesson. In the sixth year came the girl-twins with the woman; and I recognized the girls, and heard how they had been kept alive. Having heard the story, I thought, 'Their mother besought me for the children's sake, and I believed her when she said that children cannot live without father or mother; but a stranger has nursed them, and has brought them up.' And when the woman showed her love for the children that were not her own, and wept over them, I saw in her the living God and understood What men live by. And I knew that God had revealed to me the last lesson, and had forgiven my sin. And then I smiled for the third time."

XII

And the angel's body was bared, and he was clothed in light so that eye could not look on him; and his voice grew louder, as though it came not from him but from heaven above. And the angel said:

"I have learnt that all men live not by care for themselves but by love.

"It was not given to the mother to know what her children needed for their life. Nor was it given to the rich man to know what he himself needed. Nor is it given to any man to know whether, when evening comes, he will need boots for his body or slippers for his corpse.

"I remained alive when I was a man, not by care of myself, but because love was present in a passer-by, and because he and his wife pitied and loved me. The orphans remained alive not because of their mother's care, but because there was love in the heart of a woman, a stranger to them, who pitied and loved them. And all men live not by the thought they spend on their own welfare, but because love exists in man.

"I knew before that God gave life to men and desires that they should live; now I understood more than that.

"I understood that God does not wish men to live apart, and therefore he does not reveal to them what each one needs for himself; but he wishes them to live united, and therefore reveals to each of them what is necessary for all.

"I have now understood that though it seems to men that they live by care for themselves, in truth it is love alone by which they live. He who has love, is in God, and God is in him, for God is love."

And the angel sang praise to God, so that the hut trembled at his voice. The roof opened, and a column of fire rose from earth to heaven. Simon and his wife and children fell to the ground. Wings appeared upon the angel's shoulders, and he rose into the heavens.

And when Simon came to himself the hut stood as before, and there was no one in it but his own family.

GOD SEES THE TRUTH, BUT WAITS

In the town of Vladímir lived a young merchant named Iván Dmítritch Aksyónof. He had two shops and a house of his own.

Aksyónof was a handsome, fair-haired, curly-headed fellow, full of fun, and very fond of singing. When quite a young man he had been given to drink, and was riotous when he had had too much, but after he married he gave up drinking, except now and then.

One summer Aksyónof was going to the Nízhny Fair, and as he bade good-bye to his family his wife said to him, 'Iván Dmítritch, do not start to-day; I have had a bad dream about you.'

Aksyónof laughed, and said, 'You are afraid that when I get to the fair I shall go on the spree.'

His wife replied: 'I do not know what I am afraid of; all I know is that I had a bad dream. I dreamt you returned from the town, and when you took off your cap I saw that your hair was quite grey.'

Aksyónof laughed. 'That's a lucky sign,' said he. 'See if I don't sell out all my goods, and bring you some presents from the fair.'

So he said good-bye to his family, and drove away.

When he had travelled half-way, he met a merchant whom he knew, and they put up at the same inn for the night. They had some tea together, and then went to bed in adjoining rooms.

It was not Aksyónof's habit to sleep late, and, wishing to travel while it was still cool, he aroused his driver before dawn, and told him to put in the horses.

Then he made his way across to the landlord of the inn (who lived in a cottage at the back), paid his bill, and continued his journey.

When he had gone about twenty-five miles, he stopped for the horses to be fed. Aksyónof rested awhile in the passage of the inn, then he stepped out into the porch and, ordering a samovár to be heated got out his guitar and began to play.

Suddenly a tróyka drove up with tinkling bells, and an official alighted, followed by two soldiers. He came to Aksyónof and began to question him, asking him who he was and whence he came. Aksyónof answered him fully, and said, 'Won't you have some tea with me?' But the official went on cross-questioning him and asking him, 'Where did you spend last night? Were you alone, or with a fellow-merchant? Did you see the other merchant this morning? Why did you leave the inn before dawn?'

Aksyónof wondered why he was asked all these questions, but he described all that had happened, and then added, 'Why do you cross-question me as if I were a thief or a robber? I am travelling on business of my own, and there is no need to question me.'

Then the official, calling the soldiers, said, 'I am the police-officer of this district, and I question you because the merchant with whom you spent last night has been found with his throat cut. We must search your things.'

They entered the house. The soldiers and the police-officer unstrapped Aksyónof's luggage and searched it. Suddenly the officer drew a knife out of a bag, crying, 'Whose knife is this?'

Aksyónof looked, and seeing a blood-stained knife taken from his bag, he was frightened.

'How is it there is blood on this knife?'

Aksyónof tried to answer, but could hardly utter a word, and only stammered: 'I - I don't know - not mine.'

Then the police-officer said, 'This morning the merchant was found in bed with his throat cut. You are the only person who could have done it. The house was locked from inside, and no one else was there. Here is this bloodstained knife in your bag, and your face and manner betray you! Tell me how you killed him, and how much money you stole?'

Aksyónof swore he had not done it; that he had not seen the merchant after they had had tea together; that he had no money except eight thousand roubles of his own, and that the knife was not his. But his voice was broken, his face pale, and he trembled with fear as though he were guilty.

The police-officer ordered the soldiers to bind Aksyónof and to put him in the cart. As they tied his feet together and flung him into the cart,

Aksyónof crossed himself and wept. His money and goods were taken from him, and he was sent to the nearest town and imprisoned there. Enquiries as to his character were made in Vladímir. The merchants and other inhabitants of that town said that in former days he used to drink and waste his time, but that he was a good man. Then the trial came on: he was charged with murdering a merchant from Ryazán, and robbing him of twenty thousand rúbles.

His wife was in despair, and did not know what to believe. Her children were all quite small; one was a baby at her breast. Taking them all with her, she went to the town where her husband was in gaol. At first she was not allowed to see him; but, after much begging, she obtained permission from the officials, and was taken to him. When she saw her husband in prison-dress and in chains, shut up with thieves and criminals, she fell down, and did not come to her senses for a long time. Then she drew her children to her, and sat down near him. She told him of things at home, and asked about what had happened to him. He told her all, and she asked, 'What can we do now?'

'We must petition the Tsar not to let an innocent man perish.'

His wife told him that she had sent a petition to the Tsar, but that it had not been accepted.

Aksyónof did not reply, but only looked downcast.

Then his wife said, 'It was not for nothing I dreamt your hair had turned grey. You remember? You should not have started that day.' And passing her fingers through his hair, she said: 'Ványa dearest, tell your wife the truth; was it not you who did it?'

'So you, too, suspect me!' said Aksyónof, and hiding his face in his hands, he began to weep. Then a soldier came to say that the wife and children must go away; and Aksyónof said good-bye to his family for the last time.

When they were gone, Aksyónof recalled what had been said, and when he remembered that his wife also had suspected him, he said to himself, 'It seems that only God can know the truth, it is to Him alone we must appeal, and from Him alone expect mercy.'

And Aksyónof wrote no more petitions; gave up all hope, and only prayed to God.

Aksyónof was condemned to be flogged and sent to the mines. So he was flogged with a knout, and when the wounds made by the knout were healed, he was driven to Siberia with other convicts.

For twenty-six years Aksyónof lived as a convict in Siberia. His hair turned white as snow and his beard grew long, thin, and grey. All his mirth went; he stooped; he walked slowly, spoke little, and never laughed, but he often prayed.

In prison Aksyónof learnt to make boots, and earned a little money, with which he bought The Lives of the Saints. He read this book when there was light enough in the prison; and on Sundays in the prison-church he read the lessons and sang in the choir; for his voice was still good.

The prison authorities liked Aksyónof for his meekness, and his fellow-prisoners respected him: they called him 'Grandfather,' and 'The Saint.' When they wanted to petition the prison authorities about anything, they always made Aksyónof their spokesman, and when there were quarrels among the prisoners they came to him to put things right, and to judge the matter.

No news reached Aksyónof from his home, and he did not even know if his wife and children were still alive.

One day a fresh gang of convicts came to the prison. In the evening the old prisoners collected round the new ones and asked them what towns or villages they came from, and what they were sentenced for. Among the rest Aksyónof sat down near the new-comers, and listened with downcast air to what was said.

One of the new convicts, a tall, strong man of sixty, with a closely-cropped grey beard, was telling the others what he had been arrested for.

'Well, friends,' he said, 'I only took a horse that was tied to a sledge, and I was arrested and accused of stealing. I said I had only taken it to get home quicker, and had then let it go; besides, the driver was a personal friend of mine. So I said, "It's all right." "No," said they, "you stole it." But how or where I stole it they could not say. I once really did something wrong, and ought by rights to have come here long ago, but that time I was not found out. Now I have been sent here for nothing at all... Eh, but it's lies I'm telling you; I've been to Siberia before, but I did not stay long.'

'Where are you from?' asked some one.

'From Vladímir. My family are of that town. My name is Makár, and they also call me Semyónitch.'

Aksyónof raised his head and said: 'Tell me, Semyónitch, do you know anything of the merchants Aksyónof, of Vladímir? Are they still alive?'

'Know them? Of course I do. The Aksyónofs are rich, though their father is in Siberia: a sinner like ourselves, it seems! As for you, Gran'dad, how did you come here?'

Aksyónof did not like to speak of his misfortune. He only sighed, and said, 'For my sins I have been in prison these twenty-six years.'

'What sins?' asked Makár Semyónitch.

But Aksyónof only said, 'Well, well - I must have deserved it!' He would have said no more, but his companions told the new-comer how Aksyónof came to be in Siberia: how someone had killed a merchant and had put a knife among Aksyónof's things, and Aksyónof had been unjustly condemned.

When Makár Semyónitch heard this, he looked at Aksyónof, slapped his own knee, and exclaimed,

'Well this is wonderful! Really wonderful! But how old you've grown, Gran'dad!'

The others asked him why he was so surprised, and where he had seen Aksyónof before; but Makár Semyónitch did not reply. He only said: 'It's wonderful that we should meet here, lads!'

These words made Aksyónof wonder whether this man knew who had killed the merchant; so he said 'Perhaps, Semyónitch, you have heard of that affair or maybe you've seen me before?'

'How could I help hearing? The world's full of rumours. But it's long ago, and I've forgotten what I heard.'

'Perhaps you heard who killed the merchant?' asked Aksyónof.

Makár Semyónitch laughed, and replied, 'It must have been him in whose bag the knife was found! If someone else hid the knife there, "He's not a thief till he's caught," as the saying is. How could anyone put a knife into your bag while it was under your head? It would surely have woke you up?'

When Aksyónof heard these words, he felt sure this was the man who had killed the merchant. He rose and went away. All that night Aksyónof lay awake.

He felt terribly unhappy, and all sorts of images rose in his mind. There was the image of his wife as she was when he parted from her to go to the fair. He saw her as if she were present; her face and her eyes rose before him; he heard her speak and laugh. Then he saw his children, quite little, as they were at that time: one with a little cloak on, another at his mother's breast. And then he remembered himself as he used to be - young and merry. He remembered how he sat playing the guitar in the porch of the inn where he was arrested, and how free from care he had been. He saw, in his mind, the place where he was flogged, the executioner, and the people standing around; the chains, the convicts, all the twenty-six years of his prison life, and his premature old age. The thought of it all made him so wretched that he was ready to kill himself.

'And it's all that villain's doing!' thought Aksyónof. And his anger was so great against Makár Semyónitch that he longed for vengeance, even if he himself should perish for it. He kept repeating prayers all night, but could get no peace. During the day he did not go near Makár Semyónitch, nor even look at him.

A fortnight passed in this way. Aksyónof could not sleep at nights, and was so miserable that he did not know what to do.

One night as he was walking about the prison he noticed some earth that came rolling out from under one of the shelves on which the prisoners slept. He stopped to see what it was. Suddenly Makár Semyónitch crept out from under the shelf, and looked up at Aksyónof with frightened face. Aksyónof tried to pass without looking at him, but Makár seized his hand and told him that he had dug a hole under the wall, getting rid of the earth by putting it into his high-boots, and emptying it out every day on the road when the prisoners were driven to their work.

'Just you keep quiet, old man, and you shall get out too. If you blab they'll flog the life out of me, but I will kill you first.'

Aksyónof trembled with anger as he looked at his enemy. He drew his hand away, saying, 'I have no wish to escape, and you have no need to kill me; you killed me long ago! As to telling of you - I may do so or not, as God shall direct.'

Next day, when the convicts were led out to work, the convoy soldiers noticed that one or other of the prisoners emptied some earth out of his boots. The prison was searched, and the tunnel found. The Governor came and questioned all the prisoners to find out who had dug the hole. They all denied any knowledge of it. Those who knew, would not betray Makár Semyónitch, knowing he would be flogged almost to death. At last the Governor turned to Aksyónof, whom he knew to be a just man, and said:

'You are a truthful old man; tell me, before God, who dug the hole?'

Makár Semyónitch stood as if he were quite unconcerned, looking at the Governor and not so much as glancing at Aksyónof. Aksyónof's lips and hands trembled, and for a long time he could not utter a word. He thought, 'Why should I screen him who ruined my life? Let him pay for what I have suffered. But if I tell, they will probably flog the life out of him and maybe I suspect him wrongly. And, after all, what good would it be to me?'

'Well, old man,' repeated the Governor, 'tell us the truth: who has been digging under the wall?'

Aksyónof glanced at Makár Semyónitch, and said 'I cannot say, your honour. It is not God's will that I should tell! Do what you like with me; I am in your hands.'

However much the Governor tried, Aksyónof would say no more, and so the matter had to be left.

That night, when Aksyónof was lying on his bed and just beginning to doze, someone came quietly and sat down on his bed. He peered through the darkness and recognized Makár.

'What more do you want of me?' asked Aksyónof. 'Why have you come here?'

Makár Semyónitch was silent. So Aksyónof sat up and said, 'What do you want? Go away, or I will call the guard!'

Makár Semyónitch bent close over Aksyónof, and whispered, 'Iván Dmítritch, forgive me!'

'What for?' asked Aksyónof.

'It was I who killed the merchant and hid the knife among your things. I meant to kill you too, but I heard a noise outside; so I hid the knife in your bag and escaped out of the window.'

Aksyónof was silent, and did not know what to say. Makár Semyónitch slid off the bed-shelf and knelt upon the ground. 'Iván Dmítritch,' said he, 'forgive me! For the love of God, forgive me! I will confess that it was I who killed the merchant, and you will be released and can go to your home.'

'It is easy for you to talk,' said Aksyónof, 'but I have suffered for you these twenty-six years. Where could I go to now?...My wife is dead, and my children have forgotten me. I have nowhere to go...'

Makár Semyónitch did not rise, but beat his head on the floor. 'Iván Dmítritch, forgive me!' he cried. 'When they flogged me with the knout it was not so hard to bear as it is to see you now...yet you had pity on me, and did not tell. For Christ's sake forgive me, wretch that I am!' And he began to sob.

When Aksyónof heard him sobbing he, too, began to weep.

'God will forgive you!' said he. 'Maybe I am a hundred times worse than you.' And at these words his heart grew light, and the longing for home left him. He no longer had any desire to leave the prison, but only hoped for his last hour to come.

In spite of what Aksyónof had said, Maker Semyónitch confessed his guilt. But when the order for his release came, Aksyónof was already dead.

MASTER AND MAN

I

It happened in the 'seventies in winter, on the day after St. Nicholas's Day. There was a fete in the parish and the innkeeper, Vasili Andreevich Brekhunov, a Second Guild merchant, being a church elder had to go to church, and had also to entertain his relatives and friends at home.

But when the last of them had gone he at once began to prepare to drive over to see a neighbouring proprietor about a grove which he had been bargaining over for a long time. He was now in a hurry to start, lest buyers from the town might forestall him in making a profitable purchase.

The youthful landowner was asking ten thousand rubles for the grove simply because Vasili Andreevich was offering seven thousand. Seven thousand was, however, only a third of its real value. Vasili Andreevich might perhaps have got it down to his own price, for the woods were in his district and he had a long-stand agreement with the other village dealers that no one should run up the price in another's district, but he had now learnt that some timber dealers from town meant to bid for the Goryachkin grove, and he resolved to go at once and get the matter settled. So as soon as the feast was over, he took seven hundred rubles from his strong box, added to them two thousand three hundred rubles of church money he had in his keeping, so as to make up the sum to three thousand; carefully counted the notes, and having put them into his pocketbook made haste to start.

Nikita, the only one of Vasili Andreevich's labourers who was not drunk that day, ran to harness the horse. Nikita, though an habitual drunkard, was not drunk that day because since the last day before the fast, when he had drunk his coat and leather boots, he had sworn off drink and had kept his vow for two months, and was still keeping it despite the temptation of the vodka that had been drunk everywhere during the first two days of the feast.

Nikita was a peasant of about fifty from a neighbouring village, "nat a manager" as the peasants said of him, meaning that he was not the thrifty head of a household but lived most of his time away from home as a labourer. He was valued everywhere for his industry, dexterity, and strength at work, and still more for his kindly and pleasant temper. But he never settled down anywhere for long because about twice a year, or even oftener, he had a drinking bout, and then besides spending all his clothes on drink he became turbulent and quarrelsome. Vasili Andreevich himself had turned him away several times, but had afterwards taken him back again - valuing his honesty, his kindness to animals, and especially his cheapness. Vasili Andreevich did not pay Nikita the eighty rubles a year such a man was worth, but only about forty, which he gave him haphazard, in small sums, and even that mostly not in cash but in goods from his own shop and at high prices.

Nikita's wife Martha, who had once been a handsome vigorous woman, managed the homestead with the help of her son and two daughters, and did not urge Nikita to live at home: first because she had been living for some twenty years already with a cooper, a peasant from another village who lodged in their house; and secondly because though she managed her husband as she pleased when he was sober, she feared him like fire when he was drunk. Once when he had got drunk at home, Nikita, probably to make up for his submissiveness when sober, broke open her box, took out her best clothes, snatched up an axe, and chopped all her undergarments and dresses to bits. All the wages Nikita earned went to his wife, and he raised no objection to that. So now, two days before the holiday, Martha had been twice to see Vasili Andreevich and had got from him wheat flour, tea, sugar, and a quart of vodka, the lot costing three rubles, and also five rubles in cash, for which she thanked him as a special favour, though he owed Nikita at least twenty rubles.

"What agreement did we ever draw up with you?" said Vasili Andreevich to Nikita. "If you need anything, take it; you will work it off. I'm not like others to keep you waiting, and making up accounts and reckoning fines. We deal straight-forwardly. You serve me and I don't neglect you."

And when saying this Vasili Andreevich was honestly convinced that he was Nikita's benefactor, and he knew how to put it so plausibly that all those who depended on him for their money, beginning with Nikita, confirmed him in the conviction that he was their benefactor and did not overreach them.

"Yes, I understand, Vasili Andreevich. You know that I serve you and take as much pains as I would for my own father. I understand very well!" Nikita would reply. He was quite aware that Vasili Andreevich was cheating him, but at the same time he felt that it was useless to try to clear up his accounts with him or explain his side of the matter, and that as long as he had nowhere to go he must accept what he could get.

Now, having heard his master's order to harness, he went as usual cheerfully and willingly to the shed, stepping briskly and easily on his rather turned-in feet; took down from a nail the heavy tasseled leather bridle, and jingling the rings of the bit went to the closed stable where the horse he was to harness was standing by himself.

"What, feeling lonely, feeling lonely, little silly?" said Nikita in answer to the low whinny with which he was greeted by the good-tempered, medium-sized bay stallion, with a rather slanting crupper, who stood alone in the shed. "Now then, now then, there's time enough. Let me water you first," he went on, speaking to the horse just as to someone who understood the words he was using and having whisked the dusty, grooved back of the well-fed young stallion with the skirt of his coat, he put a bridle on his handsome head, straightened his ears and forelock, and having taken off his halter led him out to water.

Picking his way out of the dung-strewn stable, Mukhorty frisked, and making play with his hind leg pretended that he meant to kick Nikita, who was running at a trot beside him to the pump.

"Now then, now then, you rascal!" Nikita called out, well knowing how carefully Mukhorty threw out his hind leg just to touch his greasy sheepskin coat but not to strike him - a trick Nikita much appreciated.

After a drink of the cold water the horse sighed, moving his strong wet lips from the hairs of which transparent drops fell into the trough; then standing still as if in thought, he suddenly gave a loud snort.

"If you don't want more, you needn't. But don't go asking for any later," said Nikita quite seriously and fully explaining his conduct to Mukhorty. Then he ran back to the shed pulling the playful young horse, who wanted to gambol all over the yard, by the rein.

There was no one else in the yard except a stranger, the cook's husband, who had come for the holiday.

"Go and ask which sledge is to be harnessed - the wide one or the small one - there's a good fellow!"

The cook's husband went into the house, which stood on an iron foundation and was iron-roofed, and soon returned saying that the little one was to be harnessed. By that time Nikita had put the collar and brass-studded bellyband on Mukhorty and, carrying a light, painted shaftbow in one hand, was leading the horse with the other up to two sledges that stood in the shed.

"All right, let it be the little one!" he said, backing the intelligent horse, which all the time kept pretending to bite him, into the shafts, and with the aid of the cook's husband he proceeded to harness. When everything was nearly ready and only the reins had to be adjusted, Nikita sent the other man to the shed for some straw and to the barn for a drugget.

"There, that's all right! Now, now, don't bristle up!" said Nikita, pressing down into the sledge the freshly threshed oat straw the cook's husband had brought. "And now let's spread the sacking like this, and the drugget over it. There, like that it will be comfortable sitting," he went on, suiting the action to the words and tucking the drugget all round over the straw to make a seat.

"Thank you, dear man. Things always go quicker with two working at it!" he added. And gathering up the leather reins fastened together by a brass ring, Nikita took the driver's seat and started the impatient horse over the frozen manure which lay in the yard, towards the gate.

"Uncle Nikita! I say, Uncle, Uncle!" a high-pitched voice shouted, and a seven-year-old boy in a black sheepskin coat, new white felt boots, and a warm cap, ran hurriedly out of the house into the yard. "Take me with you!" he cried, fastening up his coat as he ran.

"All right, come along, darling!" said Nikita, and stopping the sledge he picked up the master's pale thin little son, radiant with joy, and drove out into the road.

It was past two o'clock and the day was windy, dull, and cold, with more than twenty degrees Fahrenheit of frost. Half the sky was hidden by a lowering dark cloud. In the yard it was quiet, but in the street the wind was felt more keenly. The snow swept down from a neighbouring shed and whirled about in the corner near the bath-house.

Hardly had Nikita driven out of the yard and turned the horse's head to the house, before Vasili Andreevich emerged from the high porch in front of the house with a cigarette in his mouth and wearing a cloth-covered sheepskin coat tightly girdled low at his waist, and stepped onto the hard-trodden snow which squeaked under the leather soles of his felt boots, and stopped. Taking a last whiff of his cigarette he threw it down, stepped on it, and letting the smoke escape through his moustache and looking askance at the horse that was coming up, began to tuck in his sheepskin collar on both sides of his ruddy face, clean-shaven except for the moustache, so that his breath should not moisten the collar.

"See now! The young scamp is there already!" he exclaimed when he saw his little son in the sledge. Vasili Andreevich was excited by the vodka he had drunk with his visitors, and so he was even more pleased than usual with everything that was his and all that he did. The sight of his son, whom he always thought of as his heir, now gave him great satisfaction. He looked at him, screwing up his eyes and showing his long teeth.

His wife - pregnant, thin and pale, with her head and shoulders wrapped in a shawl so that nothing of her face could be seen but her eyes - stood behind him in the vestibule to see him off.

"Now really, you ought to take Nikita with you," she said timidly, stepping out from the doorway.

Vasili Andreevich did not answer. Her words evidently annoyed him and he frowned angrily and spat.

"You have money on you," she continued in the same plaintive voice. "What if the weather gets worse! Do take him, for goodness' sake!"

"Why? Don't I know the road that I must needs take a guide?" exclaimed Vasili Andreevich, uttering every word very distinctly and compressing his lips unnaturally, as he usually did when speaking to buyers and sellers.

"Really you ought to take him. I beg you in God's name!" his wife repeated, wrapping her shawl more closely round her head.

"There, she sticks to it like a leech! ...where am I to take him?"

"I'm quite ready to go with you, Vasili Andreevich," said Nikita cheerfully. "But they must feed the horses while I am away," he added, turning to his master's wife.

"I'll look after them, Nikita dear. I'll tell Simon," replied the mistress.

"Well, Vasili Andreevich, am I to come with you?" said Nikita, awaiting a decision.

"It seems I must humour my old woman. But if you're coming you'd better put on a warmer cloak," said Vasili Andreevich, smiling again as he winked at Nikita's short sheepskin coat, which was torn under the arms and at the back, was greasy and out of shape, frayed to a fringe round the skirt, and had endured many things in its lifetime.

"Hey, dear man, come and hold the horse!" shouted Nikita to the cook's husband, who was still in the yard.

"No, I will myself, I will myself!" shrieked the little boy, pulling his hands, red with cold, out of his pickets, and seizing the cold leather reins.

"Only a moment, Father, Vasili Andreevich!" replied Nikita, and running quickly with his in-turned toes in his felt boots with their soles patched with felt, he hurried across the yard and into the workmen's hut.

"Arinushka! Get my coat down from the stove. I'm going with the master," he said, as he ran into the hut and took down his girdle from the nail on which it hung.

The workmen's cook, who had had a sleep after dinner and was now getting the samovar ready for her husband, turned cheerfully to Nikita, and infected by his hurry began to move as quickly as he did, got down his miserable worn-out cloth coat from the stove where it was drying, and began hurriedly shaking it out and smoothing it down.

"There now, you'll have a chance of a holiday with your good man," said Nikita, who from kindhearted politeness always said something to anyone he was alone with.

Then, drawing his worn narrow girdle around him, he drew in his breath, pulling in his lean stomach still more, and girdled himself as tightly as he could over his sheepskin.

"There now," he said addressing himself no longer to the cook but the girdle, as he tucked the ends in at the waist, "now you won't come undone!" And working his shoulders up and down to free his arms, he put the coat over his sheepskin, arched his back more strongly to ease his arms, poked himself under the armpits, and took down his leather-covered mittens from the shelf. "Now we're all right!"

"You ought to wrap your feet up, Nikita. Your boots are very bad."

Nikita stopped as if he had suddenly realized this. "Yes, I ought to... But they'll do like this. It isn't far!" and he ran out into the yard.

"Won't you be cold, Nikita?" said the mistress as he came up to the sledge.

"Cold? No, I'm quite warm," answered Nikita as he pushed some straw up to the forepart of the sledge so that it should cover his feet, and stowed away the whip, which the good horse would not need, at the bottom of the sledge.

Vasili Andreevich, who was wearing two fur-lined coats one over the other, was already in the sledge, his broad back filling nearly its whole rounded width, and taking the reins he immediately touched the horse. Nikita jumped in just as the sledge started, and seated himself in front on the left side, with one leg hanging over the edge.

II

The good stallion took the sledge along at a brisk pace over the smooth-frozen road through the village, the runners squeaking slightly as they went.

"Look at him hanging on there! Hand me the whip, Nikita!" shouted Vasili Andreevich, evidently enjoying the sight of his "heir," who standing on the runners was hanging on at the back of the sledge. "I'll give it you! Be off to mamma, you dog!"

The boy jumped down. The horse increased his amble and, suddenly changing foot, broke into a fast trot.

The Crosses, the village where Vasili Andreevich lived, consisted of six houses. As soon as they had passed the blacksmith's hut, the last in the village, they realized that the wind was much stronger than they had thought. The road could hardly be seen. The tracks left by the sledge-runners were immediately covered by snow and the road was only distinguished by the fact that it was higher than the rest of the ground.

There was a whirl of snow over the fields and the line where sky and earth met could not been seen. The Telyatin forest, usually clearly visible, now only loomed up occasionally and dimly through the driving snowy dust. The wind came from the left, insistently blowing over to one side the mane on Mukhorty's sleek neck and carrying aside even his fluffy tail, which was tied in a simple knot. Nikita's wide coat-collar, as he sat on the windy side, pressed close to his cheek and nose.

"This road doesn't give him a chance - it's too snowy," said Vasili Andreevich, who prided himself on his good horse. "I once drove to Pashutino with him in half an hour."

"What?" asked Nikita, who could not hear on account of his collar.

"I say I once went to Pashutino in half an hour," shouted Vasili Andreevich.

"It goes without saying that he's a good horse," replied Nikita.

They were silent for a while. But Vasili Andreevich wished to talk.

"Well, did you tell your wife not to give the cooper any vodka?" he began in the same loud tone, quite convinced that Nikita must feel flattered to be talking with so clever and important a person as himself, and he was so pleased with his jest that it did not enter his head that the remark might be unpleasant to Nikita.

The wind again prevented Nikita's hearing his master's words.

Vasili Andreevich repeated the jest about the cooper in his loud, clear voice.

"That's their business, Vasili Andreevich. I don't pry into their affairs. As long as she doesn't ill-treat our boy - God be with them."

"That's so," said Vasili Andreevich. "Well, and will you be buying a horse in spring?" he went on, changing the subject.

"Yes, I can't avoid it," answered Nikita, turning down his collar and leaning back towards his master.

The conversation now became interesting to him and he did not wish to lose a word.

"The lad's growing up. He must begin to plough for himself, but till now we've always had to hire someone," he said.

"Well, why not have the lean-cruppered one. I won't charge much for it," shouted Vasili Andreevich, feeling animated, and consequently starting on his favourite occupation - that of horse- dealing - which absorbed all his mental powers.

"Or you might let me have fifteen rubles and I'll buy one at the horse-market," said Nikita, who knew that the horse Vasili Andreevich wanted to sell him would be dear at seven rubles, but that if he took it from him it would be charged at twenty-five, and then he would be unable to draw any money for half a year.

"It's a good horse. I think of your interest as of my own - according to conscience. Brekhunov isn't a man to wrong anyone. Let the loss be mine. I'm not like others. Honestly!" he shouted in the voice in which he hypnotized his customers and dealers. "It's a real good horse."

"Quite so!" said Nikita with a sigh, and convinced that there was nothing more to listen to, he again released his collar, which immediately covered his ear and face.

They drove on in silence for about half an hour. The wind blew sharply onto Nikita's side and arm where his sheepskin was torn.

He huddled up and breathed into the collar which covered his mouth, and was not wholly cold.

"What do you think - shall we go through Karamyshevo or by the straight road?" asked Vasili Andreevich.

The road through Karamyshevo was more frequented and was well marked with a double row of high stakes. The straight road was nearer but little used and had no stakes, or only poor ones covered with snow.

Nikita thought awhile.

"Though Karamyshevo is farther, it is better going," he said.

"But by the straight road, when once we get through the hollow by the forest, it's good going - sheltered," said Vasili Andreevich, who wished to go the nearest way.

"Just a you please," said Nikita, and again let go of his collar.

Vasili Andreevich did as he had said, and having gone about half a verst came to a tall oak stake which had a few dry leaves still dangling on it, and there he turned to the left.

On turning they faced directly against the wind, and snow was beginning to fall. Vasili Andreevich, who was driving, inflated his cheeks, blowing the breath out through his moustache. Nikita dosed.

161

So they went on in silence for about ten minutes. Suddenly Vasili Andreevich began saying something.

"Eh, what?" asked Nikita, opening his eyes.

Vasili Andreevich did not answer, but bent over, looking behind them and then ahead of the horse. The sweat had curled Mukhorty's coat between his legs and on his neck.

He went at a walk.

"What is it?" Nikita asked again.

"What is it? What is it?" Vasili Andreevich mimicked him angrily. "There are no stakes to be seen! We must have got off the road!"

Well, pull up then, and I'll look for it," said Nikita, and jumping down lightly from the sledge and taking the whip from under the straw, he went off to the left from his own side of the sledge.

The snow was not deep that year, so that it was possible to walk anywhere, but still in places it was knee-deep and got into Nikita's boots. He went about feeling the ground with his feet and the whip, but could not find the road anywhere.

"Well, how it is?" asked Vasili Andreevich when Nikita came back to the sledge.

"There is no road this side. I must go to the other side and try there," said Nikita.

"There is something there in front. Go and have a look."

Nikita went to what had appeared dark, but found that it was earth which the wind had blown from the bare fields of winter oats and had strewn over the snow, colouring it. Having searched to the right also, he returned to the sledge, brushed the snow from his coat, shook it out of his boots, and seated himself once more.

"We must go to the right," he said decidedly. "The wind was blowing on our left before, but now it is straight in my face. Drive to the right," he repeated with decision.

Vasili Andreevich took his advice and turned to the right, but still there was no road. They went on in that direction for some time. The wind was as fierce as ever and it was snowing lightly.

"It seems, Vasili Andreevich, that we have gone quite astray," Nikita suddenly remarked, as if it were a pleasant thing. "what is that?" he added, pointing to some potato vines that showed up under the snow.

Vasili Andreevich stopped the perspiring horse, whose deep sides were heaving heavily.

"What is it?"

"Why, we are on the Zakharov lands. See where we've got to!"

"Nonsense!" retorted Vasili Andreevich.

"It's not nonsense, Vasili Andreevich. It's the truth," replied Nikita. "You can feel that the sledge is going over a potato-field, and there are the heaps of vines which have been carted here. It's the Zakharov factory land."

"Dear me, how we have gone astray!" said Vasili Andreevich. "What are we to do now?"

"We must go straight on, that's all. We shall come out somewhere - if not at Zakharova, then at the proprietor's farm," said Nikita.

Vasili Andreevich agreed, and drove as Nikita had indicated. So they went on for a considerable time. At times they came onto bare fields and the sledge- runners rattled over frozen lumps of earth. Sometimes they got onto a winter- rye field, or a fallow field on which they could see stalks of wormwood, and straws sticking up through the snow and swaying in the wind; sometimes they came onto deep and even white snow, above which nothing was to be seen.

The snow was falling from above and sometimes rose from below. The horse was evidently exhausted, his hair had all curled up from sweat and was covered with hoar-frost, and he went at a walk. Suddenly he stumbled and sat down in a ditch or water-course. Vasili Andreevich wanted to stop, but Nikita cried to him:

"Why stop? We've got in and must get out. Hey, pet! Hey, darling! Gee up, old fellow!" he shouted in a cheerful tone to the horse, jumping out of the sledge and himself getting stuck in the ditch.

The horse gave a start and quickly climbed out onto the frozen bank. It was evidently a ditch that had been dug there.

"Where are we now?" asked Vasili Andreevich.

"We'll soon find out!" Nikita replied. "Go on, we'll get somewhere."

"Why, this must be the Goryachkin forest!" said Vasili Andreevich, pointing to something dark that appeared amid the snow in front of them.

"We'll see what forest it is when we get there," said Nikita.

He saw that beside the black thing they had noticed, dry, oblong willow- leaves were fluttering, and so he knew it was not a forest but a settlement, but he did not wish to say so. And in fact they had not gone twenty-five yards beyond the ditch before something in front of them, evidently trees, showed up black, and they heard a new and melancholy sound. Nikita had guessed right: it was not a wood, but a row of tall willows with a few leaves still fluttering on them here and there. They had evidently been planted along the ditch round a threshing-floor. Coming up to the willows, which moaned sadly in the wind, the horse suddenly planted his forelegs above the height of the sledge, drew up his hind legs also, pulling the sledge onto higher ground, and turned to the left, no longer sinking up to his knees in snow. They were back on a road.

"Well, here we are, but heaven only knows where!" said Nikita.

The horse kept straight along the road through the drifted snow, and before they had gone another hundred yards the straight line of the dark wattle wall of a barn showed up black before them, its roof heavily covered with snow which poured down from it. after passing the barn the road turned to the wind and they drove into a snow-drift. But ahead of them was a lane with houses on either side, so evidently the snow had been blown across the road and they had to drive through the drift. And so in fact it was. Having driven through the snow they came out into a street. At the end house of the village some frozen clothes hanging on a line - shirts, one red and one white, trousers, leg- bands, and a petticoat - fluttered wildly in the wind. The white shirt in particular struggled desperately, waving its sleeves about.

"There now, either a lazy woman or a dead one has not taken her clothes down before the holiday," remarked Nikita, looking at the fluttering shirts.

III

At the entrance to the street the wind still raged and the road was thickly covered with snow, but well within the village it was calm, warm, and cheerful. At one house a dog was barking, at another a woman, covering her head with her coat, came running from somewhere and entered the door of a hut, stopping on the threshold to have a look at the passing sledge. In the middle of the village girls could be heard singing.

Here in the village there seemed to be less wind and snow, and the frost was less keen.

"Why, this is Grishkino," said Vasili Andreevich.

"So it is," responded Nikita.

It really was Grishkino, which meant that they had gone too far to the left and had traveled some six miles, not quite in the direction they aimed at, but towards their destination for all that.

From Grishkino to Goryachkin was about another four miles.

In the middle of the village they almost ran into a tall man walking down the middle of the street.

"Who are you?" shouted the man, stopping the horse, and recognizing Vasili Andreevich he immediately took hold of the shaft, went along it hand over hand till he reached the sledge, and placed himself on the driver's seat.

He was Isay, a peasant of Vasili Andreevich's acquaintance, and well known as the principal horse-thief in the district.

"Ah, Vasili Andreevich! Where are you off to?" said Isay, enveloping Nikita in the odour of the vodka he had drunk.

"We are going to Goryachkin."

"And look where you've got to! You should have gone through Molchanovka,"

"Should have, but didn't manage it," said Vasili Andreevich, holding in the horse.

"That's a good horse," said Isay, with a shrewd glance at Mukhorty, and with a practised hand he tightened the loosened know high in the horse's bushy tail.

"Are you going to stay the night?"

"No, friend. I must get on."

"Your business must be pressing. And who is this? Ah, Nikita Stepanych!"

"Who else?" replied Nikita. "But I say, good friend, how are we to avoid going astray again?"

"Where can you go astray here? Turn back straight down the street and then when you come out keep straight on. Don't take to the left. You will come out onto the high road, and then turn to the right."

"And where do we turn off the high road? As in summer, or the winter way?" asked Nikita.

"The winter way. As soon as you turn off you'll see some bushes, and opposite them there is a way-mark - a large oak, one with branches - and that's the way."

Vasili Andreevich turned the horse back and drove through the outskirts of the village.

"Why not stay the night?" Isay shouted after them.

But Vasili Andreevich did not answer and touched up the horse. Four miles of good road, two of which lay through the forest, seemed easy to manage, especially as the wind was apparently quieter and the snow had stopped.

Having driven along the trodden village street, darkened here and there by fresh manure, past the yard where the clothes hung out and where the white shirt had broken loose and was now attached only by one frozen sleeve, they again came within sound of the weird moan of the willows, and again emerged on the open fields. The storm, far from ceasing, seemed to have grown yet stronger. The road was completely covered with drifting snow, and only the stakes showed that they had not lost their way. But even the stakes ahead of them were not easy to see, since the wind blew in their faces.

Vasili Andreevich screwed up his eyes, bent down his head, and looked out for the way-marks, but trusted mainly to the horse's sagacity, letting it take its own way. And the horse really did not lose the road but followed its windings, turning how to the right and now to the left and sensing it under his feet, so that though the snow fell thicker and the wind strengthened they still continued to see way-marks now to the left and now to the right of them.

So they traveled on for about ten minutes, when suddenly, through the slanting screen of wind-driven snow, something black showed up which moved in front of the horse.

This was another sledge with fellow-travelers. Mukhorty over took them, and struck his hooves against the back of the sledge in front of him.

"Pass on... hey there... get in front!" cried voices from the sledge.

Vasili Andreevich swerved aside to pass the other sledge. In it sat three men and a woman, evidently visitors returning from a feast. One peasant was whacking the snow-covered croup of their little horse with a long switch, and the other two sitting in front waved their arms and shouted something. The woman, completely wrapped up and covered with snow, sat drowsing and bumping at the back.

"Who are you?" shouted Vasili Andreevich.

"From A-a-a..." was all that could be heard.

"I say, where are you from?"

"From A-a-a...!" one of the peasants shouted with all his might, but still it was impossible to make out who they were.

"Get along! Keep up!" shouted another, ceaselessly beating his horse with the switch.

"So you're from a feast, it seems?"

"Go on, go on! Faster, Simon! Get in front! Faster!"

The wings of the sledges bumped against one another, almost got jammed but managed to separate, and the peasants' sledge began to fall behind.

Their shaggy, big-bellied horse, all covered with snow, breathed heavily under the low shaft-bow and, evidently using the last of its strength, vainly endeavoured to escape from the switch, hobbling with its short legs through the deep snow which it threw up under itself.

Its muzzle, young-looking, with the nether lip drawn up like that of a fish, nostrils distended and ears pressed back from fear, kept up for a few seconds near Nikita's shoulder and then began to fall behind.

"Just see what liquor does!" said Nikita. "They've tired that little horse to death. What pagans!"

For a few minutes they heard the panting of the tired little horse and the drunken shouting of the peasants. Then the panting and the shouts died away, and around them nothing could be heard but the whistling of the wind in their ears and now and then the squeak of their sledge-runners over a windswept part of the road.

This encounter cheered and enlivened Vasili Andreevich, and he drove on more boldly without examining the way-marks, urging on the horse and trusting to him.

Nikita had nothing to do, and as usual in such circumstances he drowsed, making up for much sleepless time. Suddenly the horse stopped and Nikita nearly fell forward onto his nose.

"You know we're off the track again!" said Vasili Andreevich.

"How's that?"

"Why there are no way-marks to be seen. We must have got off the road again."

"Well, if we've lost the road we must find it," said Nikita curtly, and getting out and stepping lightly on his pigeon-toed feet he started once more going about on the snow.

He walked about for a long time, now disappearing and now reappearing, and finally he came back.

"There is no road here. There may be farther on," he said, getting into the sledge.

It was already growing dark. The snow-storm had not increased but had also not subsided.

"If we could only hear those peasants!" said Vasili Andreevich.

"Well they haven't caught us up. We must have gone far astray. Or maybe they have lost their way too."

"Where are we to go then?" asked Vasili Andreevich.

"Why, we must let the horse take its own way," said Nikita. "He will take us right. Let me have the reins."

Vasili Andreevich gave him the reins, the more willingly because his hands were beginning to feel frozen in his thick gloves.

Nikita took the reins, but only held them, trying not to shake them and rejoicing at his favourite's sagacity. And indeed the clever horse, turning first one ear and then the other now to one side and then to the other, began to wheel round.

"The one thing he can't do is to talk," Nikita kept saying. "See what he is doing! Go on, go on! You know best. that's it, that's it!"

The wind was now blowing from behind and it felt warmer.

"Yes, he's clever," Nikita continued, admiring the horse. "A Kirgiz horse is strong but stupid. But this one - just see what he's doing with his ears! He doesn't need any telegraph. He can scent a mile off."

Before another half-hour had passed they saw something dark ahead of them - a wood or a village - and stakes again appeared to the right. They had evidently come out onto the road.

"Why, that's Grishkino again!" Nikita suddenly exclaimed.

And indeed, there on their left was that same barn with the snow flying from it, and farther on the same line with the frozen washing, shirts and trousers, which still fluttered desperately in the wind.

Again they drove into the street and again it grew quiet, warm, and cheerful, and again they could see the manure-stained street and hear voices and songs and the barking of a dog. It was already so dark that there were lights in some of the windows.

Half-way through the village Vasili Andreevich turned the horse towards a large double-fronted brick house and stopped at the porch.

Nikita went to the lighted snow-covered window, in the rays of which flying snow-flakes glittered, and knocked at it with his whip.

"Who's there?" a voice replied to his knock.

"From Kresty, the Brekhunovs, dear fellow," answered Nikita. "Just come out for a minute."

Someone moved from the window, and a minute or two later there was the sound of the passage door as it came unstuck, then the latch of the outside door clicked and a tall white-bearded peasant, with a sheepskin coat thrown over his white holiday shirt, pushed his way out holding the door firmly against the wind, followed by a lad in a red shirt and high leather boots.

"Is that you, Andreevich?" asked the old man.

"Yes, friend, we've gone astray," said Vasili Andreevich. "We wanted to get to Goryachkin but found ourselves here. We went a second time but lost our way again."

"Just see how you have gone astray!" said the old man. "Petrushka, go and open the gate!" he added, turning to the lad in the red shirt.

"All right," said the lad in a cheerful voice, and ran back into the passage.

"But we're not staying the night," said Vasili Andreevich.

"Where will you go in the night? You'd better stay!"

"I'd be glad to, but I must go on. It's business, and it can't be helped."

"Well, warm yourself at least. The samovar is just ready."

"Warm myself? Yes, I'll do that," said Vasili Andreevich. "It won't get darker. The moon will rise and it will be lighter. Let's go in and warm ourselves, Nikita."

"Well, why not? Let us warm ourselves," replied Nikita, who was stiff with cold and anxious to warm his frozen limbs.

Vasili Andreevich went into the room with the old man, and Nikita drove through the gate opened for him by Petrushka, by whose advice he backed the horse under the penthouse. the ground was covered with manure and the tall bow over the horse's head caught against the beam. The hens and the cock had already settled to roost there, and clucked peevishly, clinging to the beam with their claws. the disturbed sheep shied and rushed aside trampling the frozen manure with their hooves. The dog yelped desperately with fright and anger and then burst out barking like a puppy at the stranger.

Nikita talked to them all, excused himself to the fowls and assured them that he would not disturb them again, rebuked the sheep for being frightened without knowing why, and kept soothing the dog, while he tied up the horse.

"Now that will be all right," he said, knocking the snow off his clothes. "Just hear how he barks!" he added, turning to the dog. "Be quiet, stupid! Be quiet. You are only troubling yourself for nothing. we're not thieves, we're friends..."

"And these are, it's said, the three domestic counsellors," remarked the lad, and with his strong arms he pushed under the pent-roof the sledge that had remained outside.

"Why counsellors?" asked Nikita.

"That's what is printed in Paulson. A thief creeps to a house - the dog barks, that means, 'Be on your guard!' The cock crows, that means, 'Get up!' The cat licks herself - that means, "A welcome guest is coming. Get ready to receive him!" said the lad with a smile.

Petrushka could read and write and knew Paulson's primer, his only book, almost by heart, and he was fond of quoting sayings from it that he thought suited the occasion, especially when he had had something to drink, as today.

"That's so," said Nikita.

"You must be chilled through and through," said Petrushka.

"Yes, I am rather," said Nikita, and they went across the yard and the passage into the house.

IV

The household to which Vasili Andreevich had come was one of the richest in the village. The family had five allotments, besides renting other land. They had six horses, three cows, two calves, and some twenty sheep. There were twenty-two members belonging to the homestead: four married sons, six grandchildren (one of whom, Petrushka, was married), two great-grandchildren, three orphans, and four daughters-in-law with their babies. It was one of the few homesteads that remained still undivided, but even here the dull internal work of disintegration which would inevitably lead to separation had already begun, starting as usual among the women. Two sons were living in Moscow as water-carriers, and one was in the army. At home now were the old man and his wife, their second son who managed the homestead, the eldest who had come from Moscow for the holiday, and all the women and children. Besides these members of the family there was a visitor, a neighbour who was godfather to one of the children.

Over the table in the room hung a lamp with a shade, which brightly lit up the tea-things, a bottle of vodka, and some refreshments, besides illuminating the brick walls, which in the far corner were hung with icons on both sides of which were pictures. At the head of the table sat Vasili Andreevich in a black sheepskin coat, sucking his frozen moustache and observing the room and the people around him with his prominent hawk-like eyes. With him sat the old, bald, white-bearded master of the house in a white homespun shirt, and next to him the son home from Moscow for the holiday - a man with a sturdy back and powerful shoulders and clad in a thin print shirt - then the second son, also broad-shouldered, who acted as head of the house, and then a lean red-haired peasant - the neighbour.

Having had a drink of vodka and something to eat, they were about to take tea, and the samovar standing on the floor beside the brick oven was already humming. The children could be seen in the top bunks and on the top of the oven. A woman sat on a lower bunk with a cradle beside her. The old housewife, her face covered with wrinkles which wrinkled even her lips, was waiting on Vasili Andreevich.

As Nikita entered the house she was offering her guest a small tumbler of thick glass which she had just filled with vodka.

"Don't refuse Vasili Andreevich, you mustn't! Wish us a merry feast. Drink it, dear!" she said.

the sight and smell of vodka, especially now when he was chilled through and tired out, much disturbed Nikita's mind. He frowned, and having shaken the snow off his cap and coat, stopped in front of the icons as if not seeing anyone, crossed himself three times, and bowed to the icons. Then, turning to the old master of the house and bowing first to him, then to all those at table, then to the women who stood by the oven, and muttering: "A merry holiday!" he beg taking off his outer things without looking at the table.

"Why, you're all covered with hoar-frost, old fellow!" said the eldest brother, looking at Nikita's snow-covered face, eyes, and beard.

Nikita took off his coat, shook it again, hung it up beside the oven, and came up to the table. He too was offered vodka. He went through a moment of painful hesitation and nearly took up the glass and emptied the clear fragrant liquid down his throat, but he glanced at Vasili Andreevich, remembered his oath and the boots that he had sold for drink, recalled the cooper, remembered his son for whom he had promised to buy a horse by spring, signed, and declined it.

"I don't drink, thank you kindly," he said frowning, and sat down on a bench near the second window.

"How's that?" asked the eldest brother.

"I just don't drink," replied Nikita without lifting his eyes but looking askance at his scanty beard and moustache and getting the icicles out of them.

"It's not good for him," said Vasili Andreevich, munching a cracknel after emptying his glass.

"Well, then, have some tea," said the kindly old hostess. "You must be chilled through, good soul. Why are you women dawdling so with the samovar?"

"It is ready," said one of the young women, and after flicking with her apron the top of the samovar which was now boiling over, she carried it with an effort to the table, raised it, and set it down with a thud.

Meanwhile Vasili Andreevich was telling how he had lost his way, how they had come back twice to this same village, and how they had gone astray and had met some drunken peasants. Their hosts were surprised, explained where and why they had missed their way, said who the tipsy people they had met were, and told them how they ought to go.

"A little child could find the way to Molchanovka from here. All you have to do is to take the right turning from the high road. There's a bush you can see just there. but you didn't even get that far!" said the neighbour.

"You's better stay the night. The women will make up beds for you," said the old woman persuasively.

"You could go on in the morning and it would be pleasanter," said the old man, confirming what his wife has said.

"I can't, friend. Business!" said Vasili Andreevich. "Lose an hour and you can't catch it up in a year," he added, remembering the grove and the dealers who might snatch that deal from him. "We shall get there, shan't we?" he said, turning to Nikita.

Nikita did not answer for some time, apparently still intent on thawing out his beard and moustache.

"If only we don't go astray again," he replied gloomily.

He was gloomy because he passionately longed for some vodka, and the only thing that could assuage that longing was tea and he had not yet been offered any.

"But we have only to reach the turning and then we shan't go wrong. The road will be through the forest the whole way," said Vasili Andreevich.

"It's just as you please, Vasili Andreevich. If we're to go, let us go," said Nikita, taking the glass of tea he was offered.

"We'll drink our tea and be off."

Nikita said nothing but only shook his head, and carefully pouring some tea into his saucer began warming his hands, the fingers of which were always swollen with hard work, over the steam. Then, biting off a tiny bit of sugar, he bowed to his hosts, said, "Your health!" and drew in the steaming liquid.

"If somebody would see us as far as the turning," said Vasili Andreevich.

"Well, we can do that," said the eldest son. "Petrushka will harness and go that far with you."

"Well, then, put in the horse, lad, and I shall be thankful to you for it."

"Oh, what for, dear man?" said the kindly old woman. "We are heartily glad to do it."

"Petrushka, go and put in the mare," said the eldest brother.

"All right," replied Petruskha with a smile, and promptly snatching his cap down from a nail he ran away to harness.

While the horse was being harnessed the talk returned to the point at which it had stopped when Vasili Andreevich drove up to the window. The old man had been complaining to his neighbour, the village elder, about his third son who had not sent him anything for the holiday though he had sent a French shawl to his wife.

"The young people are getting out of hand," said the old man.

"And how they do!" said the neighbour. "There's no managing them! They know too much. There's Demochkin now, who broke his father's arm. It's all from being too clever, it seems."

Nikita listened, watched their faces, and evidently would have liked to share in the conversation, but he was too busy drinking his tea and only nodded his head approvingly. He emptied one tumbler after another and grew warmer and warmer and more and more comfortable. The talk continued on the same subject for a long time - the harmfulness of a household dividing up - and it was clearly not an abstract discussion but concerned the question of a separation in that house; a separation demanded by the second son who sat there morosely silent.

It was evidently a sore subject and absorbed them all, but out of propriety they did not discuss their private affairs before strangers. At last, however, the old man could not restrain himself, and with tears in his eyes declared that he would not consent to a break-up of the family during his lifetime, that his house was prospering, thank God, but that if they separated they would all have to go begging.

"Just like the Matveevs," said the neighbour. "They used to have a proper house, but now they've split up none of them has anything."

"And that is what you want to happen to us," said the old man, turning to his son.

The son made no reply and there was an awkward pause. The silence was broken by Petrushka, who having harnessed the horse had returned to the hut a few minutes before this and had been listening all the time with a smile.

"There's a fable about that in Paulson," he said. "A father gave his sons a broom to break. At first they could not break it, but when they took it twig by twig they broke it easily. And it's the same here," and he gave a broad smile. "I'm ready!" he added.

"If you're ready, let's go," said Vasili Andreevich. And as to separating, don't you allow it, Grandfather. You've got everything together and you're the master. Go to the Justice of the Peace. He'll say how things should be done."

"He carries on so, carries on so," the old man continued in a whining tone. "There's no doing anything with him. It's as if the devil possessed him."

Nikita having meanwhile finished his fifth tumbler of tea laid it on its side instead of turning it upside down, hoping to be offered a sixth glass. But there was no more water in the samovar, so the hostess did not fill it up for him. Besides, Vasili Andreevich was putting his things on, so there was nothing for it but for Nikita to get up too, put back into the sugar-basin the lump of sugar he had nibbled all round, wipe his perspiring face with the skirt of his sheepskin, and go to put on his overcoat.

Having put it on he sighed deeply, thanked his hosts, said good-bye, and went out of the warm bright room into the cold dark passage, through which the wind was howling and where snow was blowing through the cracks of the shaking door, and from there into the yard.

Petrushka stood in his sheepskin in the middle of the yard by his horse, repeating some lines from Paulson's primer. He said with a smile:

"Storms with mist the sky conceal,
Snowy circles wheeling wild.
Now like savage beast 'twill howl,
and now 'tis wailing like a child."

Nikita nodded approvingly as he arranged the reins.

The old man, seeing Vasili Andreevich off, brought a lantern into the passage to show him a light, but it was blown out at once. And even in the yard it was evident that the snowstorm had become more violent.

"Well, this is weather!" thought Vasili Andreevich. "Perhaps we may not get there after all. But there is nothing to be done. Business! Besides, we have got ready, our host's horse has been harnessed, and we'll get there with god's help!"

Their aged host also thought they ought not to go, but he had already tried to persuade them to stay and had not been listened to.

"It's no use asking them again. Maybe my age makes me timid. They'll get there all right, and at least we shall get to bed in good time and without any fuss," he thought.

Petrushka did not think of danger. He knew the road and the whole district so well, and the lines about "snowy circles wheeling wild" described what was happening outside so aptly that it cheered him up. Nikita did not wish to go at all, but he had been accustomed not to have his own way and to serve others for so long that there was no one to hinder the departing travelers.

V

Vasili Andreevich went over to his sledge, found it with difficulty in the darkness, climbed in and took the reins.

"Go on in front!" he cried.

Petruskha kneeling in his low sledge started his horse. Mukhorty, who had been neighing for some time past, now scenting a mare ahead of him started after her, and they drove out into the street. They drove again through the outskirts of the village and along the same road, past the yard where the frozen linen had hung (which, however, was no longer to be seen), past the same barn, which was now snowed up almost to the roof and from which the snow was still endlessly pouring, past the same dismally moaning, whistling, and swaying willows, and again entered into the sea of blustering snow raging from above and below. The wind was so strong that when it blew from the side and the travelers steered against it, it tilted the sledges and turned the horses to one side. Petrushka drove his good mare in front at a brisk trot and kept shouting lustily. Mukhorty pressed after her.

After traveling so for about ten minutes, Petrushka turned round and shouted something. Neither Vasili Andreevich nor Nikita could hear anything because of the wind, but they guessed that they had arrived at the turning. In fact Petrushka had turned to the right, and now the wind that had blown from the side blew straight into their faces, and through the snow they saw something dark on their right. It was the bush at the turning.

"Well now, God speed you!"

"Thank you, Petrushka!"

"Storms with mist the sky conceal!" shouted Petrushka as he disappeared.

"There's a poet for you!" muttered Vasili Andreevich, pulling at the reins.

"Yes, a fine lad - a true peasant," said Nikita.

They drove on.

Nikita wrapping his coat closely about him and pressing his head down so close to his shoulders that his short beard covered his throat, sat silently, trying not to lose the warmth he had obtained while drinking tea in the house. Before him he saw the straight lines of the shafts which constantly deceived him into thinking they were on a well traveled road, and the horse's swaying crupper with his knotted tail blown to one side, and farther ahead the high shaft-bow and the swaying head and neck of the horse with its waving mane. Now and then he caught sight of a way-sign, so that he knew they were still on a road and that there was nothing for him to be concerned about.

Vasili Andreevich drove on, leaving it to the horse to keep to the road. But Mukhorty, though he had had a breathing-space in the village, ran reluctantly, and seemed now and then to get off the road, so that Vasili Andreevich had repeatedly to correct him.

"Here's a stake to the right, and another, and here's a third," Vasili Andreevich counted, "and here in front is the forest," thought he, as he looked at something dark in front of him. But what had seemed to him a forest was only a bush. The passed the bush and drove on for another hundred yards but there was no fourth way-mark nor any forest.

"We must reach the forest soon," thought Vasili Andreevich, and animated by the vodka and the tea he did not stop but shook the reins, and the good obedient horse responded, now ambling, now slowly trotting in the direction in which he was sent, though he knew that he was not going the right way. Ten minutes went by, but there was still no forest.

"There now, we must be astray again," said Vasili Andreevich, pulling up.

Nikita silently got out of the sledge and holding his coat, which the wind now wrapped closely about him and now almost tore off, started to feel about in the snow, going first to one side and then to the other. Three or four times he was completely lost to sight. At last he returned and took the reins from Vasili Andreevich's hand.

"We must go to the right," he said sternly and peremptorily, as he turned the horse.

"Well, if it's to the right, go to the right," said Vasili Andreevich, yielding up the reins to Nikita and thrusting his freezing hands into his sleeves.

Nikita did not reply.

"Now then, friend, stir yourself!" he shouted to the horse, but in spite of the shake of the reins Mukhorty moved only at a walk.

The snow in places was up to his knees, and the sledge moved by fits and starts with his every movement.

Nikita took the whip that hung over the front of the sledge and struck him once. The good horse, unused to the ship, sprang forward and moved at a trot, but immediately fell back into an amble and then to a walk. So they went on for five minutes. It was dark and the snow whirled from above and rose from below, so that sometimes the shaft-bow could not be seen. At times the sledge seemed to stand still and the field to run backwards. Suddenly the horse stopped abruptly, evidently aware of something close in front of him. Nikita again sprang lightly out, throwing down the reins, and went ahead to see what had brought him to a standstill, but hardly had he made a step in front of the horse before his feet slipped and he went rolling down an incline.

"Whoa, whoa, whoa!" he said to himself as he fell, and he tried to stop his fall but could not, and only stopped when his feet plunged into a thick layer of snow that had drifted to the bottom of the hollow.

The fringe of a drift of snow that hung on the edge of the hollow, disturbed by Nikita's fall, showered down on him and got inside his collar.

"What a thing to do!" said Nikita reproachfully, addressing the drift and the hollow and shaking the snow from under his collar.

"Nikita! Hey, Nikita!" shouted Vasili Andreevich from above.

But Nikita did not reply. He was too occupied in shaking out the snow and searching for the whip he had dropped when rolling down the incline. Having found the whip he tried to climb straight up the bank where he had rolled down, but it was impossible to do so: he kept rolling down again, and so he had to go along at the foot of the hollow to find a way up. About seven yards farther on he managed with difficulty to crawl up the incline on all fours, then he followed the edge of the hollow back to the place where the horse should have been. He could not see either horse or sledge, but as he walked against the wind he heard Vasili Andreevich's shouts and Mukhorty's neighing, calling him.

"I'm coming! I'm coming! What are you cackling for?" he muttered.

Only when he had come up to the sledge could he make out the horse, and Vasili Andreevich standing beside it and looking gigantic.

"Where the devil did you vanish to? We must go back, if only to Grishkino," he began reproaching Nikita.

"I'd be glad to get back, Vasili Andreevich, but which way are we to go? there is such a ravine here that if we once get in it we shan't get out again. I got stuck so fast there myself that I could hardly get out."

"What shall we do, then? We can't stay here! We must go somewhere!" said Vasili Andreevich.

Nikita said nothing. He seated himself in the sledge with his back to the wind, took off his boots, shook out the snow that had got into them, and taking some straw from the bottom of the sledge, carefully plugged with it a hold in his left boot.

Vasili Andreevich remained silent, as though now leaving everything to Nikita. Having put his boots on again, Nikita drew his feet into the sledge, put on his mittens and took up the reins, and directed the horse along the side of the ravine. But they had not gone a hundred yards before the horse again stopped short. The ravine was in front of him again.

Nikita again climbed out and again trudged about in the snow. He did this for a considerable time and at last appeared from the opposite side to that from which he had started.

"Vasili Andreevich, are you alive?" he called out.

"Here!" replied Vasili Andreevich. "Well, what now?"

"I can't make anything out. It's too dark. There's nothing but ravines. We must drive against the wind again."

They set off once more. Again Nikita went stumbling through the snow, again he fell in, again climbed out and trudged about, and at last quite out of breath he sat down beside the sledge.

"Well, how now?" asked Vasili Andreevich.

"Why, I am quite worn out and the horse won't go."

"Then what's to be done?"

"Why, wait a minute."

Nikita went away again but soon returned.

"Follow me!" he said, going in front of the horse.

Vasili Andreevich no longer gave orders but implicitly did what Nikita told him.

"Here, follow me!" Nikita shouted, stepping quickly to the right, and seizing the rein he led Mukhorty down towards a snow-drift.

At first the horse held back, then he jerked forward, hoping to leap the drift, but he had not the strength and sank into it up to his collar.

"Get out!" Nikita called to Vasili Andreevich who still sat in the sledge, and taking hold of one shaft he moved the sledge closer to the horse. "It's hard, brother!" he said to Mukhorty, "but it can't be helped. Make an effort! Now, now, just a little one!" he shouted.

The horse gave a tug, then another, but failed to clear himself and settled down again as if considering something.

"Now, brother, this won't do!" Nikita admonished him. "Now once more!"

Again Nikita tugged at the shaft on his side, and Vasili Andreevich did the same on the other.

Mukhorty lifted his head and then gave a sudden jerk.

"That's it! That's it!" cried Nikita. "Don't be afraid - you won't sink!"

One plunge, another, and a third, and at last Mukhorty was out of the snow- drift, and stood still, breathing heavily and shaking the snow off himself. Nikita wished to lead him farther, but Vasili Andreevich, in his two fur coats, was so out of breath that he could not walk farther and dropped into the sledge.

"Let me get my breath!" he said, unfastening the kerchief with which he had tied the collar of his fur coat at the village.

"It's all right here. You lie there," said Nikita. "I will lead him along." And with Vasili Andreevich in the sledge he led the horse by the bridle about ten paces down and then up a slight rise, and stopped.

The place where Nikita had stopped was not completely in the hollow where the snow sweeping down from the hillocks might have buried them altogether, but still it was partly sheltered from the wind by the side of the ravine. There were moments when the wind seemed to abate a little, but that did not last long and as if to make up for that respite the storm swept down with tenfold vigour and tore and whirled the more fiercely. Such a gust struck them at the moment when Vasili Andreevich, having recovered his breath, got out of the sledge and went up to Nikita to consult him as to what they should do. They both bent down involuntarily and waited till the violence of the squall should have passed. Mukhorty too laid back his ears and shook his head discontentedly. As soon as the violence of the blast had abated a little, Nikita took off his mittens, stuck them into his belt, breathed onto his hands, and began to undo the straps of the shaft-bow.

"What's that you are doing there?" asked Vasili Andreevich.

"Unharnessing. What else is there to do? I have no strength left," said Nikita as though excusing himself.

"Can't we drive somewhere?"

"No we can't. We shall only kill the horse. Why, the poor beast is not himself now," said Nikita, pointing to the horse, which was standing submissively waiting for what might come, with his steep wet sides heaving heavily. "We shall have to stay the night here," he said, as if preparing to spend the night at an inn, and he proceeded to unfasten the collar-straps. The buckles came undone.

"But shan't we be frozen?" remarked Vasili Andreevich.

"Well, if we are we can't help it," said Nikita.

VI

Although Vasili Andreevich felt quite warm in his two fur coats, especially after struggling in the snow-drift, a cold shiver ran down his back on realizing that he must really spend the night where they were. To calm himself he sat down in the sledge and got out his cigarettes and matches.

Nikita meanwhile unharnessed Mukhorty. He unstrapped the belly-band and the back-band, took away the reins, loosened the collar-strap, and removed the shaft-bow, talking to him all the time to encourage him.

"Now come out! come out!" he said, leading him clear of the shafts. "Now we'll tie you up here and I'll put down some straw and take off your bridle. When you've had a bite you'll feel more cheerful."

But Mukhorty was restless and evidently not comforted by Nikita's remarks. He stepped now on one foot and now on another, and pressed close against the sledge, turning his back to the wind and rubbing his head on Nikita's sleeve. Then, as if not to pain Nikita by refusing his offer of the straw he put before him, he hurriedly snatched a wisp out of the sledge, but immediately decided that it was now no time to think of straw and threw it down, and the wind instantly scattered it, carried it away and covered it with snow.

"Now we will set up a signal," said Nikita, and turning the front of the sledge to the wind he tied the shafts together with a strap and set them up on end in front of the sledge. "There now, when the snow covers us up, good folk will see the shafts and dig us out," he said slapping his mittens together and putting them on. "That's what the old folk taught us!"

Vasili Andreevich meanwhile had unfastened his coat, and holding its skirts up for shelter, struck one sulphur match after another on the steel box. But his hands trembled, and one match after another either did not kindle or was blown out by the wind just as he was lifting it to the cigarette. At last a match did burn up, and its flame lit up for a moment the fur of his coat, his hand with the gold ring on the bent forefinger, and the snow-sprinkled oat-strap that stuck out from under the drugget. The cigarette lighted, he eagerly took a whiff or two, inhaled the smoke, let it out through his moustache, and would have inhaled again, but the wind tore off the burning tobacco and whirled it away as it had done the straw.

But even these few puffs had cheered him.

"If we must spend the night here, we must!" he said with decision. "Wait a bit, I'll arrange a flag as well," he added, picking up the kerchief which he had thrown down in the sledge after taking it from round his collar, and drawing off his gloves and standing up on the front of the sledge and stretching himself to reach the strap, he tied the kerchief to it with a tight knot.

The kerchief immediately began to flutter wildly, now clinging round the shaft, now suddenly streaming out, stretching and flapping.

"Just see what a fine flat!" said Vasili Andreevich, admiring his handiwork and letting himself down into the sledge. "We should be warmer together, but there's not enough room for two," he added.

"I'll find a place," said Nikita. "But I must cover up the horse first - he sweated so, poor thing. Let go!" he added, drawing the drugged from under Vasili Andreevich.

Having got the drugged he folded it in two, and after taking off the breechband and pad, covered Mukhorty with it.

"Anyhow it will be warmer, silly!" he said, putting back the breechband and the pad on the horse over the drugget. Then having finished that business he returned to the sledge, and addressing Vasili Andreevich, said: "You won't need the sackcloth, will you? And let me have some straw."

And having taken these things from under Vasili Andreevich, Nikita went behind the sledge, dug out a hole for himself in the snow, put straw into it, wrapped his coat well round him, covered himself with the sackcloth, and pulling his cap well down seated himself on the straw he had spread, and leant against the wooden back of the sledge to shelter himself from the wind and the snow.

Vasili Andreevich shook his head disapprovingly at what Nikita was doing, as in general he disapproved of the peasant's stupidity and lack of education, and he began to settle himself down for the night.

He smoothed the remaining straw over the bottom of the sledge, putting more if it under his side. Then he thrust his hands into his sleeves and settled down, sheltering his head in the corner of the sledge from the wind in front.

He did not wish to sleep. He lay and thought: thought ever of the one thing that constituted the sole aim, meaning, pleasure, and pride of his life - of how much money he had made and might still make, of how much other people he knew had made and possessed, and of how those others had made and were making it, and how he, like them, might still make much more. The purchase of the Goryachkin grove was a matter of immense importance to him. By that one deal he hoped to make perhaps ten thousand rubles. He began mentally to reckon the value of the wood he had inspected in autumn, and on five acres of which he had counted all the trees.

"The oaks will go for sledge-runners. The undergrowth will take care of itself, and there'll still be some thirty sazheens of firewood left on each desyatin," said he to himself. "That means there will be at least two hundred and twenty-five rubles' worth left on each desyatin. Fifty-six desyatins means fifty-six hundred, and fifty-six hundreds, and fifty-six tens, and another fifty-six tens, and then fifty-six fives..." He saw that it came out to more than twelve thousand rubles, but could not reckon it up exactly without a counting-frame. "But I won't give ten thousand, anyhow. I'll give about eight thousand with a deduction on account of the glades. I'll grease the surveyor's palm - give him a hundred rubles, or a hundred and fifty, and he'll reckon that there are some five desyatins of glade to be deducted. And he'll let it go for eight thousand. Three thousand cash down. That'll move him, no fear!" he thought, and he pressed his pocket-book with his forearm.

"God only knows how we missed the turning. The forest ought to be there, and a watchman's hut, and dogs barking. But the damned things don't bark when they're wanted." He turned his collar down from his ear and listened, but as before only the whistling of the wind could be heard, the flapping and fluttering of the kerchief tied to the shafts, and the pelting of the snow against the woodwork of the sledge. He again covered up his ear.

"If I had known I would have stayed the night. Well, no matter, we'll get there to-morrow. It's only one day lost. And the others won't travel in such weather." Then he remembered that on the 9th he had to receive payment from but butcher for his oxen. "He meant to come himself, but he won't find me, and my wife won't know how to receive the money.

She doesn't know the right way of doing things," he thought, recalling how at their party the day before she had not known how to treat the police-officer who was their guest. "Of course she's only a woman! Where could she have seen anything? In my father's time what was our house like? Just a rich peasant's house: just an oatmill and an inn - that was the whole property. But what have I done in these fifteen years? A shop, two taverns, a flour-mill, a grain-store, two farms leased out, and a house with an iron-roofed barn," he thought proudly. "Not as it was in Father's time! Who is talked of in the whole district now? Brekhunov! And why? Because I stick to business. I take trouble, not like others who lie abed or waste their time on foolishness while I don't sleep of nights. Blizzard or no blizzard I start out. So business gets done. They think money-making is a joke. No, take pains and rack your brains! You get overtaken out of doors at night, like this, or keep awake night after night till the thoughts whirling in your head make the pillow turn," he meditated with pride. "They think people get on through luck. After all, the Moronovs are now millionaires. And why? Take pains and God gives. If only He grants me health!"

The thought that he might himself be a millionaire like Mironov, who began with nothing, so excited Vasili Andreevich that he felt the need of talking to somebody. But there was no one to talk to... If only he could have reached Goryachkin he would have talked to the landlord and shown him a thing or two.

"Just see how it blows! It will snow us up so deep that we shan't be able to get out in the morning!" he thought, listening to a gust of wind that blew against the front of the sledge, bending it and lashing the snow against it. He raised himself and looked round. All he could see through the whirling darkness of Mukhorty's dark head, his back covered by the fluttering drugget, and his thick knotted tail; while all round, in front and behind, was the same fluctuating white darkness, sometimes seeming to get a little lighter and sometimes growing denser still.

"A pity I listened to Nikita," he thought. "We ought to have driven on. We should have come out somewhere, if only back to Grishkino and stayed the night at Taras's. As it is we must sit here all night. But what was I thinking about? Yes, that God gives to those who take trouble, but not to loafers, lie- abeds, or fools. I must have a smoke!"

He sat down again, got out his cigarette-case, and stretched himself flat on his stomach, screening the matches with the skirt of his coat. But the wind found its way in and put out match after match. At last he got one to burn and lit a cigarette. He was very glad that he had managed to do what he wanted, and though the wind smoked more of the cigarette than he did, he still got two or three puffs and felt more cheerful. He again leant back, wrapped himself up, started reflecting and remembering, and suddenly and quite unexpectedly lost consciousness and fell asleep.

Suddenly something seemed to give him a push and awoke him. Whether it was Mukhorty who had pulled some straw from under him, or whether something within him had startled him, at all events it woke him, and his heart began to beat faster and faster so that the sledge seemed to tremble under him. He opened his eyes. Everything around him was just as before. "It looks lighter," he thought. "I expect it won't be long before dawn." But he at once remembered that it was lighter because the moon had risen. He sat up and looked first at the horse. Mukhorty still stood with his back to the wind, shivering all over. One side of the drugget, which was completely covered with snow, had been blown back, the breeching had slipped down and the snow-covered head with its waving forelock and mane were now more visible. Vasili Andreevich leant over the back of the sledge and looked behind. Nikita still sat in the same position in which he had settled himself. The sacking with which he was covered, and his legs, were thickly covered with snow.

"If only that peasant doesn't freeze to death! His clothes are so wretched. I may be held responsible for him. What shiftless people they are - such a want of education," thought Vasili Andreevich, and he felt like taking the drugget off the horse and putting it over Nikita, but it would be very cold to get out and move about and, moreover, the horse might freeze to death. "Why did I bring him with me? It was all her stupidity!" he thought, recalling his unloved wife, and he rolled over into his old place at the front part of the sledge. "My uncle once spent a whole night like this," he reflected, "and was all right." But another case came at once to his mind. "But when they dug Sebastian out he was dead - stiff like a frozen carcass. If I'd only stopped the night in Grishkino all this would not have happened!"

And wrapping his coat carefully round him so that none of the warmth of the fur should be wasted but should warm him all over, neck, knees, and feet, he shut his eyes and tried to sleep again. But try as he would he could not get drowsy, on the contrary he felt wide awake and animated. Again he began counting his gains and the debts due to him, again he began bragging to himself and feeling pleased with himself and his position, but all this was continually disturbed by a stealthily approaching fear and by the unpleasant regret that he had not remained in Grishkino.

"How different it would be to be lying warm on a bench!" He turned over several times in his attempts to get into a more comfortable position more sheltered from the wind, he wrapped up his legs closer, shut his eyes, and lay still. But either his legs in their strong felt boots began to ache from being bent in one position, or the wind blew in somewhere, and after lying still for a short time he again began to recall the disturbing fact that he might now have been lying quietly in the warm hut at Grishkino. He again sat up, turned about, muffled himself up, and settled down once more.

Once he fancied that he heard a distant cock-crow. He felt glad, turned down his coat-collar and listened with strained attention, but in spite of all his efforts nothing could be heard but the wind whistling between the shafts, the flapping of the kerchief, and the snow pelting against the frame of the sledge.

Nikita sat just as he had done all the time, not moving and not even answering Vasili Andreevich who had addressed him a couple of times. "He doesn't care a bit - he's probably asleep!" thought Vasili Andreevich with vexation, looking behind the sledge at Nikita who was covered with a thick layer of snow.

Vasili Andreevich got up and lay down again some twenty times. It seemed to him that the night would never end. "It must be getting near morning," he thought, getting up and looking around. "Let's have a look at my watch. It will be cold to unbutton, but if I only know that it's getting near morning I shall at any rate feel more cheerful. We could begin harnessing."

In the depth of his heart Vasili Andreevich knew that it could not yet be near morning, but he was growing more and more afraid, and wished both to get to know and yet to deceive himself. He carefully undid the fastening of his sheepskin, pushed in his hand, and felt about for a long time before he got to his waistcoat. With great difficulty he managed to draw out his silver watch with its enameled flower design, and tried to make out the time. He could not see anything without a light. Again he went down on his knees and elbows as he had done when he lighted a cigarette, got out his matches, and proceeded to strike one. This time he went to work more carefully, and feeling with his fingers for a match with the largest head and the greatest amount of phosphorus, lit it at the first try. Bringing the face of the watch under the light he could hardly believe his eyes... It was only ten minutes past twelve. Almost the whole night was still before him.

"Oh, how long the night is!" he thought, feeling a cold shudder run down his back, and having fastened his fur coat again and wrapped himself up, he snuggled into a corner of the sledge intending to wait patiently. Suddenly, above the monotonous roar of the wind, he clearly distinguished another new and living sound. It steadily strengthened, and having become quite clear diminished just as gradually. Beyond all doubt it was a wolf, and he was so near that the movement of his jaws as he changed his cry was brought down the wind. Vasili Andreevich turned back the collar of his coat and listened attentively. Mukhorty too strained to listen, moving his ears, and when the wolf had ceased its howling he shifted from foot to foot and gave a warning snort. After this Vasili Andreevich could not fall asleep again or even calm himself. The more he tried to think of his accounts, his business, his reputation, his worth and his wealth, the more and more was he mastered by fear, and regrets that he had not stayed the night at Grishkino dominated and mingled in all his thoughts.

"Devil take the forest! Things were all right without it, thank God. Ah, if we had only put up for the night!" he said to himself. "They say it's drunkards that freeze," he thought, "and I have had some drink." And observing his sensations he noticed that he was beginning to shiver, without knowing whether it was from cold or from fear. He tried to wrap himself up and lie down as before, but could no longer do so. He could not stay in one position. He wanted to get up, to do something to master the gathering fear that was rising in him and against which he felt himself powerless. He again got out his cigarettes and matches, but only three matches were left and they were bad ones. The phosphorus rubbed off them all without lighting.

"The devil take you! Damned thing! Curse you!" he muttered, not knowing whom or what he was cursing, and he flung away the crushed cigarette. He was about to throw away the matchbox too, but checked the movement of his hand and put the box in his pocket instead. He was seized with such unrest that he could no longer remain in one spot. He climbed out of the sledge and standing with his back to the wind began to shift his belt again, fastening it lower down in the waist and tightening it.

"What's the use of lying and waiting for death? Better mount the horse and get away!" The thought suddenly occurred to him. "The horse will move when he has someone on his back. As for him," he thought of Nikita - "it's all the same to him whether he lives or dies. What is his life worth? He won't grudge his life, but I have something to live for, thank God."

He untied the horse, threw the reins over his neck and tried to mount, but his coats and boots were so heavy that he failed. Then he clambered up in the sledge and tried to mount from there, but the sledge tilted under his weight, and he failed again. At last he drew Mukhorty nearer to the sledge, cautiously balanced on one side of it, and managed to lie on his stomach across the horse's back. After lying like that for a while he shifted forward once and again, threw a leg over, and finally seated himself, supporting his feet on the loose breeching straps. The shaking of the sledge awoke Nikita. He raised himself, and it seemed to Vasili Andreevich that he said something.

"Listen to such fools as you! Am I to die like this for nothing?" exclaimed Vasili Andreevich. And tucking the loose skirts of his fur coat in under his knees, he turned the horse and rode away from the sledge in the direction in which he thought the forest and the forester's hut must be.

VII

From the time he had covered himself with the sackcloth and seated himself behind the sledge, Nikita had not stirred. Like all those who live in touch with nature and have known want, he was patient and could wait for hours, even days, without growing restless or irritable. He heard his master call him, but did not answer because he did not want to move or talk. Though he still felt some warmth from the tea he had drunk and from his energetic struggle when clambering about in the snowdrift, he knew that this warmth would not last long and that he had no strength left to warm himself again by moving about, for he felt as tired as a horse when it stops and refuses to go further in spite of the whip, and its master sees that it must be fed before it can work again. The foot in the boot with a hole in it had already grown numb, and he could no longer feel his big toe. Besides that, his whole body began to feel colder and colder.

The thought that he might, and very probably would, die that night occurred to him, but did not seem particularly unpleasant or dreadful. It did not seem particularly unpleasant, because his whole life had been not a continual holiday, but on the contrary an unceasing round of toil of which he was beginning to feel weary. And it did not seem particularly dreadful, because besides the masters he had served here, like Vasili Andreevich, he always felt himself dependent on the Chief master, who had sent him into this life, and he knew that when dying he would still be in that Master's power and would not be ill-used by Him. "It seems a pity to give up what one is used to and accustomed to. But there's nothing to be done, I shall get used to the new things."

"Sins?" he thought, and remembered his drunkenness, the money that had gone on drink, how he had offended his wife, his cursing, his neglect of church and of the fasts, and all the things the priest blamed him for at confession. "Of course they are sins. But then, did I take them on of myself? That's evidently how God made me. Well, and the sins? Where am I to escape to?"

So at first he thought of what might happen to him that night, and then did not return such thoughts but gave himself up to whatever recollections came into his head of themselves. Now he thought of Martha's arrival, of the drunkenness among the workers and his own renunciation of drink, then of their present journey and of Taras's house and the talk about the breaking-up of the family, then of his own lad, and of Mukhorty now sheltered under the drugget, and then of his master who made the sledge creak as he tossed about in it. "I expect you're sorry yourself that you started out, dear man," he thought. "It would seem hard to leave a life such as his! It's not like the likes of us."

Then all these recollections began to grow confused and got mixed in his head, and he fell asleep.

But when Vasili Andreevich, getting on the horse, jerked the sledge, against the back of which Nikita was leaning, and it shifted away and hit him in the back with one of its runners, he awoke and had to change his position whether he liked it or not. Straightening his legs with difficulty and shaking the snow off them he got up, and an agonizing cold immediately penetrated his whole body. On making out what was happening he called to Vasili Andreevich to leave him the drugget which the horse no longer needed, so that he might wrap himself in it.

But Vasili Andreevich did not stop, but disappeared amid the powdery snow.

Left alone, Nikita considered for a moment what he should do. He felt that he had not the strength to go off in search of a house. It was no longer possible to sit down in his old place - it was now all filled with snow. He felt that he could not get warmer in the sledge either, for there was nothing to cover himself with, and his coat and sheepskin no longer warmed him at all. He felt as cold as though he had nothing on but a shirt. He became frightened. "Lord, heavenly Father!" he muttered, and was comforted by the consciousness that he was not alone but that there was One who heard him and would not abandon him. He gave a deep sigh, and keeping the sackcloth over his head he got inside the sledge and lay down in the place where his master had been.

But he could not get warm in the sledge either. At first he shivered all over, then the shivering ceased and little by little he began to lose consciousness. He did not know whether he was dying or falling asleep, but felt equally prepared for the one as for the other.

VIII

Meanwhile Vasili Andreevich, with his feet and the ends of the reins, urged the horse on in the direction in which for some reason he expected the forest and forester's hut to be. The snow covered his eyes and the wind seemed intent on stopping him, but bending forward and constantly lapping his coat over and pushing it between himself and the cold harness pad which prevented him from sitting properly, he kept urging the horse on. Mukhorty ambled on obediently though with difficulty, in the direction in which he was driven.

Vasili Andreevich rode for about five minutes straight ahead, as he thought, seeing nothing but the horse's head and the white waste, and hearing only the whistle of the wind about the horse's ears and his coat collar.

Suddenly a dark patch showed up in front of him. His heart beat with joy, and he rode towards the object, already seeing in imagination the walls of village houses. But the dark patch was not stationary, it kept moving; and it was not a village but some tall stalks of wormwood sticking up through the snow on the boundary between two fields, and desperately tossing about under the pressure of the wind which beat it all to one side and whistled through it. The sight of that wormwood tormented by the pitiless wind made Vasili Andreevich shudder, he knew not why, and he hurriedly began urging the horse on, not noticing that when riding up to the wormwood he had quite changed his direction and was now heading the opposite way, thought still imagining that he was riding towards where the hut should be. But the horse kept making towards the right, and Vasili Andreevich kept guiding it to the left.

Again something dark appeared in front of him. Again he rejoiced, convinced that now it was certainly a village. But once more it was the same boundary line overgrown with wormwood, once more the same wormwood desperately tossed by the wind and carrying unreasoning terror to his heart. But its being the same wormwood was not all, for beside it there was a horse's track partly snowed over. Vasili Andreevich stopped, stooped down and looked carefully. It was a horse-track only partially covered with snow, and could be none but his own horse's hoofprints. He had evidently gone round in a small circle. "I shall perish like that!" he thought, and not to give way to his terror he urged on the horse still move, peering into the snowy darkness in which he saw only flitting and fitful points of light. Once he thought he heard the barking of dogs or the howling of wolves but the sounds were so faint and indistinct that he did not know whether he heard them or merely imagined them, and he stopped and began to listen intently.

Suddenly some terrible, deafening cry resounded near his ears, and everything shivered and shook under him. He seized Mukhorty's neck, but that too was shaking all over and the terrible cry grew still more frightful. For some seconds Vasili Andreevich could not collect himself or understand what was happening. It was only that Mukhorty, whether to encourage himself or to call for help, had neighed loudly and resonantly. "Ugh, you wretch! How you frightened me, damn you!" thought Vasili Andreevich. But even when he understood the cause of his terror he could not shake it off.

"I must calm myself and think things over," he said to himself, but yet he could not stop and continued to urge the horse on, without noticing that he was now going with the wind instead of against it. His body, especially between his legs where it touched the gad of the harness and was not covered by his overcoats, was getting painfully cold, especially when the horse walked slowly. His legs and arms trembled and his breathing came fast. He saw himself perishing amid this dreadful snowy waste, and could see no means of escape.

Suddenly the horse under him tumbled into something and, sinking into a snow-drift, began to plunge and fell on his side. Vasili Andreevich jumped off, the horse struggled to his feet, plunged forward, gave one leap and another, neighed again, and dragging the drugget and the breechband after him, disappeared, leaving Vasili Andreevich alone on the snowdrift.

The latter pressed on after the horse, but the snow lay so deep and his coats were so heavy that, sinking above his knees at each step, he stopped breathless after taking not more than twenty steps. "The copse, the oxen, the leasehold, the shop, the tavern, the house with the iron-roofed barn, and my heir," thought he. "How can I leave all that? What does this mean? It cannot be!" These thoughts flashed through his mind. Then he thought of the wormwood tossed by the wind, which he had twice ridden past, and he was seized with such terror that he did not believe in the reality of what was happening to him. "Can this be a dream?" he thought, and tried to wake up but could not. It was real snow that lashed his face and covered him and chilled his right hand from which he had lost the glove, and this was a real desert in which he was now left alone like that wormwood, awaiting an inevitable, speedy, and meaningless death.

"Queen of Heaven! Holy Father Nicholas, teacher of temperance!" he thought, recalling the service of the day before and the holy icon with its black face and gilt frame and the tapers which he sold to be set before that icon which were almost immediately brought back to him scarcely burnt at all, and which he put away in the storechest. He began to pray to that same Nicholas the Wonder-Worker to save him, promising him a thanksgiving service and some candles. But he clearly and indubitably realized that the icon, its frame, the candles, the pries, and the thanksgiving service, though very important and necessary in church, could do nothing for him here, and that there was and could be no connection between those candles and services and his present disastrous plight. "I must not despair," he thought. "I must follow the horse's track before it is snowed under. He will lead me out, or I may even catch him. Only I must not hurry, or I shall stick fast and be more lost than ever."

But in spite of his resolution to go quietly, he rushed forward and even ran, continually falling, getting up and falling again. The horse's track was already hardly visible in places where the snow did not lie deep. "I am lost!" thought Vasili Andreevich. I shall lose the track and not catch the horse." But at the moment he saw something black. It was Mukhorty, and not only Mukhorty, but the sledge with the shafts and the kerchief. Mukhorty, with the sacking and the breechband twisted round to one side, was standing not in his former place but nearer to the shafts, shaking his head which the reins he was stepping on drew downwards. It turned out that Vasili Andreevich had sunk in the same ravine Nikita had previously fallen into, and that Mukhorty was bringing him back to the sledge and he had got off his back no more than fifty paces from where the sledge was.

IX

Having stumbled back to the sledge Vasili Andreevich caught hold of it and for a long time stood motionless, trying to calm himself and recover his breath. Nikita was not in his former place, but something, already covered with snow, was lying in the sledge and Vasili Andreevich concluded that this was Nikita. His terror had now quite left him, and if he felt any fear it was lest the dreadful terror should return that he had experienced when on the horse and especially when he was left alone in the snowdrift. At any cost he had to avoid that terror, and to keep it away he must do something - occupy himself with something. And the first thing he did was to turn his back to the wind and open his fur coat. Then, as soon as he recovered his breath a little, he shook the snow out of his boots and out of his left-hand glove (the right-hand glove was hopelessly lost and by this time probably lying somewhere under a dozen inches of snow); then as was his custom when going out of his shop to buy grain from the peasants, he pulled his girdle low down and tightened it and prepared for action. The first thing that occurred to him was to free Mukhorty's leg from the rein. Having done that, and tethered him to the iron cramp at the front of the sledge where he had been before, he was going round the horse's quarters to put the breechband and pad straight and cover him with the cloth, but at that moment he noticed that something was moving in the sledge and Nikita's head rose up out of the snow that covered it. Nikita, who was half frozen, rose with great difficulty and sat up, moving his hand before his nose in a strange manner just as if he were driving away flies. He waved his hand and said something, and seemed to Vasili Andreevich to be calling him. Vasili Andreevich left the cloth unadjusted and went up to the sledge.

"What is it?" he asked. "What are you saying?"

"I'm dy...ing , that's what," said Nikita brokenly and with difficulty. "Give what is owing to me to my lad, or to my wife, no matter."

"Why, are you really frozen?" asked Vasili Andreevich.

"I feel it's my death. Forgive me for Christ's sake..." said Nikita in a tearful voice, continuing to wave his hand before his face as if driving away flies.

Vasili Andreevich stood silent and motionless for half a minute. Then suddenly, with the same resolution with which he used to strike hands when making a good purchase, he took a step back and turning up his sleeves began raking the snow off Nikita and out of the sledge. Having done this he hurriedly undid his girdle, opened out his fur coat, and having pushed Nikita down, law down on top of him, covering him not only with his fur coat but with the whole of his body, which glowed with warmth. After pushing the skirts of his coat between Nikita and the sides of the sledge, and holding down its hem with his knees, Vasili Andreevich lay like that face down, with his head pressed against the front of the sledge. Here he no longer heard the horse's movements or the whistling of the wind, but only Nikita's breathing. At first and for a long time Nikita lay motionless, then he sighed deeply and moved.

"There, and you say you are dying! Lie still and get warm, that's our way..." began Vasili Andreevich.

But to his great surprise he could say no more, for tears came to his eyes and his lower jaw began to quiver rapidly. He stopped speaking and only gulped down the rising in his throat. "Seems I was badly frightened and have gone quite weak," he thought. But this weakness was not only unpleasant, but gave him a peculiar joy such as he had never felt before.

"That's our way!" he said to himself, experiencing a strange and solemn tenderness. He lay like that for a long time, wiping his eyes on the fur of his coat and tucking under his knew the right skirt, which the wind kept turning up.

But he longed so passionately to tell somebody of his joyful condition that he said: "Nikita!"

"It's comfortable, warm!" came a voice from beneath.

"There, you see, friend, I was going to perish. And you would have been frozen, and I should have..."

But again his jaws began to quiver and his eyes to fill with tears, and he could say no more.

"Well, never mind," he thought. "I know about myself what I know."

He remained silent and lay like that for a long time.

Nikita kept him warm from below and his fur coats from above. Only his hands, with which he kept his coat skirts down around Nikita's sides, and his legs which the wind kept uncovering, began to freeze, especially his right hand which had no glove. But he did not think of his legs or of his hands but only of how to warm the peasant who was lying under him. He looked out several times at Mukhorty and could see that his back was uncovered and the drugget and breeching lying on the snow, and that he ought to get up and cover him, but he could not bring himself to leave Nikita and disturb even for a moment the joyous condition he was in. He no longer felt any kind of terror.

"No fear, we shan't lose him this time!" he said to himself, referring to his getting the peasant warm with the same boastfulness with which he spoke of his buying and selling.

Vasili Andreevich lay in that way for one hour, another, and a third, but he was unconscious of the passage of time. At first impressions of the snow- storm, the sledge-shafts, and the horse with the shaft-bow shaking before his eyes, kept passing through his mind, then he remembered Nikita lying under him, then recollections of the festival, his wife, the police-officer, and the box of candles, began to mingle with these; then again Nikita, this time lying under that box, then the peasants, customers and traders, and the white walls of his house with its iron roof with Nikita lying underneath, presented themselves to his imagination. After wards all these impressions blended into one nothingness. As the colours of the rainbow unite into one white light, so all these different impressions mingled into one, and he fell asleep.

For a long time he slept without dreaming, but just before dawn the visions recommenced. It seemed to him that he was standing by the box of tapers and that Tikhon's wife was asking for a five-kopek taper for the Church fete. He wished to take one out and give it to her, but his hands would not lift, being held tight in his pockets. He wanted to walk round the box but his feet would not move and his new clean galoshes had grown to the stone floor, and he could neither lift them nor get his feet out of the galoshes. Then the taper-box was no longer a box but a bed, and suddenly Vasili Andreevich saw himself lying in his bed at home. He was lying in his bed and could not get up. Yet it was necessary for him to get up because Ivan Matveich, the police-officer, would soon call for him and he had to go with him - either to bargain for the forest or to put Mukhorty's breeching straight.

He asked his wife: "Nikolaevna, hasn't he come yet?" "No, he hasn't," she replied. He heard someone drive up to the front steps. "It must be him," "No, he's gone past." "Nikolaevna! I say Nikolaevna, isn't he here yet?" "No." He was still lying on his bed and could not get up, but was always waiting. And this waiting was uncanny and yet joyful. Then suddenly his joy was completed. He whom he was expecting came; not Ivan Matveich the police-officer, but someone else - yet it was he whom he had been waiting for. He came and called him; and it was he who had called him and told him to lie down on Nikita. And Vasili Andreevich was glad that one had come for him.

"I'm coming!" he cried joyfully, and that cry awoke him, but woke him up not at all the same person he had been when he fell asleep. He tried to get up but could not, tried to move his arm and could not, to move his leg and also could not, to turn his head and could not. He was surprised but not at all disturbed by this. He understood that this was death, and was not at all disturbed by that either. He remembered that Nikita was lying under him and that he had got warm and was alive, and it seemed to him that he was Nikita and Nikita was he, and that his life was not in himself but in Nikita. He strained his ears and heard Nikita breathing and even slightly snoring. "Nikita is alive, so I too am alive!" he said to himself triumphantly.

And he remembered his money, his shop, his house, the buying and selling, and Mironov's millions, and it was hard for him to understand why that man, called Vasili Brekhunov, had troubled himself with all those things with which he had been troubled.

"Well, it was because he did not know what the real thing was," he thought, concerning that Vasili Brekhunov. "He did not know, but now I know and know for sure. Now I know!" And again he heard the voice of the one who had called him before. "I'm coming! Coming!" he responded gladly, and his whole being was filled with joyful emotion. He felt himself free and that nothing could hold him back any longer.

After that Vasili Andreevich neither saw, heard, nor felt anything more in this world.

All around the snow still eddied. The same whirlwinds of snow circled about, covering the dead Vasili Andreevich's fur coat, the shivering Mukhorty, the sledge, now scarcely to be seen, and Nikita lying at the bottom of it, kept warm beneath his dead master.

X

Nikita awoke before daybreak. He was aroused by the cold that had begun to creep down his back. He had dreamt that he was coming from the mill with a load of his master's flour and when crossing the stream had missed the bridge and let the cart get stuck. And he saw that he had crawled under the cart and was trying to lift it by arching his back. But strange to say the cart did not move, it stuck to his back and he could neither lift it nor get out from under it. It was crushing the whole of his loins. And how cold it felt! Evidently he must crawl out. "Have done!" he exclaimed to whoever was pressing the cart down on him. "Take out the sacks!" But the cart pressed down colder and colder, and then he heard a strange knocking, awoke completely, and remembered everything. The cold cart was his dead and frozen master lying upon him. And the knock was produced by Mukhorty, who had twice struck the sledge with his hoof.

"Andreevich! Eh, Andreevich!" Nikita called cautiously, beginning to realize the truth, and straightening his back. But Vasili Andreevich did not answer and his stomach and legs were stiff and cold and heavy like iron weights.

"He must have died! May the Kingdom of Heaven be his!" thought Nikita.

He turned his head, dug with his hand through the snow about him and opened his eyes. It was daylight; the wind was whistling as before between the shafts, and the snow was falling in the same way, except that it was no longer driving against the frame of the sledge but silently covered both sledge and horse deeper and deeper, and neither the horse's movements nor his breathing were any longer to be heard.

"He must have frozen too," thought Nikita of Mukhorty, and indeed those hoof knocks against the sledge, which had awakened Nikita, were the last efforts the already numbed Mukhorty had made to keep on his feet before dying.

"O Lord God, it seems Thou are calling me too!" said Nikita. "Thy Holy Will be done. But it's uncanny... Still, a man can't die twice and must die once. If only it would come soon!"

And he again drew in his head, closed his eyes, and became unconscious, fully convinced that now he was certainly and finally dying.

It was not till noon that day that peasants dug Vasili Andreevich and Nikita out of the snow with their shovels, not more than seventy yards from the road and less than half a mile from the village.

The snow had hidden the sledge, but the shafts and the kerchief tied to them were still visible. Mukhorty, buried up to his belly in snow, with the breeching and drugget hanging down, stood all white, his dead head pressed against his frozen throat; icicles hung from his nostrils, his eyes were covered with hoar-frost as though filled with tears, and he had grown so thin in that one night that he was nothing but skin and bone.

Vasili Andreevich was stiff as a frozen carcass, and when they rolled him off Nikita his legs remained apart and his arms stretched out as they had been. His bulging hawk eyes were frozen, and his open mouth under his clipped moustache was full of snow. But Nikita though chilled through was still alive. When he had been brought to, he felt sure that he was already dead and that what was taking place with him was no longer happening in this world but in the next. When he heard the peasants shouting as they dug him out and rolled the frozen body of Vasili Andreevich from off him, he was at first surprised that in the other world peasants should be shouting in the same old way and had the same kind of body, and then when he realized that he was still in this world he was sorry rather than glad, especially when he found that the toes on both his feet were frozen.

Nikita lay in hospital for two months. They cut off three of his toes, but the others recovered so that he was still able to work and went on living for another twenty years, first as a farm-labourer, then in his old age as a watchman. He died at home as he had wished, only this year, under the icons with a lighted taper in his hands. Before he died he asked his wife's forgiveness and forgave her for the cooper. He also took leave of his son and grandchildren, and died sincerely glad that he was relieving his son and daughter-in-law of the burden of having to feed him, and that he was now really passing from this life of which he was weary into that other life which every year and every hour grew clearer and more desirable to him. Whether he is better or worse off there where he awoke after his death, whether he was disappointed or found there what he expected, we shall all soon learn.

ALYOSHA THE POT

Alyosha was the younger brother. He was called the Pot, because his mother had once sent him with a pot of milk to the deacon's wife, and he had stumbled against something and broken it. His mother had beaten him, and the children had teased him. Since then he was nicknamed the Pot. Alyosha was a tiny, thin little fellow, with ears like wings, and a huge nose. "Alyosha has a nose that looks like a dog on a hill!" the children used to call after him. Alyosha went to the village school, but was not good at lessons; besides, there was so little time to learn. His elder brother was in town, working for a merchant, so Alyosha had to help his father from a very early age. When he was no more than six he used to go out with the girls to watch the cows and sheep in the pasture, and a little later he looked after the horses by day and by night. And at twelve years of age he had already begun to plough and to drive the cart. The skill was there though the strength was not. He was always cheerful. Whenever the children made fun of him, he would either laugh or be silent. When his father scolded him he would stand mute and listen attentively, and as soon as the scolding was over would smile and go on with his work. Alyosha was nineteen when his brother was taken as a soldier. So his father placed him with the merchant as a yard-porter. He was given his brother's old boots, his father's old coat and cap, and was taken to town. Alyosha was delighted with his clothes, but the merchant was not impressed by his appearance.

"I thought you would bring me a man in Simeon's place," he said, scanning Alyosha; "and you've brought me THIS! What's the good of him?"

"He can do everything; look after horses and drive. He's a good one to work. He looks rather thin, but he's tough enough. And he's very willing."

"He looks it. All right; we'll see what we can do with him."

So Alyosha remained at the merchant's.

The family was not a large one. It consisted of the merchant's wife: her old mother: a married son poorly educated who was in his father's business: another son, a learned one who had finished school and entered the University, but having been expelled, was living at home: and a daughter who still went to school.

They did not take to Alyosha at first. He was uncouth, badly dressed, and had no manner, but they soon got used to him. Alyosha worked even better than his brother had done; he was really very willing. They sent him on all sorts of errands, but he did everything quickly and readily, going from one task to another without stopping. And so here, just as at home, all the work was put upon his shoulders. The more he did, the more he was given to do. His mistress, her old mother, the son, the daughter, the clerk, and the cook - all ordered him about, and sent him from one place to another.

"Alyosha, do this! Alyosha, do that! What! have you forgotten, Alyosha? Mind you don't forget, Alyosha!" was heard from morning till night. And Alyosha ran here, looked after this and that, forgot nothing, found time for everything, and was always cheerful.

His brother's old boots were soon worn out, and his master scolded him for going about in tatters with his toes sticking out. He ordered another pair to be bought for him in the market. Alyosha was delighted with his new boots, but was angry with his feet when they ached at the end of the day after so much running about. And then he was afraid that his father would be annoyed when he came to town for his wages, to find that his master had deducted the cost of the boots.

In the winter Alyosha used to get up before daybreak. He would chop the wood, sweep the yard, feed the cows and horses, light the stoves, clean the boots, prepare the samovars and polish them afterwards; or the clerk would get him to bring up the goods; or the cook would set him to knead the bread and clean the saucepans. Then he was sent to town on various errands, to bring the daughter home from school, or to get some olive oil for the old mother. "Why the devil have you been so long?" first one, then another, would say to him. Why should they go? Alyosha can go. "Alyosha! Alyosha!" And Alyosha ran here and there. He breakfasted in snatches while he was working, and rarely managed to get his dinner at the proper hour. The cook used to scold him for being late, but she was sorry for him all the same, and would keep something hot for his dinner and supper.

At holiday times there was more work than ever, but Alyosha liked holidays because everybody gave him a tip. Not much certainly, but it would amount up to about sixty kopeks [1s 2d] - his very own money. For Alyosha never set eyes on his wages. His father used to come and take them from the merchant, and only scold Alyosha for wearing out his boots.

When he had saved up two roubles [4s], by the advice of the cook he bought himself a red knitted jacket, and was so happy when he put it on, that he couldn't close his mouth for joy. Alyosha was not talkative; when he spoke at all, he spoke abruptly, with his head turned away. When told to do anything, or asked if he could do it, he would say yes without the smallest hesitation, and set to work at once.

Alyosha did not know any prayer; and had forgotten what his mother had taught him. But he prayed just the same, every morning and every evening, prayed with his hands, crossing himself.

He lived like this for about a year and a half, and towards the end of the second year a most startling thing happened to him. He discovered one day, to his great surprise, that, in addition to the relation of usefulness existing between people, there was also another, a peculiar relation of quite a different character. Instead of a man being wanted to clean boots, and go on errands and harness horses, he is not wanted to be of any service at all, but another human being wants to serve him and pet him. Suddenly Alyosha felt he was such a man.

He made this discovery through the cook Ustinia. She was young, had no parents, and worked as hard as Alyosha. He felt for the first time in his life that he - not his services, but he himself - was necessary to another human being. When his mother used to be sorry for him, he had taken no notice of her. It had seemed to him quite natural, as though he were feeling sorry for himself. But here was Ustinia, a perfect stranger, and sorry for him. She would save him some hot porridge, and sit watching him, her chin propped on her bare arm, with the sleeve rolled up, while he was eating it. When he looked at her she would begin to laugh, and he would laugh too.

This was such a new, strange thing to him that it frightened Alyosha.

He feared that it might interfere with his work. But he was pleased, nevertheless, and when he glanced at the trousers that Ustinia had mended for him, he would shake his head and smile. He would often think of her while at work, or when running on errands. "A fine girl, Ustinia!" he sometimes exclaimed.

Ustinia used to help him whenever she could, and he helped her. She told him all about her life; how she had lost her parents; how her aunt had taken her in and found a place for her in the town; how the merchant's son had tried to take liberties with her, and how she had rebuffed him. She liked to talk, and Alyosha liked to listen to her. He had heard that peasants who came up to work in the towns frequently got married to servant girls. On one occasion she asked him if his parents intended marrying him soon. He said that he did not know; that he did not want to marry any of the village girls.

"Have you taken a fancy to someone, then?"

"I would marry you, if you'd be willing."

"Get along with you, Alyosha the Pot; but you've found your tongue, haven't you?" she exclaimed, slapping him on the back with a towel she held in her hand. "Why shouldn't I?"

At Shrovetide Alyosha's father came to town for his wages. It had come to the ears of the merchant's wife that Alyosha wanted to marry Ustinia, and she disapproved of it. "What will be the use of her with a baby?" she thought, and informed her husband.

The merchant gave the old man Alyosha's wages.

"How is my lad getting on?" he asked. "I told you he was willing."

"That's all right, as far as it goes, but he's taken some sort of nonsense into his head. He wants to marry our cook. Now I don't approve of married servants. We won't have them in the house."

"Well, now, who would have thought the fool would think of such a thing?" the old man exclaimed. "But don't you worry. I'll soon settle that."

He went into the kitchen, and sat down at the table waiting for his son. Alyosha was out on an errand, and came back breathless.

"I thought you had some sense in you; but what's this you've taken into your head?" his father began.

"I? Nothing."

"How, nothing? They tell me you want to get married. You shall get married when the time comes. I'll find you a decent wife, not some town hussy."

His father talked and talked, while Alyosha stood still and sighed. When his father had quite finished, Alyosha smiled.

"All right. I'll drop it."

"Now that's what I call sense."

When he was left alone with Ustinia he told her what his father had said. (She had listened at the door.)

"It's no good; it can't come off. Did you hear? He was angry - won't have it at any price."

Ustinia cried into her apron.

Alyosha shook his head.

"What's to be done? We must do as we're told."

"Well, are you going to give up that nonsense, as your father told you?" his mistress asked, as he was putting up the shutters in the evening.

"To be sure we are," Alyosha replied with a smile, and then burst into tears.

From that day Alyosha went about his work as usual, and no longer talked to Ustinia about their getting married. One day in Lent the clerk told him to clear the snow from the roof. Alyosha climbed on to the roof and swept away all the snow; and, while he was still raking out some frozen lumps from the gutter, his foot slipped and he fell over. Unfortunately he did not fall on the snow, but on a piece of iron over the door. Ustinia came running up, together with the merchant's daughter.

"Have you hurt yourself, Alyosha?"

"Ah! no, it's nothing."

But he could not raise himself when he tried to, and began to smile.

He was taken into the lodge. The doctor arrived, examined him, and asked where he felt the pain.

"I feel it all over," he said. "But it doesn't matter. I'm only afraid master will be annoyed. Father ought to be told."

Alyosha lay in bed for two days, and on the third day they sent for the priest.

"Are you really going to die?" Ustinia asked.

"Of course I am. You can't go on living for ever. You must go when the time comes." Alyosha spoke rapidly as usual. "Thank you, Ustinia. You've been very good to me. What a lucky thing they didn't let us marry! Where should we have been now? It's much better as it is."

When the priest came, he prayed with his bands and with his heart. "As it is good here when you obey and do no harm to others, so it will be there," was the thought within it.

He spoke very little; he only said he was thirsty, and he seemed full of wonder at something.

He lay in wonderment, then stretched himself, and died.

THE DEATH OF IVAN ILYCH

I

During an interval in the Melvinski trial in the large building of the Law Courts the members and public prosecutor met in Ivan Egorovich Shebek's private room, where the conversation turned on the celebrated Krasovski case. Fedor Vasilievich warmly maintained that it was not subject to their jurisdiction, Ivan Egorovich maintained the contrary, while Peter Ivanovich, not having entered into the discussion at the start, took no part in it but looked through the *Gazette* which had just been handed in.

"Gentlemen," he said, "Ivan Ilych has died!"

"You don't say so!"

"Here, read it yourself," replied Peter Ivanovich, handing Fedor Vasilievich the paper still damp from the press. Surrounded by a black border were the words: "Praskovya Fedorovna Golovina, with profound sorrow, informs relatives and friends of the demise of her beloved husband Ivan Ilych Golovin, Member of the Court of Justice, which occurred on February the 4th of this year 1882. The funeral will take place on Friday at one o'clock in the afternoon."

Ivan Ilych had been a colleague of the gentlemen present and was liked by them all. He had been ill for some weeks with an illness said to be incurable. His post had been kept open for him, but there had been conjectures that in case of his death Alexeev might receive his appointment, and that either Vinnikov or Shtabel would succeed Alexeev. So on receiving the news of Ivan Ilych's death the first thought of each of the gentlemen in that private room was of the changes and promotions it might occasion among themselves or their acquaintances.

"I shall be sure to get Shtabel's place or Vinnikov's," thought Fedor Vasilievich. "I was promised that long ago, and the promotion means an extra eight hundred rubles a year for me besides the allowance."

"Now I must apply for my brother-in-law's transfer from Kaluga," thought Peter Ivanovich. "My wife will be very glad, and then she won't be able to say that I never do anything for her relations."

"I thought he would never leave his bed again," said Peter Ivanovich aloud. "It's very sad."

"But what really was the matter with him?"

"The doctors couldn't say - at least they could, but each of them said something different. When last I saw him I thought he was getting better."

"And I haven't been to see him since the holidays. I always meant to go."

"Had he any property?"

"I think his wife had a little - but something quiet trifling."

"We shall have to go to see her, but they live so terribly far away."

"Far away from you, you mean. Everything's far away from your place."

"You see, he never can forgive my living on the other side of the river," said Peter Ivanovich, smiling at Shebek. Then, still talking of the distances between different parts of the city, they returned to the Court.

Besides considerations as to the possible transfers and promotions likely to result from Ivan Ilych's death, the mere fact of the death of a near acquaintance aroused, as usual, in all who heard of it the complacent feeling that, "it is he who is dead and not I."

Each one thought or felt, "Well, he's dead but I'm alive!" But the more intimate of Ivan Ilych's acquaintances, his so-called friends, could not help thinking also that they would now have to fulfil the very tiresome demands of propriety by attending the funeral service and paying a visit of condolence to the widow.

Fedor Vasilievich and Peter Ivanovich had been his nearest acquaintances. Peter Ivanovich had studied law with Ivan Ilych and had considered himself to be under obligations to him.

Having told his wife at dinner-time of Ivan Ilych's death, and of his conjecture that it might be possible to get her brother transferred to their circuit, Peter Ivanovich sacrificed his usual nap, put on his evening clothes and drove to Ivan Ilych's house.

At the entrance stood a carriage and two cabs. Leaning against the wall in the hall downstairs near the cloak stand was a coffin-lid covered with cloth of gold, ornamented with gold cord and tassels, that had been polished up with metal powder. Two ladies in black were taking off their fur cloaks. Peter Ivanovich recognized one of them as Ivan Ilych's sister, but the other was a stranger to him. His colleague Schwartz was just coming downstairs, but on seeing Peter Ivanovich enter he stopped and winked at him, as if to say: "Ivan Ilych has made a mess of things - not like you and me."

Schwartz's face with his Piccadilly whiskers, and his slim figure in evening dress, had as usual an air of elegant solemnity which contrasted with the playfulness of his character and had a special piquancy here, or so it seemed to Peter Ivanovich.

Peter Ivanovich allowed the ladies to precede him and slowly followed them upstairs. Schwartz did not come down but remained where he was, and Peter Ivanovich understood that he wanted to arrange where they should play bridge that evening. The ladies went upstairs to the widow's room, and Schwartz with seriously compressed lips but a playful looking his eyes, indicated by a twist of his eyebrows the room to the right where the body lay.

Peter Ivanovich, like everyone else on such occasions, entered feeling uncertain what he would have to do. All he knew was that at such times it is always safe to cross oneself. But he was not quite sure whether one should make obseisances while doing so. He therefore adopted a middle course. On entering the room he began crossing himself and made a slight movement resembling a bow. At the same time, as far as the motion of his head and arm allowed, he surveyed the room. Two young men - apparently nephews, one of whom was a high-school pupil - were leaving the room, crossing themselves as they did so. An old woman was standing motionless, and a lady with strangely arched eyebrows was saying something to her in a whisper. A vigorous, resolute Church Reader, in a frock- coat, was reading something in a loud voice with an expression that precluded any contradiction. The butler's assistant, Gerasim, stepping lightly in front of Peter Ivanovich, was strewing something on the floor. Noticing this, Peter Ivanovich was immediately aware of a faint odour of a decomposing body.

The last time he had called on Ivan Ilych, Peter Ivanovich had seen Gerasim in the study. Ivan Ilych had been particularly fond of him and he was performing the duty of a sick nurse.

Peter Ivanovich continued to make the sign of the cross slightly inclining his head in an intermediate direction between the coffin, the Reader, and the icons on the table in a corner of the room. Afterwards, when it seemed to him that this movement of his arm in crossing himself had gone on too long, he stopped and began to look at the corpse.

The dead man lay, as dead men always lie, in a specially heavy way, his rigid limbs sunk in the soft cushions of the coffin, with the head forever bowed on the pillow. His yellow waxen brow with bald patches over his sunken temples was thrust up in the way peculiar to the dead, the protruding nose seeming to press on the upper lip. He was much changed and grown even thinner since Peter Ivanovich had last seen him, but, as is always the case with the dead, his face was handsomer and above all more dignified than when he was alive. The expression on the face said that what was necessary had been accomplished, and accomplished rightly. Besides this there was in that expression a reproach and a warning to the living. This warning seemed to Peter Ivanovich out of place, or at least not applicable to him. He felt a certain discomfort and so he hurriedly crossed himself once more and turned and went out of the door - too hurriedly and too regardless of propriety, as he himself was aware.

Schwartz was waiting for him in the adjoining room with legs spread wide apart and both hands toying with his top-hat behind his back. The mere sight of that playful, well-groomed, and elegant figure refreshed Peter Ivanovich. He felt that Schwartz was above all these happenings and would not surrender to any depressing influences. His very look said that this incident of a church service for Ivan Ilych could not be a sufficient reason for infringing the order of the session - in other words, that it would certainly not prevent his unwrapping a new pack of cards and shuffling them that evening while a footman placed fresh candles on the table: in fact, that there was no reason for supposing that this incident would hinder their spending the evening agreeably. Indeed he said this in a whisper as Peter Ivanovich passed him, proposing that they should meet for a game at Fedor Vasilievich's. But apparently Peter Ivanovich was not destined to play bridge that evening. Praskovya Fedorovna (a short, fat woman who despite all efforts to the contrary had continued to broaden steadily from her shoulders downwards and who had the same extraordinarily arched eyebrows as the lady who had been standing by the coffin), dressed all in black, her head covered with lace, came out of her own room with some other ladies, conducted them to the room where the dead body lay, and said: "The service will begin immediately. Please go in."

Schwartz, making an indefinite bow, stood still, evidently neither accepting nor declining this invitation. Praskovya Fedorovna recognizing Peter Ivanovich, sighed, went close up to him, took his hand, and said: "I know you were a true friend to Ivan Ilych..." and looked at him awaiting some suitable response. And Peter Ivanovich knew that, just as it had been the right thing to cross himself in that room, so what he had to do here was to press her hand, sigh, and say, "Believe me..." So he did all this and as he did it felt that the desired result had been achieved: that both he and she were touched.

"Come with me. I want to speak to you before it begins," said the widow. "Give me your arm."

Peter Ivanovich gave her his arm and they went to the inner rooms, passing Schwartz who winked at Peter Ivanovich compassionately.

"That does for our bridge! Don't object if we find another player. Perhaps you can cut in when you do escape," said his playful look.

Peter Ivanovich sighed still more deeply and despondently, and Praskovya Fedorovna pressed his arm gratefully. When they reached the drawing-room, upholstered in pink cretonne and lighted by a dim lamp, they sat down at the table - she on a sofa and Peter Ivanovich on a low pouffe, the springs of which yielded spasmodically under his weight. Praskovya Fedorovna had been on the point of warning him to take another seat, but felt that such a warning was out of keeping with her present condition and so changed her mind. As he sat down on the pouffe Peter Ivanovich recalled how Ivan Ilych had arranged this room and had consulted him regarding this pink cretonne with green leaves. The whole room was full of furniture and knick-knacks, and on her way to the sofa the lace of the widow's black shawl caught on the edge of the table. Peter Ivanovich rose to detach it, and the springs of the pouffe, relieved of his weight, rose also and gave him a push. The widow began detaching her shawl herself, and Peter Ivanovich again sat down, suppressing the rebellious springs of the pouffe under him. But the widow had not quite freed herself and Peter Ivanovich got up again, and again the pouffe rebelled and even creaked. When this was all over she took out a clean cambric handkerchief and began to weep. The episode with the shawl and the struggle with the pouffe had cooled Peter Ivanovich's emotions and he sat there with a sullen look on his face. This awkward situation was interrupted by Sokolov, Ivan Ilych's butler, who came to report that the plot in the cemetery that Praskovya Fedorovna had chosen would cost tow hundred rubles. She stopped weeping and, looking at Peter Ivanovich with the air of a victim, remarked in French that it was very hard for her. Peter Ivanovich made a silent gesture signifying his full conviction that it must indeed be so.

"Please smoke," she said in a magnanimous yet crushed voice, and turned to discuss with Sokolov the price of the plot for the grave.

Peter Ivanovich while lighting his cigarette heard her inquiring very circumstantially into the prices of different plots in the cemetery and finally decide which she would take. When that was done she gave instructions about engaging the choir. Sokolov then left the room.

"I look after everything myself," she told Peter Ivanovich, shifting the albums that lay on the table; and noticing that the table was endangered by his cigarette-ash, she immediately passed him an ash-tray, saying as she did so: "I consider it an affectation to say that my grief prevents my attending to practical affairs. On the contrary, if anything can - I won't say console me, but - distract me, it is seeing to everything concerning him." She again took out her handkerchief as if preparing to cry, but suddenly, as if mastering her feeling, she shook herself and began to speak calmly. "But there is something I want to talk to you about."

Peter Ivanovich bowed, keeping control of the springs of the pouffe, which immediately began quivering under him.

"He suffered terribly the last few days."

"Did he?" said Peter Ivanovich.

"Oh, terribly! He screamed unceasingly, not for minutes but for hours. For the last three days he screamed incessantly. It was unendurable. I cannot understand how I bore it; you could hear him three rooms off. Oh, what I have suffered!"

"Is it possible that he was conscious all that time?" asked Peter Ivanovich.

"Yes," she whispered. "To the last moment. He took leave of us a quarter of an hour before he died, and asked us to take Volodya away."

The thought of the suffering of this man he had known so intimately, first as a merry little boy, then as a schoolmate, and later as a grown-up colleague, suddenly struck Peter Ivanovich with horror, despite an unpleasant consciousness of his own and this woman's dissimulation. He again saw that brow, and that nose pressing down on the lip, and felt afraid for himself.

"Three days of frightful suffering and the death! Why, that might suddenly, at any time, happen to me," he thought, and for a moment felt terrified. But - he did not himself know how - the customary reflection at once occurred to him that this had happened to Ivan Ilych and not to him, and that it should not and could not happen to him, and that to think that it could would be yielding to depressing which he ought not to do, as Schwartz's expression plainly showed. After which reflection Peter Ivanovich felt reassured, and began to ask with interest about the details of Ivan Ilych's death, as though death was an accident natural to Ivan Ilych but certainly not to himself.

After many details of the really dreadful physical sufferings Ivan Ilych had endured (which details he learnt only from the effect those sufferings had produced on Praskovya Fedorovna's nerves) the widow apparently found it necessary to get to business.

"Oh, Peter Ivanovich, how hard it is! How terribly, terribly hard!" and she again began to weep.

Peter Ivanovich sighed and waited for her to finish blowing her nose. When she had done so he said, "Believe me..." and she again began talking and brought out what was evidently her chief concern with him - namely, to question him as to how she could obtain a grant of money from the government on the occasion of her husband's death. She made it appear that she was asking Peter Ivanovich's advice about her pension, but he soon saw that she already knew about that to the minutest detail, more even than he did himself. She knew how much could be got out of the government in consequence of her husband's death, but wanted to find out whether she could not possibly extract something more. Peter

Ivanovich tried to think of some means of doing so, but after reflecting for a while and, out of propriety, condemning the government for its niggardliness, he said he thought that nothing more could be got. Then she sighed and evidently began to devise means of getting rid of her visitor. Noticing this, he put out his cigarette, rose, pressed her hand, and went out into the anteroom.

In the dining-room where the clock stood that Ivan Ilych had liked so much and had bought at an antique shop, Peter Ivanovich met a priest and a few acquaintances who had come to attend the service, and he recognized Ivan Ilych's daughter, a handsome young woman. She was in black and her slim figure appeared slimmer than ever. She had a gloomy, determined, almost angry expression, and bowed to Peter Ivanovich as though he were in some way to blame. Behind her, with the same offended look, stood a wealthy young man, and examining magistrate, whom Peter Ivanovich also knew and who was her fiancé, as he had heard. He bowed mournfully to them and was about to pass into the death-chamber, when from under the stairs appeared the figure of Ivan Ilych's schoolboy son, who was extremely like his father. He seemed a little Ivan Ilych, such as Peter Ivanovich remembered when they studied law together. His tear-stained eyes had in them the look that is seen in the eyes of boys of thirteen or fourteen who are not pure-minded. When he saw Peter Ivanovich he scowled morosely and shamefacedly. Peter Ivanovich nodded to him and entered the death-chamber. The service began: candles, groans, incense, tears, and sobs. Peter Ivanovich stood looking gloomily down at his feet. He did not look once at the dead man, did not yield to any depressing influence, and was one of the first to leave the room. There was no one in the anteroom, but Gerasim darted out of the dead man's room, rummaged with his strong hands among the fur coats to find Peter Ivanovich's and helped him on with it.

"Well, friend Gerasim," said Peter Ivanovich, so as to say something. "It's a sad affair, isn't it?"

"It's God will. We shall all come to it someday," said Gerasim, displaying his teeth - the even white teeth of a healthy peasant - and, like a man in the thick of urgent work, he briskly opened the front door, called the coachman, helped Peter Ivanovich into the sledge, and sprang back to the porch as if in readiness for what he had to do next.

Peter Ivanovich found the fresh air particularly pleasant after the smell of incense, the dead body, and carbolic acid.

"Where to sir?" asked the coachman.

"It's not too late even now...I'll call round on Fedor Vasilievich."

He accordingly drove there and found them just finishing the first rubber, so that it was quite convenient for him to cut in.

II

Ivan Ilych's life had been most simple and most ordinary and therefore most terrible.

He had been a member of the Court of Justice, and died at the age of forty-five. His father had been an official who after serving in various ministries and departments in Petersburg had made the sort of career which brings men to positions from which by reason of their long service they cannot be dismissed, though they are obviously unfit to hold any responsible position, and for whom therefore posts are specially created, which though fictitious carry salaries of from six to ten thousand rubles that are not fictitious, and in receipt of which they live on to a great age.

Such was the Privy Councillor and superfluous member of various superfluous institutions, Ilya Epimovich Golovin.

He had three sons, of whom Ivan Ilych was the second. The eldest son was following in his father's footsteps only in another department, and was already approaching that stage in the service at which a similar sinecure would be reached. The third son was a failure. He had ruined his prospects in a number of positions and was now serving in the railway department. His father and brothers, and still more their wives, not merely disliked meeting him, but avoided remembering his existence unless compelled to do so. His sister had married Baron Greff, a Petersburg official of her father's type. Ivan Ilych was *le phenix de la famille* as people said. He was neither as cold and formal as his elder brother nor as wild as the younger, but was a happy mean between them - an intelligent polished, lively and agreeable man. He had studied with his younger brother at the School of Law, but the latter had failed to complete the course and was expelled when he was in the fifth class. Ivan Ilych finished the course well.

Even when he was at the School of Law he was just what he remained for the rest of his life: a capable, cheerful, good-natured, and sociable man, though strict in the fulfillment of what he considered to be his duty: and he considered his duty to be what was so considered by those in authority. Neither as a boy nor as a man was he a toady, but from early youth was by nature attracted to people of high station as a fly is drawn to the light, assimilating their ways and views of life and establishing friendly relations with them. All the enthusiasms of childhood and youth passed without leaving much trace on him; he succumbed to sensuality, to vanity, and latterly among the highest classes to liberalism, but always within limits which his instinct unfailingly indicated to him as correct.

At school he had done things which had formerly seemed to him very horrid and made him feel disgusted with himself when he did them; but when later on he saw that such actions were done by people of good position and that they did not regard them as wrong, he was able not exactly to regard them as right, but to forget about them entirely or not be at all troubled at remembering them.

Having graduated from the School of Law and qualified for the tenth rank of the civil service, and having received money from his father for his equipment, Ivan Ilych ordered himself clothes at Scharmer's, the fashionable tailor, hung a medallion inscribed *respice finem* on his watch-chain, took leave of his professor and the prince who was patron of the school, had a farewell dinner with his comrades at Donon's first-class restaurant, and with his new and fashionable portmanteau, linen, clothes, shaving and other toilet appliances, and a travelling rug, all purchased at the best shops, he set off for one of the provinces where through his father's influence, he had been attached to the governor as an official for special service.

In the province Ivan Ilych soon arranged as easy and agreeable a position for himself as he had had at the School of Law. He performed his official task, made his career, and at the same time amused himself pleasantly and decorously. Occasionally he paid official visits to country districts where he behaved with dignity both to his superiors and inferiors, and performed the duties entrusted to him, which related chiefly to the sectarians, with an exactness and incorruptible honesty of which he could not but feel proud.

In official matters, despite his youth and taste for frivolous gaiety, he was exceedingly reserved, punctilious, and even severe; but in society he was often amusing and witty, and always good- natured, correct in his manner, and *bon enfant*, as the governor and his wife - with whom he was like one of the family - used to say of him.

In the province he had an affair with a lady who made advances to the elegant young lawyer, and there was also a milliner; and there were carousals with aides-de-camp who visited the district, and after-supper visits to a certain outlying street of doubtful reputation; and there was too some obsequiousness to his chief and even to his chief's wife, but all this was done with such a tone of good breeding that no hard names could be applied to it. It all came under the heading of the French saying: *"Il faut que jeunesse se passe."* It was all done with clean hands, in clean linen, with French phrases, and above all among people of the best society and consequently with the approval of people of rank.

So Ivan Ilych served for five years and then came a change in his official life. The new and reformed judicial institutions were introduced, and new men were needed. Ivan Ilych became such a new man. He was offered the post of examining magistrate, and he accepted it though the post was in another province and obliged him to give up the connexions he had formed and to make new ones. His friends met to give him a send-off; they had a group photograph taken and presented him with a silver cigarette-case, and he set off to his new post.

As examining magistrate Ivan Ilych was just as *comme il faut* and decorous a man, inspiring general respect and capable of separating his official duties from his private life, as he had been when acting as an official on special service. His duties now as examining magistrate were far more interesting and attractive than before. In his former position it had been pleasant to wear an undress uniform made by Scharmer, and to pass through the crowd of petitioners and officials who were timorously awaiting an audience with the governor, and who envied him as with free and easy gait he went straight into his chief's private room to have a cup of tea and a cigarette with him. But not many people had then been directly dependent on him - only police officials and the sectarians when he went on special missions - and he liked to treat them politely, almost as comrades, as if he were letting them feel that he who had the power to crush them was treating them in this simple, friendly way. There were then but few such people. But now, as an examining magistrate, Ivan Ilych felt that everyone without exception, even the most important and self-satisfied, was in his power, and that he need only write a few words on a sheet of paper with a certain heading, and this or that important, self-satisfied person would be brought before him in the role of an accused person or a witness, and if he did not choose to allow him to sit down, would have to stand before him and answer his questions. Ivan Ilych never abused his power; he tried on the contrary to soften its expression, but the consciousness of it and the possibility of softening its effect, supplied the chief interest and attraction of his office. In his work itself, especially in his examinations, he very soon acquired a method of eliminating all considerations irrelevant to the legal aspect of the case, and reducing even the most complicated case to a form in which it would be presented on paper only in its externals, completely excluding his personal opinion of the matter, while above all observing every prescribed formality. The work was new and Ivan Ilych was one of the first men to apply the new Code of 1864.

On taking up the post of examining magistrate in a new town, he made new acquaintances and connexions, placed himself on a new footing and assumed a somewhat different tone. He took up an attitude of rather dignified aloofness towards the provincial authorities, but picked out the best circle of legal gentlemen and wealthy gentry living in the town and assumed a tone of slight dissatisfaction with the government, of moderate liberalism, and of enlightened citizenship. At the same time, without at all altering the elegance of his toilet, he ceased shaving his chin and allowed his beard to grow as it pleased.

Ivan Ilych settled down very pleasantly in this new town. The society there, which inclined towards opposition to the governor was friendly, his salary was larger, and he began to play *vint* [a form of bridge], which he found added not a little to the pleasure of life, for he had a capacity for cards, played good-humouredly, and calculated rapidly and astutely, so that he usually won.

After living there for two years he met his future wife, Praskovya Fedorovna Mikhel, who was the most attractive, clever, and brilliant girl of the set in which he moved, and among other amusements and relaxations from his labours as examining magistrate, Ivan Ilych established light and playful relations with her.

While he had been an official on special service he had been accustomed to dance, but now as an examining magistrate it was exceptional for him to do so. If he danced now, he did it as if to show that though he served under the reformed order of things, and had reached the fifth official rank, yet when it came to dancing he could do it better than most people. So at the end of an evening he sometimes danced with Praskovya Fedorovna, and it was chiefly during these dances that he captivated her. She fell in love with him. Ivan Ilych had at first no definite intention of marrying, but when the girl fell in love with him he said to himself: "Really, why shouldn't I marry?"

Praskovya Fedorovna came of a good family, was not bad looking, and had some little property. Ivan Ilych might have aspired to a more brilliant match, but even this was good. He had his salary, and she, he hoped, would have an equal income. She was well connected, and was a sweet, pretty, and thoroughly correct young woman. To say that Ivan Ilych married because he fell in love with Praskovya Fedorovna and found that she sympathized with his views of life would be as incorrect as to say that he married because his social circle approved of the match. He was swayed by both these considerations: the marriage gave him personal satisfaction, and at the same time it was considered the right thing by the most highly placed of his associates.

So Ivan Ilych got married.

The preparations for marriage and the beginning of married life, with its conjugal caresses, the new furniture, new crockery, and new linen, were very pleasant until his wife became pregnant - so that Ivan Ilych had begun to think that marriage would not impair the easy, agreeable, gay and always decorous character of his life, approved of by society and regarded by himself as natural, but would even improve it. But from the first months of his wife's pregnancy, something new, unpleasant, depressing, and unseemly, and from which there was no way of escape, unexpectedly showed itself.

His wife, without any reason - *de gaiete de coeur* as Ivan Ilych expressed it to himself - began to disturb the pleasure and propriety of their life. She began to be jealous without any cause, expected him to devote his whole attention to her, found fault with everything, and made coarse and ill-mannered scenes.

At first Ivan Ilych hoped to escape from the unpleasantness of this state of affairs by the same easy and decorous relation to life that had served him heretofore: he tried to ignore his wife's disagreeable moods, continued to live in his usual easy and pleasant way, invited friends to his house for a game of cards, and also tried going out to his club or spending his evenings with friends. But one day his wife began upbraiding him so vigorously, using such coarse words, and continued to abuse him every time he did not fulfil her demands, so resolutely and with such evident determination not to give way till he submitted - that is, till he stayed at home and was bored just as she was - that he became alarmed. He now realized that matrimony - at any rate with Praskovya Fedorovna - was not always conducive to the pleasures and amenities of life, but on the contrary often infringed both comfort and propriety, and that he must therefore entrench himself against such infringement. And Ivan Ilych began to seek for means of doing so. His official duties were the one thing that imposed upon Praskovya Fedorovna, and by means of his official work and the duties attached to it he began struggling with his wife to secure his own independence.

With the birth of their child, the attempts to feed it and the various failures in doing so, and with the real and imaginary illnesses of mother and child, in which Ivan Ilych's sympathy was demanded but about which he understood nothing, the need of securing for himself an existence outside his family life became still more imperative.

As his wife grew more irritable and exacting and Ivan Ilych transferred the center of gravity of his life more and more to his official work, so did he grow to like his work better and became more ambitious than before.

Very soon, within a year of his wedding, Ivan Ilych had realized that marriage, though it may add some comforts to life, is in fact a very intricate and difficult affair towards which in order to perform one's duty, that is, to lead a decorous life approved of by society, one must adopt a definite attitude just as towards one's official duties.

And Ivan Ilych evolved such an attitude towards married life. He only required of it those conveniences - dinner at home, housewife, and bed - which it could give him, and above all that propriety of external forms required by public opinion. For the rest he looked for lighthearted pleasure and propriety, and was very thankful when he found them, but if he met with antagonism and querulousness he at once retired into his separate fenced-off world of official duties, where he found satisfaction.

Ivan Ilych was esteemed a good official, and after three years was made Assistant Public Prosecutor. His new duties, their importance, the possibility of indicting and imprisoning anyone he chose, the publicity his speeches received, and the success he had in all these things, made his work still more attractive.

More children came. His wife became more and more querulous and ill-tempered, but the attitude Ivan Ilych had adopted towards his home life rendered him almost impervious to her grumbling.

After seven years' service in that town he was transferred to another province as Public Prosecutor. They moved, but were short of money and his wife did not like the place they moved to. Though the salary was higher the cost of living was greater, besides which two of their children died and family life became still more unpleasant for him.

Praskovya Fedorovna blamed her husband for every inconvenience they encountered in their new home. Most of the conversations between husband and wife, especially as to the children's education, led to topics which recalled former disputes, and these disputes were apt to flare up again at any moment. There remained only those rare periods of amorousness which still came to them at times but did not last long. These were islets at which they anchored for a while and then again set out upon that ocean of veiled hostility which showed itself in their aloofness from one another. This aloofness might have grieved Ivan Ilych had he considered that it ought not to exist, but he now regarded the position as normal, and even made it the goal at which he aimed in family life. His aim was to free himself more and more from those unpleasantness and to give them a semblance of harmlessness and propriety. He attained this by spending less and less time with his family, and when obliged to be at home he tried to safeguard his position by the presence of outsiders. The chief thing however was that he had his official duties. The whole interest of his life now centered in the official world and that interest absorbed him. The consciousness of his power, being able to ruin anybody he wished to ruin, the importance, even the external dignity of his entry into court, or meetings with his subordinates, his success with superiors and inferiors, and above all his masterly handling of cases, of which he was conscious - all this gave him pleasure and filled his life, together with chats with his colleagues, dinners, and bridge. So that on the whole Ivan Ilych's life continued to flow as he considered it should do - pleasantly and properly.

So things continued for another seven years. His eldest daughter was already sixteen, another child had died, and only one son was left, a schoolboy and a subject of dissension. Ivan Ilych wanted to put him in the School of Law, but to spite him Praskovya Fedorovna entered him at the High School. The daughter had been educated at home and had turned out well: the boy did not learn badly either.

III

So Ivan Ilych lived for seventeen years after his marriage. He was already a Public Prosecutor of long standing, and had declined several proposed transfers while awaiting a more desirable post, when an unanticipated and unpleasant occurrence quite upset the peaceful course of his life. He was expecting to be offered the post of presiding judge in a University town, but Happe somehow came to the front and obtained the appointment instead. Ivan Ilych became irritable, reproached Happe, and quarrelled both him and with his immediate superiors - who became colder to him and again passed him over when other appointments were made.

This was in 1880, the hardest year of Ivan Ilych's life. It was then that it became evident on the one hand that his salary was insufficient for them to live on, and on the other that he had been forgotten, and not only this, but that what was for him the greatest and most cruel injustice appeared to others a quite ordinary occurrence. Even his father did not consider it his duty to help him. Ivan Ilych felt himself abandoned by everyone, and that they regarded his position with a salary of 3,500 rubles as quite normal and even fortunate. He alone knew that with the consciousness of the injustices done him, with his wife's incessant nagging, and with the debts he had contracted by living beyond his means, his position was far from normal.

In order to save money that summer he obtained leave of absence and went with his wife to live in the country at her brother's place.

In the country, without his work, he experienced *ennui* for the first time in his life, and not only *ennui* but intolerable depression, and he decided that it was impossible to go on living like that, and that it was necessary to take energetic measures.

Having passed a sleepless night pacing up and down the veranda, he decided to go to Petersburg and bestir himself, in order to punish those who had failed to appreciate him and to get transferred to another ministry.

Next day, despite many protests from his wife and her brother, he started for Petersburg with the sole object of obtaining a post with a salary of five thousand rubles a year. He was no longer bent on any particular department, or tendency, or kind of activity. All he now wanted was an appointment to another post with a salary of five thousand rubles, either in the administration, in the banks, with the railways in one of the Empress Marya's Institutions, or even in the customs - but it had to carry with it a salary of five thousand rubles and be in a ministry other than that in which they had failed to appreciate him.

And this quest of Ivan Ilych's was crowned with remarkable and unexpected success. At Kursk an acquaintance of his, F. I. Ilyin, got into the first-class carriage, sat down beside Ivan Ilych, and told him of a telegram just received by the governor of Kursk announcing that a change was about to take place in the ministry: Peter Ivanovich was to be superseded by Ivan Semonovich.

The proposed change, apart from its significance for Russia, had a special significance for Ivan Ilych, because by bringing forward a new man, Peter Petrovich, and consequently his friend Zachar Ivanovich, it was highly favourable for Ivan Ilych, since Sachar Ivanovich was a friend and colleague of his.

In Moscow this news was confirmed, and on reaching Petersburg Ivan Ilych found Zachar Ivanovich and received a definite promise of an appointment in his former Department of Justice.

A week later he telegraphed to his wife: "Zachar in Miller's place. I shall receive appointment on presentation of report."

Thanks to this change of personnel, Ivan Ilych had unexpectedly obtained an appointment in his former ministry which placed him two states above his former colleagues besides giving him five thousand rubles salary and three thousand five hundred rubles for expenses connected with his removal. All his ill humour towards his former enemies and the whole department vanished, and Ivan Ilych was completely happy.

He returned to the country more cheerful and contented than he had been for a long time. Praskovya Fedorovna also cheered up and a truce was arranged between them. Ivan Ilych told of how he had been feted by everybody in Petersburg, how all those who had been his enemies were put to shame and now fawned on him, how envious they were of his appointment, and how much everybody in Petersburg had liked him.

Praskovya Fedorovna listened to all this and appeared to believe it. She did not contradict anything, but only made plans for their life in the town to which they were going. Ivan Ilych saw with delight that these plans were his plans, that he and his wife agreed, and that, after a stumble, his life was regaining its due and natural character of pleasant lightheartedness and decorum.

Ivan Ilych had come back for a short time only, for he had to take up his new duties on the 10th of September. Moreover, he needed time to settle into the new place, to move all his belongings from the province, and to buy and order many additional things: in a word, to make such arrangements as he had resolved on, which were almost exactly what Praskovya Fedorovna too had decided on.

Now that everything had happened so fortunately, and that he and his wife were at one in their aims and moreover saw so little of one another, they got on together better than they had done since the first years of marriage. Ivan Ilych had thought of taking his family away with him at once, but the insistence of his wife's brother and her sister-in-law, who had suddenly become particularly amiable and friendly to him and his family, induced him to depart alone.

So he departed, and the cheerful state of mind induced by his success and by the harmony between his wife and himself, the one intensifying the other, did not leave him. He found a delightful house, just the thing both he and his wife had dreamt of. Spacious, lofty reception rooms in the old style, a convenient and dignified study, rooms for his wife and daughter, a study for his son - it might have been specially built for them. Ivan Ilych himself superintended the arrangements, chose the wallpapers, supplemented the furniture (preferably with antiques which he considered particularly *comme il faut*), and supervised the upholstering. Everything progressed and progressed and approached the ideal he had set himself: even when things were only half completed they exceeded his expectations. He saw what a refined and elegant character, free from vulgarity, it would all have when it was ready. On falling asleep he pictured to himself how the reception room would look. Looking at the yet unfinished drawing room he could see the fireplace, the screen, the what-not, the little chairs dotted here and there, the dishes and plates on the walls, and the bronzes, as they would be when everything was in place. He was pleased by the thought of how his wife and daughter, who shared his taste n this matter, would be impressed by it. They were certainly not expecting as much. He had been particularly successful in finding, and buying cheaply, antiques which gave a particularly aristocratic character to the whole place. But in his letters he intentionally understated everything in order to be able to surprise them. All this so absorbed him that his new duties - though he liked his official work - interested him less than he had expected. Sometimes he even had moments of absent-mindedness during the court sessions and would consider whether he should have straight or curved cornices for his curtains. He was so interested in it all that he often did things himself, rearranging the furniture, or rehanging the curtains. Once when mounting a step-ladder to show the upholsterer, who did not understand, how he wanted the hangings draped, he made a false step and slipped, but being a strong and agile man he clung on and only knocked his side against the knob of the window frame. The bruised place was painful but the pain soon passed, and he felt particularly bright and well just then. He wrote: "I feel fifteen years younger." He thought he would have everything ready by September, but it dragged on till mid-October. But the result was charming not only in his eyes but to everyone who saw it.

In reality it was just what is usually seen in the houses of people of moderate means who want to appear rich, and therefore succeed only in resembling others like themselves: there are damasks, dark wood, plants, rugs, and dull and polished bronzes - all the things people of a certain class have in order to resemble other people of that class. His house was so like the others that it would never have been noticed, but to him it all seemed to be quite exceptional. He was very happy when he met his family at the station and brought them to the newly furnished house all lit up, where a footman in a white tie opened the door into the hall decorated with plants, and when they went on into the drawing-room and the study uttering exclamations of delight. He conducted them everywhere, drank in their praises eagerly, and beamed with pleasure. At tea that evening, when Praskovya Fedorovna among others things asked him about his fall, he laughed, and showed them how he had gone flying and had frightened the upholsterer.

"It's a good thing I'm a bit of an athlete. Another man might have been killed, but I merely knocked myself, just here; it hurts when it's touched, but it's passing off already - it's only a bruise."

So they began living in their new home - in which, as always happens, when they got thoroughly settled in they found they were just one room short - and with the increased income, which as always was just a little (some five hundred rubles) too little, but it was all very nice.

Things went particularly well at first, before everything was finally arranged and while something had still to be done: this thing bought, that thing ordered, another thing moved, and something else adjusted. Though there were some disputes between husband and wife, they were both so well satisfied and had so much to do that it all passed off without any serious quarrels. When nothing was left to arrange it became rather dull and something seemed to be lacking, but they were then making acquaintances, forming habits, and life was growing fuller.

Ivan Ilych spent his mornings at the law court and came home to diner, and at first he was generally in a good humour, though he occasionally became irritable just on account of his house. (Every spot on the tablecloth or the upholstery, and every broken window- blind string, irritated him. He had devoted so much trouble to arranging it all that every disturbance of it distressed him.) But on the whole his life ran its course as he believed life should do: easily, pleasantly, and decorously.

He got up at nine, drank his coffee, read the paper, and then put on his undress uniform and went to the law courts. There the harness in which he worked had already been stretched to fit him and he donned it without a hitch: petitioners, inquiries at the chancery, the chancery itself, and the sittings public and administrative. In all this the thing was to exclude everything fresh and vital, which always disturbs the regular course of official business, and to admit only official relations with people, and then only on official grounds. A man would come, for instance, wanting some information. Ivan Ilych, as one in whose sphere the matter did not lie, would have nothing to do with him: but if the man had some business with him in his official capacity, something that could be expressed on officially stamped paper, he would do everything, positively everything he could within the limits of such relations, and in doing so would maintain the semblance of friendly human relations, that is, would observe the courtesies of life. As soon as the official relations ended, so did everything else. Ivan Ilych possessed this capacity to separate his real life from the official side of affairs and not mix the two, in the highest degree, and by long practice and natural aptitude had brought it to such a pitch that sometimes, in the manner of a virtuoso, he would even allow himself to let the human and official relations mingle. He let himself do this just because he felt that he could at any time he chose resume the strictly official attitude again and drop the human relation. And he did it all easily, pleasantly, correctly, and even artistically. In the intervals between the sessions he smoked, drank tea, chatted a little about politics, a little about general topics, a little about cards, but most of all about official appointments. Tired, but with the feelings of a virtuoso - one of the first violins who has played his part in an orchestra with precision - he would return home to find that his wife and daughter had been out paying calls, or had a visitor, and that his son had been to school, had done his homework with his tutor, and was surely learning what is taught at High Schools. Everything was as it should be. After dinner, if they had no visitors, Ivan Ilych sometimes read a book that was being much discussed at the time, and in the evening settled down to work, that is, read official papers, compared the depositions of witnesses, and noted paragraphs of the Code applying to them. This was neither dull nor amusing. It was dull when he might have been playing bridge, but if no bridge was available it was at any rate better than doing nothing or sitting with his wife. Ivan Ilych's chief pleasure was giving little dinners to which he invited men and women of good social position, and just as his drawing-room resembled all other drawing-rooms so did his enjoyable little parties resemble all other such parties.

Once they even gave a dance. Ivan Ilych enjoyed it and everything went off well, except that it led to a violent quarrel with his wife about the cakes and sweets. Praskovya Fedorovna had made her own plans, but Ivan Ilych insisted on getting everything from an expensive confectioner and ordered too many cakes, and the quarrel occurred because some of those cakes were left over and the confectioner's bill came to forty-five rubles. It was a great and disagreeable quarrel. Praskovya Fedorovna called him "a fool and an imbecile," and he clutched at his head and made angry allusions to divorce.

But the dance itself had been enjoyable. The best people were there, and Ivan Ilych had danced with Princess Trufonova, a sister of the distinguished founder of the Society "Bear My Burden".

The pleasures connected with his work were pleasures of ambition; his social pleasures were those of vanity; but Ivan Ilych's greatest pleasure was playing bridge. He acknowledged that whatever disagreeable incident happened in his life, the pleasure that beamed like a ray of light above everything else was to sit down to bridge with good players, not noisy partners, and of course to four-handed bridge (with five players it was annoying to have to stand out, though one pretended not to mind), to play a clever and serious game (when the cards allowed it) and then to have supper and drink a glass of wine. After a game of bridge, especially if he had won a little (to win a large sum was unpleasant), Ivan Ilych went to bed in a specially good humour.

So they lived. They formed a circle of acquaintances among the best people and were visited by people of importance and by young folk. In their views as to their acquaintances, husband, wife and daughter were entirely agreed, and tacitly and unanimously kept at arm's length and shook off the various shabby friends and relations who, with much show of affection, gushed into the drawing-room with its Japanese plates on the walls. Soon these shabby friends ceased to obtrude themselves and only the best people remained in the Golovins' set.

Young men made up to Lisa, and Petrishchev, an examining magistrate and Dmitri Ivanovich Petrishchev's son and sole heir, began to be so attentive to her that Ivan Ilych had already spoken to Praskovya Fedorovna about it, and considered whether they should not arrange a party for them, or get up some private theatricals.

So they lived, and all went well, without change, and life flowed pleasantly.

IV

They were all in good health. It could not be called ill health if Ivan Ilych sometimes said that he had a queer taste in his mouth and felt some discomfort in his left side.

But this discomfort increased and, though not exactly painful, grew into a sense of pressure in his side accompanied by ill humour. And his irritability became worse and worse and began to mar the agreeable, easy, and correct life that had established itself in the Golovin family. Quarrels between husband and wife became more and more frequent, and soon the ease and amenity disappeared and even the decorum was barely maintained. Scenes again became frequent, and very few of those islets remained on which husband and wife could meet without an explosion. Praskovya Fedorovna now had good reason to say that her husband's temper was trying. With characteristic exaggeration she said he had always had a dreadful temper, and that it had needed all her good nature to put up with it for twenty years. It was true that now the quarrels were started by him. His bursts of temper always came just before dinner, often just as he began to eat his soup. Sometimes he noticed that a plate or dish was chipped, or the food was not right, or his son put his elbow on the table, or his daughter's hair was not done as he liked it, and for all this he blamed Praskovya Fedorovna. At first she retorted and said disagreeable things to him, but once or twice he fell into such a rage at the beginning of dinner that she realized it was due to some physical derangement brought on by taking food, and so she restrained herself and did not answer, but only hurried to get the dinner over. She regarded this self-restraint as highly praiseworthy. Having come to the conclusion that her husband had a dreadful temper and made her life miserable, she began to feel sorry for herself, and the more she pitied herself the more she hated her husband. She began to wish he would die; yet she did not want him to die because then his salary would cease. And this irritated her against him still more. She considered herself dreadfully unhappy just because not even his death could save her, and though she concealed her exasperation, that hidden exasperation of hers increased his irritation also.

After one scene in which Ivan Ilych had been particularly unfair and after which he had said in explanation that he certainly was irritable but that it was due to his not being well, she said that he was ill it should be attended to, and insisted on his going to see a celebrated doctor.

He went. Everything took place as he had expected and as it always does. There was the usual waiting and the important air assumed by the doctor, with which he was so familiar (resembling that which he himself assumed in court), and the sounding and listening, and the questions which called for answers that were foregone conclusions and were evidently unnecessary, and the look of importance which implied that "if only you put yourself in our hands we will arrange everything - we know indubitably how it has to be done, always in the same way for everybody alike." It was all just as it was in the law courts. The doctor put on just the same air towards him as he himself put on towards an accused person.

The doctor said that so-and-so indicated that there was so- and-so inside the patient, but if the investigation of so-and-so did not confirm this, then he must assume that and that. If he assumed that and that, then... and so on. To Ivan Ilych only one question was important: was his case serious or not? But the doctor ignored that inappropriate question. From his point of view it was not the one under consideration, the real question was to decide between a floating kidney, chronic catarrh, or appendicitis. It was not a question the doctor solved brilliantly, as it seemed to Ivan Ilych, in favour of the appendix, with the reservation that should an examination of the urine give fresh indications the matter would be reconsidered. All this was just what Ivan Ilych had himself brilliantly accomplished a thousand times in dealing with men on trial. The doctor summed up just as brilliantly, looking over his spectacles triumphantly and even gaily at the accused. From the doctor's summing up Ivan Ilych concluded that things were bad, but that for the doctor, and perhaps for everybody else, it was a matter of indifference, though for him it was bad. And this conclusion struck him painfully, arousing in him a great feeling of pity for himself and of bitterness towards the doctor's indifference to a matter of such importance.

He said nothing of this, but rose, placed the doctor's fee on the table, and remarked with a sigh: "We sick people probably often put inappropriate questions. But tell me, in general, is this complaint dangerous, or not?..."

The doctor looked at him sternly over his spectacles with one eye, as if to say: "Prisoner, if you will not keep to the questions put to you, I shall be obliged to have you removed from the court."

"I have already told you what I consider necessary and proper. The analysis may show something more." And the doctor bowed.

Ivan Ilych went out slowly, seated himself disconsolately in his sledge, and drove home. All the way home he was going over what the doctor had said, trying to translate those complicated, obscure, scientific phrases into plain language and find in them an answer to the question: "Is my condition bad? Is it very bad? Or is there as yet nothing much wrong?" And it seemed to him that the meaning of what the doctor had said was that it was very bad. Everything in the streets seemed depressing. The cabmen, the houses, the passers-by, and the shops, were dismal. His ache, this dull gnawing ache that never ceased for a moment, seemed to have acquired a new and more serious significance from the doctor's dubious remarks. Ivan Ilych now watched it with a new and oppressive feeling.

He reached home and began to tell his wife about it. She listened, but in the middle of his account his daughter came in with her hat on, ready to go out with her mother. She sat down reluctantly to listen to this tedious story, but could not stand it long, and her mother too did not hear him to the end.

"Well, I am very glad," she said. "Mind now to take your medicine regularly. Give me the prescription and I'll send Gerasim to the chemist's." And she went to get ready to go out.

While she was in the room Ivan Ilych had hardly taken time to breathe, but he sighed deeply when she left it.

"Well," he thought, "perhaps it isn't so bad after all."

He began taking his medicine and following the doctor's directions, which had been altered after the examination of the urine. But then it happened that there was a contradiction between the indications drawn from the examination of the urine and the symptoms that showed themselves. It turned out that what was happening differed from what the doctor had told him, and that he had either forgotten or blundered, or hidden something from him. He could not, however, be blamed for that, and Ivan Ilych still obeyed his orders implicitly and at first derived some comfort from doing so.

From the time of his visit to the doctor, Ivan Ilych's chief occupation was the exact fulfillment of the doctor's instructions regarding hygiene and the taking of medicine, and the observation of his pain and his excretions. His chief interest came to be people's ailments and people's health. When sickness, deaths, or recoveries were mentioned in his presence, especially when the illness resembled his own, he listened with agitation which he tried to hide, asked questions, and applied what he heard to his own case.

The pain did not grow less, but Ivan Ilych made efforts to force himself to think that he was better. And he could do this so long as nothing agitated him. But as soon as he had any unpleasantness with his wife, any lack of success in his official work, or held bad cards at bridge, he was at once acutely sensible of his disease. He had formerly borne such mischances, hoping soon to adjust what was wrong, to master it and attain success, or make a grand slam. But now every mischance upset him and plunged him into despair. He would say to himself: "there now, just as I was beginning to get better and the medicine had begun to take effect, comes this accursed misfortune, or unpleasantness..." And he was furious with the mishap, or with the people who were causing the unpleasantness and killing him, for he felt that this fury was killing him but he could not restrain it. One would have thought that it should have been clear to him that this exasperation with circumstances and people aggravated his illness, and that he ought therefore to ignore unpleasant occurrences. But he drew the very opposite conclusion: he said that he needed peace, and he watched for everything that might disturb it and became irritable at the slightest infringement of it. His condition was rendered worse by the fact that he read medical books and consulted doctors. The progress of his disease was so gradual that he could deceive himself when comparing one day with another - the difference was so slight. But when he consulted the doctors it seemed to him that he was getting worse, and even very rapidly. Yet despite this he was continually consulting them.

That month he went to see another celebrity, who told him almost the same as the first had done but put his questions rather differently, and the interview with this celebrity only increased Ivan Ilych's doubts and fears. A friend of a friend of his, a very good doctor, diagnosed his illness again quite differently from the others, and though he predicted recovery, his questions and suppositions bewildered Ivan Ilych still more and increased his doubts. A homoeopathist diagnosed the disease in yet another way, and prescribed medicine which Ivan Ilych took secretly for a week. But after a week, not feeling any improvement and having lost confidence both in the former doctor's treatment and in this one's, he became still more despondent. One day a lady acquaintance mentioned a cure effected by a wonder-working icon. Ivan Ilych caught himself listening attentively and beginning to believe that it had occurred. This incident alarmed him. "Has my mind really weakened to such an extent?" he asked himself. "Nonsense! It's all rubbish. I mustn't give way to nervous fears but having chosen a doctor must keep strictly to his treatment. That is what I will do. Now it's all settled. I won't think about it, but will follow the treatment seriously till summer, and then we shall see. From now there must be no more of this wavering!" this was easy to say but impossible to carry out. The pain in his side oppressed him and seemed to grow worse and more incessant, while the taste in his mouth grew stranger and stranger. It seemed to him that his breath had a disgusting smell, and he was conscious of a loss of appetite and strength. There was no deceiving himself: something terrible, new, and more important than anything before in his life, was taking place within him of which he alone was aware. Those about him did not understand or would not understand it, but thought everything in the world was going on as usual. That tormented Ivan Ilych more than anything. He saw that his household, especially his wife and daughter who were in a perfect whirl of visiting, did not understand anything of it and were annoyed that he was so depressed and so exacting, as if he were to blame for it. Though they tried to disguise it he saw that he was an obstacle in their path, and that his wife had adopted a definite line in regard to his illness and kept to it regardless of anything he said or did. Her attitude was this: "You know," she would say to her friends, "Ivan Ilych can't do as other people do, and keep to the treatment prescribed for him. One day he'll take his drops and keep strictly to his diet and go to bed in good time, but the next day unless I watch him he'll suddenly forget his medicine, eat sturgeon - which is forbidden - and sit up playing cards till one o'clock in the morning."

"Oh, come, when was that?" Ivan Ilych would ask in vexation. "Only once at Peter Ivanovich's."

"And yesterday with shebek."

"Well, even if I hadn't stayed up, this pain would have kept me awake."

"Be that as it may you'll never get well like that, but will always make us wretched."

Praskovya Fedorovna's attitude to Ivan Ilych's illness, as she expressed it both to others and to him, was that it was his own fault and was another of the annoyances he caused her. Ivan Ilych felt that this opinion escaped her involuntarily - but that did not make it easier for him.

At the law courts too, Ivan Ilych noticed, or thought he noticed, a strange attitude towards himself. It sometimes seemed to him that people were watching him inquisitively as a man whose place might soon be vacant. Then again, his friends would suddenly begin to chaff him in a friendly way about his low spirits, as if the awful, horrible, and unheard-of thing that was going on within him, incessantly gnawing at him and irresistibly drawing him away, was a very agreeable subject for jests. Schwartz in particular irritated him by his jocularity, vivacity, and *savoir-faire*, which reminded him of what he himself had been ten years ago.

Friends came to make up a set and they sat down to cards. They dealt, bending the new cards to soften them, and he sorted the diamonds in his hand and found he had seven. His partner said "No trumps" and supported him with two diamonds. What more could be wished for? It ought to be jolly and lively. They would make a grand slam. But suddenly Ivan Ilych was conscious of that gnawing pain, that taste in his mouth, and it seemed ridiculous that in such circumstances he should be pleased to make a grand slam.

He looked at his partner Mikhail Mikhaylovich, who rapped the table with his strong hand and instead of snatching up the tricks pushed the cards courteously and indulgently towards Ivan Ilych that he might have the pleasure of gathering them up without the trouble of stretching out his hand for them. "Does he think I am too weak to stretch out my arm?" thought Ivan Ilych, and forgetting what he was doing he over-trumped his partner, missing the grand slam by three tricks. And what was most awful of all was that he saw how upset Mikhail Mikhaylovich was about it but did not himself care. And it was dreadful to realize why he did not care.

They all saw that he was suffering, and said: "We can stop if you are tired. Take a rest." Lie down? No, he was not at all tired, and he finished the rubber. All were gloomy and silent. Ivan Ilych felt that he had diffused this gloom over them and could not dispel it. They had supper and went away, and Ivan Ilych was left alone with the consciousness that his life was poisoned and was poisoning the lives of others, and that this poison did not weaken but penetrated more and more deeply into his whole being.

With this consciousness, and with physical pain besides the terror, he must go to bed, often to lie awake the greater part of the night. Next morning he had to get up again, dress, go to the law courts, speak, and write; or if he did not go out, spend at home those twenty-four hours a day each of which was a torture. And he had to live thus all alone on the brink of an abyss, with no one who understood or pitied him.

V

So one month passed and then another. Just before the New Year his brother-in-law came to town and stayed at their house. Ivan Ilych was at the law courts and Praskovya Fedorovna had gone shopping. When Ivan Ilych came home and entered his study he found his brother-in-law there - a healthy, florid man - unpacking his portmanteau himself. He raised his head on hearing Ivan Ilych's footsteps and looked up at him for a moment without a word. That stare told Ivan Ilych everything. His brother-in-law opened his mouth to utter an exclamation of surprise but checked himself, and that action confirmed it all.

"I have changed, eh?"

"Yes, there is a change."

And after that, try as he would to get his brother-in-law to return to the subject of his looks, the latter would say nothing about it. Praskovya Fedorovna came home and her brother went out to her. Ivan Ilych locked to door and began to examine himself in the glass, first full face, then in profile. He took up a portrait of himself taken with his wife, and compared it with what he saw in the glass. The change in him was immense. Then he bared his arms to the elbow, looked at them, drew the sleeves down again, sat down on an ottoman, and grew blacker than night.

"No, no, this won't do!" he said to himself, and jumped up, went to the table, took up some law papers and began to read them, but could not continue. He unlocked the door and went into the reception-room. The door leading to the drawing-room was shut. He approached it on tiptoe and listened.

"No, you are exaggerating!" Praskovya Fedorovna was saying.

"Exaggerating! Don't you see it? Why, he's a dead man! Look at his eyes - there's no life in them. But what is it that is wrong with him?"

"No one knows. Nikolaevich [that was another doctor] said something, but I don't know what. And Seshchetitsky [this was the celebrated specialist] said quite the contrary..."

Ivan Ilych walked away, went to his own room, lay down, and began musing; "The kidney, a floating kidney." He recalled all the doctors had told him of how it detached itself and swayed about. And by an effort of imagination he tried to catch that kidney and arrest it and support it. So little was needed for this, it seemed to him. "No, I'll go to see Peter Ivanovich again." [That was the friend whose friend was a doctor.] He rang, ordered the carriage, and got ready to go.

"Where are you going, Jean?" asked his wife with a specially sad and exceptionally kind look.

This exceptionally kind look irritated him. He looked morosely at her.

"I must go to see Peter Ivanovich."

He went to see Peter Ivanovich, and together they went to see his friend, the doctor. He was in, and Ivan Ilych had a long talk with him.

Reviewing the anatomical and physiological details of what in the doctor's opinion was going on inside him, he understood it all.

There was something, a small thing, in the vermiform appendix. It might all come right. Only stimulate the energy of one organ and check the activity of another, then absorption would take place and everything would come right. He got home rather late for dinner, ate his dinner, and conversed cheerfully, but could not for a long time bring himself to go back to work in his room. At last, however, he went to his study and did what was necessary, but the consciousness that he had put something aside - an important, intimate matter which he would revert to when his work was done - never left him. When he had finished his work he remembered that this intimate matter was the thought of his vermiform appendix. But he did not give himself up to it, and went to the drawing-room for tea. There were callers there, including the examining magistrate who was a desirable match for his daughter, and they were conversing, playing the piano, and singing. Ivan Ilych, as Praskovya Fedorovna remarked, spent that evening more cheerfully than usual, but he never for a moment forgot that he had postponed the important matter of the appendix. At eleven o'clock he said goodnight and went to his bedroom. Since his illness he had slept alone in a small room next to his study. He undressed and took up a novel by Zola, but instead of reading it he fell into thought, and in his imagination that desired improvement in the vermiform appendix occurred. There was the absorption and evacuation and the re-establishment of normal activity. "Yes, that's it!" he said to himself. "One need only assist nature, that's all." He remembered his medicine, rose, took it, and lay down on his back watching for the beneficent action of the medicine and for it to lessen the pain. "I need only take it regularly and avoid all injurious influences. I am already feeling better, much better." He began touching his side: it was not painful to the touch. "There, I really don't feel it. It's much better already." He put out the light and turned on his side... "The appendix is getting better, absorption is occurring." Suddenly he felt the old, familiar, dull, gnawing pain, stubborn and serious. There was the same familiar loathsome taste in his mouth. His heart sank and he felt dazed. "My God! My God!" he muttered. "Again, again! And it will never cease." And suddenly the matter presented itself in a quite different aspect. "Vermiform appendix! Kidney!" he said to himself. "It's not a question of appendix or kidney, but of life and...death. Yes, life was there and now it is going, going and I cannot stop it. Yes. Why deceive myself? Isn't it obvious to everyone but me that I'm dying, and that it's only a question of weeks, days...it may happen this moment. There was light and now there is darkness. I was here and now I'm going there! Where?" A chill came over him, his breathing ceased, and he felt only the throbbing of his heart.

"When I am not, what will there be? There will be nothing. Then where shall I be when I am no more? Can this be dying? No, I don't want to!" He jumped up and tried to light the candle, felt for it with trembling hands, dropped candle and candlestick on the floor, and fell back on his pillow.

"What's the use? It makes no difference," he said to himself, staring with wide-open eyes into the darkness. "Death. Yes, death. And none of them knows or wishes to know it, and they have no pity for me. Now they are playing." (He heard through the door the distant sound of a song and its accompaniment.) "It's all the same to them, but they will die too! Fools! I first, and they later, but it will be the same for them. And now they are merry... the beasts!"

Anger choked him and he was agonizingly, unbearably miserable. "It is impossible that all men have been doomed to suffer this awful horror!" He raised himself.

"Something must be wrong. I must calm myself - must think it all over from the beginning." And he again began thinking. "Yes, the beginning of my illness: I knocked my side, but I was still quite well that day and the next. It hurt a little, then rather more. I saw the doctors, then followed despondency and anguish, more doctors, and I drew nearer to the abyss. My strength grew less and I kept coming nearer and nearer, and now I have wasted away and there is no light in my eyes. I think of the appendix - but this is death! I think of mending the appendix, and all the while here is death! Can it really be death?" Again terror seized him and he gasped for breath. He leant down and began feeling for the matches, pressing with his elbow on the stand beside the bed. It was in his way and hurt him, he grew furious with it, pressed on it still harder, and upset it. Breathless and in despair he fell on his back, expecting death to come immediately.

Meanwhile the visitors were leaving. Praskovya Fedorovna was seeing them off. She heard something fall and came in.

"What has happened?"

"Nothing. I knocked it over accidentally."

She went out and returned with a candle. He lay there panting heavily, like a man who has run a thousand yards, and stared upwards at her with a fixed look.

"What is it, Jean?"

"No...o...thing. I upset it." ("Why speak of it? She won't understand," he thought.)

And in truth she did not understand. She picked up the stand, lit his candle, and hurried away to see another visitor off. When she came back he still lay on his back, looking upwards.

"What is it? Do you feel worse?"

"Yes."

She shook her head and sat down.

"Do you know, Jean, I think we must ask Leshchetitsky to come and see you here."

This meant calling in the famous specialist, regardless of expense. He smiled malignantly and said "No." She remained a little longer and then went up to him and kissed his forehead.

While she was kissing him he hated her from the bottom of his soul and with difficulty refrained from pushing her away.

"Good night. Please God you'll sleep."

"Yes."

VI

Ivan Ilych saw that he was dying, and he was in continual despair.

In the depth of his heart he knew he was dying, but not only was he not accustomed to the thought, he simply did not and could not grasp it.

The syllogism he had learnt from Kiesewetter's Logic: "Caius is a man, men are mortal, therefore Caius is mortal," had always seemed to him correct as applied to Caius, but certainly not as applied to himself. That Caius - man in the abstract - was mortal, was perfectly correct, but he was not Caius, not an abstract man, but a creature quite, quite separate from all others. He had been little Vanya, with a mamma and a papa, with Mitya and Volodya, with the toys, a coachman and a nurse, afterwards with Katenka and will all the joys, griefs, and delights of childhood, boyhood, and youth. What did Caius know of the smell of that striped leather ball Vanya had been so fond of? Had Caius kissed his mother's hand like that, and did the silk of her dress rustle so for Caius? Had he rioted like that at school when the pastry was bad? Had Caius been in love like that? Could Caius preside at a session as he did? "Caius really was mortal, and it was right for him to die; but for me, little Vanya, Ivan

Ilych, with all my thoughts and emotions, it's altogether a different matter. It cannot be that I ought to die. That would be too terrible."

Such was his feeling.

"If I had to die like Caius I would have known it was so. An inner voice would have told me so, but there was nothing of the sort in me and I and all my friends felt that our case was quite different from that of Caius. and now here it is!" he said to himself. "It can't be. It's impossible! But here it is. How is this? How is one to understand it?"

He could not understand it, and tried to drive this false, incorrect, morbid thought away and to replace it by other proper and healthy thoughts. But that thought, and not the thought only but the reality itself, seemed to come and confront him.

And to replace that thought he called up a succession of others, hoping to find in them some support. He tried to get back into the former current of thoughts that had once screened the thought of death from him. But strange to say, all that had formerly shut off, hidden, and destroyed his consciousness of death, no longer had that effect. Ivan Ilych now spent most of his time in attempting to re-establish that old current. He would say to himself: "I will take up my duties again - after all I used to live by them." And banishing all doubts he would go to the law courts, enter into conversation with his colleagues, and sit carelessly as was his wont, scanning the crowd with a thoughtful look and leaning both his emaciated arms on the arms of his oak chair; bending over as usual to a colleague and drawing his papers nearer he would interchange whispers with him, and then suddenly raising his eyes and sitting erect would pronounce certain words and open the proceedings. But suddenly in the midst of those proceedings the pain in his side, regardless of the stage the proceedings had reached, would begin its own gnawing work. Ivan Ilych would turn his attention to it and try to drive the thought of it away, but without success. *It* would come and stand before him and look at him, and he would be petrified and the light would die out of his eyes, and he would again begin asking himself whether *It* alone was true. And his colleagues and subordinates would see with surprise and distress that he, the brilliant and subtle judge, was becoming confused and making mistakes. He would shake himself, try to pull himself together, manage somehow to bring the sitting to a close, and return home with the sorrowful consciousness that his judicial labours could not as formerly hide from him what he wanted them to hide, and could not deliver him from *It*. And what was worst of all was that *It* drew his attention to itself not in order to make him take some action but only that he should look at *It*, look it straight in the face: look at it and without doing anything, suffer inexpressibly.

And to save himself from this condition Ivan Ilych looked for consolations - new screens - and new screens were found and for a while seemed to save him, but then they immediately fell to pieces or rather became transparent, as if *It* penetrated them and nothing could veil *It*.

In these latter days he would go into the drawing-room he had arranged - that drawing-room where he had fallen and for the sake of which (how bitterly ridiculous it seemed) he had sacrificed his life - for he knew that his illness originated with that knock. He would enter and see that something had scratched the polished table. He would look for the cause of this and find that it was the bronze ornamentation of an album, that had got bent. He would take up the expensive album which he had lovingly arranged, and feel vexed with his daughter and her friends for their untidiness - for the album was torn here and there and some of the photographs turned upside down. He would put it carefully in order and bend the ornamentation back into position. Then it would occur to him to place all those things in another corner of the room, near the plants. He would call the footman, but his daughter or wife would come to help him. They would not agree, and his wife would contradict him, and he would dispute and grow angry. But that was all right, for then he did not think about *It*. *It* was invisible.

But then, when he was moving something himself, his wife would say: "Let the servants do it. You will hurt yourself again." And suddenly *It* would flash through the screen and he would see it. It was just a flash, and he hoped it would disappear, but he would involuntarily pay attention to his side. "It sits there as before, gnawing just the same!" And he could no longer forget *It*, but could distinctly see it looking at him from behind the flowers. "What is it all for?"

"It really is so! I lost my life over that curtain as I might have done when storming a fort. Is that possible? How terrible and how stupid. It can't be true! It can't, but it is."

He would go to his study, lie down, and again be alone with *It*: face to face with *It*. And nothing could be done with *It* except to look at it and shudder.

VII

How it happened it is impossible to say because it came about step by step, unnoticed, but in the third month of Ivan Ilych's illness, his wife, his daughter, his son, his acquaintances, the doctors, the servants, and above all he himself, were aware that the whole interest he had for other people was whether he would soon vacate his place, and at last release the living from the discomfort caused by his presence and be himself released from his sufferings.

He slept less and less. He was given opium and hypodermic injections of morphine, but this did not relieve him. The dull depression he experienced in a somnolent condition at first gave him a little relief, but only as something new, afterwards it became as distressing as the pain itself or even more so.

Special foods were prepared for him by the doctors' orders, but all those foods became increasingly distasteful and disgusting to him.

For his excretions also special arrangements had to be made, and this was a torment to him every time - a torment from the uncleanliness, the unseemliness, and the smell, and from knowing that another person had to take part in it.

But just through his most unpleasant matter, Ivan Ilych obtained comfort. Gerasim, the butler's young assistant, always came in to carry the things out. Gerasim was a clean, fresh peasant lad, grown stout on town food and always cheerful and bright. At first the sight of him, in his clean Russian peasant costume, engaged on that disgusting task embarrassed Ivan Ilych.

Once when he got up from the commode too weak to draw up his trousers, he dropped into a soft armchair and looked with horror at his bare, enfeebled thighs with the muscles so sharply marked on them.

Gerasim with a firm light tread, his heavy boots emitting a pleasant smell of tar and fresh winter air, came in wearing a clean Hessian apron, the sleeves of his print shirt tucked up over his strong bare young arms; and refraining from looking at his sick master out of consideration for his feelings, and restraining the joy of life that beamed from his face, he went up to the commode.

"Gerasim!" said Ivan Ilych in a weak voice.

"Gerasim started, evidently afraid he might have committed some blunder, and with a rapid movement turned his fresh, kind, simple young face which just showed the first downy signs of a beard.

"Yes, sir?"

"That must be very unpleasant for you. You must forgive me. I am helpless."

"Oh, why, sir," and Gerasim's eyes beamed and he showed his glistening white teeth, "what's a little trouble? It's a case of illness with you, sir."

And his deft strong hands did their accustomed task, and he went out of the room stepping lightly. Five minutes later he as lightly returned.

Ivan Ilych was still sitting in the same position in the armchair.

"Gerasim," he said when the latter had replaced the freshly- washed utensil. "Please come here and help me." Gerasim went up to him. "Lift me up. It is hard for me to get up, and I have sent Dmitri away."

Gerasim went up to him, grasped his master with his strong arms deftly but gently, in the same way that he stepped - lifted him, supported him with one hand, and with the other drew up his trousers and would have set him down again, but Ivan Ilych asked to be led to the sofa. Gerasim, without an effort and without apparent pressure, led him, almost lifting him, to the sofa and placed him on it.

"Thank you. How easily and well you do it all!"

Gerasim smiled again and turned to leave the room. But Ivan Ilych felt his presence such a comfort that he did not want to let him go.

"One thing more, please move up that chair. No, the other one - under my feet. It is easier for me when my feet are raised."

Gerasim brought the chair, set it down gently in place, and raised Ivan Ilych's legs on it. It seemed to Ivan Ilych that he felt better while Gerasim was holding up his legs.

"It's better when my legs are higher," he said. "Place that cushion under them."

Gerasim did so. He again lifted the legs and placed them, and again Ivan Ilych felt better while Gerasim held his legs. When he set them down Ivan Ilych fancied he felt worse.

"Gerasim," he said. "Are you busy now?"

"Not at all, sir," said Gerasim, who had learnt from the townsfolk how to speak to gentlefolk.

"What have you still to do?"

"What have I to do? I've done everything except chopping the logs for tomorrow."

"Then hold my legs up a bit higher, can you?"

"Of course I can. Why not?" and Gerasim raised his master's legs higher and Ivan Ilych thought that in that position he did not feel any pain at all.

"And how about the logs?"

"Don't trouble about that, sir. There's plenty of time."

Ivan Ilych told Gerasim to sit down and hold his legs, and began to talk to him. And strange to say it seemed to him that he felt better while Gerasim held his legs up.

After that Ivan Ilych would sometimes call Gerasim and get him to hold his legs on his shoulders, and he liked talking to him. Gerasim did it all easily, willingly, simply, and with a good nature that touched Ivan Ilych. Health, strength, and vitality in other people were offensive to him, but Gerasim's strength and vitality did not mortify but soothed him.

What tormented Ivan Ilych most was the deception, the lie, which for some reason they all accepted, that he was not dying but was simply ill, and he only need keep quiet and undergo a treatment and then something very good would result. He however knew that do what they would nothing would come of it, only still more agonizing suffering and death. This deception tortured him - their not wishing to admit what they all knew and what he knew, but wanting to lie to him concerning his terrible condition, and wishing and forcing him to participate in that lie. Those lies - lies enacted over him on the eve of his death and destined to degrade this awful, solemn act to the level of their visitings, their curtains, their sturgeon for dinner - were a terrible agony for Ivan Ilych. And strangely enough, many times when they were going through their antics over him he had been within a hairbreadth of calling out to them: "Stop lying! You know and I know that I am dying. Then at least stop lying about it!" But he had never had the spirit to do it. The awful, terrible act of his dying was, he could see, reduced by those about him to the level of a casual, unpleasant, and almost indecorous incident (as if someone entered a drawing room defusing an unpleasant odour) and this was done by that very decorum which he had served all his life long. He saw that no one felt for him, because no one even wished to grasp his position. Only Gerasim recognized it and pitied him. And so Ivan Ilych felt at ease only with him. He felt comforted when Gerasim supported his legs (sometimes all night long) and refused to go to bed, saying: "Don't you worry, Ivan Ilych. I'll get sleep enough later on," or when he suddenly became familiar and exclaimed: "If you weren't sick it would be another matter, but as it is, why should I grudge a little trouble?" Gerasim alone did not lie; everything showed that he alone understood the facts of the case and did not consider it necessary to disguise them, but simply felt sorry for his emaciated and enfeebled master. Once when Ivan Ilych was sending him away he even said straight out: "We shall all of us die, so why should I grudge a little trouble?" - expressing the fact that he did not think his work burdensome, because he was doing it for a dying man and hoped someone would do the same for him when his time came.

Apart from this lying, or because of it, what most tormented Ivan Ilych was that no one pitied him as he wished to be pitied. At certain moments after prolonged suffering he wished most of all (though he would have been ashamed to confess it) for someone to pity him as a sick child is pitied. He longed to be petted and comforted. he knew he was an important functionary, that he had a beard turning grey, and that therefore what he long for was impossible, but still he longed for it. and in Gerasim's attitude towards him there was something akin to what he wished for, and so that attitude comforted him. Ivan Ilych wanted to weep, wanted to be petted and cried over, and then his colleague Shebek would come, and instead of weeping and being petted, Ivan Ilych would assume a serious, severe, and profound air, and by force of habit would express his opinion on a decision of the Court of Cassation and would stubbornly insist on that view. This falsity around him and within him did more than anything else to poison his last days.

VIII

It was morning. He knew it was morning because Gerasim had gone, and Peter the footman had come and put out the candles, drawn back one of the curtains, and begun quietly to tidy up. Whether it was morning or evening, Friday or Sunday, made no difference, it was all just the same: the gnawing, unmitigated, agonizing pain, never ceasing for an instant, the consciousness of life inexorably waning but not yet extinguished, the approach of that ever dreaded and hateful Death which was the only reality, and always the same falsity. What were days, weeks, hours, in such a case?

"Will you have some tea, sir?"

"He wants things to be regular, and wishes the gentlefolk to drink tea in the morning," thought Ivan Ilych, and only said "No."

"Wouldn't you like to move onto the sofa, sir?"

"He wants to tidy up the room, and I'm in the way. I am uncleanliness and disorder," he thought, and said only:

"No, leave me alone."

The man went on bustling about. Ivan Ilych stretched out his hand. Peter came up, ready to help.

"What is it, sir?"

"My watch."

Peter took the watch which was close at hand and gave it to his master.

"Half-past eight. Are they up?"

"No sir, except Vladimir Ivanovich" (the son) "who has gone to school. Praskovya Fedorovna ordered me to wake her if you asked for her. Shall I do so?"

"No, there's no need to." "Perhaps I's better have some tea," he thought, and added aloud: "Yes, bring me some tea."

Peter went to the door, but Ivan Ilych dreaded being left alone. "How can I keep him here? Oh yes, my medicine." "Peter, give me my medicine."

"Why not? Perhaps it may still do some good." He took a spoonful and swallowed it. "No, it won't help. It's all tomfoolery, all deception," he decided as soon as he became aware of the familiar, sickly, hopeless taste. "No, I can't believe in it any longer. But the pain, why this pain? If it would only cease just for a moment!" And he moaned. Peter turned towards him. "It's all right. Go and fetch me some tea."

Peter went out. Left alone Ivan Ilych groaned not so much with pain, terrible thought that was, as from mental anguish. Always and forever the same, always these endless days and nights. If only it would come quicker! If only *what* would come quicker? Death, darkness?...No, no! anything rather than death!

when Peter returned with the tea on a tray, Ivan Ilych stared at him for a time in perplexity, not realizing who and what he was. Peter was disconcerted by that look and his embarrassment brought Ivan Ilych to himself.

"Oh, tea! All right, put it down. Only help me to wash and put on a clean shirt."

And Ivan Ilych began to wash. With pauses for rest, he washed his hands and then his face, cleaned his teeth, brushed his hair, looked in the glass. He was terrified by what he saw, especially by the limp way in which his hair clung to his pallid forehead.

While his shirt was being changed he knew that he would be still more frightened at the sight of his body, so he avoided looking at it. Finally he was ready. He drew on a dressing-gown, wrapped himself in a plaid, and sat down in the armchair to take his tea. For a moment he felt refreshed, but as soon as he began to drink the tea he was again aware of the same taste, and the pain also returned. He finished it with an effort, and then lay down stretching out his legs, and dismissed Peter.

Always the same. Now a spark of hope flashes up, then a sea of despair rages, and always pain; always pain, always despair, and always the same. When alone he had a dreadful and distressing desire to call someone, but he knew beforehand that with others present it would be still worse. "Another dose of morphine-to lose consciousness. I will tell him, the doctor, that he must think of something else. It's impossible, impossible, to go on like this."

An hour and another pass like that. But now there is a ring at the door bell. Perhaps it's the doctor? It is. He comes in fresh, hearty, plump, and cheerful, with that look on his face that seems to say: "There now, you're in a panic about something, but we'll arrange it all for you directly!" The doctor knows this expression is out of place here, but he has put it on once for all and can't take it off - like a man who has put on a frock-coat in the morning to pay a round of calls.

The doctor rubs his hands vigorously and reassuringly.

"Brr! How cold it is! There's such a sharp frost; just let me warm myself!" he says, as if it were only a matter of waiting till he was warm, and then he would put everything right.

"Well now, how are you?"

Ivan Ilych feels that the doctor would like to say: "Well, how are your affairs?" but that even he feels that this would not do, and says instead: "What sort of a night have you had?"

Ivan Ilych looks at him as much as to say: "Are you really never ashamed of lying?" But the doctor does not wish to understand this question, and Ivan Ilych says: "Just as terrible as ever. The pain never leaves me and never subsides. If only something..."

"Yes, you sick people are always like that... There, now I think I am warm enough. Even Praskovya Fedorovna, who is so particular, could find no fault with my temperature. Well, now I can say good-morning," and the doctor presses his patient's hand.

Then dropping his former playfulness, he begins with a most serious face to examine the patient, feeling his pulse and taking his temperature, and then begins the sounding and auscultation.

Ivan Ilych knows quite well and definitely that all this is nonsense and pure deception, but when the doctor, getting down on his knee, leans over him, putting his ear first higher then lower, and performs various gymnastic movements over him with a significant expression on his face, Ivan Ilych submits to it all as he used to submit to the speeches of the lawyers, though he knew very well that they were all lying and why they were lying.

The doctor, kneeling on the sofa, is still sounding him when Praskovya Fedorovna's silk dress rustles at the door and she is heard scolding Peter for not having let her know of the doctor's arrival.

She comes in, kisses her husband, and at once proceeds to prove that she has been up a long time already, and only owing to a misunderstanding failed to be there when the doctor arrived.

Ivan Ilych looks at her, scans her all over, sets against her the whiteness and plumpness and cleanness of her hands and neck, the gloss of her hair, and the sparkle of her vivacious eyes. He hates her with his whole soul. And the thrill of hatred he feels for her makes him suffer from her touch.

Her attitude towards him and his diseases is still the same. Just as the doctor had adopted a certain relation to his patient which he could not abandon, so had she formed one towards him - that he was not doing something he ought to do and was himself to blame, and that she reproached him lovingly for this - and she could not now change that attitude.

"You see he doesn't listen to me and doesn't take his medicine at the proper time. And above all he lies in a position that is no doubt bad for him - with his legs up."

She described how he made Gerasim hold his legs up.

The doctor smiled with a contemptuous affability that said: "What's to be done? These sick people do have foolish fancies of that kind, but we must forgive them."

When the examination was over the doctor looked at his watch, and then Praskovya Fedorovna announced to Ivan Ilych that it was of course as he pleased, but she had sent today for a celebrated specialist who would examine him and have a consultation with Michael Danilovich (their regular doctor).

"Please don't raise any objections. I am doing this for my own sake," she said ironically, letting it be felt that she was doing it all for his sake and only said this to leave him no right to refuse. He remained silent, knitting his brows. He felt that he was surrounded and involved in a mesh of falsity that it was hard to unravel anything.

Everything she did for him was entirely for her own sake, and she told him she was doing for herself what she actually was doing for herself, as if that was so incredible that he must understand the opposite.

At half-past eleven the celebrated specialist arrived. Again the sounding began and the significant conversations in his presence and in another room, about the kidneys and the appendix, and the questions and answers, with such an air of importance that again, instead of the real question of life and death which now alone confronted him, the question arose of the kidney and appendix which were not behaving as they ought to and would now be attached by Michael Danilovich and the specialist and forced to amend their ways.

The celebrated specialist took leave of him with a serious though not hopeless look, and in reply to the timid question Ivan Ilych, with eyes glistening with fear and hope, put to him as to whether there was a chance of recovery, said that he could not vouch for it but there was a possibility. The look of hope with which Ivan Ilych watched the doctor out was so pathetic that Praskovya Fedorovna, seeing it, even wept as she left the room to hand the doctor his fee.

The gleam of hope kindled by the doctor's encouragement did not last long. The same room, the same pictures, curtains, wall- paper, medicine bottles, were all there, and the same aching suffering body, and Ivan Ilych began to moan. They gave him a subcutaneous injection and he sank into oblivion.

It was twilight when he came to. They brought him his dinner and he swallowed some beef tea with difficulty, and then everything was the same again and night was coming on.

After dinner, at seven o'clock, Praskovya Fedorovna came into the room in evening dress, her full bosom pushed up by her corset, and with traces of powder on her face. She had reminded him in the morning that they were going to the theatre. Sarah Bernhardt was visiting the town and they had a box, which he had insisted on their taking. Now he had forgotten about it and her toilet offended him, but he concealed his vexation when he remembered that he had himself insisted on their securing a box and going because it would be an instructive and aesthetic pleasure for the children.

Praskovya Fedorovna came in, self-satisfied but yet with a rather guilty air. She sat down and asked how he was, but, as he saw, only for the sake of asking and not in order to learn about it, knowing that there was nothing to learn - and then went on to what she really wanted to say: that she would not on any account have gone but that the box had been taken and Helen and their daughter were going, as well as Petrishchev (the examining magistrate, their daughter's fiancé) and that it was out of the question to let them go alone; but that she would have much preferred to sit with him for a while; and he must be sure to follow the doctor's orders while she was away.

"Oh, and Fedor Petrovich" (the fiancé) "would like to come in. May he? And Lisa?"

"All right."

Their daughter came in in full evening dress, her fresh young flesh exposed (making a show of that very flesh which in his own case caused so much suffering), strong, healthy, evidently in love, and impatient with illness, suffering, and death, because they interfered with her happiness.

Fedor Petrovich came in too, in evening dress, his hair curled *a la Capoul*, a tight stiff collar round his long sinewy neck, an enormous white shirt-front and narrow black trousers tightly stretched over his strong thighs. He had one white glove tightly drawn on, and was holding his opera hat in his hand.

Following him the schoolboy crept in unnoticed, in a new uniform, poor little fellow, and wearing gloves. Terribly dark shadows showed under his eyes, the meaning of which Ivan Ilych knew well.

His son had always seemed pathetic to him, and now it was dreadful to see the boy's frightened look of pity. It seemed to Ivan Ilych that Vasya was the only one besides Gerasim who understood and pitied him.

They all sat down and again asked how he was. A silence followed. Lisa asked her mother about the opera glasses, and there was an altercation between mother and daughter as to who had taken them and where they had been put. This occasioned some unpleasantness.

Fedor Petrovich inquired of Ivan Ilych whether he had ever seen Sarah Bernhardt. Ivan Ilych did not at first catch the question, but then replied: "No, have you seen her before?"

"Yes, in *Adrienne Lecouvreur*."

Praskovya Fedorovna mentioned some roles in which Sarah Bernhardt was particularly good. Her daughter disagreed. Conversation sprang up as to the elegance and realism of her acting - the sort of conversation that is always repeated and is always the same.

In the midst of the conversation Fedor Petrovich glanced at Ivan Ilych and became silent. The others also looked at him and grew silent.

Ivan Ilych was staring with glittering eyes straight before him, evidently indignant with them. This had to be rectified, but it was impossible to do so. The silence had to be broken, but for a time no one dared to break it and they all became afraid that the conventional deception would suddenly become obvious and the truth become plain to all. Lisa was the first to pluck up courage and break that silence, but by trying to hide what everybody was feeling, she betrayed it.

"Well, if we are going it's time to start," she said, looking at her watch, a present from her father, and with a faint and significant smile at Fedor Petrovich relating to something known only to them. She got up with a rustle of her dress.

They all rose, said good-night, and went away.

When they had gone it seemed to Ivan Ilych that he felt better; the falsity had gone with them. But the pain remained - that same pain and that same fear that made everything monotonously alike, nothing harder and nothing easier. Everything was worse.

Again minute followed minute and hour followed hour. Everything remained the same and there was no cessation. And the inevitable end of it all became more and more terrible.

"Yes, send Gerasim here," he replied to a question Peter asked.

IX

His wife returned late at night. She came in on tiptoe, but he heard her, opened his eyes, and made haste to close them again. She wished to send Gerasim away and to sit with him herself, but he opened his eyes and said: "No, go away."

"Are you in great pain?"

"Always the same."

"Take some opium."

He agreed and took some. She went away.

Till about three in the morning he was in a state of stupefied misery. It seemed to him that he and his pain were being thrust into a narrow, deep black sack, but though they were pushed further and further in they could not be pushed to the bottom. And this, terrible enough in itself, was accompanied by suffering. He was frightened yet wanted to fall through the sack, he struggled but yet co-operated. And suddenly he broke through, fell, and regained consciousness. Gerasim was sitting at the foot of the bed dozing quietly and patiently, while he himself lay with his emaciated stockinged legs resting on Gerasim's shoulders; the same shaded candle was there and the same unceasing pain.

"Go away, Gerasim," he whispered.

"It's all right, sir. I'll stay a while."

"No. Go away."

He removed his legs from Gerasim's shoulders, turned sideways onto his arm, and felt sorry for himself. He only waited till Gerasim had gone into the next room and then restrained himself no longer but wept like a child. He wept on account of his helplessness, his terrible loneliness, the cruelty of man, the cruelty of God, and the absence of God.

"Why hast Thou done all this? Why hast Thou brought me here? Why, why dost Thou torment me so terribly?"

He did not expect an answer and yet wept because there was no answer and could be none. The pain again grew more acute, but he did not stir and did not call. He said to himself: "Go on! Strike me! But what is it for? What have I done to Thee? What is it for?"

Then he grew quiet and not only ceased weeping but even held his breath and became all attention. It was as though he were listening not to an audible voice but to the voice of his soul, to the current of thoughts arising within him.

"What is it you want?" was the first clear conception capable of expression in words, that he heard.

"What do you want? What do you want?" he repeated to himself.

"What do I want? To live and not to suffer," he answered.

And again he listened with such concentrated attention that even his pain did not distract him.

"To live? How?" asked his inner voice.

"Why, to live as I used to - well and pleasantly."

"As you lived before, well and pleasantly?" the voice repeated.

And in imagination he began to recall the best moments of his pleasant life. But strange to say none of those best moments of his pleasant life now seemed at all what they had then seemed - none of them except the first recollections of childhood. There, in childhood, there had been something really pleasant with which it would be possible to live if it could return. But the child who had experienced that happiness existed no longer, it was like a reminiscence of somebody else.

As soon as the period began which had produced the present Ivan Ilych, all that had then seemed joys now melted before his sight and turned into something trivial and often nasty?

And the further he departed from childhood and the nearer he came to the present the more worthless and doubtful were the joys. This began with the School of Law. A little that was really good was still found there - there was light-heartedness, friendship, and hope. But in the upper classes there had already been fewer of such good moments. Then during the first years of his official career, when he was in the service of the governor, some pleasant moments again occurred: they were the memories of love for a woman. Then all became confused and there was still less of what was good; later on again there was still less that was good, and the further he went the less there was. His marriage, a mere accident, then the disenchantment that followed it, his wife's bad breath and the sensuality and hypocrisy: then that deadly official life and those preoccupations about money, a year of it, and two, and ten, and twenty, and always the same thing. And the longer it lasted the more deadly it became. "It is as if I had been going downhill while I imagined I was going up. And that is really what it was. I was going up in public opinion, but to the same extent life was ebbing away from me. And now it is all done and there is only death.

"Then what does it mean? Why? It can't be that life is so senseless and horrible. But if it really has been so horrible and senseless, why must I die and die in agony? There is something wrong!

"Maybe I did not live as I ought to have done," it suddenly occurred to him. "But how could that be, when I did everything properly?" he replied, and immediately dismissed from his mind this, the sole solution of all the riddles of life and death, as something quite impossible.

"Then what do you want now? To live? Live how? Live as you lived in the law courts when the usher proclaimed 'The judge is coming!' The judge is coming, the judge!" he repeated to himself. "Here he is, the judge. But I am not guilty!" he exclaimed angrily. "What is it for?" And he ceased crying, but turning his face to the wall continued to ponder on the same question: Why, and for what purpose, is there all this horror? But however much he pondered he found no answer. And whenever the thought occurred to him, as it often did, that it all resulted from his not having lived as he ought to have done, he at once recalled the correctness of his whole life and dismissed so strange an idea.

X

Another fortnight passed. Ivan Ilych now no longer left his sofa. He would not lie in bed but lay on the sofa, facing the wall nearly all the time. He suffered ever the same unceasing agonies and in his loneliness pondered always on the same insoluble question: "What is this? Can it be that it is Death?" And the inner voice answered: "Yes, it is Death."

"Why these sufferings?" And the voice answered, "For no reason - they just are so." Beyond and besides this there was nothing.

From the very beginning of his illness, ever since he had first been to see the doctor, Ivan Ilych's life had been divided between two contrary and alternating moods: now it was despair and the expectation of this uncomprehended and terrible death, and now hope and an intently interested observation of the functioning of his organs. Now before his eyes there was only a kidney or an intestine that temporarily evaded its duty, and now only that incomprehensible and dreadful death from which it was impossible to escape.

These two states of mind had alternated from the very beginning of his illness, but the further it progressed the more doubtful and fantastic became the conception of the kidney, and the more real the sense of impending death.

He had but to call to mind what he had been three months before and what he was now, to call to mind with what regularity he had been going downhill, for every possibility of hope to be shattered.

Latterly during the loneliness in which he found himself as he lay facing the back of the sofa, a loneliness in the midst of a populous town and surrounded by numerous acquaintances and relations but that yet could not have been more complete anywhere - either at the bottom of the sea or under the earth - during that terrible loneliness Ivan Ilych had lived only in memories of the past. Pictures of his past rose before him one after another. They always began with what was nearest in time and then went back to what was most remote - to his childhood - and rested there. If he thought of the stewed prunes that had been offered him that day, his mind went back to the raw shrivelled French plums of his childhood, their peculiar flavour and the flow of saliva when he sucked their stones, and along with the memory of that taste came a whole series of memories of those days: his nurse, his brother, and their toys. "No, I mustn't thing of that...It is too painful," Ivan Ilych said to himself, and brought himself back to the present - to the button on the back of the sofa and the creases in its morocco. "Morocco is expensive, but it does not wear well: there had been a quarrel about it. It was a different kind of quarrel and a different kind of morocco that time when we tore father's portfolio and were punished, and mamma brought us some tarts..." And again his thoughts dwelt on his childhood, and again it was painful and he tried to banish them and fix his mind on something else.

Then again together with that chain of memories another series passed through his mind - of how his illness had progressed and grown worse. There also the further back he looked the more life there had been. There had been more of what was good in life and more of life itself. The two merged together. "Just as the pain went on getting worse and worse, so my life grew worse and worse," he thought. "There is one bright spot there at the back, at the beginning of life, and afterwards all becomes blacker and blacker and proceeds more and more rapidly - in inverse ration to the square of the distance from death," thought Ivan Ilych. And the example of a stone falling downwards with increasing velocity entered his mind. Life, a series of increasing sufferings, flies further and further towards its end - the most terrible suffering. "I am flying..." He shuddered, shifted himself, and tried to resist, but was already aware that resistance was impossible, and again with eyes weary of gazing but unable to cease seeing what was before them, he stared at the back of the sofa and waited - awaiting that dreadful fall and shock and destruction.

"Resistance is impossible!" he said to himself. "If I could only understand what it is all for! But that too is impossible. An explanation would be possible if it could be said that I have not lived as I ought to. But it is impossible to say that," and he remembered all the legality, correctitude, and propriety of his life. "That at any rate can certainly not be admitted," he thought, and his lips smiled ironically as if someone could see that smile and be taken in by it. "There is no explanation! Agony, death...What for?"

XI

Another two weeks went by in this way and during that fortnight an event occurred that Ivan Ilych and his wife had desired. Petrishchev formally proposed. It happened in the evening. The next day Praskovya Fedorovna came into her husband's room considering how best to inform him of it, but that very night there had been a fresh change for the worse in his condition. She found him still lying on the sofa but in a different position. He lay on his back, groaning and staring fixedly straight in front of him.

She began to remind him of his medicines, but he turned his eyes towards her with such a look that she did not finish what she was saying; so great an animosity, to her in particular, did that look express.

"For Christ's sake let me die in peace!" he said.

She would have gone away, but just then their daughter came in and went up to say good morning. He looked at her as he had done at his wife, and in reply to her inquiry about his health said dryly that he would soon free them all of himself. They were both silent and after sitting with him for a while went away.

"Is it our fault?" Lisa said to her mother. "It's as if we were to blame! I am sorry for papa, but why should we be tortured?"

The doctor came at his usual time. Ivan Ilych answered "Yes" and "No," never taking his angry eyes from him, and at last said: "You know you can do nothing for me, so leave me alone."

"We can ease your sufferings."

"You can't even do that. Let me be."

The doctor went into the drawing room and told Praskovya Fedorovna that the case was very serious and that the only resource left was opium to allay her husband's sufferings, which must be terrible.

It was true, as the doctor said, that Ivan Ilych's physical sufferings were terrible, but worse than the physical sufferings were his mental sufferings which were his chief torture.

His mental sufferings were due to the fact that that night, as he looked at Gerasim's sleepy, good-natured face with it prominent cheek-bones, the question suddenly occurred to him: "What if my whole life has been wrong?"

It occurred to him that what had appeared perfectly impossible before, namely that he had not spent his life as he should have done, might after all be true. It occurred to him that his scarcely perceptible attempts to struggle against what was considered good by the most highly placed people, those scarcely noticeable impulses which he had immediately suppressed, might have been the real thing, and all the rest false. And his professional duties and the whole arrangement of his life and of his family, and all his social and official interests, might all have been false. He tried to defend all those things to himself and suddenly felt the weakness of what he was defending. There was nothing to defend.

"But if that is so," he said to himself, "and I am leaving this life with the consciousness that I have lost all that was given me and it is impossible to rectify it - what then?"

He lay on his back and began to pass his life in review in quite a new way. In the morning when he saw first his footman, then his wife, then his daughter, and then the doctor, their every word and movement confirmed to him the awful truth that had been revealed to him during the night. In them he saw himself - all that for which he had lived - and saw clearly that it was not real at all, but a terrible and huge deception which had hidden both life and death. This consciousness intensified his physical suffering tenfold. He groaned and tossed about, and pulled at his clothing which choked and stifled him. And he hated them on that account.

He was given a large dose of opium and became unconscious, but at noon his sufferings began again. He drove everybody away and tossed from side to side.

His wife came to him and said:

"Jean, my dear, do this for me. It can't do any harm and often helps. Healthy people often do it."

He opened his eyes wide.

"What? Take communion? Why? It's unnecessary! However..."

She began to cry.

"Yes, do, my dear. I'll send for our priest. He is such a nice man."

"All right. Very well," he muttered.

When the priest came and heard his confession, Ivan Ilych was softened and seemed to feel a relief from his doubts and consequently from his sufferings, and for a moment there came a ray of hope. He again began to think of the vermiform appendix and the possibility of correcting it. He received the sacrament with tears in his eyes.

When they laid him down again afterwards he felt a moment's ease, and the hope that he might live awoke in him again. He began to think of the operation that had been suggested to him. "To live! I want to live!" he said to himself.

His wife came in to congratulate him after his communion, and when uttering the usual conventional words she added:

"You feel better, don't you?"

Without looking at her he said "Yes."

Her dress, her figure, the expression of her face, the tone of her voice, all revealed the same thing. "This is wrong, it is not as it should be. All you have lived for and still live for is falsehood and deception, hiding life and death from you." And as soon as he admitted that thought, his hatred and his agonizing physical suffering again sprang up, and with that suffering a consciousness of the unavoidable, approaching end. And to this was added a new sensation of grinding shooting pain and a feeling of suffocation.

The expression of his face when he uttered that "Yes" was dreadful. Having uttered it, he looked her straight in the eyes, turned on his face with a rapidity extraordinary in his weak state and shouted:

XII

From that moment the screaming began that continued for three days, and was so terrible that one could not hear it through two closed doors without horror. At the moment he answered his wife realized that he was lost, that there was no return, that the end had come, the very end, and his doubts were still unsolved and remained doubts.

"Oh! Oh! Oh!" he cried in various intonations. He had begun by screaming "I won't!" and continued screaming on the letter "O".

For three whole days, during which time did not exist for him, he struggled in that black sack into which he was being thrust by an invisible, resistless force. He struggled as a man condemned to death struggles in the hands of the executioner, knowing that he cannot save himself. And every moment he felt that despite all his efforts he was drawing nearer and nearer to what terrified him. he felt that his agony was due to his being thrust into that black hole and still more to his not being able to get right into it. He was hindered from getting into it by his conviction that his life had been a good one. That very justification of his life held him fast and prevented his moving forward, and it caused him most torment of all.

Suddenly some force struck him in the chest and side, making it still harder to breathe, and he fell through the hole and there at the bottom was a light. What had happened to him was like the sensation one sometimes experiences in a railway carriage when one thinks one is going backwards while one is really going forwards and suddenly becomes aware of the real direction.

"Yes, it was not the right thing," he said to himself, "but that's no matter. It can be done. But what *is* the right thing? he asked himself, and suddenly grew quiet.

This occurred at the end of the third day, two hours before his death. Just then his schoolboy son had crept softly in and gone up to the bedside. The dying man was still screaming desperately and waving his arms. His hand fell on the boy's head, and the boy caught it, pressed it to his lips, and began to cry.

At that very moment Ivan Ilych fell through and caught sight of the light, and it was revealed to him that though his life had not been what it should have been, this could still be rectified. He asked himself, "What *is* the right thing?" and grew still, listening. Then he felt that someone was kissing his hand. He opened his eyes, looked at his son, and felt sorry for him. His wife camp up to him and he glanced at her. She was gazing at him open-mouthed, with undried tears on her nose and cheek and a despairing look on her face. He felt sorry for her too.

"Yes, I am making them wretched," he thought. "They are sorry, but it will be better for them when I die." He wished to say this but had not the strength to utter it. "Besides, why speak? I must act," he thought. With a look at his wife he indicated his son and said: "Take him away...sorry for him...sorry for you too..." He tried to add, "Forgive me," but said "Forego" and waved his hand, knowing that He whose understanding mattered would understand.

And suddenly it grew clear to him that what had been oppressing him and would not leave his was all dropping away at once from two sides, from ten sides, and from all sides. He was sorry for them, he must act so as not to hurt them: release them and free himself from these sufferings. "How good and how simple!" he thought. "And the pain?" he asked himself. "What has become of it? Where are you, pain?"

He turned his attention to it.

"Yes, here it is. Well, what of it? Let the pain be."

"And death... where is it?"

He sought his former accustomed fear of death and did not find it. "Where is it? What death?" There was no fear because there was no death.

In place of death there was light.

"So that's what it is!" he suddenly exclaimed aloud. "What joy!"

To him all this happened in a single instant, and the meaning of that instant did not change. For those present his agony continued for another two hours. Something rattled in his throat, his emaciated body twitched, then the gasping and rattle became less and less frequent.

"It is finished!" said someone near him.

He heard these words and repeated them in his soul.

"Death is finished," he said to himself. "It is no more!"

He drew in a breath, stopped in the midst of a sigh, stretched out, and died.

LITTLE GIRLS WISER THAN MEN

It was an early easter. Sledging was only just over; snow still lay in the yards; and water ran in streams down the village street.

Two little girls from different houses happened to meet in a lane between two homesteads, where the dirty water after running through the farm-yards had formed a large puddle. One girl was very small, the other a little bigger. Their mothers had dressed them both in new frocks. The little one wore a blue frock the other a yellow print, and both had red kerchiefs on their heads. They had just come from church when they met, and first they showed each other their finery, and then they began to play. Soon the fancy took them to splash about in the water, and the smaller one was going to step into the puddle, shoes and all, when the elder checked her:

'Don't go in so, Malásha,' said she, 'your mother will scold you. I will take off my shoes and stockings, and you take off yours.'

They did so, and then, picking up their skirts, began walking towards each other through the puddle. The water came up to Malásha's ankles, and she said:

'It is deep, Akoúlya, I'm afraid!'

'Come on,' replied the other. 'Don't be frightened. It won't get any deeper.'

When they got near one another, Akoúlya said:

'Mind, Malásha, don't splash. Walk carefully!'

She had hardly said this, when Malásha plumped down her foot so that the water splashed right on to Akoúlya's frock. The frock was splashed, and so were Akoúlya's eyes and nose. When she saw the stains on her frock, she was angry and ran after Malásha to strike her. Malásha was frightened, and seeing that she had got herself into trouble, she scrambled out of the puddle, and prepared to run home. Just then Akoúlya's mother happened to be passing, and seeing that her daughter's skirt was splashed, and her sleeves dirty, she said:

'You naughty, dirty girl, what have you been doing?'

'Malásha did it on purpose,' replied the girl.

At this Akoúlya's mother seized Malásha, and struck her on the back of her neck. Malásha began to howl so that she could be heard all down the street. Her mother came out.

'What are you beating my girl for?' said she; and began scolding her neighbour. One word led to another and they had an angry quarrel. The men came out and a crowd collected in the street, every one shouting and no one listening. They all went on quarrelling, till one gave another a push, and the affair had very nearly come to blows, when Akoúlya's old grandmother, stepping in among them, tried to calm them.

'What are you thinking of, friends? Is it right to behave so? On a day like this, too! It is a time for rejoicing, and not for such folly as this.'

They would not listen to the old woman and nearly knocked her off her feet. And she would not have been able to quiet the crowd, if it had not been for Akoúlya and Malásha themselves. While the women were abusing each other, Akoúlya had wiped the mud off her frock, and gone back to the puddle. She took a stone and began scraping away the earth in front of the puddle to make a channel through which the water could run out into the street. Presently Malásha joined her, and with a chip of wood helped her dig the channel. Just as the men were beginning to fight, the water from the little girls' channel ran streaming into the street towards the very place where the old woman was trying to pacify the men. The girls followed it; one running each side of the little stream.

'Catch it, Malásha! Catch it!' shouted Akoúlya; while Malásha could not speak for laughing.

Highly delighted, and watching the chip float along on their stream, the little girls ran straight into the group of men; and the old woman, seeing them, said to the men:

'Are you not ashamed of yourselves? To go fighting on account of these lassies, when they themselves have forgotten all about it, and are playing happily together. Dear little souls! They are wiser than you!'

The men looked at the little girls, and were ashamed, and, laughing at themselves, went back each to his own home.

Except ye turn, and become as little children, ye shall in no wise enter into the kingdom of heaven.

FAMILY HAPPINESS

———— ❧ ————

PART I

I

We were in mourning for my mother, who had died in the autumn, and I spent all that winter alone in the country with Katya and Sonya.

Katya was an old friend of the family, our governess who had brought us all up, and I had known and loved her since my earliest recollections. Sonya was my younger sister. It was a dark and sad winter which we spent in our old house of Pokrovskoye. The weather was cold and so windy that the snowdrifts came higher than the windows; the panes were almost always dimmed by frost, and we seldom walked or drove anywhere throughout the winter. Our visitors were few, and those who came brought no addition of cheerfulness or happiness to the household. They all wore sad faces and spoke low, as if they were afraid of waking someone; they never laughed, but sighed and often shed tears as they looked at me and especially at little Sonya in her black frock. The feeling of death clung to the house; the air was still filled with the grief and horror of death. My mother's room was kept locked; and whenever I passed it on my way to bed, I felt a strange uncomfortable impulse to look into that cold empty room.

I was then seventeen; and in the very year of her death my mother was intending to move to Petersburg, in order to take me into society. The loss of my mother was a great grief to me; but I must confess to another feeling behind that grief - a feeling that though I was young and pretty (so everybody told me), I was wasting a second winter in the solitude of the country. Before the winter ended, this sense of dejection, solitude, and simple boredom increased to such an extent that I refused to leave my room or open the piano or take up a book. When Katya urged me to find some occupation, I said that I did not feel able for it; but in my heart I said, "What is the good of it? What is the good of doing anything, when the best part of my life is being wasted like this?" and to this question, tears were my only answer.

I was told that I was growing thin and losing my looks; but even this failed to interest me. What did it matter? For whom? I felt that my whole life was bound to go on in the same solitude and helpless dreariness, from which I had myself no strength and even no wish to escape. Towards the end of winter Katya became anxious about me and determined to make an effort to take me abroad. But money was needed for this, and we hardly knew how our affairs stood after my mother's death. Our guardian, who was to come and clear up our position, was expected every day.

In March he arrived.

"Well, thank God!" Katya said to me one day, when I was walking up and down the room like a shadow, without occupation, without a thought, and without a wish. "Sergey Mikhaylych has arrived; he has sent to inquire about us and means to come here for dinner. You must rouse yourself, dear Mashechka," she added, "or what will he think of you? He was so fond of you all."

Sergey Mikhaylych was our near neighbor, and, though a much younger man, had been a friend of my father's. His coming was likely to change our plans and to make it possible to leave the country; and also I had grown up in the habit of love and regard for him; and when Katya begged me to rouse myself, she guessed rightly that it would give me especial pain to show to disadvantage before him, more than before any other of our friends. Like everyone in the house, from Katya and his god-daughter Sonya down to the helper in the stables, I loved him from old habit; and also he had a special significance for me, owing to a remark which my mother had once made in my presence. "I should like you to marry a man like him," she said. At the time this seemed to me strange and even unpleasant. My ideal husband was quite different: he was to be thin, pale, and sad; and Sergey Mikhaylych was middle-aged, tall, robust, and always, as it seemed to me, in good spirits. But still my mother's words stuck in my head; and even six years before this time, when I was eleven, and he still said "thou" to me, and played with me, and called me by the pet-name of "violet" - even then I sometimes asked myself in a fright, "What shall I do, if he suddenly wants to marry me?"

Before our dinner, to which Katya made an addition of sweets and a dish of spinach, Sergey Mikhaylych arrived. From the window I watched him drive up to the house in a small sleigh; but as soon as it turned the corner, I hastened to the drawing room , meaning to pretend that his visit was a complete surprise. But when I heard his tramp and loud voice and Katya's footsteps in the hall, I lost patience and went to meet him myself. He was holding Katya's hand, talking loud, and smiling. When he saw me, he stopped and looked at me for a time without bowing. I was uncomfortable and felt myself blushing.

"Can this be really you?" he said in his plain decisive way, walking towards me with his arms apart. "Is so great a change possible? How grown-up you are! I used to call you "violet", but now you are a rose in full bloom!'

He took my hand in his own large hand and pressed it so hard that it almost hurt. Expecting him to kiss my hand, I bent towards him, but he only pressed it again and looked straight into my eyes with the old firmness and cheerfulness in his face.

It was six years since I had seen him last. He was much changed - older and darker in complexion; and he now wore whiskers which did not become him at all; but much remained the same - his simple manner, the large features of his honest open face, his bright intelligent eyes, his friendly, almost boyish, smile.

Five minutes later he had ceased to be a visitor and had become the friend of us all, even of the servants, whose visible eagerness to wait on him proved their pleasure at his arrival.

He behaved quite unlike the neighbors who had visited us after my mother's death. They had thought it necessary to be silent when they sat with us, and to shed tears. He, on the contrary, was cheerful and talkative, and said not a word about my mother, so that this indifference seemed strange to me at first and even improper on the part of so close a friend. But I understood later that what seemed indifference was sincerity, and I felt grateful for it. In the evening Katya poured out tea, sitting in her old place in the drawing room, where she used to sit in my mother's lifetime; our old butler Grigori had hunted out one of my father's pipes and brought it to him; and he began to walk up and down the room as he used to do in past days.

"How many terrible changes there are in this house, when one thinks of it all!" he said, stopping in his walk.

"Yes," said Katya with a sigh; and then she put the lid on the samovar and looked at him, quite ready to burst out crying.

"I suppose you remember your father?" he said, turning to me.

"Not clearly," I answered.

"How happy you would have been together now!" he added in a low voice, looking thoughtfully at my face above the eyes. "I was very fond of him," he added in a still lower tone, and it seemed to me that his eyes were shining more than usual.

"And now God has taken her too!" said Katya; and at once she laid her napkin on the teapot, took out her handkerchief, and began to cry.

"Yes, the changes in this house are terrible," he repeated, turning away. "Sonya, show me your toys," he added after a little and went off to the parlor. When he had gone, I looked at Katya with eyes full of tears.

"What a splendid friend he is!" she said. And, though he was no relation, I did really feel a kind of warmth and comfort in the sympathy of this good man.

I could hear him moving about in the parlor with Sonya, and the sound of her high childish voice. I sent tea to him there; and I heard him sit down at the piano and strike the keys with Sonya's little hands.

Then his voice came - "Marya Aleksandrovna, come here and play something."

I liked his easy behavior to me and his friendly tone of command; I got up and went to him.

"Play this," he said, opening a book of Beethoven's music at the adagio of the "Moonlight Sonata." "Let me hear how you play," he added, and went off to a corner of the room, carrying his cup with him.

I somehow felt that with him it was impossible to refuse or to say beforehand that I played badly: I sat down obediently at the piano and began to play as well as I could; yet I was afraid of criticism, because I knew that he understood and enjoyed music. The adagio suited the remembrance of past days evoked by our conversation at tea, and I believe that I played it fairly well. But he would not let me play the scherzo. "No," he said, coming up to me; "you don't play that right; don't go on; but the first movement was not bad; you seem to be musical." This moderate praise pleased me so much that I even reddened. I felt it pleasant and strange that a friend of my father's, and his contemporary, should no longer treat me like a child but speak to me seriously. Katya now went upstairs to put Sonya to bed, and we were left alone in the parlor.

He talked to me about my father, and about the beginning of their friendship and the happy days they had spent together, while I was still busy with lesson-books and toys; and his talk put my father before me in quite a new light, as a man of simple and delightful character. He asked me too about my tastes, what I read and what I intended to do, and gave me advice. The man of mirth and jest who used to tease me and make me toys had disappeared; here was a serious, simple, and affectionate friend, for whom I could not help feeling respect and sympathy. It was easy and pleasant to talk to him; and yet I felt an involuntary strain also. I was anxious about each word I spoke: I wished so much to earn for my own sake the love which had been given me already merely because I was my father's daughter.

After putting Sonya to bed, Katya joined us and began to complain to him of my apathy, about which I had said nothing.

"So she never told me the most important thing of all!" he said, smiling and shaking his head reproachfully at me.

"Why tell you?" I said. "It is very tiresome to talk about, and it will pass off." (I really felt now, not only that my dejection would pass off, but that it had already passed off, or rather had never existed.)

"It is a bad thing," he said, "not to be able to stand solitude. Can it be that you are a young lady?"

"Of course, I am a young lady," I answered laughing.

"Well, I can't praise a young lady who is alive only when people are admiring her, but as soon as she is left alone, collapses and finds nothing to her taste - one who is all for show and has no resources in herself."

"You have a flattering opinion of me!" I said, just for the sake of saying something.

He was silent for a little. Then he said: "Yes; your likeness to your father means something. There is something in you...," and his kind attentive look again flattered me and made me feel a pleasant embarrassment.

I noticed now for the first time that his face, which gave one at first the impression of high spirits, had also an expression peculiar to himself - bright at first and then more and more attentive and rather sad.

"You ought not to be bored and you cannot be," he said; "you have music, which you appreciate, books, study; your whole life lies before you, and now or never is the time to prepare for it and save yourself future regrets. A year hence it will be too late."

He spoke to me like a father or an uncle, and I felt that he kept a constant check upon himself, in order to keep on my level. Though I was hurt that he considered me as inferior to himself, I was pleased that for me alone he thought it necessary to try to be different.

For the rest of the evening he talked about business with Katya.

"Well, goodbye, dear friends," he said. Then he got up, came towards me and took my hand. When shall we see you again?" asked Katya.

"In spring," he answered, still holding my hand. "I shall go now to Danilovka" (this was another property of ours), "look into things there and make what arrangements I can; then I go to Moscow on business of my own; and in summer we shall meet again."

"Must you really be away so long?" I asked, and I felt terribly grieved. I had really hoped to see him every day, and I felt a sudden shock of regret, and a fear that my depression would return. And my face and voice just have made this plain.

"You must find more to do and not get depressed," he said; and I thought his tone too cool and unconcerned. "I shall put you through an examination in spring," he added, letting go my hand and not looking at me.

When we saw him off in the hall, he put on his fur coat in a hurry and still avoided looking at me. "He is taking a deal of trouble for nothing!" I thought. "Does he think me so anxious that he should look at me? He is a good man, a very good man; but that's all."

That evening, however, Katya and I sat up late, talking, not about him but about our plans for the summer, and where we should spend next winter and what we should do then. I had ceased to ask that terrible question - what is the good of it all? Now it seemed quite plain and simple: the proper object of life was happiness, and I promised myself much happiness ahead. It seemed as if our gloomy old house had suddenly become fully of light and life.

II

Meanwhile spring arrived. My old dejection passed away and gave place to the unrest which spring brings with it, full of dreams and vague hopes and desires. Instead of living as I had done at the beginning of winter, I read and played the piano and gave lessons to Sonya; but also I often went into the garden and wandered for long alone through the avenues, or sat on a bench there; and Heaven knows what my thoughts and wishes and hopes were at such times. Sometimes at night, especially if there was a moon, I sat by my bedroom window till dawn; sometimes, when Katya was not watching, I stole out into the garden wearing only a wrapper and ran through the dew as far as the pond; and once I went all the way to the open fields and walked right round the garden alone at night.

I find it difficult now to recall and understand the dreams which then filled my imagination. Even when I can recall them, I find it hard to believe that my dreams were just like that: they were so strange and so remote from life. Sergey Mikhaylych kept his promise: he returned from his travels at the end of May. His first visit to us was in the evening and was quite unexpected. We were sitting in the veranda, preparing for tea. By this time the garden was all green, and the nightingales had taken up their quarters for the whole of St. Peter's Fast in the leafy borders. The tops of the round lilac bushes had a sprinkling of white and purple - a sign that their flowers were ready to open. The foliage of the birch avenue was all transparent in the light of the setting sun. In the veranda there was shade and freshness. The evening dew was sure to be heavy in the grass. Out of doors beyond the garden the last sounds of day were audible, and the noise of the sheep and cattle, as they were driven home. Nikon, the half-witted boy, was driving his water-cart along the path outside the veranda, and a cold stream of water from the sprinkler made dark circles on the mould round the stems and supports of the dahlias. In our veranda the polished samovar shone and hissed on the white table-cloth; there were cracknels and biscuits and cream on the table. Katya was busy washing the cups with her plump hands. I was too hungry after bathing to wait for tea, and was eating bread with thick fresh cream. I was wearing a gingham blouse with loose sleeves, and my hair, still wet, was covered with a kerchief. Katya saw him first, even before he came in.

"You, Sergey Mikhaylych!" she cried. "Why, we were just talking about you."

I got up, meaning to go and change my dress, but he caught me just by the door.

"Why stand on such ceremony in the country?" he said, looking with a smile at the kerchief on my head. "You don't mind the presence of your butler, and I am really the same to you as Grigori is." But I felt just then that he was looking at me in a way quite unlike Grigori's way, and I was uncomfortable.

"I shall come back at once," I said, as I left them.

"But what is wrong?" he called out after me; "it's just the dress of a young peasant woman."

"How strangely he looked at me!" I said to myself as I was quickly changing upstairs. "Well, I'm glad he has come; things will be more lively." After a look in the glass I ran gaily downstairs and into the veranda; I was out of breath and did not disguise my haste. He was sitting at the table, talking to Katya about our affairs. He glanced at me and smiled; then he went on talking. From what he said it appeared that our affairs were in capital shape: it was now possible for us, after spending the summer in the country, to go either to Petersburg for Sonya's education, or abroad.

"If only you would go abroad with us -" said Katya; "without you we shall be quite lost there."

"Oh, I should like to go round the world with you," he said, half in jest and half in earnest.

"All right," I said; let us start off and go round the world."

He smiled and shook his head.

"What about my mother? What about my business, he said. "But that's not the question just now: I want to know how you have been spending your time. Not depressed again, I hope?

When I told him that I had been busy and not bored during his absence, and when Katya confirmed my report, he praised me as if he had a right to do so, and his words and looks were kind, as they might have been to a child. I felt obliged to tell him, in detail and with perfect frankness, all my good actions, and to confess, as if I were in church, all that he might disapprove of. The evening was so fine that we stayed in the veranda after tea was cleared away; and the conversation interested me so much that I did not notice how we ceased by degrees to hear any sound of the servants indoors. The scent of flowers grew stronger and came from all sides; the grass was drenched with dew; a nightingale struck up in a lilac bush close by and then stopped on hearing our voices; the starry sky seemed to come down lower over our heads.

It was growing dusk, but I did not notice it till a bat suddenly and silently flew in beneath the veranda awning and began to flutter round my white shawl. I shrank back against the wall and nearly cried out; but the bat as silently and swiftly dived out from under the awning and disappeared in the half-darkness of the garden.

"How fond I am of this place of yours!" he said, changing the conversation;

"I wish I could spend all my life here, sitting in this veranda."

"Well, do then!" said Katya.

"That's all very well," he said, "but life won't sit still."

"Why don't you marry?" asked Katya; you would make an excellent husband.

"Because I like sitting still?" and he laughed. "No, Katerina Karlovna, too late for you and me to marry. People have long ceased to think of me as a marrying man, and I am even surer of it myself; and I declare I have felt quite comfortable since the matter was settled."

It seemed to me that he said this in an unnaturally persuasive way.

"Nonsense!" said Katya; "a man of thirty-six makes out that he is too old!"

"Too old indeed," he went on, "when all one wants is to sit still. For a man who is going to marry that's not enough. Just you ask her," he added, nodding at me; "people of her age should marry, and you and I can rejoice in their happiness."

The sadness and constraint latent in his voice was not lost upon me. He was silent for a little, and neither Katya nor I spoke.

"Well, just fancy," he went on, turning a little on his seat; "suppose that by some mischance I married a girl of seventeen, Masha, if you like - I mean, Marya Aleksandrovna. The instance is good; I am glad it turned up; there could not be a better instance."

I laughed; but I could not understand why he was glad, or what it was that had turned up.

"Just tell me honestly, with your hand on your heart," he said, turning as if playfully to me, "would it not be a misfortune for you to unite your life with that of an old worn-out man who only wants to sit still, whereas Heaven knows what wishes are fermenting in that heart of yours?"

I felt uncomfortable and was silent, not knowing how to answer him.

"I am not making you a proposal, you know," he said, laughing; "but am I really the kind of husband you dream of when walking alone in the avenue at twilight? It would be a misfortune, would it not?"

"No, not a misfortune," I began.

"But a bad thing," he ended my sentence.

"Perhaps; but I may be mistaken..." He interrupted me again.

"There, you see! She is quite right, and I am grateful to her for her frankness, and very glad to have had this conversation. And there is something else to be said" - he added: "for me too it would be a very great misfortune."

"How odd you are! You have not changed in the least," said Katya, and then left the veranda, to order supper to be served.

When she had gone, we were both silent and all was still around us, but for one exception. A nightingale, which had sung last night by fitful snatches, now flooded the garden with a steady stream of song, and was soon answered by another from the dell below, which had not sung till that evening. The nearer bird stopped and seemed to listen for a moment, and then broke out again still louder than before, pouring out his song in piercing long drawn cadences. There was a regal calm in the birds' voices, as they floated through the realm of night which belongs to those birds and not to man. The gardener walked past to his sleeping-quarters in the greenhouse, and the noise of his heavy boots grew fainter and fainter along the path. Someone whistled twice sharply at the foot of the hill; and then all was still again. The rustling of leaves could just be heard; the veranda awning flapped; a faint perfume, floating in the air, came down on the veranda and filled it. I felt silence awkward after what had been said, but what to say I did not know. I looked at him. His eyes, bright in the half-darkness, turned towards me.

"How good life is!" he said.

I sighed, I don't know why.

"Well?" he asked.

"Life is good," I repeated after him.

Again we were silent, and again I felt uncomfortable. I could not help fancying that I had wounded him by agreeing that he was old; and I wished to comfort him but did not know how.

"Well, I must be saying good-bye," he said, rising; "my mother expects me for supper; I have hardly seen her all day."

"I meant to play you the new sonata," I said.

"That must wait," he replied; and I thought that he spoke coldly. "Good-bye."

I felt still more certain that I had wounded him, and I was sorry. Katya and I went to the steps to see him off and stood for a while in the open, looking along the road where he had disappeared from view. When we ceased to hear the sound of his horse's hoofs, I walked round the house to the veranda, and again sat looking into the garden; and all I wished to see and hear, I still saw and heard for a long time in the dewy mist filled with the sounds of night.

He came a second time, and a third; and the awkwardness arising from that strange conversation passed away entirely, never to return. During that whole summer he came two or three times a week; and I grew so accustomed to his presence, that, when he failed to come for some time, Ii missed him and felt angry with him, and thought he was behaving badly in deserting me. He treated me like a boy whose company he liked, asked me questions, invited the most cordial frankness on my part, gave me advice and encouragement, or sometimes scolded and checked me. But in spite of his constant effort to keep on my level, I was aware that behind the part of him which I could understand there remained an entire region of mystery, into which he did not consider it necessary to admit me; and this fact did much to preserve my respect for him and his attraction for me. I knew from Katya and from our neighbors that he had not only to care for his old mother with whom he lived, and to manage his own estate and our affairs, but was also responsible for some public business which was the source of serious worries; but what view he took of all this, what were his convictions, plans, and hopes, I could not in the least find out from him. Whenever I turned the conversation to his affairs, he frowned in a way peculiar to himself and seemed to imply, "Please stop! That is no business of yours;" and then he changed the subject. This hurt me at first; but I soon grew accustomed to confining our talk to my affairs, and felt this to be quite natural.

There was another thing which displeased me at first and then became pleasant to me. This was his complete indifference and even contempt for my personal appearance. Never by word or look did he simply that I was pretty; on the contrary, he frowned and laughed, whenever the word was applied to me in his presence. He even liked to find fault with my looks and tease me about them. On special days Katya liked to dress me out in fine clothes and to arrange my hair effectively; but my finery met only with mockery from him, which pained kind-hearted Katya and at first disconcerted me. She had made up her mind that he admired me; and she could not understand how a man could help wishing a woman whom he admired to appear to the utmost advantage. But I soon understood what he wanted. He wished to make sure that I had not a trace of affectation. And when I understood this I was really quite free from affectation in the clothes I wore, or the arrangement of my hair, or my movements; but a very obvious form of affectation took its place - an affectation of simplicity, at a time when I could not yet be really simple. That he loved me, I knew; but I did not yet ask myself whether he loved me as a child or as a woman. I valued his love; I felt that he thought me better than all other young women in the world, and I could not help wishing him to go on being deceived about me. Without wishing to deceive him, I did deceive him, and I became better myself while deceiving him. I felt it a better and worthier course to show him to good points of my heart and mind than of my body. My hair, hands, face, ways - all these, whether good or bad, he had appraised at once and knew so well, that I could add nothing to my external appearance except the wish to deceive him. But my mind and heart he did not know, because he loved them, and because they were in the very process of growth and development; and on this point I could and did deceive him. And how easy I felt in his company, once I understood this clearly! My causeless bashfulness and awkward movements completely disappeared. Whether he saw me from in front, or in profile, sitting or standing, with my hair up or my hair down, I felt that he knew me from head to foot, and I fancied, was satisfied with me as I was. If, contrary to his habit, he had suddenly said to me as other people did, that I had a pretty face, I believe that I should not have liked it at all. But, on the other hand, how light and happy my heart was when, after I had said something, he looked hard at me and said, hiding emotion under a mask of raillery:

"Yes, there is something in you! You are a fine girl - that I must tell you."

And for what did I receive such rewards, which filled my heart with pride and joy? Merely for saying that I felt for old Grigori in his love for his little granddaughter; or because the reading of some poem or novel moved me to tears; or because I liked Mozart better than Schulhof. And I was surprised at my own quickness in guessing what was good and worthy of love, when I certainly did not know then what was good and worthy to be loved. Most of my former tastes and habits did not please him; and a mere look of his, or a twitch of his eyebrow was enough to show that he did not like what I was trying to say; and I felt at once that my own standard was changed. Sometimes, when he was about to give me a piece of advice, I seemed to know beforehand what he would say. When he looked in my face and asked me a question, his very look would draw out of me the answer he wanted. All my thoughts and feelings of that time were not really mine: they were his thoughts and feelings, which had suddenly become mine and passed into my life and lighted it up. Quite unconsciously I began to look at everything with different eyes - at Katya and the servants and Sonya and myself and my occupations. Books, which I used to read merely to escape boredom, now became one of the chief pleasures of my life, merely because he brought me the books and we read and discussed them together. The lessons I gave to Sonya had been a burdensome obligation which I forced myself to go through from a sense of duty; but, after he was present at a lesson, it became a joy to me to watch Sonya's progress. It used to seem to me an impossibility to learn a whole piece of music by heart; but now, when I knew that he would hear it and might praise it, I would play a single movement forty times over without stopping, till poor Katya stuffed her ears with cottonwool, while I was still not weary of it. The same old sonatas seemed quite different in the expression, and came out quite changed and much improved. Even Katya, whom I knew and loved like a second self, became different in my eyes. I now understood for the first time that she was not in the least bound to be the mother, friend, and slave that she was to us. Now I appreciated all the self-sacrifice and devotion of this affectionate creature, and all my obligations to her; and I began to love her even better. It was he too who taught me to take quite a new view of our serfs and servants and maids. It is an absurd confession to make - but I had spent seventeen years among these people and yet knew less about than about strangers whom I had never seen; it had never once occurred to me that they had their affections and wishes and sorrows, just as I had. Our garden and woods and fields which I had known so long, became suddenly new and beautiful to me. He was right in saying that the only certain happiness in life is to live for others. At the time his words seemed to me strange, and I did not understand them; but by degrees this became a conviction with me, without thinking about it. He revealed to me a whole new world of joys in the present, without changing anything in my life, without adding anything except himself to each impression in my mind. All that had surrounded me from childhood without saying anything to me, suddenly came to life. The mere sight of him made everything begin to speak and press for admittance to my heart, filling it with happiness.

Often during that summer, when I went upstairs to my room and lay down on my bed, the old unhappiness of spring with its desires and hopes for the future gave place to a passionate happiness in the present. Unable to sleep, I often got up and sat on Katya's bed and told her how perfectly happy I was, though I now realize that this was quite unnecessary, as she could see it for herself. But when told me that she was quite content and perfectly happy, and kissed me. I believed her - it seemed to me so necessary and just that everyone should be happy. But Katya could think of sleep too; and sometimes, pretending to be angry, she drove me from her bed and went to sleep, while I turned over and over in my mind all that made me so happy. Sometimes I got up and said my prayers over again, praying in my own words and thanking God for all the happiness he had given me.

All was quiet in the room; there was only the even breathing of Katya in her sleep, and the ticking of the clock by her bed, while I turned from side to side and whispered words of prayer, or crossed myself and kissed the cross round my neck. The door was shut and the windows shuttered; perhaps a fly or gnat hung buzzing in the air. I felt a wish never to leave that room - a wish that dawn might never come, that my present frame of mind might never change. I felt that my dreams and thoughts and prayers were live things, living there in the dark with me, hovering about my bed, and standing over me. And every thought was his thought, and every feeling his feeling. I did not know yet that this was love; I thought that things might go on so forever, and that this feeling involved no consequences.

III

One day when the corn was being carried, I went with Katya and Sonya to our favorite seat in the garden, in the shade of the lime trees and above the dell, beyond which the fields and woods lay open before us. It was three days since Sergey Mikhaylych had been to see us; we were expecting him, all the more because our bailiff reported that he had promised to visit the harvest field. At two o'clock we saw him ride on to the rye field. With a smile and a glance at me, Katya ordered peaches and cherries, of which he was very fond, to be brought; then she lay down on the bench and began to doze. I tore off a crooked flat lime tree branch, which made my hand wet with its juicy leaves and juicy bark. Then I fanned Katya with it and went on with my book, breaking off from time to time, to look at the field path along which he must come. Sonya was making a dolls' house at the root of an old lime tree. The day was sultry, windless, and steaming; the clouds were packing and growing blacker; all morning a thunderstorm had been gathering, and I felt restless, as I always did before thunder. But by afternoon the clouds began to part, the sun sailed out into a clear sky, and only in one quarter was there a faint fumbling. A single heavy cloud, lowering above the horizon and mingling with the dust from the fields, was rent from time to time by pale zigzags of lightning which ran down to the ground. It was clear that for today the storm would pass off, with us at all events. The road beyond the garden was visible in places, and we could see a procession of high creaking carts slowly moving along it with their load of sheaves, while the empty carts rattled at a faster pace to meet them, with swaying legs and shirts fluttering in them. The thick dust neither blew away nor settled down - it stood still beyond the fence, and we could see it through the transparent foliage of the garden trees. A little farther off, in the stackyard, the same voices and the same creaking of wheels were audible; and the same yellow sheaves that had moves slowly past the fence were now flying aloft, and I could see the oval stacks gradually rising higher, and their conspicuous pointed tops, and the laborers swarming upon them. On the dusty field in front more carts were moving and more yellow sheaves were visible; and the noise of the carts, with the sound of talking and singing, came to us from a distance. At one side the bare stubble, with strips of fallow covered with wormwood, came more and more into view. Lower down, to the right, the gay dresses of the women were visible, as they bent down and swung their arms to bind the sheaves. Here the bare stubble looked untidy; but the disorder was cleared by degrees, as the pretty sheaves were ranged at close intervals. It seemed as if summer had suddenly turned to autumn before my eyes. The dust and heat were everywhere, except in our favorite nook in the garden; and everywhere, in this heat and dust and under the burning sun, the laborers carried on their heavy task with talk and noise.

Meanwhile Katya slept so sweetly on our shady bench, beneath her white cambric handkerchief, the black juicy cherries glistened so temptingly on the plate, our dresses were so clean and fresh, the water in the jug was so bright with rainbow colors in the sun, and I felt so happy. "How can I help it?" I thought; "am I to blame for being happy? And how can I share my happiness? How and to whom can I surrender all myself and all my happiness?"

By this time the sun had sunk behind the tops of the birch avenue, the dust was settling on the fields, the distance became clearer and brighter in the slanting light. The clouds had dispersed altogether; I could see through the trees the thatch of three new corn stacks. The laborers came down off the stacks; the carts hurried past, evidently for the last time, with a loud noise of shouting; the women, with rakes over their shoulders and straw bands in their belts, walked home past us, singing loudly; and still there was no sign of Sergey Mikhaylych, though I had seen him ride down the hill long ago. Suddenly he appeared upon the avenue, coming from a quarter where I was not looking for him. He had walked round by the dell. He came quickly towards me, with his hat off and radiant with high spirits. Seeing that Katya was asleep, he bit his lip, closed his eyes, and advanced on tiptoe; I saw at once that he was in that peculiar mood of causeless merriment which I always delighted to see in him, and which we called "wild ecstasy". He was just like a schoolboy playing truant; his whole figure, from head to foot, breathed content, happiness, and boyish frolic.

"Well, young violet, how are you? All right?" he said in a whisper, coming up to me and taking my hand. Then, in answer to my question, "Oh, I'm splendid today, I feel like a boy of thirteen - I want to play at horses and climb trees."

"Is it wild ecstasy?" I asked, looking into his laughing eyes, and feeling that the "wild ecstasy" was infecting me.

"Yes," he answered, winking and checking a smile. "But I don't see why you need hit Katerina Karlovna on the nose."

With my eyes on him I had gone on waving the branch, without noticing that I had knocked the handkerchief off Katya's face and was now brushing her with the leaves. I laughed.

"She will say she was awake all the time," I whispered, as if not to awake Katya; but that was not my real reason - it was only that I liked to whisper to him.

He moved his lips in imitation of me, pretending that my voice was too low for him to hear. Catching sight of the dish of cherries, he pretended to steal it, and carried it off to Sonya under the lime tree, where he sat down on her dolls. Sonya was angry at first, but he soon made his peace with her by starting a game, to see which of them could eat cherries faster.

"If you like, I will send for more cherries," I said; "or let us go ourselves."

He took the dish and set the dolls on it, and we all three started for the orchard. Sonya ran behind us, laughing and pulling at his coat, to make him surrender the dolls. He gave them up and then turned to me, speaking more seriously.

"You really are a violet," he said, still speaking low, though there was no longer any fear of waking anybody; "when I came to you out of all that dust and heat and toil, I positively smelt violets at once. But not the sweet violet - you know, that early dark violet that smells of melting snow and spring grass."

"Is harvest going on well?" I asked, in order to hide the happy agitation which his words produced in me.

"First rate! Our people are always splendid. The more you know them, the better you like them."

"Yes," I said; "before you came I was watching them from the garden, and suddenly I felt ashamed to be so comfortable myself while they were hard at work, and so..."

He interrupted me, with a kind but grave look: "Don't talk like that, my dear; it is too sacred a matter to talk of lightly. God forbid that you should use fine phrases about that!"

"But it is only to you I say this."

"All right, I understand. But what about those cherries?"

The orchard was locked, and no gardener to be seen: he had sent them all off to help with the harvest. Sonya ran to fetch the key. But he would not wait for her: climbing up a corner of the wall, he raised the net and jumped down on the other side.

His voice came over the wall - "If you want some, give me the dish."

"No," I said; "I want to pick for myself. I shall fetch the key; Sonya won't find it."

But suddenly I felt that I must see what he was doing there and what he looked like - that I must watch his movements while he supposed that no one saw him. Besides I was simply unwilling just then to lose sight of him for a single minute. running on tiptoe through the nettles to the other side of the orchard where the wall was lower, I mounted on an empty cask, till the top of the wall was on a level with my waist, and then leaned over into the orchard. I looked at the gnarled old trees, with their broad dented leaves and the ripe black cherries hanging straight and heavy among the foliage; then I pushed my head under the net, and from under the knotted bough of an old cherry tree I caught sight of Sergey Mikhaylych. He evidently thought that I had gone away and that no one was watching him. With his hat off and his eyes shut, he was sitting on the fork of an old tree and carefully rolling into a ball a lump of cherry tree gum. Suddenly he shrugged his shoulders, opened his eyes, muttered something, and smiled. Both words and smile were so unlike him that I felt ashamed of myself for eavesdropping. It seemed to me that he had said, "Masha!" "Impossible," I thought. "Darling Masha!" he said again, in a lower and more tender tone. There was possible doubt about the two words this time. My heart beat hard, and such a passionate joy - illicit joy, as I felt - took hold of me, that I clutched at the wall, fearing to fall and betray myself. Startled by the sound of my movement, he looked round - he dropped his eyes instantly, and his face turned red, even scarlet, like a child's. He tried to speak, but in vain; again and again his face positively flamed up. Still he smiled as he looked at me, and I smiled too. Then his whole face grew radiant with happiness. He had ceased to be the old uncle who spoiled or scolded me; he was a man on my level, who loved and feared me as I loved and feared him. We looked at one another without speaking. But suddenly he frowned; the smile and light in his eyes disappeared, and he resumed his cold paternal tone, just as if we were doing something wrong and he was repenting and calling on me to repent.

"You had better get down, or you will hurt yourself," he said; "and do put your hair straight; just think what you look like?"

"What makes him pretend? What makes him want to give me pain?" I thought in my vexation. And the same instant brought an irresistible desire to upset his composure again and test my power over him.

"No," I said; "I mean to pick for myself." I caught hold of the nearest branch and climbed to the top of the wall; then, before he had time to catch me, I jumped down on the other side.

"What foolish things you do!" he muttered, flushing again and trying to hide his confusion under a pretence of annoyance; "you might really have hurt yourself. But how do you mean to get out of this?"

He was even more confused than before, but this time his confusion frightened rather than pleased me. It infected me too and made me blush; avoiding his eye and not knowing what to say, I began to pick cherries though I had nothing to put them in. I reproached myself, I repented of what I had done, I was frightened; I felt that I had lost his good opinion forever by my folly. Both of us were silent and embarrassed. From this difficult situation Sonya rescued us by running back with the key in her hand. For some time we both addressed our conversation to her and said nothing to each other. When we returned to Katya, who assured us that she had never been asleep and was listening all the time, I calmed down, and he tried to drop into his fatherly patronizing manner again, but I was not taken in by it. A discussion which we had had some days before came back clear before me.

Katya had been saying that it was easier for a man to be in love and declare his love than for a woman.

"A man may say that he is in love, and a woman can't," she said.

"I disagree," said he; "a man has no business to say, and can't say that he is in love."

"Why not?" I asked.

"Because it never can be true. What sort of a revelation is that, that a man is in love? A man seems to think that whenever he says the word, something will go pop! - that some miracle will be worked, signs and wonders, with all the big guns firing at once! In my opinion," he went on, "whoever solemnly brings out the words "I love you" is either deceiving himself or, which is even worse, deceiving others."

"Then how is a woman to know that a man is in love with her, unless he tells her?" asked Katya.

"That I don't know," he answered; "every man has his own way of telling things. If the feeling exists, it will out somehow. But when I read novels, I always fancy the crestfallen look of Lieut. Strelsky or Alfred, when he says, "I love you, Eleanora", and expects something wonderful to happen at once, and no change at all takes place in either of them - their eyes and their noses and their whole selves remain exactly as they were."

Even then I had felt that this banter covered something serious that had reference to myself. But Katya resented his disrespectful treatment of the heroes in novels.

"You are never serious," she said; "but tell me truthfully, have you never yourself told a woman that you loved her?"

"Never, and never gone down on one knee," he answered, laughing; "and never will."

This conversation I now recalled, and I reflected that there was no need for him to tell me that he loved me. "I know that he loves me," I thought, "and all his endeavors to seem indifferent will not change my opinion."

He said little to me throughout the evening, but in every word he said to Katya and Sonya and in every look and movement of his I saw love and felt no doubt of it. I was only vexed and sorry for him, that he thought it necessary still to hide his feelings and pretend coldness, when it was all so clear, and when it would have been so simple and easy to be boundlessly happy. But my jumping down to him in the orchard weighed on me like a crime. I kept feeling that he would cease to respect me and was angry with me.

After tea I went to the piano, and he followed me.

"Play me something - it is long since I heard you," he said, catching me up in the parlor.

"I was just going to," I said. Then I looked straight in his face and said quickly, "Sergèy Mikhaylych, you are not angry with me, are you?"

"What for?" he asked.

"For not obeying you this afternoon," I said, blushing.

He understood me: he shook his head and made a grimace, which implied that I deserved a scolding but that he did not feel able to give it.

"So it's all right, and we are friends again?" I said, sitting down at the piano.

"Of course!" he said.

In the drawing room, a large lofty room, there were only two lighted candles on the piano, the rest of the room remaining in half-darkness. Outside the open windows the summer night was bright. All was silent, except when the sound of Katya's footsteps in the unlighted parlor was heard occasionally, or when his horse, which was tied up under the window, snorted or stamped his hoof on the burdocks that grew there. He sat behind me, where I could not see him; but everywhere - in the half-darkness of the room, in every sound, in myself - I felt his presence. Every look, every movement of his, though I could not see them, found an echo in my heart. I played a sonata of Mozart's which he had brought me and which I had learnt in his presence and for him. I was not thinking at all of what I was playing, but I believe that I played it well, and I thought that he was pleased. I was conscious of his pleasure, and conscious too, though I never looked at him, of the gaze fixed on me from behind. Still moving my fingers mechanically. I turned round quite involuntarily and looked at him. The night had grown brighter, and his head stood out on a background of darkness. He was sitting with his head propped on his hands, and his eyes shone as they gazed at me. Catching his look, I smiled and stopped playing. He smiled too and shook his head reproachfully at the music, for me to go on. When I stopped, the moon had grown brighter and was riding high in the heavens; and the faint light of the candles was supplemented by a new silvery light which came in through the windows and fell on the floor. Katya called out that it was really too bad - that I had stopped at the best part of the piece, and that I was playing badly. But he declared that I had never played so well; and then he began to walk about the rooms - through the drawing room to the unlighted parlor and back again to the drawing room, and each time he looked at me and smiled. I smiled too; I wanted even to laugh with no reason; I was so happy at something that had happened that very day. Katya and I were standing by the piano; and each time that he vanished through the drawing room door, I started kissing her in my favorite place, the soft part of her neck under the chin; and each time he came back, I made a solemn face and refrained with difficulty from laughing.

"What is the matter with her today?" Katya asked him.

He only smiled at me without answering; he knew what was the matter with me.

"Just look what a night it is!" he called out from the parlor, where he had stopped by the open French window looking into the garden.

We joined him; and it really was such a night as I have never seen since. The full moon shone above the house and behind us, so that we could not see it, and half the shadow, thrown by the roof and pillars of the house and by the veranda awning, lay slanting and foreshortened on the gravel-path and the strip of turf beyond. Everything else was bright and saturated with the silver of the dew and the moonlight. The broad garden path, on one side of which the shadows of the dahlias and their supports lay aslant, all bright and cold, and shining on the inequalities of the gravel, ran on till it vanished in the mist. Through the trees the roof of the greenhouse shone bright, and a growing mist rose from the dell. The lilac bushes, already partly leafless, were all bright to the center. Each flower was distinguishable apart, and all were drenched with dew. In the avenues light and shade were so mingled that they looked, not like paths and trees but like transparent houses, swaying and moving. To our right, in the shadow of the house, everything was black, indistinguishable, and uncanny. But all the brighter for the surrounding darkness was the top of a poplar, with a fantastic crown of leaves, which for some strange reason remained there close to the house, towering into the bright light, instead of flying away into the dim distance, into the retreating dark blue of the sky.

"Let us go for a walk," I said.

Katya agreed, but said I must put on galoshes.

"I don't want them, Katya," I said; "Sergey Mikhaylych will give me his arm."

As if that would prevent me from wetting my feet! But to us three this seemed perfectly natural at the time. Though he never used to offer me his arm, I now took it of my own accord, and he saw nothing strange in it. We all went down from the veranda together. That whole world, that sky, that garden, that air, were different from those that I knew.

We were walking along an avenue, and it seemed to me, whenever I looked ahead, that we could go no farther in the same direction, that the world of the possible ended there, and that the whole scene must remain fixed for ever in its beauty. But we still moved on, and the magic wall kept parting to let us in; and still we found the familiar garden with trees and paths and withered leaves. And we were really walking along the paths, treading on patches of light and shade; and a withered leaf was really crackling under my foot, and a live twig brushing my face. And that was really he, walking steadily and slowly at my side, and carefully supporting my arm; and that was really Katya walking beside us with her creaking shoes. And that must be the moon in the sky, shining down on us through the motionless branches.

But at each step the magic wall closed up again behind us and in front, and I ceased to believe in the possibility of advancing father - I ceased to believe in the reality of it all.

"Oh, there's a frog!" cried Katya.

"Who said that? and why?" I thought. But then I realized it was Katya, and that she was afraid of frogs. Then I looked at the ground and saw a little frog which gave a jump and then stood still in front of me, while its tiny shadow was reflected on the shining clay of the path.

"You're not afraid of frogs, are you?" he asked.

I turned and looked at him. Just where we were there was a gap of one tree in the lime avenue, and I could see his face clearly - it was so handsome and so happy!

Though he had spoken of my fear of frogs, I knew that he meant to say, "I love you, my dear one!" "I love you, I love you" was repeated by his look, by his arm; by the light, the shadow, and the air all repeated the same words.

We had gone all round the garden. Katya's short steps had kept up with us, but now she was tired and out of breath. She said it was time to go in; and I felt very sorry for her. "Poor thing!" I thought; "why does not she feel as we do? Why are we not all young and happy, like this night and like him and me?"

We went in, but it was a long time before he went away, though the cocks had crowed, and everyone in the house was asleep, and his horse, tethered under the window, snorted continually and stamped his hoof on the burdocks. Katya never reminded us of the hour, and we sat on talking of the merest trifles and not thinking of the time, till it was past two. The cocks were crowing for the third time and the dawn was breaking when he rode away. He said good bye as usual and made no special allusion; but I knew that from that day he was mine, and that I should never lose him now. As soon as I had confessed to myself that I loved him, I took Katya into my confidence. She rejoiced in the news as was touched by my telling her; but she was actually able - poor thing! - to go to bed and sleep! For me, I walked for a long, long time about the veranda; then I went down to the garden where, recalling each word, each movement, I walked along the same avenues through which I had walked with him. I did not sleep at all that night, and saw sunrise and early dawn for the first time in my life. And never again did I see such a night and such a morning. "Only why does he not tell me plainly that he loves me?" I thought; "what makes him invent obstacles and call himself old, when all is so simple and so splendid? What makes him waste this golden time which may never return? Let him say "I love you" - say it in plain words; let him take my hand in his and bent over it and say "I love you". Let him blush and look down before me; and then I will tell him all. No! Not tell him, but throw my arms round him and press close to him and weep." But then a thought came to me - "What if I am mistaken and he does not love me?"

I was startled by this fear - God knows where it might have led me. I recalled his embarrassment and mine, when I jumped down to him in the orchard; and my heart grew very heavy. Tears gushed from my eyes, and I began to pray. A strange thought occurred to me, calming me and bringing hope with it. I resolved to begin fasting on that day, to take the Communion on my birthday, and on that same day to be betrothed to him.

How this result would come to pass I had no idea; but from that moment I believed and felt sure it would be so. The dawn had fully come and the laborers were getting up when I went back to my room.

IV

The Fast of the Assumption falling in August, no one in the house was surprised by my intention of fasting.

During the whole of the week he never once came to see us; but, far from being surprised or vexed or made uneasy by his absence, I was glad of it - I did not expect him until my birthday. Each day during the week I got up early. While the horses were being harnessed, I walked in the garden alone, turning over in my mind the sins of the day before, and considering what I must do today, so as to be satisfied with my day and not spoil it by a singles in. It seemed so easy to me then to abstain from sin altogether; only a trifling effort seemed necessary. When the horses came round, I got into the carriage with Katya or one of the maids, and we drove to the church two miles away. While entering the church, I always recalled the prayer for those who "come unto the Temple in the fear of God", and tried to get just that frame of mind when mounting the two grass- grown steps up to the building. At that hour there were not more than a dozen worshippers - household servants or peasant women keeping the Fast. They bowed to me, and I returned their bows with studied humility. Then, with what seemed to me a great effort of courage, I went myself and got candles from the man who kept them, an old soldier and an Elder; and I placed the candles before the icons. Through the central door of the altar-screen I could see the altar cloth which my mother had worked; on the screen were the two angels which had seemed so big to me when I was little, and the dove with a golden halo which had fascinated me long ago. Behind the choir stood the old batter font, where I had been christened myself and stood godmother to so many of the servants' children. The old priest came out, wearing a cope made of the pall that had covered my father's coffin, and began to read in the same voice that I had heard all my life - at services held in our house, at Sonya's christening, at memorial services for my father, and at my mother's funeral. The same old quavering voice of the deacon rose in the choir; and the same old woman, whom I could remember at every service in that church, crouched by the wall, fixing her streaming eyes on an icon in the choir, pressing her folded fingers against her faded kerchief, and muttering with her toothless gums. And these objects were no longer merely curious to me, merely interesting from old recollections - each had become important and sacred in my eyes and seemed charged with profound meaning. I listened to each word of the prayers and tried to suit my feeling to it; and if I failed to understand, I prayed silently that God would enlighten me, or made up a prayer of my own in place of what I had failed to catch. When the penitential prayers were repeated, I recalled my past life, and that innocent childish past seemed to me so black when compared to the present brightness of my soul, that I wept and was horrified at myself; but I felt too that all those sins would be forgiven, and that if my sins had been even greater, my repentance would be all the sweeter. At the end of the service when the priest said, "The blessing of the Lord be upon you!" I seemed to feel an immediate sensation of physical well-being, of a mysterious light and warmth that instantly filled my heart. The service over, the priest came and asked me whether he should come to our house to say Mass, and what hour would suit me; and I thanked him for the suggestion, intended, as I thought, to please me, but said that I would come to church instead, walking or driving.

"Is that not too much trouble?" he asked. And I was at a loss for an answer, fearing to commit a sin of pride.

After the Mass, if Katya was not with me, I always sent the carriage home and walked back alone, bowing humbly to all who passed, and trying to find an opportunity of giving help or advice. I was eager to sacrifice myself for someone, to help in lifting a fallen cart, to rock a child's cradle, to give up the path to others by stepping into the mud. One evening I heard the bailiff report to Katya that Simon, one of our serfs, had come to beg some boards to make a coffin for his daughter, and a ruble to pay the priest for the funeral; the bailiff had given what he asked. "Are they as poor as that?" I asked. "Very poor, Miss," the bailiff answered; "they have no salt to their food." My heart ached to hear this, and yet I felt a kind of pleasure too. Pretending to Katya that I was merely going for a walk, I ran upstairs, got out all my money (it was very little but it was all I had), crossed myself, and started off alone, through the veranda and the garden, on my way to Simon's hut. It stood at the end of the village, and no one saw me as I went up to the window, placed the money on the sill, and tapped on the pane. Someone came out, making the door creak, and hailed me; but I hurried home, cold and shaking with fear like a criminal. Katya asked where I had been and what was the matter with me; but I did not answer, and did not even understand what she was saying. Everything suddenly seemed to me so petty and insignificant. I locked myself up in my own room, and walked up and down alone for a long time, unable to do anything, unable to think, unable to understand my own feelings. I thought of the joy of the whole family, and of what they would say of their benefactor; and I felt sorry that I had not given them the money myself. I thought too of what Sergey Mikhaylych would say, if he knew what I had done; and I was glad to think that no one would ever find out. I was so happy, and I felt myself and everyone else so bad, and yet was so kindly disposed to myself and to all the world, that the thought of death came to me as a dream of happiness. I smiled and prayed and wept, and felt at that moment a burning passion of love for all the world, myself included. Between services I used to read the Gospel; and the book became more and more intelligible to me, and the story of that divine life simpler and more touching; and the depths of thought and feeling I found in studying it became more awful and impenetrable. On the other hand, how clear and simple everything seemed to me when I rose from the study of this book and looked again on life around me and reflected on it! It was so difficult, I felt, to lead a bad life, and so simple to love everyone and be loved. All were so kind and gentle to me; even Sonya, whose lessons I had not broken off, was quite different - trying to understand and please me and not to vex me. Everyone treated me as I treated them. Thinking over my enemies, of whom I must ask pardon before confession, I could only remember one - one of our neighbors, a girl whom I had made fun of in company a year ago, and who had ceased to visit us. I wrote to her, confessing my fault and asking her forgiveness. She replied that she forgave me and wished me to forgive her. I cried for joy over her simple words, and saw in them, at the time, a deep and touching feeling. My old nurse cried, when I asked her to forgive me. "What makes them all so kind to me? What have I done to deserve their love?" I asked myself. Sergey Mikhaylych would come into my mind, and I thought for long about him. I could not help it, and I did not consider these thoughts sinful. But my thoughts of him were quite different from what they had been on the night when I first realized that I loved him: he seemed to me now like a second self, and became a part of every plan for the future. The inferiority which I had always felt in his presence had vanished entirely: I felt myself his equal and could understand him thoroughly from the moral elevation I had reached. What had seemed strange in him was now quite clear to me. Now I could see what he meant by saying to live for others was the only true happiness, and I agreed with him perfectly. I believed that our life together would be endlessly happy and untroubled. I looked forward, not to foreign tours or fashionable society or display, but to a quite different scene - a quiet family life in the country, with constant self-sacrifice, constant mutual love, and constant recognition in all things of the kind hand of Providence.

I carried out my plan of taking the Communion on my birthday. When I came back from church that day, my heart was so swelling with happiness that I was afraid of life, afraid of any feeling that might break in on that happiness. We had hardly left the carriage for the steps in front of the house, when there was a sound of wheels on the bridge, and I saw Sergey Mikhaylych drive up in his well-known trap. He congratulated me, and we went together to the parlour. Never since I had known him had I been so much at my ease with him and so self- possessed as on that morning. I felt in myself a whole new world out of his reach and beyond his comprehension. I was not conscious of the slightest embarrassment in speaking to him. He must have understood the cause of this feeling; for he was tender and gentle beyond his wont and showed a kind of reverent consideration for me. When I made for the piano, he locked it and put the key in his pocket.

"Don't spoil your present mood," he said, "you have the sweetest of all music in your soul just now."

I was grateful for his words, and yet I was not quite pleased at his understanding too easily and clearly what ought to have been an exclusive secret in my heart. At dinner he said that he had come to congratulate me and also to say goodbye; for he must go to Moscow tomorrow. He looked at Katya as he spoke; but then he stole a glance at me, and I saw that he was afraid he might detect signs of emotion on my face. But I was neither surprised nor agitated; I did not even ask whether he would be long away. I knew he would say this, and I knew that he would not go. How did I know? I cannot explain that to myself now; but on that memorable day it seemed that I knew everything that had been and that would be. It was like a delightful dream, when all that happens seems to have happened already and to be quite familiar, and it will all happen over again, and one knows that it will happen.

He meant to go away immediately after dinner; but, as Katya was tired after church and went to lie down for a little, he had to wait until she woke up in order to say goodbye to her. The sun shone into the drawing room, and we went out to the veranda. When we were seated, I began at once, quite calmly, the conversation that was bound to fix the fate of my heart. I began to speak, no sooner and no later, but at the very moment when we sat down, before our talk had taken any turn or color that might have hindered me from saying what I meant to say. I cannot tell myself where it came from - my coolness and determination and preciseness of expression. It was if something independent of my will was speaking through my lips. He sat opposite me with his elbows resting on the rails of the veranda; he pulled a lilac-branch towards him and stripped the leaves off it. When I began to speak, he let go the branch and leaned his head on one hand. His attitude might have shown either perfect calmness or strong emotion.

"Why are you going?" I asked, significantly, deliberately, and looking straight at him.

He did not answer at once.

"Business!" he muttered at last and dropped his eyes.

I realized how difficult he found it to lie to me, and in reply to such a frank question.

"Listen," I said; you know what today is to me, how important for many reasons. If I question you, it is not to show an interest in your doings (you know that I have become intimate with you and fond of you) - I ask you this question, because I must know the answer. Why are you going?"

"It is very hard for me to tell you the true reason," he said. "During this week I have thought much about you and about myself, and have decided that I must go. You understand why; and if you care for me, you will ask no questions." He put up a hand to rub his forehead and cover his eyes. "I find it very difficult... But you will understand."

My heart began to beat fast.

"I cannot understand you," I said; I cannot! you must tell me; in God's name and for the sake of this day tell me what you please, and I shall hear it with calmness," I said.

He changed his position, glanced at me, and again drew the lilac-twig towards him.

"Well!" he said, after a short silence and in a voice that tried in vain to seem steady, "it's a foolish business and impossible to put into words, and I feel the difficulty, but I will try to explain it to you," he added, frowning as if in bodily pain.

"Well?" I said.

"Just imagine the existence of a man - let us call him A - who has left youth far behind, and of a woman whom we may call B, who is young and happy and has seen nothing as yet of life or of the world. Family circumstances of various kinds brought them together, and he grew to love her as a daughter, and had no fear that his love would change its nature."

He stopped, but I did not interrupt him.

"But he forgot that B was so young, that life was still all a May-game to her," he went on with a sudden swiftness and determination and without looking at me, "and that it was easy to fall in love with her in a different way, and that this would amuse her. He made a mistake and was suddenly aware of another feeling, as heavy as remorse, making its way into his heart, and he was afraid. He was afraid that their old friendly relations would be destroyed, and he made up his mind to go away before that happened." As he said this, he began again to rub his eyes with a pretence of indifference, and to close them.

"Why was he afraid to love differently?" I asked very low; but I restrained my emotion and spoke in an even voice. He evidently thought that I was not serious; for he answered as if he were hurt.

"You are young, and I am not young. You want amusement, and I want something different. Amuse yourself, if you like, but not with me. If you do, I shall take it seriously; and then I shall be unhappy, and you will repent. That is what A said," he added; "however, this is all nonsense; but you understand why I am going. And don't let us continue this conversation. Please not!"

"No! no!" I said, "We must continue it," and tears began to tremble in my voice. "Did he love her, or not?

He did not answer.

"If he did not love her, why did he treat her as a child and pretend to love her?" I asked.

"Yes, A behaved badly," he interrupted me quickly; "but it all came to an end and they parted friends."

"This is horrible! Is there no other ending?" I said with a great effort and then felt afraid of what I had said.

"Yes, there is," he said, showing a face full of emotion and looking straight at me. "There are two different endings. But, for God's sake, listen to me quietly and don't interrupt. Some say" - here he stood up and smiled with a smile that was heavy with pain - "some say that A went off his head, fell passionately in love with B, and told her so. But she only laughed. To her it was all a jest, but to him a matter of life and death."

I shuddered and tried to interrupt him - tried to say that he must not dare to speak for me; but he checked me, laying his hand on mine.

"Wait!" he said, and his voice shook. "The other story is that she took pity on him, and fancied, poor child, from her ignorance of the world, that she really could love him, and so consented to be his wife. And he, in his madness, believed it - believed that his whole life could begin anew;

but she saw herself that she had deceived him and that he had deceived her... But let us drop the subject finally," he ended, clearly unable to say more; and then he began to walk up and down in silence before me.

Thought he had asked that subject should be dropped, I saw that his whole soul was hanging on my answer. I tried to speak, but the pain at my heart kept me dumb. I glanced at him - he was pale and his lower lip trembled. I felt sorry for him. With a sudden effort I broke the bonds of silence which had held me fast, and began to speak in a low inward voice, which I feared would break every moment.

"There is a third ending to the story," I said, and then paused, but he said nothing; "the third ending is that he did not love her, but hurt her, hurt her, and thought that he was right; and he left her and was actually proud of himself. You have been pretending, not I; I have loved you since the first day we met, loved you," I repeated, and at the word "loved" my low inward voice changed, without intention of mine, to a wild cry which frightened me myself.

He stood pale before me, his lip trembled more and more violently, and two tears came out upon his cheeks.

"It is wrong!" I almost screamed, feeling that I was choking with angry unshed tears. "Why do you do it?" I cried and got up to leave him.

But he would not let me go. His head was resting on my knees, his lips were kissing my still trembling hands, and his tears were wetting them. "My God! if I had only known!" he whispered.

"Why? why?" I kept on repeating, but in my heart there was happiness, happiness which had now come back, after so nearly departing for ever.

Five minutes later Sonya was rushing upstairs to Katya and proclaiming all over the house that Masha intended to marry Sergey Mikhaylych.

V

There were no reasons for putting off our wedding, and neither he nor I wished for delay. Katya, it is true, thought we ought to go to Moscow, to buy and order wedding clothes; and his mother tried to insist that, before the wedding, he must set up a new carriage, but new furniture, and repaper the whole house. But we two together carried our point, that all these things, if they were really indispensable, should be done afterwards, and that we should be married within a fortnight after my birthday, quietly, without wedding clothes, with a party, without best men and supper and champagne, and all the other conventional features of a wedding. He told me how dissatisfied his mother was that there should be no band, no mountain of luggage, no renovation of the whole house - so unlike her own marriage which had cost thirty thousand rubles; and he told of the solemn and secret confabulations which she held in her store room with her housekeeper, Maryushka, rummaging the chests and discussing carpets, curtains, and salvers as indispensable conditions of our happiness. At our house Katya did just the same with my old nurse, Kuzminichna. It was impossible to treat the matter lightly with Katya. She was firmly convinced that he and I, when discussing our future, were merely talking the sentimental nonsense natural to people in our position; and that our real future happiness depended on the hemming of table cloths and napkins and the proper cutting out and stitching of underclothing. Several times a day secret information passed between the two houses, to communicate what was going forward in each; and though the external relations between Katya and his mother were most affectionate, yet a slightly hostile though very subtle diplomacy was already perceptible in their dealings. I now became more intimate with Tatyana Semyonovna, the mother of Sergey Mikhaylych, an old-fashioned lady, strict and formal in the management of her household. Her son loved her, and not merely because she was his mother: he thought her the best, cleverest, kindest, and most affectionate woman in the world. She was always kind to us and to me especially, and was glad that her son should be getting married; but when I was with her after our engagement, I always felt that she wished me to understand that, in her opinion, her son might have looked higher, and that it would be as well for me to keep that in mind. I understood her meaning perfectly and thought her quite right.

During that fortnight he and I met every day. He came to dinner regularly and stayed on till midnight. But though he said - and I knew he was speaking the truth - that he had no life apart from me, yet he never spent the whole day with me, and tried to go on with his ordinary occupations. Our outward relations remained unchanged to the very day of our marriage: we went on saying "you" and not "thou" to each other; he did not even kiss my hand; he did not seek, but even avoided, opportunities of being alone with me. It was as if he feared to yield to the harmful excess of tenderness he felt. I don't know which of us had changed; but I now felt myself entirely his equal; I no longer found in him the pretence of simplicity which had displeased me earlier; and I often delighted to see in him, not a grown man inspiring respect and awe but a loving and wildly happy child. "How mistaken I was about him!" I often thought; "he is just such another human being as myself!" It seemed to me now, that his whole character was before me and that I thoroughly understood it. And how simple was every feature of his character, and how congenial to my own! Even his plans for our future life together were just my plans, only more clearly and better expressed in his words.

The weather was bad just then, and we spent most of our time indoors. The corner between the piano and the window was the scene of our best intimate talks. The candle light was reflected on the blackness of the window near us; from time to time drops struck the glistening pane and rolled down. The rain pattered on the roof; the water splashed in a puddle under the spout; it felt damp near the window; but our corner seemed all the brighter and warmer and happier for that.

"Do you know, there is something I have long wished to say to you," he began one night when we were sitting up late in our corner; "I was thinking of it all the time you were playing."

"Don't say it, I know all about it," I replied.

"All right! Mum's the word!"

"No! What is it?" I asked.

"Well, it is this. You remember the story I told you about A and B?"

"I should just think I did! What a stupid story! Lucky that it ended as it did!"

"Yes. I was very near destroying my happiness by my own act. You saved me. But the main thing is that I was always telling lies then, and I'm ashamed of it, and I want to have my say out now."

"Please don't! You really mustn't!"

"Don't be frightened," he said, smiling. "I only want to justify myself. When I began then, I meant to argue."

"It is always a mistake to argue," I said.

"Yes, I argued wrong. After all my disappointments and mistakes in life, I told myself firmly when I came to the country this year, that love was no more for me, and that all I had to do was to grow old decently. So for a long time, I was unable to clear up my feeling towards you, or to make out where it might lead me. I hoped, and I didn't hope: at one time I thought you were trifling with me; at another I felt sure of you but could not decide what to do. But after that evening, you remember when we walked in the garden at night, I got alarmed: the present happiness seemed too great to be real. What if I allowed myself to hope and then failed? But of course I was thinking only of myself, for I am disgustingly selfish."

He stopped and looked at me.

"But it was not all nonsense that I said then. It was possible and right for me to have fears. I take so much from you and can give so little. You are still a child, a bud that has yet to open; you have never been in love before, and I..."

"Yes, do tell me the truth..." I began, and then stopped, afraid of his answer. "No, never mind," I added.

"Have I been in love before? is that it?" he said, guessing my thoughts at once. "That I can tell you. No, never before - nothing a t all like what I feel now." But a sudden painful recollection seemed to flash across his mind. "No," he said sadly; "in this too I need your compassion, in order to have the right to love you. Well, was I not bound to think twice before saying that I loved you? What do I give you? Love, no doubt."

"And is that little?" I asked, looking him in the face.

"Yes, my dear, it is little to give you," he continued; "you have youth and beauty. I often lie awake at night from happiness, and all the time I think of our future life together. I have lived through much, and now I think I have found what is needed for happiness. A quiet secluded life in the country, with the possibility of being useful to people to whom it is easy to do good, and who are not accustomed to have it done to them; then work which one hopes may be of some use; then rest, nature, books, music, love for one's neighbor - such is my idea of happiness. And then, on the top of all that, you for a mate, and children perhaps - what more can He hear of man desire?"

"It should be enough," I said.

"Enough for me whose youth is over," he went on, "but not for you. Life is still before you, and you will perhaps seek happiness, and perhaps find it, in something different. You think now that this is happiness, because you love me."

"You are wrong," I said; "I have always desired just that quiet domestic life and prized it. And you only say just what I have thought."

He smiled.

"So you think, my dear; but that is not enough for you. You have youth and beauty," he repeated thoughtfully.

But I was angry because he disbelieved me and seemed to cast my youth and beauty in my teeth.

"Why do you love me then?" I asked angrily; "for my youth or for myself?"

"I don't know, but I love you," he answered, looking at me with his attentive and attractive gaze.

I did not reply and involuntarily looked into his eyes. Suddenly a strange thing happened to me: first I ceased to see what was around me; then his face seemed to vanish till only the eyes were left, shining over against mine; next the eyes seemed to be in my own head, and then all became confused - I could see nothing and was forced to shut my eyes, in order to break loose from the feeling of pleasure and fear which his gaze was producing in me...

The day before our wedding day, the weather cleared up towards evening. The rains which had begun in summer gave place to clear weather, and we had our first autumn evening, bright and cold. It was a wet, cold, shining world, and the garden showed for the first time the spaciousness and color and bareness of autumn. The sky was clear, cold, and pale. I went to bed happy in the thought that tomorrow, our wedding day, would be fine. I awoke with the sun, and the thought that this very day... seemed alarming and surprising. I went out into the garden. The sun had just risen and shone fitfully through the meager yellow leaves of the lime avenue. The path was strewn with rustling leaves, clusters of mountain ash berries hung red and wrinkled on the boughs, with a sprinkling of frost-bitten crumpled leaves; the dahlias were black and wrinkled. The first rime lay like silver on the pale green of the grass and on the broken burdock plants round the house. In the clear cold sky there was not, and could not be, a single cloud.

"Can it possibly be today?" I asked myself, incredulous of my own happiness. "Is it possible that I shall wake tomorrow, not here but in that strange house with the pillars? Is it possible that I shall never again wait for his coming and meet him, and sit up late with Katya to talk about him? Shall I never sit with him beside the piano in our drawing room? Never see him off and feel uneasy about him on dark nights?" But I remembered that he promised yesterday to pay a last visit, and that Katya had insisted on my trying on my wedding dress, and had said "For tomorrow". I believed for a moment that it was all real, and then doubted again. "Can it be that after today I shall be living there with a mother-in-law, without Nadezhda or Grigori or Katya? Shall I go to bed without kissing my old nurse good night and hearing her say, while she signs me with the cross from old custom, "Good night, Miss"? Shall I never again teach Sonya and play with her and knock through the wall to her in the morning and hear her hearty laugh? Shall I become from today someone that I myself do not know? And is a new world, that will realize my hopes and desires, opening before me? And will that new world last forever?" alone with these thoughts I was depressed and impatient for his arrival. He came early, and it required his presence to convince me that I should really be his wife that very day, and the prospect ceased to frighten me.

Before dinner we walked to our church, to attend a memorial service for my father.

"If only he were living now!" I thought as we were returning and I leant silently on the arm of him who had been the dearest friend of the object of my thoughts. During the service, while I pressed my forehead against the cold stone of the chapel floor, I called up my father so vividly;

I was so convinced that he understood me and approved my choice, that I felt as if his spirit were still hovering over us and blessing me. And my recollections and hopes, my joy and sadness, made up one solemn and satisfied feeling which was in harmony with the fresh still air, the silence, the bare fields and pale sky, from which the bright but powerless rays, trying in vain to burn my cheek, fell over all the landscape. My companion seemed to understand and share my feeling. He walked slowly and silently; and his face, at which I glanced from time to time, expressed the same serious mood between joy and sorrow which I shared with nature.

Suddenly he turned to me, and I saw that he intended to speak. "Suppose he starts some other subject than that which is in my mind?" I thought. But he began to speak of my father and did not even name him.

"He once said to me in just, "you should marry my Masha", " he began.

"He would have been happy now," I answered, pressing closer the arm which held mine.

"You were a child then," he went on, looking into my eyes; "I loved those eyes and used to kiss them only because they were like his, never thinking they would be so dear to me for their own sake. I used to call you Masha then."

"I want you to say 'thou' to me," I said.

"I was just going to," he answered; "I feel for the first time that thou art entirely mine;" and his calm happy gaze that drew me to him rested on me.

We went on along the foot path over the beaten and trampled stubble; our voices and footsteps were the only sounds. On one side the brownish stubble stretched over a hollow to a distant leafless wood; across it at some distance a peasant was noiselessly ploughing a black strip which grew wider and wider. A drove of horses scattered under the hill seemed close to us. On the other side, as far as the garden and our house peeping through the trees, a field of winter corn, thawed by the sun, showed black with occasional patches of green. The winter sun shone over everything, and everything was covered with long gossamer spider's webs, which floated in the air round us, lay on the frost-dried stubble, and got into our eyes and hair and clothes. When we spoke, the sound of our voices hung in the motionless air above us, as if we two were alone in the whole world - alone under that azure vault, in which the beams of the winter sun played and flashed without scorching.

I too wished to say "thou" to him, but I felt ashamed.

"Why dost thou walk so fast?" I said quickly and almost in a whisper; I could not help blushing.

He slackened his pace, and the gaze he turned on me was even more affectionate, gay, and happy.

At home we found that his mother and the inevitable guests had arrived already, and I was never alone with him again till we came out of church to drive to Nikolskoe.

The church was nearly empty: I just caught a glimpse of his mother standing up straight on a mat by the choir and of Katya wearing a cap with purple ribbons and with tears on her cheeks, and of two or three of our servants looking curiously at me. I did not look at him, but felt his presence there beside me. I attended to the words of the prayers and repeated them, but they found no echo in my heart. Unable to pray, I looked listlessly at the icons, the candles, the embroidered cross on the priest's cope, the screen, and the window, and took nothing in. I only felt that something strange was being done to me. At last the priest turned to us with the cross in his hand, congratulated us, and said, "I christened you and by God's mercy have lived to marry you." Katya and his mother kissed us, and Grigori's voice was heard, calling up the carriage. But I was only frightened and disappointed: all was over, but nothing extraordinary, nothing worthy of the Sacrament I had just received, had taken place in myself. He and I exchanged kisses, but the kiss seemed strange and not expressive of our feeling. "Is this all?" I thought. We went out of church, the sound of wheels reverberated under the vaulted roof, the fresh air blew on my face, he put on his hat and handed me into the carriage. Through the window I could see a frosty moon with a halo round it. He sat down beside me and shut the door after him. I felt a sudden pang. The assurance of his proceedings seemed to me insulting. Katya called out that I should put something on my head; the wheels rumbled on the stone and then moved along the soft road, and we were off. Huddling in a corner, I looked out at the distant fields and the road flying past in the cold glitter of the moon. Without looking at him, I felt his presence beside me. "Is this all I have got from the moment, of which I expected so much?" I thought; and still it seemed humiliating and insulting to be sitting alone with him, and so close. I turned to him, intending to speak; but the words would not come, as if my love had vanished, giving place to a feeling of mortification and alarm.

"Till this moment I did not believe it was possible," he said in a low voice in answer to my look.

"But I am afraid somehow," I said.

"Afraid of me, my dear?" he said, taking my hand and bending over it.

My hand lay lifeless in his, and the cold at my heart was painful.

"Yes," I whispered.

But at that moment my heart began to beat faster, my hand trembled and pressed his, I grew hot, my eyes sought his in the half darkness, and all at once I felt that I did not fear him, that this fear was love - a new love still more tender and stronger than the old. I felt that I was wholly his, and that I was happy in his power over me.

PART II

I

Days, weeks, two whole months of seclusion in the country slipped by unnoticed, as we thought then; and yet those two months comprised feelings, emotions, and happiness, sufficient for a lifetime. Our plans for the regulation of our life in the country were not carried out at all in the way that we expected; but the reality was not inferior to our ideal. There was none of that hard work, performance of duty, self-sacrifice, and life for others, which I had pictured to myself before our marriage; there was, on the contrary, merely a selfish feeling of love for one another, a wish to be loved, a constant causeless gaiety and entire oblivion of all the world. It is true that my husband sometimes went to his study to work, or drove to town on business, or walked about attending to the management of the estate; but I saw what it cost him to tear himself away from me. He confessed later that every occupation, in my absence, seemed to him mere nonsense in which it was impossible to take any interest. It was just the same with me. If I read, or played the piano, or passed my time with his mother, or taught in the school, I did so only because each of these occupations was connected with him and won his approval; but whenever the thought of him was not associated with any duty, my hands fell by my sides and it seemed to me absurd to think that anything existed apart from him. Perhaps it was a wrong and selfish feeling, but it gave me happiness and lifted me high above all the world. He alone existed on earth for me, and I considered him the best and most faultless man in the world; so that I could not live for anything else than for him, and my one object was to realize his conception of me. And in his eyes I was the first and most excellent woman in the world, the possessor of all possible virtues; and I strove to be that woman in the opinion of the first and best of men.

He came to my room one day while I was praying. I looked round at him and went on with my prayers. Not wishing to interrupt me, he sat down at a table and opened a book. But I thought he was looking at me and looked round myself. He smiled, I laughed, and had to stop my prayers.

"Have you prayed already?" I asked.

"Yes. But you go; I'll go away."

"You do say your prayers, I hope?"

He made no answer and was about to leave the room when I stopped him.

"Darling, for my sake, please repeat the prayers with me!" He stood up beside me, dropped his arms awkwardly, and began, with a serious face and some hesitation. Occasionally he turned towards me, seeking signs of approval and aid in my face.

When he came to an end, I laughed and embraced him.

"I feel just as if I were ten! And you do it all!" he said, blushing and kissing my hands.

Our house was one of those old-fashioned country houses in which several generations have passed their lives together under one roof, respecting and loving one another. It was all redolent of good sound family traditions, which as soon as I entered it seemed to become mine too. The management of the household was carried on by Tatyana Semyonovna, my mother-in- law, on old- fashioned lines. Of grace and beauty there was not much; but, from the servants down to the furniture and food, there was abundance of everything, and a general cleanliness, solidity, and order, which inspired respect. The drawing room furniture was arranged symmetrically; there were portraits on the walls, and the floor was covered with home-made carpets and mats. In the morning-room there was an old piano, with chiffoniers of two different patterns, sofas, and little carved tables with bronze ornaments. My sitting room, specially arranged by Tatyana Semyonovna, contained the best furniture in the house, of many styles and periods, including an old pierglass, which I was frightened to look into at first, but came to value as an old friend. Though Tatyana Semyonovna's voice was never heard, the whole household went like a clock. The number of servants was far too large (they all wore soft boots with no heels, because Tatyana Semyonovna had an intense dislike for stamping heels and creaking soles); but they all seemed proud of their calling, trembled before their old mistress, treated my husband and me with an affectionate air of patronage, and performed their duties, to all appearance, with extreme satisfaction. Every Saturday the floors were scoured and the carpets beaten without fail; on the first of every month there was a religious service in the house and holy water was sprinkled; on Tatyana Semyonovna's name day and on her son's (and on mine too, beginning from that autumn) an entertainment was regularly provided for the whole neighborhood. And all this had gone on without a break ever since the beginning of Tatyana Semyonovna's life.

My husband took no part in the household management, he attended only to the farm- work and the laborers, and gave much time to this. Even in winter he got up so early that I often woke to find him gone. He generally came back for early tea, which we drank alone together; and at that time, when the worries and vexations of the farm were over, he was almost always in that state of high spirits which we called "wild ecstasy". I often made him tell me what he had been doing in the morning, and he gave such absurd accounts that we both laughed till we cried. Sometimes I insisted on a serious account, and he gave it, restraining a smile. I watched his eyes and moving lips and took nothing in: the sight of him and the sound of his voice was pleasure enough.

"Well, what have I been saying? Repeat it," he would sometimes say. But I could repeat nothing. It seemed so absurd that he should talk to me of any other subject than ourselves. As if it mattered in the least what went on in the world outside! It was at a much later time that I began to some extent to understand and take an interest in his occupations. Tatyana Semyonovna never appeared before dinner: she breakfasted alone and said good morning to us by deputy. In our exclusive little world of frantic happiness a voice form the staid orderly region in which she dwelt was quite startling: I often lost self- control and could only laugh without speaking, when the maid stood before me with folded hands and made her formal report: "The mistress bade me inquire how you slept after your walk yesterday evening; and about her I was to report that she had pain in her side all night, and a stupid dog barked in the village and kept her awake; and also I was to ask how you liked the bread this morning, and to tell you that it was not Taras who baked today, but Nikolashka who was trying his hand for the first time; and she says his baking is not at all bad, especially the cracknels: but the tea-rusks were over-baked." Before dinner we saw little of each other: he wrote or went out again while I played the piano or read; but at four o'clock we all met in the drawing room before dinner. Tatyana Semyonovna sailed out of her own room, and certain poor and pious maiden ladies, of whom there were always two or three living in the house, made their appearance also. Every day without fail my husband by old habit offered his arm to his mother, to take her in to dinner; but she insisted that I should take the other, so that every day, without fail, we stuck in the doors and got in each other's way. She also presided at dinner, where the conversation, if rather solemn, was polite and sensible. The commonplace talk between my husband and me was a pleasant interruption to the formality of those entertainments. Sometimes there were squabbles between mother and son and they bantered one another; and I especially enjoyed the scenes, because they were the best proof of the strong and tender love which united the two. After dinner Tatyana Semyonovna went to the parlor, where she sat in an armchair and ground her snuff or cut the leaves of new books, while we read aloud or went off to the piano in the morning room. We read much together at this time, but music was our favorite and best enjoyment, always evoking fresh chords in our hearts and as it were revealing each afresh to the other. While I played his favorite pieces, he sat on a distant sofa where I could hardly see him. He was ashamed to betray the impression produced on him by the music; but often, when he was not expecting it, I rose from the piano, went up to him, and tried to detect on his face signs of emotion - the unnatural brightness and moistness of the eyes, which he tried in vain to conceal. Tatyana Semyonovna, though she often wanted to take a look at us there, was also anxious to put no constraint upon us. So she always passed through the room with an air of indifference and a pretence of being busy; but I knew that she had no real reason for going to her room and returning so soon. In the evening I poured out tea in the large drawing room, and all the household met again. This solemn ceremony of distributing cups and glasses before the solemnly shining samovar made me nervous for a long time. I felt myself still unworthy of such a distinction, too young and frivolous to turn the tap of such a big samovar, to put glasses on Nikita's salver, saying "For Peter Ivanovich", "For Marya Minichna", to ask "Is it sweet enough?" and to leave out limps of sugar for Nurse and other deserving persons. "Capital! capital! Just like a grown-up person!" was a frequent comment from my husband, which only increased my confusion.

After tea Tatyana Semyonovna played patience or listened to Marya Minichna telling fortunes by the cards. Then she kissed us both and signed us with the cross, and we went off to our own rooms. But we generally sat up together till midnight, and that was our best and pleasantest time. He told me stories of his past life; we made plans and sometimes even talked philosophy; but we tried always to speak low, for fear we should be heard upstairs and reported to Tatyana Semyonovna, who insisted on our going to bed early. Sometimes we grew hungry; and then we stole off to the pantry, secured a cold supper by the good offices of Nikita, and ate it in my sitting room by the light of one candle. He and I lived like strangers in that big old house, where the uncompromising spirit of the past and of Tatyana Semyonovna ruled supreme. Not she only, but the servants, the old ladies, the furniture, even the pictures, inspired me with respect and a little alarm, and made me feel that he and I were a little out of place in that house and must always be very careful and cautious in our doings. Thinking it over now, I see that many things - the pressure of that unvarying routine, and that crowd of idle and inquisitive servants - were uncomfortable and oppressive; but at the time that very constraint made our love for one another still keener. Not I only, but he also, never grumbled openly at anything; on the contrary he shut his eyes to what was amiss. Dmitriy Sidorov, one of the footmen, was a great smoker;

and regularly every day, when we two were in the morning room after dinner, he went to my husband's study to take tobacco from the jar; and it was a sight to see Sergey Mikhaylych creeping on tiptoe to me with a face between delight and terror, and a wink and a warning forefinger, while he pointed at Dmitriy Sidorov, who was quite unconscious of being watched. Then, when Dmitriy Sidorov had gone away without having seen us, in his joy that all had passed off successfully, he declared (as he did on every other occasion) that I was a darling, and kissed me. At times his calm connivance and apparent indifference to everything annoyed me, and I took it for weakness, never noticing that I acted in the same way myself. "It's like a child who dares not show his will," I thought.

"My dear! my dear!" he said once when I told him that his weakness surprised me; "how can a man, as happy as I am, be dissatisfied with anything? Better to give way myself than to put compulsion on others; of that I have long been convinced. There is no condition in which one cannot be happy; but our life is such bliss! I simply cannot be angry; to me now nothing seems bad, but only pitiful and amusing. Above all - le mieux est l'ennemi du bien. Will you believe it, when I hear a ring at the bell, or receive a letter, or even wake up in the morning, I'm frightened. Life must go on, something may change; and nothing can be better than the present."

I believed him but did not understand him. I was happy; but I took that as a matter of course, the invariable experience of people in our position, and believed that there was somewhere, I knew not where, a different happiness, not greater but different.

So two months went by and winter came with its cold and snow; and, in spite of his company, I began to feel lonely, that life was repeating itself, that there was nothing new either in him or in myself, and that we were merely going back to what had been before. He began to give more time to business which kept him away from me, and my old feeling returned, that there was a special department of his mind into which he was unwilling to admit me. His unbroken calmness provoked me. I loved him as much as ever and was as happy as ever in his love; but my love, instead of increasing, stood still; and another new and disquieting sensation began to creep into my heart. To love him was not enough for me after the happiness I had felt in falling in love. I wanted movement and not a calm course of existence.

I wanted excitement and danger and the chance to sacrifice myself for my love. I felt in myself a superabundance of energy which found no outlet in our quiet life. I had fits of depression which I was ashamed of and tried to conceal from him, and fits of excessive tenderness and high spirits which alarmed him. He realized my state of mind before I did, and proposed a visit to Petersburg; but I begged him to give this up and not to change our manner of life or spoil our happiness. Happy indeed I was; but I was tormented by the thought that this happiness cost me no effort and no sacrifice, though I was even painfully conscious of my power to fact both. I loved him and saw that I was all in all to him; but I wanted everyone to see our love; I wanted to love him in spite of obstacles. My mind, and even my senses, were fully occupied; but there was another feeling of youth and craving for movement, which found no satisfaction in our quiet life. What made him say that, whenever I liked, we could go to town? Had he not said so I might have realized that my uncomfortable feelings were my own fault and dangerous nonsense, and that the sacrifice I desired was there before me, in the task of overcoming these feelings. I was haunted by the thought that I could escape from depression by a mere change from the country; and at the same time I felt ashamed and sorry to tear him away, out of selfish motives, from all he cared for. So time went on, the snow grew deeper, and there we remained together, all alone and just the same as before, while outside I knew there was noise and glitter and excitement, and hosts of people suffering or rejoicing without one thought of us and our remote existence. I suffered most from the feeling that custom was daily petrifying our lives into one fixed shape, that our minds were losing their freedom and becoming enslaved to the steady passionless course of time. The morning always found us cheerful; we were polite at dinner, and affectionate in the evening. "It is all right," I thought, "to do good to others and lead upright lives, as he says; but there is time for that later; and there are other things, for which the time is now or never." I wanted, not what I had got, but a life of struggle; I wanted feeling to be the guide of life, and not life to guide feeling. If only I could go with him to the edge of a precipice and say, "One step, and I shall fall over - one movement, and I shall be lost!" then, pale with fear, he would catch me in his strong arms and hold me over the edge till my blood froze, and then carry me off whither he pleased.

This state of feeling even affected my health, and I began to suffer from nerves. One morning I was worse than usual. He had come back from the estate office out of sorts, which was a rare thing with him. I noticed it at once and asked what was the matter. He would not tell me and said it was of no importance. I found out afterwards that the police inspector, out of spite against my husband, was summoning our peasants, making illegal demands on them, and using threats to them. My husband could not swallow this at once; he could not feel it merely "pitiful and amusing". He was provoked, and therefore unwilling to speak of it to me. But it seemed to me that he did not wish to speak to about it because he considered me a mere child, incapable of understanding his concerns. I turned from him and said no more. I then told the servant to ask Marya Minichna, who was staying in the house, to join us at breakfast. I ate my breakfast very fast and took her to the morning room where I began to talk loudly to her about some trifle which did not interest me in the least. He walked about the room, glancing at us from time to time. This made me more and more inclined to talk and even to laugh; all that I said myself, and all that Marya Minichna said, seemed to me laughable. Without a word to me he went off to his study and shut the door behind him. When I ceased to hear him, all my high spirits vanished at once; indeed Marya Minichna was surprised and asked what was the matter. I sat down on a sofa without answering, and felt ready to cry. "What has he got on his mind?" I wondered; "some trifle which he thinks important; but, if he tried to tell it me, I should soon show him it was mere nonsense. But he must needs think that I won't understand, must humiliate me by his majestic composure, and always be in the right as against me. But I too am in the right when I find things tiresome and trivial," I reflected; "and I do well to want an active life rather than to stagnate in one spot and feel life flowing past me. I want to move forward, to have some new experience every day and every hour, whereas he wants to stand still and to keep me standing beside him. And how easy it would be for him to gratify me! He need not take me to town; he need only be like me and not put compulsion on himself and regulate his feelings, but live simply. That is the advice he gives me, but he is not simple himself. That is what is the matter."

I felt the tears rising and knew that I was irritated with him. My irritation frightened me, and I went to his study. He was sitting at the table, writing. Hearing my step, he looked up for a moment and then went on writing; he seemed calm and unconcerned. His look vexed me: instead of going up to him, I stood beside his writing table, opened a book, and began to look at it. He broke off his writing again and looked at me.

"Masha, are you out of sorts?" he asked.

I replied with a cold look, as much as to say, "You are very polite, but what is the use of asking?" He shook his head and smiled with a tender timid air; but his smile, for the first time, drew no answering smile from me.

"What happened to you today?" I asked; "why did you not tell me?"

"Nothing much - a trifling nuisance," he said. "But I might tell you now. Two of our serfs went off to the town..."

But I would not let him go on.

"Why would you not tell me, when I asked you at breakfast?:

"I was angry then and should have said something foolish."

"I wished to know then."

"Why?"

"Why do you suppose that I can never help you in anything?"

"Not help me!" he said, dropping his pen. "Why, I believe that without you I could not live. You not only help me in everything I do, but you do it yourself. You are very wide of the mark," he said, and laughed. "My life depends on you. I am pleased with things, only because you are there, because I need you..."

"Yes, I know; I am a delightful child who must be humored and kept quiet," I said in a voice that astonished him, so that he looked up as if this was a new experience; "but I don't want to be quiet and calm; that is more in your line, and too much in your line," I added.

"Well," he began quickly, interrupting me and evidently afraid to let me continue, "When I tell you the facts, I should like to know your opinion."

"I don't want to hear them now," I answered. I did want to hear the story, but I found it so pleasant to break down his composure. "I don't want to play at life," I said, "but to live, as you do yourself."

His face, which reflected every feeling so quickly and so vividly, now expressed pain and intense attention.

"I want to share your life, to...," but I could not go on - his face showed such deep distress. He was silent for a moment.

"But what part of my life do you not share?" he asked; "is it because I, and not you, have to bother with the inspector and with tipsy laborers?"

"That's not the only thing," I said.

"For God's sake try to understand me, my dear!" he cried. "I know that excitement is always painful; I have learnt that from the experience of life. I love you, and I can't but wish to save you from excitement. My life consists of my love for you; so you should not make life impossible for me."

"You are always in the right," I said without looking at him.

I was vexed again by his calmness and coolness while I was conscious of annoyance and some feeling akin to penitence.

"Masha, what is the matter?" he asked. "The question is not, which of us is in the right - not at all; but rather, what grievances have you against me? Take time before you answer, and tell me all that is in your mind. You are dissatisfied with me: and you are, no doubt, right; but let me understand what I have done wrong."

But how could I put my feeling into words? That he understood me at once, that I again stood before him like a child, that I could do nothing without his understanding and foreseeing it - all this only increased my agitation.

"I have no complaint to make of you," I said; "I am merely bored and want not to be bored. But you say that it can't be helped, and, as always, you are right."

I looked at him as I spoke. I had gained my object: his calmness had disappeared, and I read fear and pain in his face.

"Masha," he began in a low troubled voice, "this is no mere trifle: the happiness of our lives is at stake. Please hear me out without answering. Why do you wish to torment me?"

But I interrupted him.

"Oh, I know you will turn out to be right. Words are useless; of course you are right." I spoke coldly, as if some evil spirit were speaking with my voice.

"If you only knew what you are doing!" he said, and his voice shook.

I burst out crying and felt relieved. He sat down beside me and said nothing. I felt sorry for him, ashamed of myself, and annoyed at what I had done. I avoided looking at him. I felt that any look from him at that moment must express severity or perplexity. At last I looked up and saw his eyes: they were fixed on me with a tender gentle expression that seemed to ask for pardon. I caught his hand and said,

"Forgive me! I don't know myself what I have been saying."

"But I do; and you spoke the truth."

"What do you mean?" I asked.

"That we must go to Petersburg," he said; "there is nothing for us to do here just now."

"As you please," I said.

He took me in his arms and kissed me.

"You must forgive me," he said; "for I am to blame."

That evening I played to him for a long time, while he walked about the room. He had a habit of muttering to himself; and when I asked him what he was muttering, he always thought for a moment and then told me exactly what it was. It was generally verse, and sometimes mere nonsense, but I could always judge of his mood by it. When I asked him now, he stood still, thought an instant, and then repeated two lines from Lermontov:

He is his madness prays for storms,

And dreams that storms will bring him peace.

"He is really more than human," I thought; "he knows everything. How can one help loving him?"

I got up, took his arm, and began to walk up and down with him, trying to keep step.

"Well?" he asked, smiling and looking at me.

"All right," I whispered. And then a sudden fit of merriment came over us both: our eyes laughed, we took longer and longer steps, and rose higher and higher on tiptoe. Prancing in this manner, to the profound dissatisfaction of the butler and astonishment of my mother-in-law, who was playing patience in the parlor, we proceeded through the house till we reached the dining room; there we stopped, looked at one another, and burst out laughing.

A fortnight later, before Christmas, we were in Petersburg.

II

The journey to Petersburg, a week in Moscow, visits to my own relations and my husband's, settling down in our new quarters, travel, new towns and new faces - all this passed before me like a dream. It was all so new, various, and delightful, so warmly and brightly lighted up by his presence and his live, that our quiet life in the country seemed to me something very remote and unimportant. I had expected to find people in society proud and cold; but to my great surprise, I was received everywhere with unfeigned cordiality and pleasure, not only by relations, but also by strangers. I seemed to be the one object of their thoughts, and my arrival the one thing they wanted, to complete their happiness. I was surprised too to discover in what seemed to me the very best society a number of people acquainted with my husband, though he had never spoken of them to me; and I often felt it odd and disagreeable to hear him now speak disapprovingly of some of these people who seemed to me so kind. I could not understand his coolness towards them or his endeavors to avoid many acquaintances that seemed to me flattering. Surely, the more kind people one knows, the better; and here everyone was kind.

"This is how we must manage, you see," he said to me before we left the country; "here we are little Croesueses, but in town we shall not be at all rich. So we must not stay after Easter, or go into society, or we shall get into difficulties. For your sake too I should not wish it."

"Why should we go into society?" I asked; "we shall have a look at the theaters, see our relations, go to the opera, hear some good music, and be ready to come home before Easter."

But these plans were forgotten the moment we got the Petersburg. I found myself at once in such a new and delightful world, surrounded by so many pleasures and confronted by such novel interests, that I instantly, though unconsciously, turned my back on my past life and its plans. "All that was preparatory, a mere playing at life; but here is the real thing! And there is the future too!" Such were my thoughts. The restlessness and symptoms of depression which had troubled me at home vanished at once and entirely, as if by magic. My love for my husband grew calmer, and I ceased to wonder whether he loved me less. Indeed I could not doubt his love: every thought of mine was understood at once, every feeling shared, and every wish gratified by him. His composure, if it still existed, no longer provoked me. I also began to realize that he not only loved me but was proud of me. If we paid a call, or made some new acquaintance, or gave an evening party at which I, trembling inwardly from fear of disgracing myself, acted as hostess, he often said when it was over: "Bravo, young woman! capital! You needn't be frightened; a real success!" And his praise gave me great pleasure. Soon after our arrival he wrote to his mother and asked me to add a postscript, but refused to let me see his letter; of course I insisted on reading it; and he had said: "You would not know Masha again, I don't myself. Where does she get that charming graceful self- confidence and ease, such social gifts with such simplicity and charm and kindliness? Everybody is delighted with her. I can't admire her enough myself, and should be more in love with her than ever, if that were possible."

Now I know what I am like," I thought. In my joy and pride I felt that I love him more than before. My success with all our new acquaintances was a complete surprise to me. I heard on all sides, how this uncle had taken a special fancy for me, and that aunt was raving about me; I was told by one admirer that I had no rival among the Petersburg ladies, and assured by another, a lady, that I might, if I cared, lead the fashion in society. A cousin of my husband's, in particular, a Princess D., middle-aged and very much at home in society, fell in love with me at first sight and paid me compliments which turned my head. The first time that she invited me to a ball and spoke to my husband about it, he turned to me and asked if I wished to go; I could just detect a sly smile on his face. I nodded assent and felt that I was blushing.

"She looks like a criminal when confessing what she wishes," he said with a good-natured laugh.

"But you said that we must not go into society, and you don't care for it yourself," I answered, smiling and looking imploringly at him.

"Let us go, if you want to very much," he said.

"Really, we had better not."

"Do you want to? Very badly?" he asked again.

I said nothing.

"Society in itself is no great harm," he went on; "but unsatisfied social aspirations are a bad and ugly business. We must certainly accept, and we will."

"To tell you the truth," I said, "I never in my life longed for anything as much as I do for this ball."

So we went, and my delight exceeded all my expectations. It seemed to me, more than ever, that I was the center round which everything revolved, that for my sake alone this great room was lighted up and the band played, and that this crowd of people had assembled to admire me. From the hairdresser and the lady's maid to my partners and the old gentlemen promenading the ball room, all alike seemed to make it plain that they were in love with me. The general verdict formed at the ball about me and reported by my cousin, came to this: I was quite unlike the other women and had a rural simplicity and charm of my own. I was so flattered by my success that I frankly told my husband I should like to attend two or three more balls during the season, and "so get thoroughly sick of them," I added; but I did not mean what I said.

He agreed readily; and he went with me at first with obvious satisfaction. He took pleasure in my success, and seemed to have quite forgotten his former warning or to have changed his opinion.

But a time came when he was evidently bored and wearied by the life we were leading. I was too busy, however, to think about that. Even if I sometimes noticed his eyes fixed questioningly on me with a serious attentive gaze, I did not realize its meaning. I was utterly blinded by this sudden affection which I seemed to evoke in all our new acquaintances, and confused by the unfamiliar atmosphere of luxury, refinement, and novelty. It pleased me so much to find myself in these surroundings not merely his equal but his superior, and yet to love him better and more independently than before, that I could not understand what he could object to for me in society life. I had a new sense of pride and self-satisfaction when my entry at a ball attracted all eyes, while he, as if ashamed to confess his ownership of me in public, made haste to leave my side and efface himself in the crowd of black coats. "Wait a little!" I often said in my heart, when I identified his obscure and sometimes woebegone figure at the end of the room - "Wait till we get home! Then you will see and understand for whose sake I try to be beautiful and brilliant, and what it is I love in all that surrounds me this evening!" I really believed that my success pleased me only because it enabled me to give it up for his sake. One danger I recognized as possible - that I might be carried away by a fancy for some new acquaintance, and that my husband might grow jealous. But he trusted me so absolutely, and seemed so undisturbed and indifferent, and all the young men were so inferior to him, that I was not alarmed by this one danger. Yet the attention of so many people in society gave me satisfaction, flattered my vanity, and made me think that there was some merit in my love for my husband. Thus I became more offhand and self-confident in my behavior to him.

"Oh, I saw you this evening carrying on a most animated conversation with Mme N.," I said one night on returning from a ball, shaking my finger at him. He had really been talking to this lady, who was a well-known figure in Petersburg society. He was more silent and depressed than usual, and I said this to rouse him up.

"What is too good of talking like that, for you especially, Masha?" he said with half-closed teeth and frowning as if in pain. "Leave that to others; it does not suit you and me. Pretence of that sort may spoil the true relation between us, which I still hope may come back."

I was ashamed and said nothing.

"Will it ever come back, Masha, do you think? he asked.

"It never was spoilt and never will be," I said; and I really believed this then.

"God grant that you are right!" he said; "if not, we ought to be going home."

But he only spoke like this once - in general he seemed as satisfied as I was, and I was so gay and so happy! I comforted myself too by thinking, "If he is bored sometimes, I endured the same thing for his sake in the country. If the relation between us has become a little different, everything will be the same again in summer, when we shall be alone in our house at Nikolskoye with Tatyana Semyonovna."

So the winter slipped by, and we stayed on, in spite of our plans, over Easter in Petersburg. A week later we were preparing to start; our packing was all done; my husband who had bought things - plants for the garden and presents for people at Nikolskoye, was in a specially cheerful and affectionate mood. Just then Princess D. came and begged us to stay till the Saturday, in order to be present at a reception to be given by Countess R. The countess was very anxious to secure me, because a foreign prince, who was visiting Petersburg and had seen me already at a ball, wished to make my acquaintance; indeed this was his motive for attending the reception, and he declared that I was the most beautiful woman in Russia. All the world was to be there; and, in a word, it would really be too bad, if I did not go too.

My husband was talking to someone at the other end of the drawing room.

"So you will go, won't you, Mary?" said the Princess.

"We meant to start for the country the day after tomorrow," I answered undecidedly, glancing at my husband. Our eyes met, and he turned away at once.

"I must persuade him to stay," she said, "and then we can go on Saturday and turn all heads. All right?"

"It would upset our plans; and we have packed," I answered, beginning to give way.

"She had better go this evening and make her curtsey to the Prince," my husband called out from the other end of the room; and he spoke in a tone of suppressed irritation which I had never heard from him before.

"I declare he's jealous, for the first time in his life," said the lady, laughing. "But it's not for the sake of the Prince I urge it, Sergey Mikhaylych, but for all our sakes. The Countess was so anxious to have her."

"It rests with her entirely," my husband said coldly, and then left the room.

I saw that he was much disturbed, and this pained me. I gave no positive promise. As soon as our visitor left, I went to my husband. He was walking up and down his room, thinking, and neither saw nor heard me when I came in on tiptoe.

Looking at him, I said to myself: "He is dreaming already of his dear Nikolskoye, our morning coffee in the bright drawing room, the land and the laborers, our evenings in the music room, and our secret midnight suppers." Then I decided in my own heart: "Not for all the balls and all the flattering princes in the world will I give up his glad confusion and tender cares." I was just about to say that I did not wish to go to the ball and would refuse, when he looked round, saw me, and frowned. His face, which had been gentle and thoughtful, changed at once to its old expression of sagacity, penetration, and patronizing composure. He would not show himself to me as a mere man, but had to be a demigod on a pedestal.

"Well, my dear?" he asked, turning towards me with an unconcerned air.

I said nothing. I was provoked, because he was hiding his real self from me, and would not continue to be the man I loved.

"Do you want to go to this reception on Saturday?" he asked.

"I did, but you disapprove. Besides, our things are all packed," I said.

Never before had I heard such coldness in his tone to me, and never before seen such coldness in his eye.

"I shall order the things to be unpacked," he said, "and I shall stay till Tuesday. So you can go to the party, if you like. I hope you will; but I shall not go."

Without looking at me, he began to walk about the room jerkily, as his habit was when perturbed.

"I simply can't understand you," I said, following him with my eyes from where I stood. "You say that you never lose self-control" (he had never really said so); "then why do you talk to me so strangely? I am ready on your account to sacrifice this pleasure, and then you, in a sarcastic tone which is new from you to me, insist that I should go."

"So you make a sacrifice!" he threw special emphasis on the last word. "Well, so do I. What could be better? We compete in generosity - what an example of family happiness!"

Such harsh and contemptuous language I had never heard from his lips before. I was not abashed, but mortified by his contempt; and his harshness did not frighten me but made me harsh too. How could he speak thus, he who was always so frank and simple and dreaded insincerity in our speech to one another? And what had I done that he should speak so? I really intended to sacrifice for his sake a pleasure in which I could see no harm; and a moment ago I loved him and understood his feelings as well as ever. We had changed parts: now he avoided direct and plain words, and I desired them.

"You are much changed," I said, with a sigh. "How am I guilty before you? It is not this party - you have something else, some old count against me. Why this insincerity? You used to be so afraid of it yourself. Tell me plainly what you complain of." "What will he say?" thought I, and reflected with some complacency that I had done nothing all winter which he could find fault with.

I went into the middle of the room, so that he had to pass close to me, and looked at him. I thought, "He will come and clasp me in his arms, and there will be an end of it." I was even sorry that I should not have the chance of proving him wrong. But he stopped at the far end of the room and looked at me.

"Do you not understand yet?" he asked.

"No, I don't."

"Then I must explain. What I feel, and cannot help feeling, positively sickens me for the first time in my life." He stopped, evidently startled by the harsh sound of his own voice.

"What do you mean?" I asked, with tears of indignation in my eyes.

"It sickens me that the Prince admired you, and you therefore run to meet him, forgetting your husband and yourself and womanly dignity; and you wilfully misunderstand what your want of self-respect makes your husband feel for you: you actually come to your husband and speak of the "sacrifice" you are making, by which you mean - "To show myself to His Highness is a great pleasure to me, but I 'sacrifice' it.'"

The longer he spoke, the more he was excited by the sound of his own voice, which was hard and rough and cruel. I had never seen him, had never thought of seeing him, like that. The blood rushed to my heart and I was frightened; but I felt that I had nothing to be ashamed of, and the excitement of wounded vanity made me eager to punish him.

"I have long been expecting this," I said. "Go on. Go on!"

"What you expected, I don't know," he went on; "but I might well expect the worst, when I saw you day after day sharing the dirtiness and idleness and luxury of this foolish society, and it has come at last. Never have I felt such shame and pain as now - pain for myself, when your friend thrusts her unclean fingers into my heart and speaks of my jealousy! - jealousy of a man whom neither you nor I know; and you refuse to understand me and offer to make a sacrifice for me - and what sacrifice? I am ashamed for you, for your degradation!....Sacrifice!" he repeated again.

"Ah, so this is a husband's power," thought I: "to insult and humiliate a perfectly innocent woman. Such may be a husband's rights, but I will not submit to them." I felt the blood leave my face and a strange distension of my nostrils, as I said, "No! I make no sacrifice on your account. I shall go to the party on Saturday without fail."

"And I hope you may enjoy it. But all is over between us two!" he cried out in a fit of unrestrained fury. "But you shall not torture me any longer! I was a fool, when I...", but his lips quivered, and he refrained with a visible effort from ending the sentence.

I feared and hated him at that moment. I wished to say a great deal to him and punish him for all his insults; but if I had opened my mouth, I should have lost my dignity by bursting into tears. I said nothing and left the room. But as soon as I ceased to hear his footsteps, I was horrified at what we had done. I feared that the tie which had made all my happiness might really be snapped forever; and I thought of going back. But then I wondered: "Is he calm enough now to understand me, if I mutely stretch out my hand and look at him? Will he realize my generosity? What if he calls my grief a mere pretense? Or he may feel sure that he is right and accept my repentance and forgive me with unruffled pride. And why, oh why, did he whom I loved so well insult me so cruelly?"

I went not to him but to my own room, where I sat for a long time and cried. I recalled with horror each word of our conversation, and substituted different words, kind words, for those that we had spoken, and added others; and then again I remembered the reality with horror and a feeling of injury. In the evening I went down for tea and met my husband in the presence of a friend who was staying with us; and it seemed to me that a wide gulf had opened between us from that day. Our friend asked me when we were to start; and before I could speak, my husband answered:

"On Tuesday," he said; "we have to stay for Countess R.'s reception." He turned to me: "I believe you intend to go?" he asked.

His matter-of-fact tone frightened me, and I looked at him timidly. His eyes were directed straight at me with an unkind and scornful expression; his voice was cold and even.

"Yes," I answered.

When we were alone that evening, he came up to me and held out his hand.

"Please forget what I said to you today," he began.

As I took his hand, a smile quivered on my lips and the tears were ready to flow; but he took his hand away and sat down on an armchair at some distance, as if fearing a sentimental scene. "Is it possible that he still thinks himself in the right?" I wondered; and, though I was quite ready to explain and to beg that we might not go to the party, the words died on my lips.

"I must write to my mother that we have put off our departure," he said; "otherwise she will be uneasy."

"When do you think of going?" I asked.

"On Tuesday, after the reception," he replied.

"I hope it is not on my account," I said, looking into his eyes; but those eyes merely looked - they said nothing, and a veil seemed to cover them from me. His face seemed to me to have grown suddenly old and disagreeable.

We went to the reception, and good friendly relations between us seemed to have been restored, but these relations were quite different from what they had been.

At the party I was sitting with other ladies when the Prince came up to me, so that I had to stand up in order to speak to him. As I rose, my eyes involuntarily sought my husband. He was looking at me from the other end of the room, and now turned away. I was seized by a sudden sense of shame and pain; in my confusion I blushed all over my face and neck under the Prince's eye. But I was forced to stand and listen, while he spoke, eyeing me from his superior height. Our conversation was soon over: there was no room for him beside me, and he, no doubt, felt that I was uncomfortable with him. We talked of the last ball, of where I should spend the summer, and so on. As he left me, he expressed a wish to make the acquaintance of my husband, and I saw them meet and begin a conversation at the far end of the room. The Prince evidently said something about me; for he smiled in the middle of their talk and looked in my direction.

My husband suddenly flushed up. He made a low bow and turned away from the prince without being dismissed. I blushed too: I was ashamed of the impression which I and, still more, my husband must have made on the Prince. Everyone, I thought, must have noticed my awkward shyness when I was presented, and my husband's eccentric behavior. "Heaven knows how they will interpret such conduct? Perhaps they know already about my scene with my husband!"

Princess D. drove me home, and on the way I spoke to her about my husband. My patience was at an end, and I told her the whole story of what had taken place between us owing to this unlucky party. To calm me, she said that such differences were very common and quite unimportant, and that our quarrel would leave no trace behind. She explained to me her view of my husband's character - that he had become very stiff and unsociable. I agreed, and believed that I had learned to judge him myself more calmly and more truly.

But when I was alone with my husband later, the thought that I had sat in judgment upon him weighed like a crime upon my conscience; and I felt that the gulf which divided us had grown still greater.

III

From that day there was a complete change in our life and our relations to each other. We were no longer as happy when we were alone together as before. To certain subjects we gave a wide berth, and conversation flowed more easily in the presence of a third person. When the talk turned on life in the country, or on a ball, we were uneasy and shrank from looking at one another. Both of us knew where the gulf between us lay, and seemed afraid to approach it. I was convinced that he was proud and irascible, and that I must be careful not to touch him on his weak point. He was equally sure that I disliked the country and was dying for social distraction, and that he must put up with this unfortunate taste of mine. We both avoided frank conversation on these topics, and each misjudged the other. We had long ceased to think each other the most perfect people in the world; each now judged the other in secret, and measured the offender by the standard of other people. I fell ill before we left Petersburg, and we went from there to a house near town, from which my husband went on alone, to join his mother at Nikolskoye. By that time I was well enough to have gone with him, but he urged me to stay on the pretext of my health. I knew, however, that he was really afraid we should be uncomfortable together in the country; so I did not insist much, and he went off alone. I felt it dull and solitary in his absence; but when he came back, I saw that he did not add to my life what he had added formerly. In the old days every thought and experience weighed on me like a crime till I had imparted it to him; every action and word of his seemed to me a model of perfection; we often laughed for joy at the mere sight of each other. But these relations had changed, so imperceptibly that we had not even noticed their disappearance. Separate interests and cares, which we no longer tried to share, made their appearance, and even the fact of our estrangement ceased to trouble us. The idea became familiar, and, before a year had passed, each could look at the other without confusion. His fits of boyish merriment with me had quite vanished; his mood of calm indulgence to all that passed, which used to provoke me, had disappeared; there was an end of those penetrating looks which used to confuse and delight me, an end of the ecstasies and prayers which we once shared in common. We did not even meet often: he was continually absent, with no fears or regrets for leaving me alone; and I was constantly in society, where I did not need him.

There were no further scenes or quarrels between us. I tried to satisfy him, he carried out all my wishes, and we seemed to love each other.

When we were by ourselves, which we seldom were, I felt neither joy nor excitement nor embarrassment in his company: it seemed like being alone. I realized that he was my husband and no mere stranger, a good man, and as familiar to me as my own self. I was convinced that I knew just what he would say and do, and how he would look; and if anything he did surprised me, I concluded that he had made a mistake. I expected nothing from him. In a word, he was my husband - and that was all. It seemed to me that things must be so, as a matter of course, and that no other relations between us had ever existed. When he left home, especially at first, I was lonely and frightened and felt keenly my need of support; when he came back, I ran to his arms with joy, though two hours later my joy was quite forgotten, and I found nothing to say to him. Only at moments which sometimes occurred between us of quiet undemonstrative affection, I felt something wrong and some pain at my heart, and I seemed to read the same story in his eyes. I was conscious of a limit to tenderness, which he seemingly would not, and I could not, overstep. This saddened me sometimes; but I had no leisure to reflect on anything, and my regret for a change which I vaguely realized I tried to drown in the distractions which were always within my reach. Fashionable life, which had dazzled me at first by its glitter and flattery of my self-love, now took entire command of my nature, became a habit, laid its fetters upon me, and monopolized my capacity for feeling. I could not bear solitude, and was afraid to reflect on my position. My whole day, from late in the morning till late at night, was taken up by the claims of society; even if I stayed at home, my time was not my own. This no longer seemed to me either gay or dull, but it seemed that so, and not otherwise, it always had to be.

So three years passed, during which our relations to one another remained unchanged and seemed to have taken a fixed shape which could not become either better or worse. Though two events of importance in our family life took place during that time, neither of them changed my own life. These were the birth of my first child and the death of Tatyana Semyonovna. At first the feeling of motherhood did take hold of me with such power, and produce in me such a passion of unanticipated joy, that I believed this would prove the beginning of a new life for me. But, in the course of two months, when I began to go out again, my feeling grew weaker and weaker, till it passed into mere habit and the lifeless performance of a duty. My husband, on the contrary, from the birth of our first boy, became his old self again - gentle, composed, and home-loving, and transferred to the child his old tenderness and gaiety. Many a night when I went, dressed for a ball, to the nursery, to sign the child with the cross before he slept, I found my husband there and felt his eyes fixed on me with something of reproof in their serious gaze. Then I was ashamed and even shocked by my own callousness, and asked myself if I was worse than other women. "But it can't be helped," I said to myself; "I love my child, but to sit beside him all day long would bore me; and nothing will make me pretend what I do not really feel."

His mother's death was a great sorrow to my husband; he said that he found it painful to go on living at Nikolskoye. For myself, although I mourned for her and sympathized with my husband's sorrow, yet I found life in that house easier and pleasanter after her death. Most of those three years we spent in town: I went only once to Nikolskoye for two months; and the third year we went abroad and spent the summer at Baden.

I was then twenty-one; our financial position was, I believed, satisfactory; my domestic life gave me all that I asked of it; everyone I knew, it seemed to me, loved me; my health was good; I was the best-dressed woman in Baden; I knew that I was good looking; the weather was fine; I enjoyed the atmosphere of beauty and refinement; and, in short, I was in excellent spirits. They had once been even higher at Nikolskoye, when my happiness was in myself and came from the feeling that I deserved to be happy, and from the anticipation of still greater happiness to come. That was a different state of things; but I did very well this summer also. I had no special wishes or hopes of fears; it seemed to me that my life was full and my conscience easy. Among all the visitors at Baden that season there was no one man whom I preferred to the rest, or even to our old ambassador, Prince K., who was assiduous in his attentions to me. One was young, and another old; one was English and fair, another French and wore a beard - to me they were all alike, but all indispensable. Indistinguishable as they were, they together made up the atmosphere which I found so pleasant. But there was one, an Italian marquis, who stood out from the rest by reason of the boldness with which he expressed his admiration. He seized every opportunity of being with me - danced with me, rode with me, and met me at the casino; and everywhere he spoke to me of my charms. Several times I saw him from my windows loitering round our hotel, and the fixed gaze of his bright eyes often troubled me, and made me blush and turn away. He was young, handsome, and well-mannered; and above all, by his smile and the expression of his brow, he resembled my husband, though much handsomer than he. He struck me by this likeness, though in general, in his lips, eyes, and long chin, there was something coarse and animal which contrasted with my husband's charming expression of kindness and noble serenity. I supposed him to be passionately in love with me, and thought of him sometimes with proud commiseration. When I tried at times to soothe him and change his tone to one of easy, half-friendly confidence, he resented the suggestion with vehemence, and continued to disquiet me by a smoldering passion which was ready at any moment to burst forth. Though I would not own it even to myself, I feared him and often thought of him against my sill. My husband knew him, and greeted him - even more than other acquaintances of ours who regarded him only as my husband - with coldness and disdain.

Towards the end of the season I fell ill and stayed indoors for a fortnight. The first evening that I went out again to hear the band, I learnt that Lady S., an Englishwoman famous for her beauty, who had long been expected, had arrived in my absence. My return was welcomed, and a group gathered round me; but a more distinguished group attended the beautiful stranger. She and her beauty was the one subject of conversation around me. When I saw her, she was really beautiful, but her self-satisfied expression struck me as disagreeable, and I said so. That day everything that had formerly seemed amusing, seemed dull. Lady S. arranged an expedition to ruined castle for the next day; but I declined to be of the party. Almost everyone else went; and my opinion of Baden underwent a complete change. Everything and everybody seemed to me stupid and tiresome; I wanted to cry, to break off my cure, to return to Russia. There was some evil feeling in my soul, but I did not yet acknowledge it to myself. Pretending that I was not strong, I ceased to appear at crowded parties; if I went out, it was only in the morning by me, to drink the waters; and my only companion was Mme M., a Russian lady, with whom I sometimes took drives in the surrounding country. My husband was absent: he had gone to Heidelberg for a time, intending to return to Russia when my cure was over, and only paid me occasional visits at Baden.

One day when Lady S. had carried off all the company on a hunting expedition, Mme M. and I drove in the afternoon to the castle. While our carriage moved slowly along the winding road, bordered by ancient chestnut-trees and commanding a vista of the pretty and pleasant country round Baden, with the setting sun lighting it up, our conversation took a more serious turn than had ever happened to us before. I had known my companion for a long time; but she appeared to me now in a new light, as a well-principled and intelligent woman, to whom it was possible to speak without reserve, and whose friendship was worth having. We spoke of our private concerns, of our children, of the emptiness of life at Baden, till we felt a longing for Russia and the Russian countryside. When we entered the castle we were still under the impression of this serious feeling. Within the walls there was shade and coolness; the sunlight played from above upon the ruins. Steps and voices were audible. The landscape, charming enough but cold to a Russian eye, lay before us in the frame made by a doorway. We sat down to rest and watched the sunset in silence. The voices now sounded louder, and I thought I heard my own name. I listened and could not help overhearing every word. I recognized the voices: the speakers were the Italian marquis and a French friend of his whom I knew also. They were talking of me and of Lady S., and the Frenchman was comparing us as rival beauties. Though he said nothing insulting, his words made my pulse quicken. He explained in detail the good points of us both. I was already a mother, while Lady S. was only nineteen; though I had the advantage in hair, my rival had a better figure. "Besides," he added, "Lady S. is a real grandee dame, and the other is nothing in particular, only one of those obscure Russian princesses who turn up here nowadays in such numbers." He ended by saying that I was wise in not attempting to compete with Lady S., and that I was completely buried as far as Baden was concerned.

"I am sorry for her - unless indeed she takes a fancy to console herself with you," he added with a hard ringing laugh.

"If she goes away, I follow her" - the words were blurted out in an Italian accent.

"Happy man! He is still capable of a passion!" laughed the Frenchman.

"Passion!" said the other voice and then was still for a moment. "It is a necessity to me: I cannot live without it. To make life a romance is the one thing worth doing. And with me romance never breaks off in the middle, and this affair I shall carry through to the end."

"Bonne chance, mon ami!" said the Frenchman.

They now turned a corner, and the voices stopped. Then we heard them coming down the steps, and a few minutes later they came out upon us by a side door. They were much surprised to see us. I blushed when the marquis approached me, and felt afraid when we left the castle and he offered me his arm. I could not refuse, and we set off for the carriage, walking behind Mme M. and his friend. I was mortified by what the Frenchman had said of me, though I secretly admitted that he had only put in words what I felt myself; but the plain speaking of the Italian had surprised and upset me by its coarseness. I was tormented by the thought that, though I had overheard him, he showed no fear of me. It was hateful to have him so close to me; and I walked fast after the other couple, not looking at him or answering him and trying to hold his arm in such a way as not to hear him. He spoke of the fine view, of the unexpected pleasure of our meeting, and so on; but I was not listening. My thoughts were with my husband, my child, my country; I felt ashamed distressed, anxious; I was in a hurry to get back to my solitary room in the Hotel de Bade, there to think at leisure of the storm of feeling that had just risen in my heart. But Mme M. walked slowly, it was still a long way to the carriage, and my escort seemed to loiter on purpose as if he wished to detain me. "None of that!" I thought, and resolutely quickened my pace. But it soon became unmistakable that he was detaining me and even pressing my arm. Mme M. turned a corner, and we were quite alone. I was afraid.

"Excuse me," I said coldly and tried to free my arm; but the lace of my sleeve caught on a button of his coat. Bending towards me, he began to unfasten it, and his ungloved fingers touched my arm. A feeling new to me, half horror and half pleasure, sent an icy shiver down my back. I looked at him, intending by my coldness to convey all the contempt I felt for him; but my look expressed nothing but fear and excitement. His liquid blazing eyes, right up against my face, stared strangely at me, at my neck and breast; both his hands fingered my arm above the wrist; his parted lips were saying that he loved me, and that I was all the world to him; and those lips were coming nearer and nearer, and those hands were squeezing mine harder and harder and burning me. A fever ran through my veins, my sight grew dim, I trembled, and the words intended to check him died in my throat. Suddenly I felt a kiss on my cheek. Trembling all over and turning cold, I stood still and stared at him. Unable to speak or move, I stood there, horrified, expectant, even desirous. It was over in a moment, but the moment was horrible! In that short time I saw him exactly as he was - the low straight forehead (that forehead so like my husband's!) under the straw hat; the handsome regular nose and dilated nostrils; the long waxed mustache and short beard; the close-shaved cheeks and sunburned neck. I hated and feared him; he was utterly repugnant and alien to me. And yet the excitement and passion of this hateful strange man raised a powerful echo in my own heart; I felt an irresistible longing to surrender myself to the kisses of that coarse handsome mouth, and to the pressure of those white hands with their delicate veins and jewelled fingers; I was tempted to throw myself headlong into the abyss of forbidden delights that had suddenly opened up before me.

"I am so unhappy already," I thought; "let more and more storms of unhappiness burst over my head!"

He put one arm round me and bent towards my face. "Better so!" I thought: "let sin and shame cover me ever deeper and deeper!"

"Je vous aime!" he whispered in the voice which was so like my husband's. At once I thought of my husband and child, as creatures once precious to me who had now passed altogether out of my life. At that moment I heard Mme M's voice; she called to me from round the corner. I came to myself, tore my hand away without looking at him, and almost ran after her: I only looked at him after she and I were already seated in the carriage. Then I saw him raise his hat and ask some commonplace question with a smile. He little knew the inexpressible aversion I felt for him at that moment.

My life seemed so wretched, the future so hopeless, the past so black! When Mme M. spoke, her words meant nothing to me. I thought that she talked only of our pity, and to hide the contempt I aroused in her. In every word and every look I seemed to detect this contempt and insulting pity. The shame of that kiss burned my cheek, and the thought of my husband and child was more than I could bear. When I was alone in my own room, I tried to think over my position; but I was afraid to be alone. Without drinking the tea which was brought me, and uncertain of my own motives, I got ready with feverish haste to catch the evening train and join my husband at Heidelberg.

I found seats for myself and my maid in an empty carriage. When the train started and the fresh air blew through the window on my face, I grew more composed and pictured my past and future to myself more clearly. The course of our married life from the time of our first visit to Petersburg now presented itself to me in a new light, and lay like a reproach on my conscience. For the first time I clearly recalled our start at Nikolskoye and our plans for the future; and for the first time I asked myself what happiness had my husband had since then. I felt that I had behaved badly to him. "By why", I asked myself, "did he not stop me? Why did he make pretences? Why did he always avoid explanations? Why did he insult me? Why did he not use the power of his love to influence me? Or did he not love me?" But whether he was to blame or not, I still felt the kiss of that strange man upon my cheek. The nearer we got to Heidelberg, the clearer grew my picture of my husband, and the more I dreaded our meeting. "I shall tell him all," I thought, "and wipe out everything with tears of repentance; and he will forgive me." But I did not know myself what I meant by "everything"; and I did not believe in my heart that he would forgive me.

As soon as I entered my husband's room and saw his calm though surprised expression, I felt at once that I had nothing to tell him, no confession to make, and nothing to ask forgiveness for. I had to suppress my unspoken grief and penitence.

"What put this into your head?" he asked. "I meant to go to Baden tomorrow." Then he looked more closely at me and seemed to take alarm. "What's the matter with you? What has happened?" he said.

"Nothing at all," I replied, almost breaking down. "I am not going back. Let us go home, tomorrow if you like, to Russia."

For some time he said nothing but looked at me attentively. Then he said, "But do tell me what has happened to you."

I blushed involuntarily and looked down. There came into his eyes a flash of anger and displeasure. Afraid of what he might imagine, I said with a power of pretence that surprised myself:

"Nothing at all has happened. It was merely that I grew weary and sad by myself; and I have been thinking a great deal of our way of life and of you. I have long been to blame towards you. Why do you take me abroad, when you can't bear it yourself? I have long been to blame. Let us go back to Nikolskoye and settle there forever."

"Spare us these sentimental scenes, my dear," he said coldly. "To go back to Nikolskoye is a good idea, for our money is running short; but the notion of stopping there 'forever' is fanciful. I know you would not settle down. Have some tea, and you will feel better," and he rose to ring for the waiter.

I imagined all he might be thinking about me; and I was offended by the horrible thoughts which I ascribed to him when I encountered the dubious and shame-faced look he directed at me. "He will not and cannot understand me." I said I would go and look at the child, and I left the room. I wished to be alone, and to cry and cry and cry...

IV

The house at Nikolskoye, so long unheated and uninhabited, came to life again; but much of the past was dead beyond recall. Tatyana Semyonovna was no more, and we were now alone together. But far from desiring such close companionship, we even found it irksome. To me that winter was the more trying because I was in bad health, from which In only recovered after the birth of my second son. My husband and I were still on the same terms as during our life in Petersburg: we were coldly friendly to each other; but in the country each room and wall and sofa recalled what he had once been to me, and what I had lost. It was if some unforgiven grievance held us apart, as if he were punishing me and pretending not to be aware of it. But there was nothing to ask pardon for, no penalty to deprecate; my punishment was merely this, that he did not give his whole heart and mind to me as he used to do; but he did not give it to anyone or to anything; as though he had no longer a heart to give. Sometimes it occurred to me that he was only pretending to be like that, in order to hurt me, and that the old feeling was still alive in his breast; and I tried to call it forth. But I always failed: he always seemed to avoid frankness, evidently suspecting me of insincerity, and dreading the folly of any emotional display. I could read in his face and the tone of his voice, "What is the good of talking? I know all the facts already, and I know what is on the tip of your tongue, and I know that you will say one thing and do another." At first I was mortified by his dread of frankness, but I came later to think that it was rather the absence, on his part, of any need of frankness. It would never have occurred to me now, to tell him of a sudden that I loved him, or to ask him to repeat the prayers with me or listen while Ii played the piano. Our intercourse came to be regulated by a fixed code of good manners. We lived our separate lives: he had his own occupations in which I was not needed, and which I no longer wished to share, while I continued my idle life which no longer vexed or grieved him. The children were still too young to form a bond between us.

But spring came round and brought Katya and Sonya to spend the summer with us in the country. as the house at Nikolskoye was under repair, we went to live at my old home at Pokrovskoye. The old house was unchanged- the veranda, the folding table and the piano in the sunny drawing room, and my old bedroom with its white curtains and the dreams of my girlhood which I seemed to have left behind me there. In that room there were two beds: one had been mine, and in it now my plump little Kokosha lay sprawling, when I went at night to sign him with the cross; the other was a crib, in which the little face of my baby, Vanya, peeped out from his swaddling clothes. Often when I had made the sign over them and remained standing in the middle of the quiet room, suddenly there rose up from all the corners, from the walls and curtains, old forgotten visions of youth. Old voices began to sing the songs of my girlhood. Where were those visions now? Where were those dear old sweet songs? All that I had hardly dared to hope for had come to pass. My vague confused dreams had become a reality, and the reality had become an oppressive, difficult, and joyless life. All remained the same - the garden visible through the window, the grass, the path, the very same bench over there above the dell, the same song of the nightingale by the pond, the same lilacs in full bloom, the same moon shining above the house; and yet, in everything such a terrible inconceivable change! Such coldness in all that might have been near and dear! Just as in old times Katya and I sit quietly alone together in the parlour and talk, and talk of him. But Katya has grown wrinkled and pale; and her eyes no longer shine with joy and hope, but express only sympathy, sorrow, and regret. We do not go into raptures as we used to, we judge him coolly; we do not wonder what we have done to deserve such happiness, or long to proclaim our thoughts to all the world. No! we whisper together like conspirators and ask each other for the hundredth time why all has changed so sadly. Yet he was still the same man, save for the deeper furrow between his eyebrows and the whiter hair on his temples; but his serious attentive look was constantly veiled from me by a cloud. And I am the same woman, but without love or desire for love, with no longing for work and not content with myself. My religious ecstasies, my love for my husband, the fullness of my former life - all these now seem utterly remote and visionary. Once it seemed so plain and right that to live for others was happiness; but now it has become unintelligible. Why live for others, when life had no attraction even for oneself?

I had given up my music altogether since the time of our first visit to Petersburg; but now the old piano and the old music tempted me to begin again.

One day I was not well and stayed indoors alone. My husband had taken Katya and Sonya to see the new buildings at Nikolskoye. Tea was laid; I went downstairs and while waiting for them sat down at the piano. I opened the "Moonlight sonata" and began to play. There was no one within sight or sound, the windows were open over the garden, and the familiar sounds floated through the room with a solemn sadness. At the end of the first movement I looked round instinctively to the corner where he used once to sit and listen to my playing. He was not there; his chair, long unmoved, was still in its place; through the window I could see a lilac bush against the light of the setting sun; the freshness of evening streamed in through the open windows. I rested my elbows on the piano and covered my face with both hands; and so I sat for a long time, thinking. I recalled with pain the irrevocable past, and timidly imagined the future. But for me there seemed to be no future, no desires at all and no hopes. "Can life be over for me?" I thought with horror; then I looked up, and, trying to forget and not to think, I began playing the same movement over again. "Oh, God!" I prayed, "forgive me if I have sinned, or restore to me all that once blossomed in my heart, or teach me what to do and how to live now." There was a sound of wheels on the grass and before the steps of the house; then I heard cautious and familiar footsteps pass along the veranda and cease; but my heart no longer replied to the sound. When I stopped playing the footsteps were behind me and a hand was laid on my shoulder.

"How clever of you to think of playing that!" he said.

I said nothing.

"Have you had tea?" he asked.

I shook my head without looking at him - I was unwilling to let him see the signs of emotion on my face.

"They'll be here immediately," he said; "the horse gave trouble, and they got out on the high road to walk home."

"Let us wait for them," I said, and went out to the veranda, hoping that he would follow; but he asked about the children and went upstairs to see them. Once more his presence and simple kindly voice made me doubt if I had really lost anything. What more could I wish? "He is kind and gentle, a good husband, a good father; I don't know myself what more I want." I sat down under the veranda awning on the very bench on which

I had sat when we became engaged. The sun had set, it was growing dark, and a little spring rain cloud hung over the house and garden, and only behind the trees the horizon was clear, with the fading glow of twilight, in which one star had just begun to twinkle. The landscape, covered by the shadow of the cloud, seemed waiting for the light spring shower. There was not a breath of wind; not a single leaf or blade of grass stirred; the scent of lilac and bird cherry was so strong in the garden and veranda that it seemed as if all the air was in flower; it came in wafts, now stronger and now weaker, till one longed to shut both eyes and hears and drink in that fragrance only. The dahlias and rose bushes, not yet in flower, stood motionless on the black mould of the border, looking as if they were growing slowly upwards on their white-shaved props; beyond the dell, the frogs were making the most of their time before the rain drove them to the pond, croaking busily and loudly. Only the high continuous note of water falling at some distance rose above their croaking. From time to time the nightingales called to one another, and I could hear them flitting restlessly from bush to bush. Again this spring a nightingale had tried to build in a bush under the window, and I heard her fly off across the avenue when I went into the veranda. From there she whistled once and then stopped; she, too, was expecting the rain.

I tried in vain to calm my feelings: I had a sense of anticipation and regret.

He came downstairs again and sat down beside me.

"I am afraid they will get wet," he said.

"Yes," I answered; and we sat for long without speaking.

The cloud came down lower and lower with no wind. The air grew stiller and more fragrant. Suddenly a drop fell on the canvas awning and seemed to rebound from it; then another broke on the gravel path; soon there was a splash on the burdock leaves, and a fresh shower of big drops came down faster and faster. Nightingales and frogs were both dumb; only the high note of the falling water, though the rain made it seem more distant, still went on; and a bird, which must have sheltered among the dry leaves near the veranda, steadily repeated its two unvarying notes. My husband got up to go in.

"Where are you going?" I asked, trying to keep him; "it is so pleasant here."

"We must send them an umbrella and galoshes," he replied.

"Don't trouble - it will soon be over."

He thought I was right, and we remained together in the veranda. I rested one hand upon the wet slippery rail and put my head out. The fresh rain wetted my hair and neck in places. The cloud, growing lighter and thinner, was passing overhead; the steady patter of the rain gave place to occasional drops that fell from the sky or dripped from the trees. The frogs began to croak again in the dell; the nightingales woke up and began to call from the dripping bushes from one side and then from another. The whole prospect before us grew clear.

"How delightful!" he said, seating himself on the veranda rail and passing a hand over my wet hair.

This simple caress had on me the effect of a reproach: I felt inclined to cry.

"What more can a man need?" he said; "I am so content now that I want nothing; I am perfectly happy!"

He told me a different story once, I thought. He had said that, however great his happiness might be, he always wanted more and more. Now he is calm and contented; while my heart is full of unspoken repentance and unshed tears.

"I think it delightful too," I said; "but I am sad just because of the beauty of it all. All is so fair and lovely outside me, while my own heart is confused and baffled and full of vague unsatisfied longing. Is it possible that there is no element of pain, no yearning for the past, in your enjoyment of nature?"

He took his hand off my head and was silent for a little.

"I used to feel that too," he said, as though recalling it, "especially in spring. I used to sit up all night too, with my hopes and fears for company, and good company they were! But life was all before me then. Now it is all behind me, and I am content with what I have. I find life capital," he added with such careless confidence, that I believed, whatever pain it gave me to hear it, that it was the truth.

"But is there nothing you wish for?" I asked.

"I don't ask for impossibilities," he said, guessing my thoughts. "You go and get your head wet," he added, stroking my head like a child's and again passing his hand over the wet hair; "you envy the leaves and the grass their wetting from the rain, and you would like yourself to be the grass and the leaves and the rain. But I am contented to enjoy them and everything else that is good and young and happy."

"And do you regret nothing of the past?" I asked, while my heart grew heavier and heavier.

Again he thought for a time before replying. I saw that he wished to reply with perfect frankness.

"Nothing," he said shortly.

"Not true! not true!" I said, turning towards him and looking into his eyes. "Do you really not regret the past?"

"No!" he repeated; "I am grateful for it, but I don't regret it."

"But would you not like to have it back?" I asked.

"No; I might as well wish to have wings. It is impossible."

"And would you not alter the past? Do you not reproach yourself or me?"

"No, never! It was all for the best."

"Listen to me!" I said touching his arm to make him look round. "Why did you never tell me that you wished me to live as you really wished me to? Why did you give me a freedom for which I was unfit? Why did you stop teaching me? If you had wished it, if you had guided me differently, none of all this would have happened!" said I in a voice that increasingly expressed cold displeasure and reproach in place of the love of former days.

"What would not have happened?" he asked, turning to me in surprise. "As it is, there is nothing wrong. Things are all right, quite all right," he added with a smile.

"Does he really not understand?" I thought; "or still worse, does he not wish to understand?"

Then I suddenly broke out. "Had you acted differently, I should not now be punished, for no fault at all, by your indifference and even contempt, and you would not have taken from me unjustly all that I valued in life!"

"What do you mean, my dear one?" he asked - he seemed not to understand me.

"No! don't interrupt me! You have taken from me your confidence, your love, even your respect; for I cannot believe, when I think of the past, that you still love me. No! don't speak! I must once for all say out what has long been torturing me. Is it my fault that I knew nothing of life, and that you left me to learn experience for myself? Is it my fault that now, when I have gained the knowledge and have been struggling for nearly a year to come back to you, you push me away and pretend not to understand what I want? And you always do it so that it is impossible to reproach you, while I am guilty and unhappy. Yes, you wish to drive me out again to that life which might rob us both of happiness."

"How did I show that!" he asked in evident alarm and surprise.

"No later than yesterday you said, and you constantly say, that I can never settle down here, and that we must spend this winter too at Petersburg; and I hate Petersburg!" I went on, "Instead of supporting me, you avoid all plain speaking, you never say a single frank affectionate word to me. And then, when I fall utterly, you will reproach me and rejoice in my fall."

"Stop!" he said with cold severity. "You have no right to say that. It only proves that you are ill-disposed towards me, that you don't..."

"That I don't love you? Don't hesitate to say it!" I cried, and the tears began to flow. I sat down on the bench and covered my face with my handkerchief.

"So that is how he understood me!" I thought, trying to restrain the sobs which choked me. "gone, gone is our former love!" said a voice at my heart. He did not come close or try to comfort me. He was hurt by what I had said. When he spoke, his tone was cool and dry.

"I don't know what you reproach me with," he began. "If you mean that I don't love you as I once did..."

"Did love!" I said, with my face buried in the handkerchief, while the bitter tears fell still more abundantly.

"If so, time is to blame for that, and we ourselves. Each time of life has its own kind of love." He was silent for a moment. "Shall I tell you the whole truth, if you really wish for frankness? In that summer when I first knew you, I used to lie awake all night, thinking about you, and I made that love myself, and it grew and grew in my heart. So again, in Petersburg and abroad, in the course of horrible sleepless nights, I strove to shatter and destroy that love, which had come to torture me. I did not destroy it, but I destroyed that part of it which gave me pain. Then I grew calm; and I feel love still, but it is a different kind of love."

"You call it love, but I call it torture!" I said. "Why did you allow me to go into society, if you thought so badly of it that you ceased to love me on that account?"

"No, it was not society, my dear," he said.

"Why did you not exercise your authority?" I went on: "why did you not lock me up or kill me? That would have been better than the loss of all that formed my happiness. I should have been happy, instead of being ashamed."

I began to sob again and hid my face.

Just then Katya and Sonya, wet and cheerful, came out to the veranda, laughing and talking loudly. They were silent as soon as they saw us, and went in again immediately.

We remained silent for a long time. I had had my cry out and felt relieved. I glanced at him. He was sitting with his head resting on his hand; he intended to make some reply to my glance, but only sighed deeply and resumed his former position.

I went up to him and removed his hand. His eyes turned thoughtfully to my face.

"Yes," he began, as if continuing his thoughts aloud, "all of us, and especially you women, must have personal experience of all the nonsense of life, in order to get back to life itself; the evidence of other people is no good. At that time you had not got near the end of that charming nonsense which I admired in you. So I let you go through it alone, feeling that I had no right to put pressure on you, though my own time for that sort of thing was long past."

"If you loved me," I said, "how could you stand beside me and suffer me to go through it?"

"Because it was impossible for you to take my word for it, though you would have tried to. Personal experience was necessary, and now you have had it."

"There was much calculation in all that," I said, "but little love."

And again we were silent.

"What you said just now is severe, but it is true," he began, rising suddenly and beginning to walk about the veranda. "Yes, it is true. I was to blame," he added, stopping opposite me; "I ought either to have kept myself from loving you at all, or to have loved you in a simpler way."

"Let us forget it all," I said timidly.

"No," he said; "the past can never come back, never;" and his voice softened as he spoke.

"It is restored already," I said, laying a hand on his shoulder.

He took my hand away and pressed it.

"I was wrong when I said that I did not regret the past. I do regret it; I weep for that past love which can never return. Who is to blame, I do not know. Love remains, but not the old love; its place remains, but it all wasted away and has lost all strength and substance; recollections are still left, and gratitude; but..."

"Do not say that!" I broke in. "Let all be as it was before! Surely that is possible?" I asked, looking into his eyes; but their gaze was clear and calm, and did not look deeply into mine.

Even while I spoke, I knew that my wishes and my petition were impossible. He smiled calmly and gently; and I thought it the smile of an old man.

"How young you are still!" he said, "and I am so old. What you seek in me is no longer there. Why deceive ourselves?" he added, still smiling.

I stood silent opposite to him, and my heart grew calmer.

"Don't let us try to repeat life," he went on. "Don't let us make pretences to ourselves. Let us be thankful that there is an end of the old emotions and excitements. The excitement of searching is over for us; our quest is done, and happiness enough has fallen to our lot. Now we must stand aside and make room - for him, if you like," he said, pointing to the nurse who was carrying Vanya out and had stopped at the veranda door. "that's the truth, my dear one," he said, drawing down my head and kissing it, not a lover any longer but an old friend.

The fragrant freshness of the night rose ever stronger and sweeter from the garden; the sounds and the silence grew more solemn; star after star began to twinkle overhead. I looked at him, and suddenly my heart grew light; it seemed that the cause of my suffering had been removed like an aching nerve. Suddenly I realized clearly and calmly that the past feeling, like the past time itself, was gone beyond recall, and that it would be not only impossible but painful and uncomfortable to bring it back. And after all, was that time so good which seemed to me so happy? And it was all so long, long ago!

"Time for tea!" he said, and we went together to the parlour. At the door we met the nurse with the baby. I took him in my arms, covered his bare little red legs, pressed him to me, and kissed him with the lightest touch of my lips. Half asleep, he moved the parted fingers of one creased little hand and opened dim little eyes, as if he was looking for something or recalling something. All at once his eyes rested on me, a spark of consciousness shone in them, the little pouting lips, parted before, now met and opened in a smile. "Mine, mine, mine!" I thought, pressing him to my breast with such an impulse of joy in every limb that I found it hard to restrain myself from hurting him. I fell to kissing the cold little feet, his stomach and hand and head with its thin covering of down. My husband came up to me, and I quickly covered the child's face and uncovered it again.

"Ivan Sergeich!" said my husband, tickling him under the chin. But I made haste to cover Ivan Sergeich up again. None but I had any business to look long at him. I glanced at my husband. His eyes smiled as he looked at me; and Ii looked into them with an ease and happiness which I had not felt for a long time.

That day ended the romance of our marriage; the old feeling became a precious irrecoverable remembrance; but a new feeling of love for my children and the father of my children laid the foundation of a new life and a quite different happiness; and that life and happiness have lasted to the present time.

WORK, DEATH AND SICKNESS

A LEGEND

This is a legend current among the South American Indians.

God, say they, at first made men so that they had no need to work: they needed neither houses, nor clothes, nor food, and they all lived till they were a hundred, and did not know what illness was.

When, after some time, God looked to see how people were living, he saw that instead of being happy in their life, they had quarrelled with one another, and, each caring for himself, had brought matters to such a pass that far from enjoying life, they cursed it.

Then God said to himself: 'This comes of their living separately, each for himself.' And to change this state of things, God so arranged matters that it became impossible for people to live without working. To avoid suffering from cold and hunger, they were now obliged to build dwellings, and to dig the ground, and to grow and gather fruits and grain.

'Work will bring them together,' thought God.

'They cannot make their tools, prepare and transport their timber, build their houses, sow and gather their harvests, spin and weave, and make their clothes, each one alone by himself.'

'It will make them understand that the more heartily they work together, the more they will have and the better they will live; and this will unite them.'

Time passed on, and again God came to see how men were living, and whether they were now happy.

But he found them living worse than before. They worked together (that they could not help doing), but not all together, being broken up into little groups. And each group tried to snatch work from other groups, and they hindered one another, wasting time and strength in their struggles, so that things went ill with them all.

Having seen that this, too, was not well, God decided so as to arrange things that man should not know the time of his death, but might die at any moment; and he announced this to them.

'Knowing that each of them may die at any moment,' thought God, 'they will not, by grasping at gains that may last so short a time, spoil the hours of life allotted to them.'

But it turned out otherwise. When God returned to see how people were living, he saw that their life was as bad as ever.

Those who were strongest, availing themselves of the fact that men might die at any time, subdued those who were weaker, killing some and threatening others with death. And it came about that the strongest and their descendants did no work, and suffered from the weariness of idleness, while those who were weaker had to work beyond their strength, and suffered from lack of rest. Each set of men feared and hated the other. And the life of man became yet more unhappy.

Having seen all this, God, to mend matters, decided to make use of one last means; he sent all kinds of sickness among men. God thought that when all men were exposed to sickness they would understand that those who are well should have pity on those who are sick, and should help them, that when they themselves fall ill those who are well might in turn help them.

And again God went away, but when He came back to see how men lived now that they were subject to sicknesses, he saw that their life was worse even than before. The very sickness that in God's purpose should have united men, had divided them more than ever. Those men who were strong enough to make others work, forced them also to wait on them in times of sickness; but they did not, in their turn, look after others who were ill. And those who were forced to work for others and to look after them when sick, were so worn with work that they had no time to look after their own sick, but left them without attendance. That the sight of sick folk might not disturb the pleasures of the wealthy, houses were arranged in which these poor people suffered and died, far from those whose sympathy might have cheered them, and in the arms of hired people who nursed them without compassion, or even with disgust.

Moreover, people considered many of the illnesses infectious, and, fearing to catch them, not only avoided the sick, but even separated themselves from those who attended the sick.

Then God said to Himself: 'If even this means will not bring men to understand wherein their happiness lies, let them be taught by suffering.' And God left men to themselves.

And, left to themselves, men lived long before they understood that they all ought to, and might be, happy. Only in the very latest times have a few of them begun to understand that work ought not to be a bugbear to some and like galley-slavery for others, but should be a common and happy occupation, uniting all men. They have begun to understand that with death constantly threatening each of us, the only reasonable business of every man is to spend the years, months, hours, and minutes, allotted him - in unity and love. They have begun to understand that sickness, far from dividing men, should, on the contrary, give opportunity for loving union with one another.

WHERE LOVE IS, GOD IS

In a certain town there lived a cobbler, Martin Avdéiteh by name. He had a tiny room in a basement, the one window of which looked out on to the street. Through it one could only see the feet of those who passed by, but Martin recognized the people by their boots. He had lived long in the place and had many acquaintances. There was hardly a pair of boots in the neighbourhood that had not been once or twice through his hands, so he often saw his own handiwork through the window. Some he had re-soled, some patched, some stitched up, and to some he had even put fresh uppers. He had plenty to do, for he worked well, used good material, did not charge too much, and could be relied on. If he could do a job by the day required, he undertook it; if not, he told the truth and gave no false promises; so he was well known and never short of work.

Martin had always been a good man; but in his old age he began to think more about his soul and to draw nearer to God. While he still worked for a master, before he set up on his own account, his wife had died, leaving him with a three-year old son. None of his elder children had lived, they had all died in infancy. At first Martin thought of sending his little son to his sister's in the country, but then he felt sorry to part with the boy, thinking: 'It would be hard for my little Kapitón to have to grow up in a strange family; I will keep him with me.'

Martin left his master and went into lodgings with his little son. But he had no luck with his children. No sooner had the boy reached an age when he could help his father and be a support as well as a joy to him, than he fell ill and, after being laid up for a week with a burning fever, died. Martin buried his son, and gave way to despair so great and overwhelming that he murmured against God. In his sorrow he prayed again and again that he too might die, reproaching God for having taken the son he loved, his only son while he, old as he was, remained alive. After that Martin left off going to church.

One day an old man from Martin's native village who had been a pilgrim for the last eight years, called in on his way from Tróitsa Monastery. Martin opened his heart to him, and told him of his sorrow.

'I no longer even wish to live, holy man,' he said. 'All I ask of God is that I soon may die. I am now quite without hope in the world.'

The old man replied: 'You have no right to say such things, Martin. We cannot judge God's ways. Not our reasoning, but God's will, decides. If God willed that your son should die and you should live, it must be best so. As to your despair - that comes because you wish to live for your own happiness.'

'What else should one live for?' asked Martin.

'For God, Martin,' said the old man. 'He gives you life, and you must live for Him. When you have learnt to live for Him, you will grieve no more, and all will seem easy to you.'

Martin was silent awhile, and then asked: 'But how is one to live for God?'

The old man answered: 'How one may live for God has been shown us by Christ. Can you read? Then buy the Gospels, and read them: there you will see how God would have you live. You have it all there.'

These words sank deep into Martin's heart, and that same day he went and bought himself a Testament in large print, and began to read.

At first he meant only to read on holidays, but having once begun he found it made his heart so light that he read every day. Sometimes he was so absorbed in his reading that the oil in his lamp burnt out before he could tear himself away from the book. He continued to read every night, and the more he read the more clearly he understood what God required of him, and how he might live for God. And his heart grew lighter and lighter. Before, when he went to bed he used to lie with a heavy heart, moaning as he thought of his little Kapitón; but now he only repeated again and again: 'Glory to Thee, glory to Thee, O Lord! Thy will be done!'

From that time Martin's whole life changed. Formerly, on holidays he used to go and have tea at the public house, and did not even refuse a glass or two of vódka. Sometimes, after having had a drop with a friend, he left the public house not drunk, but rather merry, and would say foolish things: shout at a man, or abuse him. Now, all that sort of thing passed away from him. His life became peaceful and joyful. He sat down to his work in the morning, and when he had finished his day's work he took the lamp down from the wall, stood it on the table, fetched his book from the shelf, opened it, and sat down to read. The more he read the better he understood, and the clearer and happier he felt in his mind.

It happened once that Martin sat up late, absorbed in his book. He was reading Luke's Gospel; and in the sixth chapter he came upon the verses:

'To him that smiteth thee on the one cheek offer also the other; and from him that taketh away thy cloke withhold not thy coat also. Give to every man that asketh thee; and of him that taketh away thy goods ask them not again. And as ye would that men should do to you, do ye also to them likewise.'

He also read the verses where our Lord says:

'And why call ye me, Lord, Lord, and do not the things which I say? Whosoever cometh to me, and heareth my sayings, and doeth them, I will shew you to whom he is like: He is like a man which built an house, and digged deep, and laid the foundation on a rock: and when the flood arose, the stream beat vehemently upon that house, and could not shake it: for it was founded upon a rock. But he that heareth and doeth not, is like a man that without a foundation built an house upon the earth, against which the stream did beat vehemently, and immediately it fell; and the ruin of that house was great.'

When Martin read these words his soul was glad within him. He took off his spectacles and laid them on the book, and leaning his elbows on the table pondered over what he had read. He tried his own life by the standard of those words, asking himself:

'Is my house built on the rock, or on sand? If it stands on the rock, it is well. It seems easy enough while one sits here alone, and one thinks one has done all that God commands; but as soon as I cease to be on my guard, I sin again. Still I will persevere. It brings such joy. Help me, O Lord!'

He thought all this, and was about to go to bed, but was loth to leave his book. So he went on reading the seventh chapter - about the centurion, the widow's son, and the answer to John's disciples - and he came to the part where a rich Pharisee invited the Lord to his house; and he read how the woman who was a sinner, anointed his feet and washed them with her tears, and how he justified her. Coming to the forty-fourth verse, he read:

'And turning to the woman, he said unto Simon, Seest thou this woman? I entered into thine house thou gavest me no water for my feet: but she hath wetted my feet with her tears, and wiped them with her hair. Thou gavest me no kiss; but she, since the time I came in, hath not ceased to kiss my feet. My head with oil thou didst not anoint: but she hath anointed my feet with ointment.'

He read these verses and thought: 'He gave no water for his feet, gave no kiss, his head with oil he did not anoint...' And Martin took off his spectacles once more, laid them on his book, and pondered.

'He must have been like me, that Pharisee. He too thought only of himself - how to get a cup of tea, how to keep warm and comfortable; never a thought of his guest. He took care of himself, but for his guest he cared nothing at all. Yet who was the guest? The Lord himself! If he came to me, should I behave like that?'

Then Martin laid his head upon both his arms and, before he was aware of it, he fell asleep.

'Martin!' he suddenly heard a voice, as if someone had breathed the word above his ear.

He started from his sleep. 'Who's there?' he asked.

He turned round and looked at the door; no one was there. He called again. Then he heard quite distinctly: 'Martin, Martin! Look out into the street to-morrow, for I shall come.'

Martin roused himself, rose from his chair and rubbed his eyes, but did not know whether he had heard these words in a dream or awake. He put out the lamp and lay down to sleep.

Next morning he rose before daylight, and after saying his prayers he lit the fire and prepared his cabbage soup and buckwheat porridge. Then he lit the samovár, put on his apron, and sat down by the window to his work. As he sat working Martin thought over what had happened the night before. At times it seemed to him like a dream, and at times he thought that he had really heard the voice. 'Such things have happened before now,' thought he.

So he sat by the window, looking out into the street more than he worked, and whenever anyone passed in unfamiliar boots he would stoop and look up, so as to see not the feet only but the face of the passer-by as well. A house-porter passed in new felt boots; then a water-carrier. Presently an old soldier of Nicholas' reign came near the window spade in hand. Martin knew him by his boots, which were shabby old felt ones, goloshed with leather. The old man was called Stepániteh: a neighbouring tradesman kept him in his house for charity, and his duty was to help the house-porter. He began to clear away the snow before Martin's window. Martin glanced at him and then went on with his work.

'I must be growing crazy with age,' said Martin, laughing at his fancy. 'Stepánitch comes to clear away the snow, and I must needs imagine it's Christ coming to visit me. Old dotard that I am!'

Yet after he had made a dozen stitches he felt drawn to look out of the window again. He saw that Stepánitch had leaned his spade against the wall, and was either resting himself or trying to get warm. The man was old and broken down, and had evidently not enough strength even to clear away the snow.

'What if I called him in and gave him some tea?' thought Martin. 'The samovár is just on the boil.'

He stuck his awl in its place, and rose; and putting the samovár on the table, made tea. Then he tapped the window with his fingers. Stepánitch turned and came to the window. Martin beckoned to him to come in, and went himself to open the door.

'Come in,' he said, 'and warm yourself a bit. I'm sure you must be cold.'

'May God bless you!' Stepánitch answered. 'My bones do ache to be sure.' He came in, first shaking off the snow, and lest he should leave marks on the floor he began wiping his feet; but as he did so he tottered and nearly fell.

'Don't trouble to wipe your feet,' said Martin 'I'll wipe up the floor - it's all in the day's work. Come, friend, sit down and have some tea.'

Filling two tumblers, he passed one to his visitor, and pouring his own out into the saucer, began to blow on it.

Stepániteh emptied his glass, and, turning it upside down, put the remains of his piece of sugar on the top. He began to express his thanks, but it was plain that he would be glad of some more.

'Have another glass,' said Martin, refilling the visitor's tumbler and his own. But while he drank his tea Martin kept looking out into the street.

'Are you expecting any one?' asked the visitor.

'Am I expecting any one? Well, now, I'm ashamed to tell you. It isn't that I really expect any one; but I heard something last night which I can't get out of my mind Whether it was a vision, or only a fancy, I can't tell. You see, friend, last night I was reading the Gospel, about Christ the Lord, how he suffered, and how he walked on earth. You have heard tell of it, I dare say.'

'I have heard tell of it,' answered Stepánitch; 'but I'm an ignorant man and not able to read.'

'Well, you see, I was reading of how he walked on earth. I came to that part, you know, where he went to a Pharisee who did not receive him well. Well, friend, as I read about it, I thought now that man did not receive Christ the Lord with proper honour. Suppose such a thing could happen to such a man as myself, I thought, what would I not do to receive him! But that man gave him no reception at all. Well, friend, as I was thinking of this, I began to doze, and as I dozed I heard someone call me by name. I got up, and thought I heard someone whispering, "Expect me; I will come to-morrow." This happened twice over. And to tell you the truth, it sank so into my mind that, though I am ashamed of it myself, I keep on expecting him, the dear Lord!'

Stepánitch shook his head in silence, finished his tumbler and laid it on its side; but Martin stood it up again and refilled it for him.

'Here drink another glass, bless you! And I was thinking too, how he walked on earth and despised no one, but went mostly among common folk: He went with plain people, and chose his disciples from among the likes of us, from workmen like us, sinners that we are. "He who raises himself," he said, "shall be humbled and he who humbles himself shall be raised." "You call me Lord," he said, "and I will wash your feet." "He who would be first," he said, "let him be the servant of all; because," he said, "blessed are the poor, the humble, the meek, and the merciful."'

Stepánitch forgot his tea. He was an old man easily moved to tears, and as he sat and listened the tears ran down his cheeks.

'Come, drink some more,' said Martin. But Stepánitch crossed himself, thanked him, moved away his tumbler, and rose.

'Thank you, Martin Avdéitch,' he said, 'you have given me food and comfort both for soul and body.'

'You're very welcome. Come again another time. I am glad to have a guest,' said Martin.

Stepánitch went away; and Martin poured out the last of the tea and drank it up. Then he put away the tea things and sat down to his work, stitching the back seam of a boot. And as he stitched he kept looking out of the window, waiting for Christ, and thinking about him and his doings. And his head was full of Christ's sayings.

Two soldiers went by: one in Government boots the other in boots of his own; then the master of a neighbouring house, in shining goloshes; then a baker carrying a basket. All these passed on. Then a woman came up in worsted stockings and peasant-made shoes. She passed the window, but stopped by the wall. Martin glanced up at her through the window, and saw that she was a stranger, poorly dressed, and with a baby in her arms. She stopped by the wall with her back to the wind, trying to wrap the baby up though she had hardly anything to wrap it in. The woman had only summer clothes on, and even they were shabby and worn. Through the window Martin heard the baby crying, and the woman trying to soothe it, but unable to do so. Martin rose and going out of the door and up the steps he called to her.

'My dear, I say, my dear!'

The woman heard, and turned round.

'Why do you stand out there with the baby in the cold? Come inside. You can wrap him up better in a warm place. Come this way!'

The woman was surprised to see an old man in an apron, with spectacles on his nose, calling to her, but she followed him in.

They went down the steps, entered the little room, and the old man led her to the bed.

'There, sit down, my dear, near the stove. Warm yourself, and feed the baby.'

'Haven't any milk. I have eaten nothing myself since early morning,' said the woman, but still she took the baby to her breast.

Martin shook his head. He brought out a basin and some bread. Then he opened the oven door and poured some cabbage soup into the basin. He took out the porridge pot also but the porridge was not yet ready, so he spread a cloth on the table and served only the soup and bread.

'Sit down and eat, my dear, and I'll mind the baby. Why, bless me, I've had children of my own; I know how to manage them.'

The woman crossed herself, and sitting down at the table began to eat, while Martin put the baby on the bed and sat down by it. He chucked and chucked, but having no teeth he could not do it well and the baby continued to cry. Then Martin tried poking at him with his finger; he drove his finger straight at the baby's mouth and then quickly drew it back, and did this again and again. He did not let the baby take his finger in its mouth, because it was all black with cobbler's wax. But the baby first grew quiet watching the finger, and then began to laugh. And Martin felt quite pleased.

The woman sat eating and talking, and told him who she was, and where she had been.

'I'm a soldier's wife,' said she. 'They sent my husband somewhere, far away, eight months ago, and I have heard nothing of him since. I had a place as cook till my baby was born, but then they would not keep me with a child. For three months now I have been struggling, unable to find a place, and I've had to sell all I had for food. I tried to go as a wet-nurse, but no one would have me; they said I was too starved-looking and thin. Now I have just been to see a tradesman's wife (a woman from our village is in service with her) and she has promised to take me. I thought it was all settled at last, but she tells me not to come till next week. It is far to her place, and I am fagged out, and baby is quite starved, poor mite. Fortunately our landlady has pity on us, and lets us lodge free, else I don't know what we should do.'

Martin sighed. 'Haven't you any warmer clothing?' he asked.

'How could I get warm clothing?' said she. 'Why I pawned my last shawl for sixpence yesterday.'

Then the woman came and took the child, and Martin got up. He went and looked among some things that were hanging on the wall, and brought back an old cloak.

'Here,' he said, 'tho_vgh it's a worn-out old thing, it will do to wrap him up in.'

The woman looked at the cloak, then at the old man, and taking it, burst into tears. Martin turned away, and groping under the bed brought out a small trunk. He fumbled about in it, and again sat down opposite the woman. And the woman said:

'The Lord bless you, friend. Surely Christ must have sent me to your window, else the child would have frozen. It was mild when I started, but now see how cold it has turned. Surely it must have been Christ who made you look out of your window and take pity on me, poor wretch!'

Martin smiled and said; 'It is quite true; it was he made me do it. It was no mere chance made me look out.'

And he told the woman his dream, and how he had heard the Lord's voice promising to visit him that day.

'Who knows? All things are possible,' said the woman. And she got up and threw the cloak over her shoulders, wrapping it round herself and round the baby. Then she bowed, and thanked Martin once more.

'Take this for Christ's sake,' said Martin, and gave her sixpence to get her shawl out of pawn. The woman crossed herself, and Martin did the same, and then he saw her out.

After the woman had gone, Martin ate some cabbage soup, cleared the things away, and sat down to work again. He sat and worked, but did not forget the window, and every time a shadow fell on it he looked up at once to see who was passing. People he knew and strangers passed by, but no one remarkable.

After a while Martin saw an apple-woman stop just in front of his window. She had a large basket, but there did not seem to be many apples left in it; she had evidently sold most of her stock. On her back she had a sack full of chips, which she was taking home. No doubt she had gathered them at some place where building was going on. The sack evidently hurt her, and she wanted to shift it from one shoulder to the other, so she put it down on the footpath and, placing her basket on a post, began to shake down the chips in the sack. While she was doing this a boy in a tattered cap ran up, snatched an apple out of the basket, and tried to slip away; but the old woman noticed it, and turning, caught the boy by his sleeve. He began to struggle, trying to free himself, but the old woman held on with both hands, knocked his cap off his head, and seized hold of his hair. The boy screamed and the old woman scolded. Martin dropped his awl, not waiting to stick it in its place, and rushed out of the door. Stumbling up the steps, and dropping his spectacles in his hurry, he ran out into the street. The old woman was pulling the boy's hair and scolding him, and threatening to take him to the police. The lad was struggling and protesting, saying, 'I did not take it. What are you beating me for? Let me go!'

Martin separated them. He took the boy by the hand and said, 'Let him go, Granny. Forgive him for Christ's sake.'

'I'll pay him out, so that he won't forget it for a year! I'll take the rascal to the police!'

Martin began entreating the old woman.

'Let him go, Granny. He won't do it again. Let him go for Christ's sake!'

The old woman let go, and the boy wished to run away, but Martin stopped him

'Ask the Granny's forgiveness!' said he. 'And don't do it another time. I saw you take the apple.'

The boy began to cry and to beg pardon.

'That's right. And now here's an apple for you, and Martin took an apple from the basket and gave it to the boy, saying, 'I will pay you, Granny.'

'You will spoil them that way, the young rascals,' said the old woman. 'He ought to be whipped so that he should remember it for a week.'

'Oh, Granny, Granny,' said Martin, 'that's our way - but it's not God's way. If he should be whipped for stealing an apple, what should be done to us for our sins?'

The old woman was silent.

And Martin told her the parable of the lord who forgave his servant a large debt, and how the servant went out and seized his debtor by the throat. The old woman listened to it all, and the boy, too, stood by and listened.

'God bids us forgive,' said Martin, 'or else we shall not be forgiven. Forgive every one; and a thoughtless youngster most of all.'

The old woman wagged her head and sighed.

'It's true enough,' said she, 'but they are getting terribly spoilt.'

'Then we old ones must show them better ways,' Martin replied.

'That's just what I say,' said the old woman. 'I have had seven of them myself, and only one daughter is left.' And the old woman began to tell how and where she was living with her daughter, and how many grandchildren she had. 'There now,' she said, 'I have but little strength left, yet I work hard for the sake of my grandchildren; and nice children they are, too. No one comes out to meet me but the children. Little Annie, now, won't leave me for any one. "It's grandmother, dear grandmother, darling grandmother."' And the old woman completely softened at the thought.

'Of course, it was only his childishness, God help him,' said she, referring to the boy.

As the old woman was about to hoist her sack on her back, the lad sprang forward to her, saying, 'Let me carry it for you, Granny. I'm going that way.'

The old woman nodded her head, and put the sack on the boy's back, and they went down the street together, the old woman quite forgetting to ask Martin to pay for the apple. Martin stood and watched them as they went along talking to each other.

When they were out of sight Martin went back to the house. Having found his spectacles unbroken on the steps, he picked up his awl and sat down again to work. He worked a little, but could soon not see to pass the bristle through the holes in the leather; and presently he noticed the lamplighter passing on his way to light the street lamps.

'Seems it's time to light up,' thought he. So he trimmed his lamp, hung it up, and sat down again to work. He finished off one boot and, turning it about, examined it. It was all right. Then he gathered his tools together, swept up the cuttings, put away the bristles and the thread and the awls, and, taking down the lamp, placed it on the table. Then he took the Gospels from the shelf. He meant to open them at the place he had marked the day before with a bit of morocco, but the book opened at another place. As Martin opened it, his yesterday's dream came back to his mind, and no sooner had he thought of it than he seemed to hear footsteps, as though someone were moving behind him. Martin turned round, and it seemed to him as if people were standing in the dark corner, but he could not make out who they were. And a voice whispered in his ear: 'Martin, Martin, don't you know me?'

'Who is it?' muttered Martin.

'It is I,' said the voice. And out of the dark corner stepped Stepánitch, who smiled and vanishing like a cloud was seen no more.

'It is I,' said the voice again. And out of the darkness stepped the woman with the baby in her arms and the woman smiled and the baby laughed, and they too vanished.

'It is I,' said the voice once more. And the old woman and the boy with the apple stepped out and both smiled, and then they too vanished.

And Martin's soul grew glad. He crossed himself put on his spectacles, and began reading the Gospel just where it had opened; and at the top of the page he read

'I was an hungered, and ye gave me meat: I was thirsty, and ye gave me drink: I was a stranger, and ye took me in.'

And at the bottom of the page he read

'Inasmuch as ye did it unto one of these my brethren even these least, ye did it unto me' (Matt. xxv).

And Martin understood that his dream had come true; and that the Saviour had really come to him that day, and he had welcomed him.

HOW MUCH LAND DOES A MAN NEED?

—— ⊷⊶ ——

I

An elder sister came to visit her younger sister in the country. The elder was married to a tradesman in town, the younger to a peasant in the village. As the sisters sat over their tea talking, the elder began to boast of the advantages of town life: saying how comfortably they lived there, how well they dressed, what fine clothes her children wore what good things they ate and drank, and how she went to the theatre, promenades, and entertainments.

The younger sister was piqued, and in turn disparage the life of a tradesman, and stood up for that of a peasant.

'I would not change my way of life for yours,' said she. We may live roughly, but at least we are free from anxiety. You live in better style than we do but though you often earn more than you need, you are very likely to lose all you have. You know the proverb, "Loss and gain are brothers twain." It often happens that people who are wealthy one day are begging their bread the next. Our way is safer. Though a peasant's life is not a fat one, it is a long one. We shall never grow rich, but we shall always have enough to eat.'

The elder sister said sneeringly:

'Enough? Yes, if you like to share with the pigs and the calves! What do you know of elegance or manners! However much your goodman may slave, you will die as you are living - on a dung heap - and your children the same.'

'Well, what of that?' replied the younger. 'Of course our work is rough and coarse. But, on the other hand, it is sure; and we need not bow to anyone. But you, in your towns, are surrounded by temptations; to-day all may be right, but to-morrow the Evil One may tempt your husband with cards, wine, or women, and all will go to ruin. Don't such things happen often enough?'

Pahóm, the master of the house, was lying on the top of the oven, and he listened to the women's chatter.

'It is perfectly true,' thought he. 'Busy as we are from childhood tilling mother earth, we peasants have no time to let any nonsense settle in our heads. Our only trouble is that we haven't land enough. If I had plenty of land, I shouldn't fear the Devil himself!'

The women finished their tea, chatted a while about dress, and then cleared away the tea-things and lay down to sleep.

But the Devil had been sitting behind the oven, and had heard all that was said. He was pleased that the peasant's wife had led her husband into boasting, and that he had said that if he had plenty of land he would not fear the Devil himself.

'All right,' thought the Devil. 'We will have a tussle. I'll give you land enough; and by means of that land I will get you into my power.'

II

Close to the village there lived a lady, a small landowner, who had an estate of about three hundred acres. She had always lived on good terms with the peasants, until she engaged as her steward an old soldier, who took to burdening the people with fines. However careful Pahóm tried to be, it happened again and again that now a horse of his got among the lady's oats, now a cow strayed into her garden, now his calves found their way into her meadows - and he always had to pay a fine.

Pahóm paid up, but grumbled, and, going home in a temper, was rough with his family. All through that summer, Pahóm had much trouble because of this steward; and he was even glad when winter came and the cattle had to be stabled. Though he grudged the fodder when they could no longer graze on the pasture-land, at least he was free from anxiety about them.

In the winter the news got about that the lady was going to sell her land, and that the keeper of the inn on the high road was bargaining for it. When the peasants heard this they were very much alarmed.

'Well', thought they, 'if the innkeeper gets the land, he will worry us with fines worse than the lady's steward. We all depend on that estate.'

So the peasants went on behalf of their Commune and asked the lady not to sell the land to the innkeeper offering her a better price for it themselves. The lady agreed to let them have it. Then the peasants tried to arrange for the Commune to buy the whole estate so that it might be held by them all in common. They met twice to discuss it, but could not settle the matter; the Evil One sowed discord among them, and they could not agree. So they decided to buy the land individually, each according to his means; and the lady agreed to this plan as she had to the other.

Presently Pahóm heard that a neighbour of his was buying fifty acres, and that the lady had consented to accept one half in cash and to wait a year for the other half. Pahóm felt envious

'Look at that,' thought he, 'the land is all being sold, and I shall get none of it.' So he spoke to his wife.

'Other people are buying,' said he, 'and we must also buy twenty acres or so. Life is becoming impossible. That steward is simply crushing us with his fines.'

So they put their heads together and considered how they could manage to buy it. They had one hundred roubles laid by. They sold a colt, and one half of their bees; hired out one of their sons as a labourer, and took his wages in advance; borrowed the rest from a brother-in-law, and so scraped together half the purchase money.

Having done this, Pahóm chose out a farm of forty acres, some of it wooded, and went to the lady to bargain for it. They came to an agreement, and he shook hands with her upon it, and paid her a deposit in advance. Then they went to town and signed the deeds; he paying half the price down, and undertaking to pay the remainder within two years.

So now Pahóm had land of his own. He borrowed seed, and sowed it on the land he had bought. The harvest was a good one, and within a year he had managed to pay off his debts both to the lady and to his brother-in-law. So he became a landowner, ploughing and sowing his own land, making hay on his own land, cutting his own trees, and feeding his cattle on his own pasture. When he went out to plough his fields, or to look at his growing corn, or at his grass-meadows, his heart would fill with joy. The grass that grew and the flowers that bloomed there, seemed to him unlike any that grew elsewhere. Formerly, when he had passed by that land it had appeared the same as any other land, but now it seemed quite different.

III

So Pahóm was well-contented, and everything would have been right if the neighbouring peasants would only not have trespassed on his corn-fields and meadows. He appealed to them most civilly, but they still went on: now the Communal herdsmen would let the village cows stray into his meadows; then horses from the night pasture would get among his corn. Pahóm turned them out again and again, and forgave their owners, and for a long time he forbore from prosecuting any one. But at last he lost patience and complained to the District Court. He knew it was the peasants' want of land, and no evil intent on their part, that caused the trouble; but he thought:

'I cannot go on overlooking it, or they will destroy all I have. They must be taught a lesson.'

So he had them up, gave them one lesson, and then another, and two or three of the peasants were fined. After a time Pahóm's neighbours began to bear him a grudge for this, and would now and then let their cattle on to his land on purpose. One peasant even got into Pahóm's wood at night and cut down five young lime trees for their bark. Pahóm passing through the wood one day noticed something white. He came nearer, and saw the stripped trunks lying on the ground, and close by stood the stumps, where the trees had been. Pahóm was furious.

'If he had only cut one here and there it would have been bad enough,' thought Pahóm, 'but the rascal has actually cut down a whole clump. If I could only find out who did this, I would pay him out.'

He racked his brains as to who it could be. Finally he decided: 'It must be Simon - no one else could have done it.' So he went to Simon's homestead to have a look round, but he found nothing, and only had an angry scene. However, he now felt more certain than ever that Simon had done it, and he lodged a complaint. Simon was summoned. The case was tried, and re-tried, and at the end of it all Simon was acquitted, there being no evidence against him. Pahóm felt still more aggrieved, and let his anger loose upon the Elder and the Judges.

'You let thieves grease your palms,' said he. 'If you were honest folk yourselves, you would not let a thief go free.'

So Pahóm quarrelled with the Judges and with his neighbours. Threats to burn his building began to be uttered. So though Pahóm had more land, his place in the Commune was much worse than before.

About this time a rumour got about that many people were moving to new parts. 'There's no need for me to leave my land,' thought Pahóm. 'But some of the others might leave our village and then there would be more room for us. I would take over their land myself, and make my estate a bit bigger. I could then live more at ease. As it is, I am still too cramped to be comfortable.

One day Pahóm was sitting at home, when a peasant, passing through the village, happened to call in. He was allowed to stay the night, and supper was given him. Pahóm had a talk with this peasant and asked him where he came from. The stranger answered that he came from beyond the Volga, where he had been working. One word led to another, and the man went on to say that many people were settling in those parts. He told how some people from his village had settled there. They had joined the Commune, and had had twenty-five acres per man granted them. The land was so good, he said, that the rye sown on it grew as high as a horse, and so thick that five cuts of a sickle made a sheaf. One peasant, he said, had brought nothing with him but his bare hands, and now he had six horses and two cows of his own.

Pahóm's heart kindled with desire. He thought:

'Why should I suffer in this narrow hole, if one can live so well elsewhere? I will sell my land and my homestead here, and with the money I will start afresh over there and get everything new. In this crowded place one is always having trouble. But I must first go and find out all about it myself.

Towards summer he got ready and started. He went down the Volga on a steamer to Samára, then walked another three hundred miles on foot, and at last reached the place. It was just as the stranger had said. The peasants had plenty of land: every man had twenty-five acres of Communal land given him for his use, and anyone who had money could buy, besides, at two shillings an acre as much good freehold land as he wanted.

Having found out all he wished to know, Pahóm returned home as autumn came on, and began selling off his belongings. He sold his land at a profit, sold his homestead and all his cattle, and withdrew from membership of the Commune. He only waited till the spring, and then started with his family for the new settlement.

IV

As soon as Pahóm and his family arrived at their new abode, he applied for admission into the Commune of a large village. He stood treat to the Elders, and obtained the necessary documents. Five shares of Communal land were given him for his own and his sons' use: that is to say - 125 acres (not all together but in different fields) besides the use of the Communal pasture. Pahóm put up the buildings he needed, and bought cattle. Of the Communal land alone he had three times as much as at his former home, and the land was good corn-land. He was ten times better off than he had been. He had plenty of arable land and pasturage, and could keep as many head of cattle as he liked.

At first, in the bustle of building and settling down, Pahóm was pleased with it all, but when he got used to it he began to think that even here he had not enough land. The first year, he sowed wheat on his share of the Communal land, and had a good crop. He wanted to go on sowing wheat, but had not enough Communal land for the purpose, and what he had already used was not available; for in those parts wheat is only sown on virgin soil or on fallow land. It is sown for one or two years, and then the land lies fallow till it is again overgrown with prairie grass. There were many who wanted such land, and there was not enough for all; so that people quarrelled about it. Those who were better off, wanted it for growing wheat, and those who were poor, wanted it to let to dealers, so that they might raise money to pay their taxes. Pahóm wanted to sow more wheat; so he rented land from a dealer for a year. He sowed much wheat and had a fine crop, but the land was too far from the village - the wheat had to be carted more than ten miles. After a time Pahóm noticed that some peasant-dealers were living on separate farms, and were growing wealthy; and he thought:

'If I were to buy some freehold land, and have a homestead on it, it would be a different thing altogether. Then it would all be nice and compact.'

The question of buying freehold land recurred to him again and again.

He went on in the same way for three years: renting land and sowing wheat. The seasons turned out well and the crops were good, so that he began to lay money by. He might have gone on living contentedly, but he grew tired of having to rent other people's land every year, and having to scramble for it. Wherever there was good land to be had, the peasants would rush for it and it was taken up at once, so that unless you were sharp about it you got none. It happened in the third year that he and a dealer together rented a piece of pasture land from some peasants; and they had already ploughed it up, when there was some dispute, and the peasants went to law about it, and things fell out so that the labour was all lost.

'If it were my own land,' thought Pahóm, 'I should be independent, and there would not be all this unpleasantness.'

So Pahóm began looking out for land which he could buy; and he came across a peasant who had bought thirteen hundred acres, but having got into difficulties was willing to sell again cheap. Pahóm bargained and haggled with him, and at last they settled the price at 1,500 roubles, part in cash and part to be paid later. They had all but clinched the matter, when a passing dealer happened to stop at Pahóm's one day to get a feed for his horses. He drank tea with Pahóm, and they had a talk. The dealer said that he was just returning from the land of the Bashkírs, far away, where he had bought thirteen thousand acres of land, all for 1,000 roubles. Pahóm questioned him further, and the tradesman said:

'All one need do is to make friends with the chiefs. I gave away about one hundred roubles, worth of dressing-gowns and carpets, besides a case of tea, and I gave wine to those who would drink it; and I got the land for less than two pence an acre. And he showed Pahóm the title-deeds, saying:

'The land lies near a river, and the whole prairie is virgin soil.'

Pahóm plied him with questions, and the tradesman said:

'There is more land there than you could cover if you walked a year, and it all belongs to the Bashkírs. They are as simple as sheep, and land can be got almost for nothing.'

'There now,' thought Pahóm, 'with my one thousand roubles, why should I get only thirteen hundred acres, and saddle myself with a debt besides. If I take it out there, I can get more than ten times as much for the money.'

V

Pahóm inquired how to get to the place, and as soon as the tradesman had left him, he prepared to go there himself. He left his wife to look after the homestead, and started on his journey taking his man with him. They stopped at a town on their way, and bought a case of tea, some wine, and other presents, as the tradesman had advised. On and on they went until they had gone more than three hundred miles, and on the seventh day they came to a place where the Bashkírs had pitched their tents. It was all just as the tradesman had said. The people lived on the steppes, by a river, in felt-covered tents. They neither tilled the ground, nor ate bread. Their cattle and horses grazed in herds on the steppe. The colts were tethered behind the tents, and the mares were driven to them twice a day. The mares were milked, and from the milk kumiss was made. It was the women who prepared kumiss, and they also made cheese. As far as the men were concerned, drinking kumiss and tea, eating mutton, and playing on their pipes, was all they cared about. They were all stout and merry, and all the summer long they never thought of doing any work. They were quite ignorant, and knew no Russian, but were good-natured enough.

As soon as they saw Pahóm, they came out of their tents and gathered round their visitor. An interpreter was found, and Pahóm told them he had come about some land. The Bashkírs seemed very glad they took Pahóm and led him into one of the best tents, where they made him sit on some down cushions placed on a carpet, while they sat round him. They gave him tea and kumiss, and had a sheep killed, and gave him mutton to eat. Pahóm took presents out of his cart and distributed them among the Bashkírs, and divided amongst them the tea. The Bashkírs were delighted. They talked a great deal among themselves, and then told the interpreter to translate.

'They wish to tell you,' said the interpreter, 'that they like you, and that it is our custom to do all we can to please a guest and to repay him for his gifts. You have given us presents, now tell us which of the things we possess please you best, that we may present them to you.'

'What pleases me best here,' answered Pahóm 'is your land. Our land is crowded, and the soil is exhausted; but you have plenty of land and it is good land. I never saw the like of it.'

The interpreter translated. The Bashkírs talked among themselves for a while. Pahóm could not understand what they were saying, but saw that they were much amused, and that they shouted and laughed. Then they were silent and looked at Pahóm while the interpreter said:

'They wish me to tell you that in return for your presents they will gladly give you as much land as you want. You have only to point it out with your hand and it is yours.'

The Bashkírs talked again for a while and began to dispute. Pahóm asked what they were disputing about, and the interpreter told him that some of them thought they ought to ask their Chief about the land and not act in his absence, while others thought there was no need to wait for his return.

VI

While the Bashkírs were disputing, a man in a large fox-fur cap appeared on the scene. They all became silent and rose to their feet. The interpreter said, 'This is our Chief himself.'

Pahóm immediately fetched the best dressing-gown and five pounds of tea, and offered these to the Chief. The Chief accepted them, and seated himself in the place of honour. The Bashkírs at once began telling him something. The Chief listened for a while, then made a sign with his head for them to be silent, and addressing himself to Pahóm, said in Russian:

'Well, let it be so. Choose whatever piece of land you like; we have plenty of it.'

'How can I take as much as I like?' thought Pahóm. 'I must get a deed to make it secure, or else they may say, "It is yours," and afterwards may take it away again.'

'Thank you for your kind words,' he said aloud. 'You have much land, and I only want a little. But I should like to be sure which bit is mine.

Could it not be measured and made over to me? Life and death are in God's hands. You good people give it to me, but your children might wish to take it away again.'

'You are quite right,' said the Chief. 'We will make it over to you.'

'I heard that a dealer had been here,' continued Pahóm, 'and that you gave him a little land, too, and signed title-deeds to that effect. I should like to have it done in the same way.'

The Chief understood.

'Yes,' replied he, 'that can be done quite easily. We have a scribe, and we will go to town with you and have the deed properly sealed.'

'And what will be the price?' asked Pahóm.

'Our price is always the same: one thousand roubles a day.'

Pahóm did not understand.

'A day? What measure is that? How many acres would that be?'

'We do not know how to reckon it out,' said the Chief. 'We sell it by the day. As much as you can go round on your feet in a day is yours, and the price is one thousand roubles a day.'

Pahóm was surprised.

'But in a day you can get round a large tract of land,' he said.

The Chief laughed.

'It will all be yours!' said he. 'But there is one condition: If you don't return on the same day to the spot whence you started, your money is lost.'

'But how am I to mark the way that I have gone?'

'Why, we shall go to any spot you like, and stay there. You must start from that spot and make your round, taking a spade with you. Wherever you think necessary, make a mark. At every turning, dig a hole and pile up the turf; then afterwards we will go round with a plough from hole to hole. You may make as large a circuit as you please, but before the sun sets you must return to the place you started from. All the land you cover will be yours.'

Pahóm was delighted. It was decided to start early next morning. They talked a while, and after drinking some more kumiss and eating some more mutton, they had tea again, and then the night came on. They gave Pahóm a feather-bed to sleep on, and the Bashkírs dispersed for the night, promising to assemble the next morning at daybreak and ride out before sunrise to the appointed spot.

VII

Pahóm lay on the feather-bed, but could not sleep. He kept thinking about the land.

'What a large tract I will mark off!' thought he. 'I can easily do thirty-five miles in a day. The days are long now, and within a circuit of thirty-five miles what a lot of land there will be! I will sell the poorer land, or let it to peasants, but I'll pick out the best and farm it. I will buy two ox-teams, and hire two more labourers. About a hundred and fifty acres shall be plough-land, and I will pasture cattle on the rest.'

Pahóm lay awake all night, and dozed off only just before dawn. Hardly were his eyes closed when he had a dream. He thought he was lying in that same tent, and heard somebody chuckling outside. He wondered who it could be, and rose and went out and he saw the Bashkír Chief sitting in front of the tent holding his sides and rolling about with laughter. Going nearer to the Chief, Pahóm asked: 'What are you laughing at?' But he saw that it was no longer the Chief, but the dealer who had recently stopped at his house and had told him about the land. Just as Pahóm was going to ask, 'Have you been here long?' he saw that it was not the dealer, but the peasant who had come up from the Volga, long ago, to Pahóm's old home. Then he saw that it was not the peasant either, but the Devil himself with hoofs and horns sitting there and chuckling, and before him lay a man barefoot, prostrate on the ground, with only trousers and a shirt on. And Pahóm dreamt that he looked more attentively to see what sort of a man it was that was lying there, and he saw that the man was dead and that it was himself! He awoke horror-struck.

'What things one does dream,' thought he.

Looking round he saw through the open door that the dawn was breaking.

'It's time to wake them up,' thought he. 'We ought to be starting.'

He got up, roused his man (who was sleeping in his cart), bade him harness; and went to call the Bashkírs.

'It's time to go to the steppe to measure the land,' he said.

The Bashkírs rose and assembled, and the Chief came too. Then they began drinking kumiss again, and offered Pahóm some tea, but he would not wait.

'If we are to go, let us go. It is high time,' said he.

VIII

The Bashkírs got ready and they all started: some mounted on horses, and some in carts. Pahóm drove in his own small cart with his servant, and took a spade with him. When they reached the steppe, the morning red was beginning to kindle. They ascended a hillock (called by the Bashkírs a shikhan) and dismounting from their carts and their horses, gathered in one spot. The Chief came up to Pahóm and stretching out his arm towards the plain:

'See,' said he, 'all this, as far as your eye can reach, is ours. You may have any part of it you like.'

Pahóm's eyes glistened: it was all virgin soil, as flat as the palm of your hand, as black as the seed of a poppy, and in the hollows different kinds of grasses grew breast high.

The Chief took off his fox-fur cap, placed it on the ground and said:

'This will be the mark. Start from here, and return here again. All the land you go round shall be yours.'

Pahóm took out his money and put it on the cap. Then he took off his outer coat, remaining in his sleeveless under-coat. He unfastened his girdle and tied it tight below his stomach, put a little bag of bread into the breast of his coat, and tying a flask of water to his girdle, he drew up the tops of his boots, took the spade from his man, and stood ready to start. He considered for some moments which way he had better go - it was tempting everywhere.

'No matter,' he concluded, 'I will go towards the rising sun.'

He turned his face to the east, stretched himself and waited for the sun to appear above the rim.

'I must lose no time,' he thought, 'and it is easier walking while it is still cool.'

The sun's rays had hardly flashed above the horizon, before Pahóm, carrying the spade over his shoulder went down into the steppe.

Pahóm started walking neither slowly nor quickly. After having gone a thousand yards he stopped, dug a hole, and placed pieces of turf one on another to make it more visible. Then he went on; and now that he had walked off his stiffness he quickened his pace. After a while he dug another hole.

Pahóm looked back. The hillock could be distinctly seen in the sunlight, with the people on it, and the glittering tyres of the cart-wheels. At a rough guess Pahóm concluded that he had walked three miles. It was growing warmer; he took off his under-coat, flung it across his shoulder, and went on again. It had grown quite warm now; he looked at the sun, it was time to think of breakfast.

'The first shift is done, but there are four in a day, and it is too soon yet to turn. But I will just take off my boots,' said he to himself.

He sat down, took off his boots, stuck them into his girdle, and went on. It was easy walking now.

'I will go on for another three miles,' thought he, 'and then turn to the left. This spot is so fine, that it would be a pity to lose it. The further one goes, the better the land seems.'

He went straight on for a while, and when he looked round, the hillock was scarcely visible and the people on it looked like black ants, and he could just see something glistening there in the sun.

'Ah,' thought Pahóm, 'I have gone far enough in this direction, it is time to turn. Besides I am in a regular sweat, and very thirsty.'

He stopped, dug a large hole, and heaped up pieces of turf. Next he untied his flask, had a drink, and then turned sharply to the left. He went on and on; the grass was high, and it was very hot.

Pahóm began to grow tired: he looked at the sun and saw that it was noon.

'Well,' he thought, 'I must have a rest.'

He sat down, and ate some bread and drank some water; but he did not lie down, thinking that if he did he might fall asleep. After sitting a little while, he went on again. At first he walked easily: the food had strengthened him; but it had become terribly hot, and he felt sleepy; still he went on, thinking: 'An hour to suffer, a life-time to live.'

He went a long way in this direction also, and was about to turn to the left again, when he perceived a damp hollow: 'It would be a pity to leave that out,' he thought. 'Flax would do well there.' So he went on past the hollow, and dug a hole on the other side of it before he turned the corner. Pahóm looked towards the hillock. The heat made the air hazy: it seemed to be quivering, and through the haze the people on the hillock could scarcely be seen.

'Ah!' thought Pahóm, 'I have made the sides too long; I must make this one shorter.' And he went along the third side stepping faster. He looked at the sun: it was nearly half way to the horizon, and he had not yet done two miles of the third side of the square. He was still ten miles from the goal.

'No,' he thought, 'though it will make my land lop-sided, I must hurry back in a straight line now. I might go too far, and as it is I have a great deal of land.'

So Pahóm hurriedly dug a hole, and turned straight towards the hillock.

IX

Pahóm went straight towards the hillock, but he now walked with difficulty. He was done up with the heat, his bare feet were cut and bruised, and his legs began to fail. He longed to rest, but it was impossible if he meant to get back before sunset. The sun waits for no man, and it was sinking lower and lower.

'Oh dear,' he thought, 'if only I have not blundered trying for too much! What if I am too late?'

He looked towards the hillock and at the sun. He was still far from his goal, and the sun was already near the rim

Pahóm walked on and on; it was very hard walking, but he went quicker and quicker. He pressed on, but was still far from the place. He began running, threw away his coat, his boots, his flask, and his cap, and kept only the spade which he used as a support.

'What shall I do,' he thought again, 'I have grasped too much, and ruined the whole affair. I can't get there before the sun sets.'

And this fear made him still more breathless. Pahóm went on running, his soaking shirt and trousers stuck to him, and his mouth was parched. His breast was working like a blacksmith's bellows, his heart was beating like a hammer, and his legs were giving way as if they did not belong to him. Pahóm was seized with terror lest he should die of the strain.

Though afraid of death, he could not stop. 'After having run all that way they will call me a fool if I stop now,' thought he. And he ran on and on, and drew near and heard the Bashkírs yelling and shouting to him, and their cries inflamed his heart still more. He gathered his last strength and ran on.

The sun was close to the rim, and cloaked in mist looked large, and red as blood. Now, yes now, it was about to set! The sun was quite low, but he was also quite near his aim. Pahóm could already see the people on the hillock waving their arms to hurry him up. He could see the fox-fur cap on the ground, and the money on it, and the Chief sitting on the ground holding his sides. And Pahóm remembered his dream.

'There is plenty of land,' thought he, 'but will God let me live on it? I have lost my life, I have lost my life! I shall never reach that spot!'

Pahóm looked at the sun, which had reached the earth: one side of it had already disappeared. With all his remaining strength he rushed on, bending his body forward so that his legs could hardly follow fast enough to keep him from falling. Just as he reached the hillock it suddenly grew dark. He looked up - the sun had already set! He gave a cry: 'All my labour has been in vain,' thought he, and was about to stop, but he heard the Bashkírs still shouting, and remembered that though to him, from below, the sun seemed to have set, they on the hillock could still see it. He took a long breath and ran up the hillock. It was still light there. He reached the top and saw the cap. Before it sat the Chief laughing and holding his sides. Again Pahóm remembered his dream, and he uttered a cry: his legs gave way beneath him, he fell forward and reached the cap with his hands.

'Ah, that's a fine fellow!' exclaimed the Chief 'He has gained much land!'

Pahóm's servant came running up and tried to raise him, but he saw that blood was flogging from his mouth. Pahóm was dead!

The Bashkírs clicked their tongues to show their pity.

His servant picked up the spade and dug a grave long enough for Pahóm to be in, and buried him in it. Six feet from his head to his heels was all he needed.

THREE DEATHS

—∞∞∞—

I

It was autumn.

Along the highway came two equipages at a brisk pace. In the first carriage sat two women. One was a lady, thin and pale; the other, her maid, with a brilliant red complexion, and plump. Her short, dry locks escaped from under a faded cap; her red hand, in a torn glove, put them back with a jerk. Her full bosom, incased in a tapestry shawl, breathed of health; her keen black eyes now gazed through the window at the fields hurrying by them, now rested on her mistress, now peered solicitously into the corners of the coach.

Before the maid's face swung the lady's bonnet on the rack; on her knees lay a puppy; her feet were raised by packages lying on the floor, and could almost be heard drumming upon them above the noise of the creaking of the springs and the rattling of the windows.

The lady, with her hands resting in her lap and her eyes shut, feebly swayed on the cushions which supported her back, and, slightly frowning, tried to suppress her cough.

She wore a white nightcap, and a blue neckerchief twisted around her delicate pale neck. A straight line, disappearing under the cap, parted her perfectly smooth blond hair, which was pomaded; and there was a dry deathly appearance about the whiteness of the skin, in this wide parting. The withered and rather sallow skin was loosely drawn over her delicate and pretty features, and there was a hectic flush on the cheeks and cheekbones. Her lips were dry and restless, her thin eyelashes had lost their curve, and a cloth traveling capote made straight folds over her sunken chest. Although her eyes were closed, her face gave the impression of weariness, irascibility, and habitual suffering.

The lackey, leaning back was napping on the coachbox. The yamshchik, or hired driver, shouting in a clear voice, urged on his four powerful and sweaty horses, occasionally looking back at the other driver, who was shouting just behind them in an open barouche. The tires of the wheels, in their even and rapid course, left wide parallel tracks on the limy mud of the highway.

The sky was gray and cold, a moist mist was falling over the fields and the road. It was suffocating in the carriage, and smelt of eau-de-Cologne and dust. The invalid leaned back her head, and slowly opened her eyes. Her great eyes were brilliant, and of a beautiful dark color.

"Again!" said she, nervously, pushing away with her beautiful attenuated hand the end of her maid's cloak, which occasionally hit against her leg. Her mouth contracted painfully.

Matriosha raised her cloak in both hands, lifting herself up on her strong legs, and then sat down again, farther away. Her fresh face was suffused with a brilliant scarlet.

The invalid's beautiful dark eyes eagerly followed the maid's motions; and then with both hands she took hold of the seat, and did her best to raise herself a little higher, but her strength was not sufficient.

Again her mouth became contracted, and her whole face took on an expression of unavailing, angry irony.

"If you would only help me... ah! It's not necessary. I can do it myself. Only have the goodness not to put those pillows behind me. On the whole, you had better not touch them, if you don't understand!"

The lady closed her eyes, and then again, quickly raising the lids, gazed at her maid.

Matriosha looked at her, and gnawed her red lower lip. A heavy sigh escaped from the sick woman's breast; but the sigh was not ended, but was merged in a fit of coughing. She scowled, and turned her face away, clutching her chest with both hands. When the coughing fit was over, she once more shut her eyes, and continued to sit motionless. The coach and the barouche rolled into a village. Matriosha drew her fat hand from under her shawl, and made the sign of the cross.

"What is this?" demanded the lady.

"A post-station, madame."

"Why did you cross yourself, I should like to know?"

"The church, madame."

The invalid lady looked out of the window, and began slowly to cross herself, gazing with all her eyes at the great village church, in front of which her carriage was now passing.

The two vehicles came to a stop together at the post-house. The sick woman's husband and the doctor dismounted from the barouche, and came to the coach.

"How are you feeling?" asked the doctor, taking her pulse.

"Well, my dear, aren't you fatigued?" asked the husband in French. "Wouldn't you like to get out?"

Matriosha, gathering up the bundles, squeezed herself into the corner, so as not to interfere with the conversation.

"No matter, it's all the same thing," replied the invalid. "I will not get out."

The husband, after standing there a little, went into the post-house. Matriosha, jumping from the coach, tiptoed across the muddy road into the enclosure.

"If I am miserable, there is no reason why the rest of you should not have breakfast," said the sick woman, smiling faintly to the doctor, who was standing by her window.

"I makes no difference to them how I am," she remarked to herself as the doctor, turning from her with slow step, started to run up the steps of the station-house. "They are well, and it's all the same to them. O my God!"

"How now, Edouard Ivanovitch?" said the husband, as he met the doctor, and rubbing his hands with a gay smile. "I have ordered my traveling-case brought; what do you say to that?"

"That's worth while," replied the doctor.

"Well, now, how about her?" asked the husband, with a sigh, lowering his voice and raising his brows.

"I have told you that she cannot reach Moscow, much less Italy, especially in such weather."

"What is to be done, then? Oh! My God! My God!"

The husband covered his eyes with his hand.

"Give it here," he added, addressing his man, who came bringing the traveling-case.

"You'll have to stop somewhere on the route," replied the doctor, shrugging his shoulders.

"But tell me, what can I do?" rejoined the husband. "I have employed every argument to keep her from going; I have spoken to her of our means, and of our children whom we should have to leave behind, and of my business. She would not hear a word. She has made her plans for living abroad, as if she were well. But if I should tell her what her real condition is, it would kill her."

"Well, she is a dead woman now; you may as well know it, Vasili Dmitritch. A person cannot live without lungs, and there is no way of making lungs grow again. It is melancholy, it is hard, but what is to be done about it? It is my business and yours to make her last days as easy as possible. The confessor is the person needed here."

"Oh, my God! Now just perceive how I am situated, in speaking to her of her last will. Let come whatever may, yet I cannot speak of that. And yet you know how good she is."

"Try at least to persuade her to wait until the roads are frozen," said the doctor, shaking his head significantly; "something might happen during the journey."

"Aksiusha, oh, Aksiusha!" cried the superintendent's daughter, throwing a cloak over her head, and tiptoeing down the muddy back steps. "Come along. Let us have a look at the Shirkinskaya lady; they say she got lung trouble, and they're taking her abroad. I never saw how any one looked in consumption."

Aksiusha jumped down from the door-sill; and the two girls, hand in hand, hurried out of the gates. Shortening their steps, they walked by the coach, and stared in at the lowered window. The invalid bent her head toward them; but, when she saw their inquisitiveness, she frowned and turned away.

"Oh, de-e-ar!" said the superintendent's daughter, vigorously shaking her head. "How wonderfully pretty she used to be, and how she has changed! It is terrible! Did you see? Did you see, Aksiusha?"

"Yes, and how thin she is!" assented Aksiusha. "Let us go by and look again; we'll make believe we are going to the well. Did you see, she turned away from us; still I got a good view of her. Isn't it too bad, Masha?"

"Yes, but what terrible mud!" replied Masha, and both of them started to run back within the gates.

"It's evident that I have become a fright," thought the sick woman. "But we must hurry, hurry, and get abroad, and there I shall soon get well."

"Well, and how are you, my dear?" inquired the husband, coming to the coach with still a morsel of something in his mouth.

"Always one and the same question," thought the sick woman, "and he's even eating!"

"It's no consequence," she murmured, between her teeth.

"Do you know, my dear, I am afraid that this journey in such weather will only make you worse. Edouard Ivanovitch says the same thing. Hadn't we better turn back?"

She maintained an angry silence.

"Maybe the weather will improve, the roads will become good, and that would be better for you; then at least we could start all together."

"Pardon me. If I had not listened to you so long, I should at this moment be at Berlin and have entirely recovered."

"What's to be done, my angel? It was impossible, as you know. But now if you would wait a month, you would be ever so much better; I could finish up my business, and we could take the children with us."

"The children are well, and I am not."

"But just see here, my love, if in this weather you should grow worse on the road... At least we should be at home."

"What is the use of being at home? Die at home?" replied the invalid, peevishly.

But the word die evidently startled her, and she turned on her husband a supplicating and inquiring look. He dropped his eyes, and said nothing.

The sick woman's mouth suddenly contracted in a childish fashion, and the tears sprang to her eyes. Her husband covered his face with his handkerchief, and silently turned from the coach.

"No, I will go," cried the invalid; and, lifting her eyes to the sky, she clasped her hands, and began to whisper incoherent words. "My God! Why must it be?" she said, and the tears flowed more violently.

She prayed long and fervently, but still there was just the same sense of constriction and pain in her chest, just the same gray melancholy in the sky and the fields and the road; just the same autumnal mist, neither thicker nor more tenuous, but ever the same it in its monotony, falling on the muddy highway, on the roofs, on the carriage, and on the sheepskin coats of the drivers, who were talking in strong, gay voices, as they were oiling and adjusting the carriage.

II

The coach was ready, but the driver loitered. He had gone into the drivers' room [izba]. In the izba it was warm, close, dark, and suffocating, smelling of human occupation, of cooking bread, of cabbage, and of sheepskin garments.

Several drivers were in the room; the cook was engaged near the oven, on top of which lay a sick man wrapped up in his sheepskins.

"Uncle Khveodor! Hey! Uncle Khveodor," called a young man, the driver, in a tulup, and with his knout in his belt, coming into the room, and addressing the sick man.

"What do you want, rattlepate? What are you calling to Fyedka [Footnote: Fyedka and Fyedya are diminutives of Feodor (Theodore), mispronounced by the yamshchik.] for?" asked one of the drivers. "There's your carriage waiting for you."

"I want to borrow his boots. Mine are worn out," replied the young fellow, tossing back his curls and straightening his mittens in his belt. "Why? Is he asleep? Say, Uncle Khvodor!" he insisted, going to the oven.

"What is it?" a weak voice was heard saying, and an emaciated face was lifted up from the oven.

A broad, gaunt hand, bloodless and covered with hairs, pulled up his overcoat over the dirty shirt that covered his bony shoulder. "Give me something to drink, brother; what is it you want?"

The young fellow handed him a small dish of water.

"I say, Fyedya," said he, hesitating, "I reckon you won't want your new boots now; let me have them? Probably you won't need them anymore."

The sick man, dropping his weary head down to the lacquered bowl, and dipping his thin, hanging mustache into the brown water, drank feebly and eagerly.

His tangled beard was unclean; his sunken, clouded eyes were with difficulty raised to the young man's face. When he had finished drinking, he tried to raise his hand to wipe his wet lips, but his strength failed him, and he wiped them on the sleeve of his overcoat. Silently, and breathing with difficulty through his nose, he looked straight into the young man's eyes, and tried to collect his strength.

"Maybe you have promised them to someone else?" said the young driver. "If that's so, all right. The worst of it is, it is wet outside, and I have to go out to my work, and so I said to myself, 'I reckon I'll ask Fyedka for his boots; I reckon he won't be needing them.' But may you will need them, - just say."

Something began to bubble up and rumble in the sick man's chest; he bent over, and began to strangle, with a cough that rattled in his throat.

"Now I should like to know where he would need them?" unexpectedly snapped out the cook, angrily addressing the whole hovel. "This is the second month that he has not crept down from the oven. Just see how he is all broken up! And you can hear how it must hurt him inside. Where would he need boots? They would not think of burying him in new ones! And it was time long ago, God pardon me the sin of saying so. Just see how he chokes! He ought to be taken from this room to another, or somewhere. They say there's hospitals in the city; but what's you going to do? He takes up the whole room, and that's too much. There isn't any room at all. And yet you are expected to keep neat."

"Hey! Seryoha, come along, take your place, the people are waiting," cried the head man of the station, coming to the door.

Seryoha started to go without waiting for his reply, but the sick man during his cough intimated by his eyes that he was going to speak.

"You take the boots, Seryoha," said he, conquering the cough, and getting his breath a little. "Only, do you hear, buy me a stone when I am dead," he added hoarsely.

"Thank you, uncle; then I will take them, and as for the stone, - yei-yei! - I will buy you one." There, children, you are witnesses," the sick man was able to articulate, and then once more he bent over and began to choke.

"All right, we have heard," said one of the drivers. "But run, Seryoha, or else the starosta will be after you again. You know Lady Shirkinskaya is sick."

Seryoha quickly pulled off his ragged, unwieldy boots, and flung them under the bench. Uncle Feodor's new ones fitted his feet exactly, and the yung driver could not keep his eyes off them as he went to the carriage.

"Ek! What splendid boots! Here's some grease," called another driver with the grease-pot in his hand, as Seryoha mounted to his box and gathered up the reins. "Get them for nothing?"

"So you're jealous, are you?" cried Seryoha, lifting up and tucking around his legs the tails of his overcoat. "Of with you, my darlings," he cried to the horses, cracking his knout; and the coach and barouche, with their occupants, trunks, and other belongings, were hidden in the thick autumnal mist, and rapidly whirled away over the wet road.

The sick driver remained on the oven in the stifling hovel, and, not being able to throw off the phlegm, by a supreme effort turned over on the other side, and stopped coughing.

Till evening there was a continual coming and going, and eating of meals in the room, and the sick man was not noticed. Before night came on, the cook climbed up on the oven, and got the sheepskin coat from the farther side of his legs.

"Don't be angry with me, Nastasya," exclaimed the sick man. "I shall soon leave your room."

"All right, all right, it's of no consequence," muttered the woman. "But what is the matter with you, uncle? Tell me."

"All my inwards are gnawed out. God knows what it is!"

"And I don't doubt your gullet hurts you when you cough so!"

"It hurts me all over. My death is at hand, that's what it is. Okh! Okh! Okh!" groaned the sick man.

"Mow cover up your legs this way," said Nastasya, comfortably arranging the overcoat so that it would cover him, and then getting down from the oven.

During the night the room was faintly lighted by a single taper. Nastasya and a dozen drivers were sleeping, snoring loudly, on the floor and the benches. Only the sick man feebly hawked and coughed, and tossed on the oven.

In the morning no sound was heard from him.

"I saw something wonderful in my sleep," said the cook, as she stretched herself in the early twilight the next morning. "I seemed to see Uncle Khveodor get down from the oven and go out to cut wood. 'Look here,' says he, 'I'm going to help you, Nastya;' and I says to him, 'How can you split wood?' but he seizes the hatchet, and begins to cut so fast, so fast that nothing but chips fly. 'Why,' sais I, 'haven't you been sick?' - 'No,' says he, 'I am well,' and he kind of lifted up the ax, and I was scared; and I screamed and woke up. He can't be dead, can he? - Uncle Khveodor! Hey, uncle!"

Feodor did not move.

"Now he can't be dead, can he? Go and see," said one of the drivers, who had just waked up.

The emaciated hand, covered with reddish hair, that hung down from the oven, was cold and pale.

"Go tell the superintendent; it seems he is dead," said the driver.

Feodor had no relatives. He was a stranger. On the next day they buried him in the new burying-ground behind the grove; and Nastasya for many days had to tell everybody of the vision which she had seen, and how she had been the first to discover that Uncle Feodor was dead.

III

Spring had come.

Along the wet streets of the city swift streamlets ran purling between heaps of dung-covered ice; bright were the colors of people's dresses and the tones of their voices, as they hurried along. In the walled gardens, the buds on the trees were burgeoning, and the fresh breeze swayed their branches with a soft gentle murmur. Everywhere transparent drops were forming and falling.

The sparrows chattered incoherently, and fluttered about on their little wings. On the sunny side, on the walls, houses, and trees, all was full of life and brilliancy. The sky, and the earth, and the heart of man overflowed with youth and joy.

In front of a great seigniorial mansion, in one of the principal streets, fresh straw had been laid down; in the house lay that same moribund invalid whom we saw hastening abroad.

Near the closed doors of her room stood the sick lady's husband, and a lady well along in years. On a divan sat the confessor, with cast-down eyes, holding something wrapped up under his stole. In one corner, in a Voltaire easy-chair, reclined an old lady, the sick woman's mother, weeping violently.

Near her stood the maid, holding a clean handkerchief, ready for the old lady's use when she should ask for it. Another maid was rubbing the old lady's temples, and blowing on her gray head underneath her cap.

"Well, Christ be with you, my dear," said the husband to the elderly lady who was standing with him near the door: "she has such confidence in you; you know how to talk with her; go and speak with her a little while, my darling, please go!"

He was about to open the door for her; but his cousin held him back, putting her handkerchief several times to her eyes, and shaking her head.

"There, now she will not see that I have been weeping," said she, and, opening the door herself, went to the invalid.

The husband was in the greatest excitement, and seemed quite beside himself. He started to go over to the old mother, but, after taking a few steps, he turned around, walked the length of the room, and approached the priest.

The priest looked at him, raised his brows toward heaven, and sighed. The thick gray beard also was lifted and fell again.

"My God! My God!" said the husband.

"What can you do?" exclaimed the confessor, sighing and again lifting up his brows and beard, and letting them drop.

"And the old mother there!" exclaimed the husband almost in despair. "She will not be able to endure it. You see, she loved her so, she loved her so, that she... I don't know. You might try, father, to calm her a little, and persuade her to go away."

The confessor arose and went over to the old lady.

"It is true, no one can appreciate a mother's heart," said he, "but God is compassionate."

The old lady's face was suddenly convulsed, and a hysterical sob shook her frame.

"God is compassionate," repeated the priest, when she had grown a little calmer. "I will tell you, in my parish there was a sick man, and much worse than Marya Dmitrievna, and he, though he was only a shopkeeper, was cured in a very short time, by means of herbs. And this very same shopkeeper is now in Moscow. I have told Vasili Dmitrievitch about him; it might be tried, you know. At all events, it would satisfy the invalid. With God, all things are possible."

"No, she won't get well," persisted the old lady. "Why should God have taken her, and not me?"

And again the hysterical sobbing overcame her, so violently that she fainted away.

The invalid's husband hid his face in his hands, and rushed from the room.

In the corridor the first person whom he met was a six-year-old boy, who was chasing his little sister with all his might and main.

"Do you bid me take the children to their mamasha?" inquired the nurse.

"No, she does not like to see them. They distract her."

The lad stopped for a moment, and, after looking eagerly into his father's face, he cut a dido with his leg, and with merry shouts ran on.

"I'm playing whe's a horse, papasha," cried the little fellow, pointing to his sister.

Meantime, in the next room, the cousin had taken her seat near the sick woman, and was skilfully bringing the conversation by degrees round so as to prepare her for the thought of death. The doctor stood by the window, mixing some draught.

The invalid, in a white capote, all surrounded by cushions, was sitting up in bed, and gazed silently at her cousin.

"Ah, my dear!" she exclaimed, unexpectedly interrupting her, "don't try to prepare me; don't treat me like a little child! I am a Christian woman. I know all about it. I know that I have not long to live; I know that if my husband had heeded me sooner, I should have been in Italy, and possibly, yes probably, should have been well by this time. They all told him so. But what is to be done? It's as God saw fit. We all of us have sinned, I know that; but I hope in the mercy of God, that all will be pardoned, ought to be pardoned. I am trying to sound my own heart. I also have committed many sins, my love. But how much I have suffered in atonement! I have tried to bear my sufferings patiently."

"Then shall I have the confessor come in, my love? It will be all the easier for you, after you have been absolved," said the cousin.

The sick woman dropped her head in token of assent. "O God! Pardon me, a sinner," she whispered.

The cousin went out, and beckoned to the confessor. "She is an angel," she said to the husband, with tears in her eyes. The husband wept. The priest went into the sick room; the old lady still remained unconscious, and in the room beyond all was perfectly quiet. At the end of five minutes the confessor came out, and, taking off his stole, arranged his hair.

"Thanks be to the Lord, she is calmer now," said he. "She wishes to see you."

The cousin and the husband went to the sick-room. The invalid, gently weeping, was gazing at the images.

"I congratulate you, my love," said the husband.

"Thank you. How well I feel now! What ineffable joy I experience!" said the sick woman, and a faint smile played over her thin lips. "How merciful God is! Is He not? He is merciful and omnipotent!"

And again with an eager prayer she turned her tearful eyes toward the holy images.

Then suddenly something seemed to occur to her mind. She beckoned to her husband.

"You are never willing to do what I desire," said she, in a weak and querulous voice.

The husband, stretching his neck, listened to her submissively.

"What is it, my love?"

"How many times I have told you that these doctors don't know anything! There are simple women doctors; they make cures. That's what the good father said. A shopkeeper... Send for him."

"For whom, my love?"

"Good heavens! You can never understand me." And the dying woman frowned, and closed her eyes.

The doctor came to her, and took her hand. Her pulse was evidently growing feebler and feebler. He made a sign to the husband. The sick woman remarked this gesture, and looked around in fright. The cousin turned away to hide her tears.

"Don't weep, don't torment yourselves on my account," said the invalid. "That takes away from me my last comfort."

"You are an angel!" exclaimed the cousin, kissing her hand.

"No, kiss me here. They only kiss the hands of those who are dead. My God! My God!"

That same evening the sick woman was a corpse, and the corpse in the coffin lay in the parlor of the great mansion. In the immense room, the doors of which were closed, sat the clerk, and with a monstrous voice read the Psalms of David through his nose.

The bright glare from the wax candles in the lofty silver candelabra fell on the white brow of the dead, on the heavy waxen hands, on the stiff folds of the cerement which brought out into awful relief the knees and the feet.

The clerk, not varying his tones, continued to read on steadily, and in the silence of the chamber of death his words rang out and died away. Occasionally from distant rooms came the voice of children and their romping.

"Thou hidest thy face, they are troubled; thou takest away their breath, they die and return to their dust.

"Thou sendest forth thy Spirit, they are created; and thou renewest the fact of the earth.

"The glory of the Lord shall endure forever."

The face of the dead was stern and majestic. But there was no motion either on the pure cold brow, or the firmly closed lips. She was all attention! But did she perhaps now understand these majestic words?

IV

At the end of a month, over the grave of the dead a stone chapel was erected. Over the driver's there was as yet no stone, and only the fresh green grass sprouted over the mound which served as the sole record of the past existence of a man.

"It will be a sin and a shame, Seryoha," said the cook at the station-house one day, "if you don't buy a gravestone for Khveodor. You kept saying, 'it's winter, winter,' but now why don't you keep your word? I heard it all. He has already come back once to ask why you don't do it; if you don't buy him one, he will come again, he will choke you."

"Well, now, have I denied it?" urged Seryoha. "I am going to buy him a stone, as I said I would. I can get one for a ruble and a half. I have not forgotten about it; I'll have to get it. As soon as I happen to be in town, then I'll buy him one."

"You ought at least to put up a cross, that's what you ought to do," said an old driver. It isn't right at all. You're wearing those boots now."

"Yes. But where could I get him a cross? You wouldn't want to make one out of an old piece of stick, would you?"

"What is that you say? Make one out of an old piece of stick? No; take your ax, go out to the wood a little earlier than usual, and you can hew him one. Take a little ash tree, and you can make one. You can have a covered cross. If you go then, you won't have to give the watchman a little drink of vodka. One doesn't want to give vodka for every trifle. Now, yesterday I broke my axletree, and I go and hew out a new one of green wood. No one said a word."

Early the next morning, almost before dawn, Seryoha took his ax, and went to the wood.

Over all things hung a cold, dead veil of falling mist, as yet untouched by the rays of the sun.

The east gradually grew brighter, reflecting its pale light over the vault of heaven still covered by light clouds. Not a single grass-blade below, now a single leaf on the topmost branches of the tree-top, waved. Only from time to time could be heard the sound of fluttering wings in the thicket, or a rustling on the ground broke in on the silence of the forest.

Suddenly a strange sound, foreign to this nature, resounded and died away at the edge of the forest. Again the noise sounded, and was monotonously repeated again and again, at the foot of one of the ancient, immovable trees. A tree-top began to shake in an extraordinary manner; the juicy leaves whispered something; and the warbler, sitting on one of the branches, flew off a couple of times with a shrill cry, and wagging its tail, finally perched on another tree.

The ax rang more and more frequently; the white chips, full of sap, were scattered upon the dewy grass, and a slight cracking was heard beneath the blows.

The tree trembled with all its body, leaned over, and quickly straightened itself, shuddering with fear on its base.

For an instant all was still, then once more the tree bent over; a crash was heard in its trunk; and, tearing the thicket, and dragging down the branches, it plunged toward the damp earth.

The noise of the ax and of footsteps ceased.

The warbler uttered a cry, and flew higher. The branch which she grazed with her wings shook for an instant, and then came to rest like all the others their foliage.

The trees, more joyously than ever, extended their motionless branches over the new space that had been made in their midst.

The first sunbeams, breaking through the cloud, gleamed in the sky, and shone along the earth and heavens.

The mist, in billows, began to float along the hollows; the dew, gleaming, played on the green foliage; translucent white clouds hurried along their azure path.

The birds hopped about in the thicket, and, as if beside themselves, voiced their happiness; the juicy leaves joyfully and contentedly whispered on the tree-tops; and the branches of the living trees slowly and majestically waved over the dead and fallen tree.

ILYÁS

There once lived, in the Government of Oufá a Bashkír named Ilyás. His father, who died a year after he had found his son a wife, did not leave him much property. Ilyás then had only seven mares, two cows, and about a score of sheep. He was a good manager, however, and soon began to acquire more. He and his wife worked from morn till night; rising earlier than others and going later to bed; and his possessions increased year by year. Living in this way, Ilyás little by little acquired great wealth. At the end of thirty-five years he had 200 horses, 150 head of cattle, and 1,200 sheep. Hired labourers tended his flocks and herds, and hired women milked his mares and cows, and made kumiss, butter and cheese. Ilyás had abundance of everything, and everyone in the district envied him. They said of him:

'Ilyás is a fortunate man: he has plenty of everything. This world must be a pleasant place for him.'

People of position heard of Ilyás and sought his acquaintance. Visitors came to him from afar; and he welcomed every one, and gave them food and drink. Whoever might come, there was always kumiss, tea, sherbet, and mutton to set before them. Whenever visitors arrived a sheep would be killed, or sometimes two; and if many guests came he would even slaughter a mare for them.

Ilyás had three children: two sons and a daughter; and he married them all off. While he was poor, his sons worked with him, and looked after the flocks and herds themselves; but when he grew rich they got spoiled and one of them took to drink. The eldest was killed in a brawl; and the younger, who had married a self-willed woman, ceased to obey his father, and they could not live together any more.

So they parted, and Ilyás gave his son a house and some of the cattle; and this diminished his wealth. Soon after that, a disease broke out among Ilyás's sheep, and many died. Then followed a bad harvest, and the hay crop failed; and many cattle died that winter. Then the Kirghíz captured his best herd of horses; and Ilyás's property dwindled away. It became smaller and smaller, while at the same time his strength grew less; till, by the time he was seventy years old, he had begun to sell his furs, carpets, saddles, and tents. At last he had to part with his remaining cattle, and found himself face to face with want. Before he knew how it had happened, he had lost everything, and in their old age he and his wife had to go into service. Ilyás had nothing left, except the clothes on his back, a fur cloak, a cup, his indoor shoes and overshoes, and his wife, Sham-Shemagi, who also was old by this time. The son who had parted from him had gone into a far country, and his daughter was dead, so that there was no one to help the old couple.

Their neighbour, Muhammad-Shah, took pity on them. Muhammad-Shah was neither rich nor poor, but lived comfortably, and was a good man. He remembered Ilyás's hospitality, and pitying him, said:

'Come and live with me, Ilyás, you and your old woman. In summer you can work in my melon-garden as much as your strength allows, and in winter feed my cattle; and Sham-Shemagi shall milk my mares and make kumiss. I will feed and clothe you both. When you need anything, tell me, and you shall have it.'

Ilyás thanked his neighbour, and he and his wife took service with Muhammad-Shah as labourers. At first the position seemed hard to them, but they got used to it, and lived on, working as much as their strength allowed.

Muhammad-Shah found it was to his advantage to keep such people, because, having been masters themselves, they knew how to manage and were not lazy, but did all the work they could. Yet it grieved Muhammad-Shah to see people brought so low who had been of such high standing.

It happened once that some of Muhammad-Shah's relatives came from a great distance to visit him, and a Mullah came too. Muhammad-Shah told Ilyás to catch a sheep and kill it. Ilyás skinned the sheep, and boiled it, and sent it in to the guests. The guests ate the mutton, had some tea, and then began drinking kumiss. As they were sitting with their host on down cushions on a carpet, conversing and sipping kumiss from their cups, Ilyás, having finished his work passed by the open door. Muhammad-Shah, seeing him pass, said to one of the guests:

'Did you notice that old man who passed just now?'

'Yes,' said the visitor, 'what is there remarkable about him?'

'Only this - that he was once the richest man among us,' replied the host. 'His name is Ilyás. You may have heard of him.'

'Of course I have heard of him,' the guest answered 'I never saw him before, but his fame has spread far and wide.'

'Yes, and now he has nothing left,' said Muhammad-Shah, 'and he lives with me as my labourer, and his old woman is here too - she milks the mares.'

The guest was astonished: he clicked with his tongue, shook his head, and said:

'Fortune turns like a wheel. One man it lifts, another it sets down! Does not the old man grieve over all he has lost?'

'Who can tell. He lives quietly and peacefully, and works well.'

'May I speak to him?' asked the guest. 'I should like to ask him about his life.'

'Why not?' replied the master, and he called from the kibítka in which they were sitting:

'Babay;' (which in the Bashkir tongue means 'Grandfather') 'come in and have a cup of kumiss with us, and call your wife here also.'

Ilyás entered with his wife; and after exchanging greetings with his master and the guests, he repeated a prayer, and seated himself near the door. His wife passed in behind the curtain and sat down with her mistress.

A Cap of kumiss was handed to Ilyás; he wished the guests and his master good health, bowed, drank a little, and put down the cup.

'Well, Daddy,' said the guest who had wished to speak to him, 'I suppose you feel rather sad at the sight of us. It must remind you of your former prosperity, and of your present sorrows.'

Ilyás smiled, and said:

'If I were to tell you what is happiness and what is misfortune, you would not believe me. You had better ask my wife. She is a woman, and what is in her heart is on her tongue. She will tell you the whole truth.'

The guest turned towards the curtain.

'Well, Granny,' he cried, 'tell me how your former happiness compares with your present misfortune.'

And Sham-Shemagi answered from behind the curtain:

'This is what I think about it: My old man and I lived for fifty years seeking happiness and not finding it; and it is only now, these last two years, since we had nothing left and have lived as labourers, that we have found real happiness, and we wish for nothing better than our present lot.'

The guests were astonished, and so was the master; he even rose and drew the curtain back, so as to see the old woman's face. There she stood with her arms folded, looking at her old husband, and smiling; and he smiled back at her. The old woman went on:

'I speak the truth and do not jest. For half a century we sought for happiness, and as long as we were rich we never found it. Now that we have nothing left, and have taken service as labourers, we have found such happiness that we want nothing better.'

'But in what does your happiness consist?' asked the guest.

'Why, in this,' she replied, 'when we were rich my husband and I had so many cares that we had no time to talk to one another, or to think of our souls, or to pray to God. Now we had visitors, and had to consider what food to set before them, and what presents to give them, lest they should speak ill of us. When they left, we had to look after our labourers who were always trying to shirk work and get the best food, while we wanted to get all we could out of them. So we sinned. Then we were in fear lest a wolf should kill a foal or a calf, or thieves steal our horses. We lay awake at night, worrying lest the ewes should overlie their lambs, and we got up again and again to see that all was well. One thing attended to, another care would spring up: how, for instance, to get enough fodder for the winter. And besides that, my old man and I used to disagree. He would say we must do so and so, and I would differ from him; and then we disputed - sinning again. So we passed from one trouble to another, from one sin to another, and found no happiness.'

'Well, and now?'

'Now, when my husband and I wake in the morning, we always have a loving word for one another and we live peacefully, having nothing to quarrel about. We have no care but how best to serve our master. We work as much as our strength allows and do it with a will, that our master may not lose but profit by us. When we come in, dinner or supper is ready and there is kumiss to drink. We have fuel to burn when it is cold and we have our fur cloak. And we have time to talk, time to think of our souls, and time to pray. For fifty years we sought happiness, but only now at last have we found it.'

The guests laughed.

But Ilyás said:

'Do not laugh, friends. It is not a matter for jesting - it is the truth of life. We also were foolish at first, and wept at the loss of our wealth; but now God has shown us the truth, and we tell it, not for our own consolation, but for your good.'

And the Mullah said:

'That is a wise speech. Ilyás has spoken the exact truth. The same is said in Holy Writ.'

And the guests ceased laughing and became thoughtful.